The Color of
Death

BY ELIZABETH LOWELL

Amber Beach
Jade Island
Pearl Cove
Midnight in Ruby Bayou
Moving Target
Running Scared
Die in Plain Sight
The Color of Death

The Color of Death

ELIZABETH LOWELL

wm

WILLIAM MORROW
An Imprint of HarperCollins*Publishers*

This is a work of fiction. The characters, incidents, and dialogue are products of the author's imagination and are not to be construed as real. Any resemblance to actual events or persons, living or dead, is entirely coincidental.

HarperCollins books may be purchased for educational, business, or sales promotional use. For information please write: Special Markets Department, HarperCollins Publishers Inc., 10 East 53rd Street, New York, NY 10022.

FIRST EDITION

Designed by Mia Risberg

Printed on acid-free paper

Library of Congress Cataloging-in-Publication Data

Lowell, Elizabeth, 1944–
    The color of death / by Elizabeth Lowell.—1st ed.
        p.   cm.
    ISBN 0-06-050413-7 (acid-free paper)
        1. Women   detectives—Fiction.   2. Gem-cutting   industry—
    Fiction.   3. Brothers—Death—Fiction.   4. Jewelry trade—
    Fiction.   I. Title.

PS3562.O8847C65 2004
813'.54—dc22   2003071003

04   05   06   07   08   WBC/RRD   10   9   8   7   6   5   4   3   2   1

*To the many people
who enrich my life.*

You know who you are.

The Color of
Death

Chapter 1

Sanibel, Florida
November

Lee Mandel spent a lot of time looking over his shoulder. It came with the job. But as he stretched contentedly in the February sun, he wasn't thinking about watching his back. He was smiling at the server who had the lithe body and optimism only people under thirty could manage.

"Hey, you *sure* you've got the best shrimp on Sanibel Island?" Lee teased.

"You bet your ass, sir."

Lee laughed and waved off the server. "I'll have the usual. And coffee as fast as your big feet can manage. Oh, and bring a couple extra to-go bags, okay?"

The young man grinned, reached behind his back, and pulled out two white paper bags with the café's SoupOr Shrimp logo printed in bright red down the side.

"These do?" He dropped them in front of Lee. "I grabbed them as soon as I saw you coming up the stairs."

Uneasiness snaked through Lee. He was becoming predictable. In his business that was not only stupid, it was dangerous. But he hadn't seen anyone following him when he drove over the bridges from the mainland to Sanibel Island. Besides, once the contents of the courier packet were transferred to a wrinkled takeout bag, no one would suspect what Lee knew for a fact: the gems were worth a million, minimum. Wholesale.

In the future, he'd use something even less noticeable, maybe a brown paper bag like the winos. Usually the couriers who were carrying unique goods didn't have to worry as much as the guys carrying watches and engagement rings.

Usually, but not always.

For the last few years there had been rumors of a new gang working, one that targeted only the very highest end of portable and valuable goods. The good news was that the gang wasn't as rough as the South Americans. The new boys were slick and quiet.

The server and his tight butt disappeared back into the dark, smoky café, leaving Lee alone to enjoy the winter sun. He shifted his chair so that his back was to the wall of the building and wondered what his sister, Kate, was doing now that she'd finished cutting and polishing the Seven Sins. Probably she was getting ready to hit the gem show circuit again and see if she could find some rough that would repay her time and effort to cut it.

Maybe if Mom and Dad let up on the grandchild subject, she'd slow down and find a good man. As it is, they're driving her nuts as surely as they drove me.

Guilt whispered through him. He should tell his parents. He really should, especially now that he'd found the man he wanted to spend his life with. He just didn't want the crap that would come after he came out of the closet, the tears and the where-did-we-go-wrong questions.

His parents hadn't gone wrong. He just wasn't the son they'd expected. End of sad story.

Conversation floated around Lee. Some of it came from the open-air ground-level parking lot directly under him. Nearly everything on Sanibel Island was built on stilts. When the hurricanes came, most of the mess just washed through underneath the buildings, leaving the higher living quarters more or less intact.

"But I *want* to see the *treasure!*"

The young girl's voice was high, stubborn, and all too clear as she emerged from a car out in the sunstruck parking lot that tourists invariably chose. Lee smiled slightly at the idea of sizzling upholstery and steering wheels too hot to hold, and he wondered if the snowbirds were afraid of the shadows between the pillars holding up the small shopping center.

"We saw the Atocha stuff last year. Big deal." The parental voice was frayed and impatient. "All they want to do in that so-called museum is sell overpriced pieces of eight to the next sucker coming through the door."

"I don't *care*. I want to see the gold coins and *emeralds*."

Lee tuned out the girl's whine even as he wondered what she would say if she saw the seven extraordinary sapphires that were locked in the trunk of his car. Most of the time he didn't know what he was carrying in the anonymous packets he took from point A to point B for various courier companies, including the one his family owned. He enjoyed the freedom of being freelance. On this job, he just happened to be the son of the company's owner and the brother of the cutter, so he knew what the Seven Sins were and how much they were worth.

Kate had been so excited about being commissioned to cut the extra fine quality sapphire rough that she'd called him and described the stones to him the way he'd describe a lover. He'd visited her twice in Arizona and been amazed at the progress from shapeless, dull bluish stone to exquisitely faceted gems that burned with an extraordinary blue color.

He'd enjoyed watching Kate's excitement. For once it had seemed like she was years younger than he was, instead of eight years older. Not that he blamed her for being thrilled. It was a real coup for a relatively young cutter to score a high-end job like the rough from Arthur McCloud, one of the foremost collectors of gemstones in the world. She'd even asked that Lee courier the rough to her and then courier the cut and polished Seven Sins back to McCloud. Keeping it in the family, as it were.

Squinting against the sun, Lee stared at the modest watch strapped to his left wrist. Quarter of eleven. Plenty of time. From the café, it was maybe fifteen minutes over a small bridge connecting Sanibel and Captiva islands. With luck he'd have an hour after he dropped off the stones on Captiva to go shelling on the falling tide and still make his flight out of Fort Myers to Los Angeles. On Friday, ninety percent of the traffic would be heading over the bridges into Sanibel; he'd be going the opposite direction. It should be an easy drive all the way in to the airport.

He stretched again. In his shorts, golf shirt, and sandals, he blended right in with the rest of the population. Not too tall. Not too short. Not too fat. Not too tan. Not too anything. Couriers were as anonymous as their parcels. If he'd been in Manhattan, he would have worn a dark suit and charcoal overcoat. Seattle would have required a high-tech rain jacket and a cup of espresso mounted permanently in one hand. No umbrella. No one in the Pacific NorthWet bothered.

The faint sound of a car responding to the call of an electronic key disturbed Lee. He sat upright and mentally reviewed the cars he'd seen when he parked in the lot just beneath him, near the stairway. Except for his white rental car, there hadn't been any close to the stairs.

Most of the shops opened at eleven, and that was twenty minutes away. The only other vehicles he'd noticed were parked well to the back, away from the stairs. The cars and light trucks almost certainly belonged to employees following orders to make it easy for the paying customers to park close to the stairs leading to the shops.

He stood and glanced over the railing to the ground one story below. No one. The whining girl and her family had gone inside the café, apparently preferring smoke to fresh air. For the moment, he was as alone as anyone ever was in the winter tourist mecca of Sanibel Island.

From beneath him came the muffled thump of a trunk closing.

Frowning, he hurried down the stairs. The transition from full

Florida sunlight to the full-shade gloom of the parking lot made him hesitate. He glanced quickly around the area.

Nothing moved in the cool shadows.

Telling himself he was being paranoid, Lee crossed quickly to his car. He punched the electronic key and unlocked the trunk.

It was empty.

"Son of a bitch!"

Frantically he leaned in and felt around. Smaller than his palm, worth more than he would make in a lifetime, the package holding the Seven Sins could have shifted, maybe fallen into the wheel well.

They have to be here.

From the darkness beyond the car came a slight scuff, as though someone was trying to sneak past him to the bright sun. At least it seemed like sneaking until he spun around and saw a familiar face.

Relieved, he smiled and said, "Hey, I didn't expect to see you on this coast."

"You shouldn't have seen me at all."

There was a soft sound, then a grunt as a bullet slammed through flesh and bone to Lee's heart. He collapsed into the trunk.

This can't be happening.

But it was. The world was spinning away and he wasn't part of it anymore, color swirling down to black.

Norm . . . Katie . . . can you hear me? I love . . .

The trunk slammed down, hiding death.

Chapter 2

Little Miami
Two days later

Jaime "Seguro" Jimenez de los Santos knew it was his lucky day when the door of his pawnshop opened and a platinum blonde with maximum boobs and a shrink-wrap dress sauntered toward him. Platform heels added five inches to her height and made her ass swing real nice. His only complaint was that the dress began at the neck and covered all that flesh.

Then he took another look and realized that the breasts came from a high-class gel bra, the kind drag queens wear. The skirt almost made up for it, though. It was so short he could see the bottom of her butt cheeks. Or his, more likely.

Ni modo. Seguro liked lovers both ways, as long as he got to be the pitcher.

The door closed, shutting out the impatient horns, the stink of badly tuned engines, and the cascading accents of Spanish from six nations. Through the heat and dust-glazed windows, tired palm trees swayed over the worn cinder-block buildings lining the crowded street.

A heavy floral perfume washed over Seguro as the woman leaned against the counter. Her makeup was as bold as her dress. Her eyes were the blue of a rare clear day in muggy Florida.

"*Buen dia, señorita,*" Seguro said informally, giving her the thorough leer that his culture and her dress required. "*¿Como le puedo ayudar?*"

"English, if you can, *por favor,*" she said, pronouncing the two Spanish words as though they were English. She had a husky, almost hoarse voice. "My *español* sucks."

"*Sí,* how can I help you?"

"Someone told me you give the best price around for loose stones."

He hesitated.

"You know," she said earnestly, "loose stones—gems that aren't set? Do you understand?"

"*Sí,* yes, I understand. Who told you that?"

"Someone in L.A. Los Angeles. My boyfriend's from there. His buddy said you had a cousin that had a cousin that . . ." She shrugged, making everything sway from top to bottom. "My boyfriend's not a Santos but he did time with one, if you get what I mean."

Seguro grinned and nodded quickly, accepting her explanation. Most of the contacts a man needed to succeed in life were already in his extended family. The rest he could make in the joint. "*Sí.* I know. I meet some people that way."

"Damn useful," she agreed. With both hands she lifted her big canvas tote and smacked it onto the counter. "I got some shit you'll like."

He made an all-purpose sound and idly wondered if she was really a he. No sign of a beard shadow, but it was hard to be sure underneath all that makeup. In any case, many of *los maricones* had their beards permanently removed.

She pawed through the tote and pulled out an antacid bottle. Before Seguro took the plastic antacid container, he spread a worn piece of dark cloth on the countertop. Then he uncapped the bottle and poured the contents out on the cloth. Instead of the rush of small stones he had expected, a big, thumb-sized rectangle of deep blue bounced out onto the counter. He grabbed the gem and centered it on the dark cloth. His breath came in.

And stayed.

"I want fifty thousand," she said.

His head snapped up. The blue eyes looking across the counter at him were lighter than the big stone but just as hard.

"We see" was all Seguro said.

"The sapphire is worth a lot more than fifty grand."

"To someone, yes. To me? I no think so." He shrugged fluidly. "I see."

She tapped long, stoplight-red acrylic fingernails on the counter. "Fine. You see. But hurry it up. I got a plane to catch. Big vacation in Aruba with my boyfriend."

"Ah, I hear it is pretty there."

"I'll send you a card."

Seguro pulled out a jeweler's loupe and began looking at the large blue stone. Except for the occasional impatient tap of fake fingernails on the counter, it was quiet in the shop.

"Well?" she said when he finally looked up.

"I need a friend to look at it."

She put her hands on her narrow hips in what could have been impatience or challenge. "Like I said, I'm in a hurry."

"I regret, but . . ." He shrugged again.

"What can you give me *now*?"

"Two thousand."

"Thirty."

"Two thousand, one hundred."

"This is bullshit. The stone's worth two hundred thousand, easy."

"Then take it and sell it for that sum."

"Fifteen thousand."

"Two thousand, one hundred and fifty," he said patiently. "I am sorry, *Señor*—er, *Señorita*—but I am no expert. I already say double what I should because you are a fine person that knows the cousin of my cousin from the joint. I can do no more. I am very sorry."

"Well, fuck! I want it in cash. Right now."

"But of course. Wait here for me, yes?"

"Just hurry up. You aren't the only pawnshop in Little Miami."

Seguro went to the small room in the back of the pawnshop, locked the door behind him, and went to the safe. Hurriedly he counted hundreds into a pile, then added a fifty-dollar bill. When he reopened the door to the shop, the woman was still there.

She held out her hand, palm up.

He counted the money into her blunt palm, then waited while she counted it again for herself.

"You made yourself a hell of a buy," she said bitterly. "A real steal."

Seguro grinned. "I never doubt it. *Buena suerte.*"

No sooner had the front door shut behind the blonde than he rushed over and locked it. He flipped the sign to CLOSED and pulled down the blinds behind the wrought-iron bars that covered the windows.

Then he stood and shook. He had little doubt that the sapphire was real.

As real as death.

He would have to be very, very careful what he did next or he would be as dead as the previous owner no doubt was.

¡Dios!

He needed connections for this one. The kind of connections people whispered about because to speak the names aloud was to get your throat slit. He mentally went through a list of names and rejected them. Then he came to one that made him pause.

Eduardo.

The brother-in-law of his wife's cousin lived in L.A. He worked in the jewelry trade. He would help. He had the connections no one spoke of aloud. He could sell the gem without getting caught.

Without getting killed.

Chapter 3

Glendale, Arizona
Five days later

Kate Chandler couldn't concentrate. With a muttered curse she looked away from the microscope that held a nice piece of tsavorite rough. She'd been studying the deep green specimen, trying to decide how to cut it in a way that would maximize both size and brilliance in the final stone.

Usually, she loved holding all that potential in her hand, making the decisions that would transform rather ordinary-looking rough into dazzling gems. But right now she was having a hard time caring about anything but the phone that didn't ring.

"Damn it, Lee," she said. *"Call."*

She checked the window of the cell phone that lay within reach on her worktable. The cell hadn't been out of her sight for days, no matter where she went in her house.

No new calls. No missed calls. Nothing but silence and a fear that grew deeper with every passing second.

Impatiently, she punched in Norm Gallagher's number.

Norm picked it up instantly. "Lee?"

Kate's stomach clenched. "No. Just me, Kate. I was hoping . . ."

"He hasn't called." Norm's voice was bleak, hoarse, like he had a cold or had been crying. "What are we going to do?"

"I . . ." She took a breath. "I haven't told Mom and Dad, but I called the FBI and told them Lee had been kidnapped. They didn't want to listen to me. They gave me a verbal pat on the head and told me to leave it all to the Florida authorities. I told them the Florida cops were idiots who were more interested in smearing Lee than in finding him."

"Lee's right," Norm said. "You're a pistol. I can't wait to meet you and the family."

"One big happy reunion," Kate said, forcing herself to sound cheerful instead of bone-deep worried.

Afraid for Lee.

Cold right to her soul.

"Norm . . ."

"Yes?"

"I'm scared. I didn't tell you before and Dad would have a cow if he knew I was telling you now, but Lee's rental car was turned in a day late and the package he was carrying never arrived."

There was a long silence followed by the sounds of a man swallowing hard not to show emotion. "No sign of . . . foul play?"

"No."

"You don't sound happy about that."

"I'm not. I'm scared and mad and . . . scared." Kate closed her eyes, yanked her hair clip out of her dark hair, and massaged her scalp. *Lee, where the hell are you?*

"I'm scared too," Norm said. "I got past mad after the first twenty-four hours."

"This is so unlike Lee," she whispered. "Even if he forgot to call me after he delivered the Seven Sins, he's just plain nuts for you. He'd call you, no matter what."

Norm gave up swallowing and let the tears clog his throat. "Thanks, Katie."

"It's the truth."

"Do you suppose he had some kind of accident and doesn't remember his name?"

Kate leaned against her worktable, hearing the same fear in Norm's voice that was twisting through her, the words neither one of them wanted to say aloud: *What if Lee is dead?*

"I've called every hospital between Fort Myers, where he picked up the rental car, and Captiva Island, where he was supposed to make the delivery," Kate said. "No one has admitted an amnesia patient in the past five days, or any John Doe patient that doesn't know his own name."

"They're sure?"

Kate didn't answer. Norm's words had been more a cry for hope than a real question.

"Call me the instant you hear anything," she said.

"You too."

She cut the connection and let her own tears come, grief and fear mixed together, shaking her.

Chapter 4

Scottsdale, Arizona
Five months later
Tuesday morning
9:30 A.M.

Heart pounding, Kate looked over the crowded conference. She tried not to think about the eerie mechanical voice on her answering machine, telling her that she would die if she didn't stop asking questions and trying to find out what had happened to Lee Mandel, why no one had seen him, why he hadn't called anyone, even the older sister who had always loved him no matter what a handful he was.

But she'd kept asking anyway. Just more carefully. She'd focused on the missing gems rather than on the brother she was afraid she'd never see again.

She watched the room with dark eyes that had seen a lot of people yearning over a lot of gems. No one glanced back at her, not even the man leaning against the far wall, a heavy show catalogue in his hands and a shuttered expression on his face. Except for him, everyone was poring over the gleaming wealth laid out beneath glass.

The real show wouldn't open for days, but some nice goods were already on public display. The preshow booths were a kind of dress rehearsal featuring the dealers who couldn't, wouldn't, or hadn't been invited to pay the stiff stall rentals for the main show. A handful of these excluded merchants had pooled their money to rent a large conference room off the lobby of the hotel for the week before the main show. Purcell Colored Gems was one of the second-tier merchants that had set up a booth.

Yesterday Kate had seen one of the Seven Sins on display there.

The Purcells hadn't been helpful when she'd asked where the gem came from, but she'd found a way around them. Now all she had to do was make sure they didn't find out.

Breathe slow and deep, like you're making the first cut on a piece of really good rough.

The silent advice didn't slow Kate's heartbeat, but the thought of shaping colorful rough material into brilliant, eternally dreaming gems did the trick. Working with rough stone always calmed her. She didn't know why. She just knew it did.

That's the way, she told herself. *Slow and steady. This is the easy part.*

She had good hands. She'd always had them, even when she was only eleven and entertaining neighborhood kids by pulling pennies out of their ears.

Breathe slow and move fast and be grateful the emerald-cut Sin didn't turn up in one of the private showings in a dealer's room. That would have been much harder to pull off.

Quietly, Kate let out another long breath and stepped into the conference room. The booths spread out in front of her belonged to the second- and third-tier gem dealers and jewelers. Even so, the booths were a universe away from the crowds of bead and gimcrack sellers haggling and sweating on the clogged public parking lots where temporary open-air booths had been set up beneath the desert's blazing April sun.

Inside Phoenix's newest, most luxurious hotel-spa, all was tranquil, cool, and lightly scented with flowers. If Kate's sensitive nostrils also picked up the oily, pervasive smell of greed wafting through the conference area, it didn't offend her. Shortly after she'd had her first period, she'd realized that the presence of gems made some humans sweat. The fact that she could look at gorgeous jewels without thinking in dollar signs gave her an edge over a lot of people in the trade.

She shook down the long sleeves of her raspberry silk jacket, felt the small weight poised just above the edge of her left palm, and took a last slow breath.

I'll make those FBI bastards listen, Lee.

I swear it.

Chapter 5

Scottsdale
Tuesday
9:32 A.M.

Sam Groves leaned against the Scottsdale Royale's expensively papered wall and thumbed through a catalogue of upcoming attractions that would appear when the real gem show got under way. The catalogue was thick enough to take several days to read, but long before that he would have moved on, changed his clothes, put on a hat, and altered his profile. Simple enough disguises, because most people were simple. Especially with all the colored pretties scattered around. Like big tits, big gems often had a negative effect on the IQ of the men looking at them.

Sam enjoyed tits and gems as much as any man, but he managed to keep his mind on his job. He was sixteen years into the FBI and hoped to make twenty before someone added up the "doesn't play well with others" and "colors outside the lines" flags in his file, and then kicked his "runs with scissors" ass out of the Bureau.

No matter how hard Sam tried, when someone asked his opinion, he gave it. All of it, no matter how disagreeable it might be to the people who asked.

Good thing you're bright, boy, 'cuz you sure ain't politic.

That's what his first SAC—special agent in charge—had told Sam fifteen years ago. Nothing had changed since then. The Bureau got even with him by delaying his promotions and assigning him to low-profile jobs. So instead of tracking international and domestic terrorists with the other Bureau hotshots, he was part of a special task force trying to break a ring of jewel hijackers that had plagued the gem trade in the past five years.

But even on what should have been a straightforward assignment, Sam's offbeat way of looking at the world had gotten him into trouble.

Tough titty. Sam flipped another page and scanned another breathless advertisement describing rubies as the colored gem investment of the century. *I've weathered worse than Mr. "Legend in His Own Mind" Sizemore. In less than five years I'll have my pension and my own business, and the politically correct assholes who can't see beyond their own brown noses can take a flying leap.*

Silently, Sam repeated his personal mantra while he handled an assignment any schoolboy could have covered.

A shimmer of raspberry silk caught his eye. He glanced across the room. Though not beautiful, the woman held his attention. Black hair ruthlessly pulled back from her face. Medium height. Nicely curved—not showgirl nice, but the kind of real flesh that men liked to hold close. Expensive-looking suit and low heels with matching leather handbag. No obvious jewelry.

She moved confidently, yet his investigator's gut told him that she was on edge.

Intrigued, he drifted closer without ever looking directly at her. When he saw that she was heading for the Purcell booth, his interest sharpened. If someone offered them quality goods, Mike and Lois had a reputation for not asking embarrassing questions about previous owners and bills of sale. Naturally, the price they paid for the goods reflected their tight lips. In all, the Purcells were just the kind of folks a gem hijacker might be looking for.

After all, there wasn't much point in clouting a gem shipment if you couldn't turn the tiny pretties into big mounds of anonymous green cash.

Chapter 6

Scottsdale
Tuesday
9:33 A.M.

Kate was so relieved to find Mike Purcell alone in the booth that she gave him a radiant smile. He responded with a leer. When his wife, Lois, wasn't around, Purcell had the reputation of being a real hound. Until yesterday, Kate hadn't thought much about the gossip. Then she'd learned firsthand just how true the gossip was, and she'd chosen her outfit for today accordingly.

She braced her smile to keep it from slipping, eased her right hand down her blouse to undo a few buttons, and told herself that it was all for a good cause. Apparently unaware of the gap in her clothing, she stepped closer to the case and bent over it.

"Come back to look at the blue sapphire?" Purcell asked slyly, leaning forward over the display case, close enough to sense her body heat. "Or maybe you have something else in mind."

Her smile stiffened, but he didn't notice. His eyes were on the cleavage she'd so generously displayed. She swallowed hard and settled into the odious business of flirting with a man she'd rather have scraped off her shoes.

"Well, you never know." Kate stroked the hollow of her throat lightly, hoping to distract him from her breasts. It worked for about two seconds. "That is one mighty fine gemstone," she said in a carefully breathless voice.

The sapphire was indeed unusual, but not quite to the point of being a showstopper. At least, good old Purcell must have thought so or he wouldn't have displayed it so openly.

Kate thought Purcell was wrong. That was a gem guaranteed to raise the heart rate of any dealer who saw it.

Maybe Purcell just couldn't resist strutting the stone in front of the other second-tier dealers, she thought, gritting her teeth against her sudden distaste for the man who was older than her father. *Or maybe he knows that McCloud wasn't supposed to tell anyone about the Seven Sins, so he thinks it's safe. Either way, Purcell is slime.*

But all she said aloud was, "Emerald-cut sapphires of that size and quality don't come on the market every day."

"Day?" Purcell straightened and reached into the case without looking away from the smooth, firm tits he'd love to squeeze. "Honeypot, sapphires like this are rarer than a faithful woman. I ought to know. I've helped more than one of the little darlings do the adultery dance. And unlike this sapphire, I gave those gals a real thorough deep-heat treatment, if you get my meaning."

Kate's smile became all teeth. She made a sound like a terrier sinking canines into a rat. "I still can't believe that the gem hasn't ever been heated. May I look at it again?"

"What are you offering?"

Same as last time, you jackal. A cheap peep show. "I won't be able to say until I look at it again. Reassurance, you know?" Kate said. "I just can't believe it's worth more than twenty-five thousand a carat. Before my client starts rounding up that kind of money, I have to be sure. I mean, this is only the preshow, after all. Lots of world-class gems haven't even been put out yet. Surely you understand?"

The husky hesitation in her voice made Purcell's palms hot. He'd seen bigger tits, but hers were here, now, and he wanted to see more of them.

"Oh, what the hell," he said, pulling out the small box that held the sapphire. "You handled those tweezers real well yesterday, just like a pro. Need a loupe?"

"No, thanks. I brought my own this time. I didn't want to take a chance on dropping yours again."

Besides, only an idiot used the same distraction twice, but pointing that out wasn't any part of Kate's agenda.

He grinned. "You didn't do any harm. You can go looking for a loupe in my lap any old time you want to."

Kate didn't think her acting skills were up to answering. Then she thought of Lee, missing for five months, almost certainly dead, and— *Don't go there,* she told herself roughly. *Crying doesn't do a damn bit of good, especially now. Suck it up. You have a job to do.*

"You're way too kind, Mr. Purcell," she said hoarsely. "I felt like such a fool."

"You felt just fine from where I was sitting."

She swallowed hard and fished in the pocket of her jacket. When her fingers wrapped around the cool curve of the loupe, it steadied her. She took out the small 10x magnifying glass and looked at Purcell expectantly.

He waited, hoping that she would come around the glass like she had yesterday. He'd really liked squeezing that firm ass between his thighs and the heavy display case.

She didn't move.

"View's better from here," he said.

She shook her head. "No, you'll just get me all flustered again. I have to keep my mind on my business."

"You sure, honeypot?"

"That you'd get me flustered? I sure am." *And this time I might not be able to stop myself from parking my foot in your crotch.* "You have a way of making a woman forget what she's doing."

He laughed. "So they tell me."

He took the clear top off the box, nudged it toward her, and handed her a pair of jeweler's tweezers.

Ignoring the slick feel of his fingers rubbing over her palm, she positioned the tweezers and picked up the thirty-carat stone. Holding the loupe to one eye, she brought the sapphire closer until it was in focus.

The color was everything a blue sapphire should be. The inclusions didn't detract from the brilliance. The cut was superb.

Show time.

She set the gem back in its box and simultaneously fumbled with the loupe. It smacked against her collarbone and slid down between her breasts. She gave a stifled little shriek and went after the loupe with her right hand. As she fished around in her bra, she flashed more skin at Purcell.

She needn't have worried about holding his attention. He was staring at her breasts so hard he was sweating.

"You turn me into all thumbs," Kate said, smiling at Purcell, "but—"

The rest of her words were lost in a gasp as large masculine fingers closed over her left hand, all but crushing it.

"C'mon, get a move on it," said a rough, impatient voice. "We're late. I've been looking all over hell for you."

Kate went cold as she glanced up into a stranger's hard gem-blue eyes.

Chapter 7

Scottsdale
Tuesday
9:40 A.M.

Sam Groves dragged his prey away from Purcell's booth and out into the hotel lobby.

"Let go of me," Kate said in a low, furious voice.

"Or you'll scream?" he asked without interest.

She said something under her breath.

"Yeah, that's what I thought," he said. "Don't want to call attention to yourself, do you?"

"Mr.—"

"Groves. Sam Groves." He crowded her against a potted plant the size of a delivery truck and took a credential holder out of his hip pocket. A badge flashed gold. "Special Agent, FBI. Any questions?"

"What the hell do you think you're doing?"

"That's my question." He turned over her hand, the hand that he hadn't released from his grip. One blunt finger traced the delicate bump of wax or glue or whatever had held the stone out of sight in her sleeve until it was time to make the switch. "A quick scrape, the stone drops, and it's switched before the mark knows what happened."

She gave him a look that said his deodorant had failed her sniff test.

"Open up," he said, "or I'll have to hurt your fingers."

"You already have."

"You're making me cry." He squeezed harder. "Open up."

"How can I?" she retorted, struggling quietly, uselessly against his grip.

Her dark brown eyes glared up at her captor. If he was bothered by her, attracted to her, or repelled by her, he didn't show it. His attitude made it real clear that he wasn't going to be distracted by a little skin. If anything, he looked bored.

But not careless. Her fingers were white and the hidden stone bit into her flesh from the force of his grip.

He replaced his credentials and moved his hand to her wrist without giving her a chance to escape. "Open up."

With an odd smile, she uncurled her fingers. A forty-carat emerald-cut blue sapphire gleamed on her palm.

"Surprise, surprise," he said. "Something stuck to your delicate little fingers. Who are you going to sell this to?"

"No one."

"Yeah? You're just switching stones for the hell of it?"

"Something like that."

"You must think I'm as stupid as Purcell."

Kate met Sam's cool blue eyes straight on. The man might be a lot of things, but stupid wasn't one of them. Normally, she would have been attracted to his intelligence and old-fashioned male strength. Not today. Today she wished she'd never met the son of a bitch.

"I'm sure you're very bright for a federal robot," she said. "But that doesn't mean you're right. I'm not a thief."

Sam's dark eyebrows rose. He'd met some confident con men in his time, but she was something else.

Federal robot.

He almost laughed. If she only knew how wide of the mark that shot was.

"Not a thief, huh?" he asked lazily. "That blue stone in your hand says you're a liar."

"You're assuming that the stone is valuable enough to be worth stealing."

"I sure am."

"The stone's only real value lies in the time a cutter spent on it."

"Oh, yeah, right," he said, not bothering to hide his impatience.

Kate's chin tilted up. The more her heartbeat settled down from being caught, the madder she got. "I can prove it."

"How?"

"Pick a dealer. Any dealer. Show them the stone and see what they say."

For a long moment, Sam simply looked at his unexpected captive. She had the kind of classy face that made a man want to please her, dark eyes that looked earnest, fine bones, rich black hair, and an unmistakably female shape that the loose clothing couldn't hide. Overall impression was of fresh, businesslike femininity. Intelligent too. Quick in more than one sense of the word.

If he hadn't seen her pull the switch himself, he would have believed her innocent act.

But he'd seen the switch.

Then he remembered just how much eyewitness testimony was really worth—slightly less than a handful of warm spit. Three eyewitnesses would earnestly tell you that the guy was tall, short, average, thin, fat, average, hairy, bald, average, and looked just like you.

He glanced at his watch. The strike force meeting wouldn't start for another twenty minutes. Whatever else the woman might or might not be, she was more interesting than the pages of the catalogue he'd been thumbing through since the booths opened at nine. She smelled better too.

And there was always the chance if he crowded her hard enough, she might volunteer some interesting leads into the gem-fencing community. So far the strike force hadn't done much but spend public funds following leads that didn't pan out.

"Okay, Ms. . . ."

"Natalie," Kate said quickly, hoping her mother wouldn't care if her name was borrowed.

"You have a middle and a last name?"

She'd already decided that Smith or Jones was a nonstarter. So she grabbed the first words she thought of: her profession and her mother's maiden name. "Cutter. Middle name Harrison."

"All right, Ms. Natalie Harrison Cutter. You have any ID?"

She was ready for that too. "Up in my room. You aren't going there."

Sam decided to let it go for now. Without releasing his grip on her, he plucked the stone from her palm. "We'll just walk back to the conference room and see what some dealers think of this stone."

"Let go of me," she said, tugging against his grip.

"Not unless you'd rather wear handcuffs. I've seen you move, sweetheart. Quick and slick."

Kate locked her teeth together against the anger and adrenaline that wanted to spill out in a rush of scathing words. "Typical condescending FBI," she said distinctly. "*Sweetheart.*"

The left corner of Sam's mouth tilted up. "You know a lot of us federal robots, do you?"

"Let's say I'm familiar with the breed."

"The kind of familiarity that leads to contempt?"

Kate's sideways look said it all.

He grinned. "I like your style."

"I'll change it."

"Come with me, Ms. 'No ID' Natalie. We'll see how wide your sassy streak is."

"If I were a man, you wouldn't call it sassy."

"If you were a man, Purcell wouldn't have been so busy looking at your tits that he took his eyes off the main point—gems. What goes around, comes around. Sweetheart."

She shot him a dark glance, saw that she was being baited, and gritted her teeth.

Then she followed him because there was no other choice except to be dragged behind like a sulky child.

Sam selected the second booth on the left, well away from Purcell. The woman behind the counter was neatly turned out in a Southwest-style jacket and black slacks. Her gray hair was cut close, as were her nails. Gems were arranged in the case like a rainbow. While not a very original design, the multicolored arc of gems was striking.

"Good morning, ma'am," Sam said. "Beautiful display you have."

The woman smiled, responding to the approval and warmth in his voice. The fact that the rest of the package was male and easy moving didn't hurt. She might have been old enough to be his mother, but her eyesight was just fine.

"Thank you," she said. "We try to please."

Kate bit the inside of her cheek to keep from screaming—or laughing. Sam was reeling the woman in the same way Kate had reeled in Purcell.

Only Sam didn't have to undo a single button.

Life really isn't fair, Kate thought angrily. *Why couldn't he have been as sleazy as Purcell? But, no. He's a one hundred percent pure FBI male. Clean-shaven. Confident. Condescending.*

Oh, lucky me.

"I'm sure you do just that," Sam said, smiling at the dealer. "If you're not too busy, I need your opinion on something."

The woman waved one hand. "If a line forms behind you, I'll kick you out. Until then, how can I help you?"

Sam held out his hand, palm up. The sapphire glowed like a huge blue eye stolen from an alien idol.

The woman's breath came in with an audible sound.

"I say this is worth a lot of money." Sam tilted his head toward his captive. "My sweetheart here doesn't think so. Can you settle the argument for us?"

"That looks like the stone Mike Purcell was bragging on."

"Purcell?" Kate said quickly. "We didn't get it from him. My, uh, sweetie won it in a poker game last night."

"Yeah, she gave me hell on the half shell when I got in late," Sam said.

"If you'd come home a winner," Kate said with lethal sincerity, "I wouldn't have cared when you got in."

"Hey, fifty-eight big ones for a stone like this is winning in any man's book."

"May I examine it?" the dealer asked, pulling a black velvet pad closer and reaching for loupe and tweezers.

"Sure."

The dealer put the loupe to her eye with one hand. With the other, she used the tweezers to pick up the stone and bring it into focus in front of the loupe. She studied it intently for a long moment, shifted a tiny gooseneck light to a better angle, and looked again.

"What are you looking for?" Sam asked.

"Pear-shaped bubbles or curved growth lines," she said absently. "They're sure signs of a synthetic."

"See any?" he pressed.

"Not yet."

Sam gave his captive a sideways look that was just short of predatory.

The dealer set aside the loupe. "I have a spectroscope on the counter behind me . . . ?"

"Sure, use it," Sam said. "I want to be real certain. Unless it will harm the stone."

"None of the tests I use are destructive to the gem."

"You have a microscope too?" Kate asked.

"Of course."

"Then just cut to the chase," Kate said. "If the stone is a Chatham synthetic, you'll still get the black bar at four hundred and fifty on the spectroscope, just like a natural."

The dealer gave Kate a speculative look and passed up the spectroscope for the binocular microscope. She set it on the countertop, put the sapphire in the stone holder, and bent over the eyepieces.

"What will that tell you?" Sam asked his captive.

"If she uses that microscope very carefully—"

"I'm GIA certified," the dealer interrupted mildly. "I know how to use a microscope." She glanced up at Kate. "What am I going to see?"

"Hexagonal or triangular platinum platelets," Kate said succinctly.

The dealer looked at Sam. "Why are you wasting my time? Your girlfriend knows more about sapphires than most of the people in this room."

"He doesn't trust me," Kate said. "That's why we're not married. Just *sweethearts*."

Sam buried a laugh. Damned if the quick-tongued little con didn't appeal to him.

The dealer turned back to the microscope. She gave the stone a good look before she finally straightened. "I'm afraid your, um, sweetheart is correct. The stone isn't worth what you paid for it."

"Yeah? How come?" Sam said, disappointed. "Sure looks good to me."

"Do you know much about colored gems?" the dealer asked.

"Nope."

"Like I told you, *sweetheart*," Kate said. "It's pretty, but it's not worth breaking a sweat over."

"No problem," he said easily. "I'm always willing to learn. And sweat."

Kate rolled her eyes.

The dealer smiled. "The stone is a Chatham synthetic. Uncommon, yes, thank God. All the other synthetics fail the spectroscope test."

"You mean that stone isn't a sapphire?" Sam asked.

"Oh, it's blue sapphire, no question." The dealer looked at Sam's expression and sighed. "Obviously, you have trouble believing in the expertise of a woman. There are a lot of male specialists who could do a formal appraisal of this stone, but it will take several days to several weeks and cost you hundreds of dollars."

"Help me out here," Sam said, frowning. "It's really a sapphire?"

Subtly, Kate tested his hold on her wrist. No change. No discreet escape possible.

Hell.

"Blue sapphire, yes," the dealer said. "Sapphires come in all colors except red."

Sam made an encouraging sound.

"When sapphires are red," the dealer said, "they're called rubies. Both sapphire and ruby have essentially the same specific gravity and—barring the impurities that give color—the same chemical composition."

He managed to look intelligent and confused at the same time. It was one of his best faces for questioning people. "So why isn't this, uh, blue sapphire worth anything?"

"It's synthetic," the dealer said patiently. "Man-made. When you buy gems, you're buying color, rarity, and clarity. The synthetics only have two out of three."

"Not enough to be in the money," Sam said.

"No. Although this is quite well done," she added, handing back the stone. "The cut is exquisite. Unusual to see that kind of exacting work in synthetic goods. Most of them are machine cut and polished according to a bean counter's formula for maximum return."

Damn right it's exquisite, Kate thought. *I cut it myself.*

And that was one bit of news she wasn't sharing unless she had to.

Sam made a rumbling, grumbling kind of sound that managed to be cuddly rather than fierce. He shoved the stone deep into his jeans pocket. "Why would anyone put all that effort into a fake?"

"Synthetic," the woman corrected instantly.

"Whatever."

"There are several possibilities."

"Such as?"

"Well," the dealer said, "the most likely explanation is that the owner of a natural blue sapphire of that size might have an identically cut synthetic and wear it instead of the more costly stone. It's a way of keeping down insurance rates."

Sam nodded.

"It's also a way of protecting valuable stones from thieves," the dealer continued. "Most gem thieves, particularly the South American gangs, couldn't tell glass from synthetic from natural."

Sam managed not to grimace over the mention of South American gangs. He heard enough of that song from his supervisory special agent and from Ted Sizemore.

You'd think that there was only one nationality of gang on the whole frigging planet.

"Really?" Sam asked. "I wouldn't have thought gem thieves were that stupid."

"There are one or two real smart ones out there," the dealer said unhappily. "I've heard rumors that some dealers were making decoy shipments to thwart those hijackers when there were some particularly fine gems to protect. Perhaps your well-cut stone came from one of those decoys."

"Thanks for your time," Sam said, turning away.

Kate followed because she didn't have a choice. She looked narrowly at him as she lengthened her stride to keep pace.

"Well, sweetheart, what next?" she asked.

His smile was a lot less easygoing than the one he'd given to the dealer. "We go somewhere quiet and talk."

"No."

He raised his left eyebrow. "Why?"

"I don't want to and you don't want to force me."

"What makes you think that?"

"Because you're undercover and don't want to be burned over something that's going nowhere in terms of a bust." She smiled a razor kind of smile. "Right?"

He thought about it. "Close enough. For now."

"Now is all there is."

She jerked her wrist.

He held on just long enough to let her know that she wasn't escaping, he was letting her go. Then he watched her retreat with the lazy interest of a predator that wasn't particularly hungry at the moment. Whatever her game was, it wasn't part of the reason he was in Scottsdale. Until that changed, she was off his menu.

He had bigger fish to catch, gut, and fry.

Chapter 8

Scottsdale
Tuesday
10:03 A.M.

The FBI's crime strike force had a formal headquarters in a million-dollar motor coach that was parked off to one side of the Scottsdale Royale's employee lot. The strike force's informal headquarters was Ted Sizemore's suite at the Royale, or whatever suite Sizemore took in whatever city was hosting a gem show big enough to draw dealers and the thieves and hijackers who preyed on them.

When Sam walked into the suite, he saw that the door to the other side of the suite was closed. He took the hint and left his SSA and Sizemore alone to talk about whatever part of the Good Old Days turned their crank. Patrick Kennedy and Sizemore went back a long way. Thirty-three years, to be precise.

Sam grabbed a cup of bad coffee from the urn that room service had set up. Then he pulled a pack of peanut butter and cheese crackers from his sports coat pocket. Not much as brunches went, and it was all he was going to get. Sizemore might buy coffee for the strike force, but his idea of food was pretzels and beer.

A lean man still in his twenties walked in. "Hey, Sam, what's happening?"

"Sweet fuck all. How about you?"

"The same." Mario yawned and stretched. Like Sam, he was wearing casual civilian clothes. Unlike Sam, Mario was a detective for the Phoenix PD. "The cell traffic we're picking up is all about meeting for lunch at the local Taco Hell. I came close to falling asleep, and your SAC was in the HQ with me."

Sam shook his head. "Bad form. Doug's a bear about staying awake on the job. Takes snoring as a personal insult." He lifted his mug. "Have some coffee."

"How lousy is it?"

Sam took a swallow. "How lousy is your imagination?"

"That bad, huh? Must be why 'Our Hero' Sizemore drinks beer."

A shrug was Sam's only answer. Anyone who had beer with every meal wasn't Sam's idea of a hero. "Who's on the earphones now?"

"Bailey. You should hear him bitch. An NYPD detective is too good for that shit. Just ask him."

"No thanks."

"What a prick." Mario grabbed a handful of pretzels and ignored the bucket of iced beer. He pulled a can of Pepsi from his jacket pocket, popped the top, and spewed brown foam in all directions. Then he came closer to Sam and said softly, "We're picking up more Spanish calls."

"Sizemore will be happy to hear it."

"Some of the maids have cell phones." Mario winked and made a pumping motion with his arm. "Real scrubwomen."

Sam snickered. He knew enough Spanglish—the creole of border Spanish and English—to catch the reference to maids who made a little extra working in the sheets before they changed them.

More men and two women filed in. The first woman was a bright, barely-thirty-year-old NYPD detective whose marriage had just crashed and burned because of her career demands. Too bad, how sad, and about three out of four law-enforcement officers had stories to match. The second woman was the Legend's daughter, Sharon Sizemore, a former FBI special agent who had been sacked for sleeping with her SAC. It was old news, but the kind of thing that made the rounds of the FBI grapevine whenever her name came up. Since her exit from the FBI, she had worked for her father's security consultation service.

The men walking in behind her were between twenty-five and forty-five years old, short hair, clean shaven, like a herd of fraternity brothers in uniformly casual clothes. One of them wore Nikes. Another wore sandals, no socks. A third wore cowboy boots. The men started talking among themselves and shaking hands with everyone in the room.

Sam sighed. Party time. Too bad he wasn't a party animal. But he'd learned to howdy and shake with the best of them, so he made the rounds of FBI special agents, LAPD, NYPD, Las Vegas PD, plus other various local law-enforcement officers. When he got to Raul Mendoza, Sam's smile became real. Mendoza was the BCIS— Bureau of Citizenship and Immigration Services—agent, the Department of Homeland Security's representative on the crime strike force. Based in Florida, he specialized in South American gangs. In Los Angeles, Mendoza had chased illegals who ran drugs to pay off their smuggler, but he'd adjusted real fast to gems. He was politic, media-wise, and headed for the top.

All the qualities Sam didn't have.

Mendoza was also a damn good investigator, which was what Sam cared about. He saluted him with a mug of coffee. Grinning, the BCIS agent returned the favor.

The noise level subsided somewhat when the SAC Doug Smith walked in, looked over the crowd, and headed straight for the coffee, where Sam had gone back for seconds.

"'Afternoon, boss," Sam said, pouring him a mug of lethal brew. "Heard you snored over the phone logs."

"Bullshit. That was Mario." Doug yawned hugely and took the mug of dark black liquid. He glared at it, scrubbed one blunt hand through sandy hair that got grayer and thinner every year, and sighed. He swallowed a gulp of coffee, grimaced, and swallowed more. "Thanks. I think."

"Those triple shifts will kill you," Sam said, smiling slightly.

"I took four hours off to sleep. Anything new?"

Before Sam could mention his no-ID gem thief, the inner door of the suite opened and two men walked out.

Ted Sizemore was the first. He moved with a confidence that was just short of a swagger. At sixty-three, with two successful careers under his belt, he'd earned the right. Unlike everyone else in the room, he was wearing a suit. The navy blue cloth had pinstripes so narrow they almost vanished. His shirt was white and crisp, his tie dark maroon with just the suggestion of diagonal navy stripes. His shoes were wing tips with a finish that could double as a shaving mirror. He might not carry FBI credentials anymore, but he hadn't forgotten the old uniform.

The second man was SSA Patrick Kennedy. More than a decade younger than Sizemore, Kennedy was one of the Legend's biggest admirers. The fact that Kennedy had worked with Sizemore in the Bureau for about twenty years probably had something to do with it. The fact that Sizemore could conjure up the media with a snap of his fingers might have had a lot more. Positive media hits were as neces-sary for promotion as investigative and bureaucratic skills. Kennedy's next career hike was riding on the outcome of the crime strike force he oversaw. Sizemore was a great unofficial asset, just as the FBI was a great unofficial asset for the Legend's security business.

Sam drank more coffee and wondered if one hand ever got tired of washing the other. He chewed his last peanut butter and cheese cracker, washed it down with more coffee, and waited for someone to pull his finger out and start the whole time-wasting dance.

Meetings sucked.

Sizemore opened a bottle of beer, scooped up a big handful of pretzels from the nearby bowl, and settled into the best chair in the suite, which just happened to be within reach of the goodies. His love of food in general and beer in particular showed in his belly and his jawline. He wasn't at the triple-chin stage yet, but he was headed there.

"Hey, Ted, good to see you," Doug said. "Heard you had a rough flight out from L.A."

"They don't build the damn planes the way they used to," Size-more said, shifting his weight more comfortably in the overstuffed chair. "Don't fly 'em as good either." He took a drink and shrugged. "We arrived rubber side down. These days that's all you can ask for."

Doug and Sizemore traded bad flight stories while the politically adept among the strike force laughed and offered their own horror stories. Sam didn't think having to stay in cheap quarters at a ho-tel—even though his own apartment was only half an hour away from the action—qualified as a horror story. Kennedy wanted every-one to travel and sleep and work together. What Kennedy wanted, he got.

Good thing I don't even have a pet rock, Sam thought. *Sure enough, it would be against FBI regs.*

Sam wondered if his stomach could take more coffee. The burn-ing in his gut told him the answer. Maybe Sizemore had a point with the beer. If nothing else, it was cheaper than the bottled water the hotel so thoughtfully left out with a six dollar price tag around its neck.

The tap water tasted lousy, but it was free. Sam headed for the bathroom. By the time he'd drunk one mug of lukewarm tap water and gone back for a refill, Kennedy had pulled out a notebook and was getting down to business. Standing a few feet behind Sizemore, Sharon took notes by murmuring into a tiny microphone whose head was hidden in her thick, chin-length brown hair. The tiny recording device was invisible behind her ear. She was dressed in a business suit and low heels, which served to minimize her female at-tributes. Brown hair, brown eyes, brown suit, ordinary build. Easy to overlook even if the room wasn't crowded.

But she has the latest spy-tech equipment, Sam thought. *Damn, I'd like to have what she's wearing instead of the crap Uncle Sam sup-plied to the strike force. I'd need Rasta hair to hide the stuff we use.*

". . . and Mendoza," Kennedy said, "tell your men to ride that border harder. The assholes we're looking for don't use passports and paved truck crossings."

"What about the airports?" Mendoza asked.

"Sky Harbor will be covered, even though we don't expect much. Pass out photos of the known gang members and be watching all the flights that originate or connect south of the border."

Mendoza nodded as though he'd been told something unusually insightful. "I'm on it."

Sam looked at his warm water and asked, "What about the secondary airport in Scottsdale?"

"You volunteering?" Kennedy shot back.

"If that's where you want me."

"Don't tempt me."

Sam drank the rest of his water and thought about going back for more.

"Okay, I want *everybody*," Kennedy glared at Sam, "to keep in mind that we're dealing with a highly organized, very fluid group of South American ex-military, some of whom were trained by various U.S. special forces to fight drug dealers but decided it was more profitable to hit jewelry couriers in the U.S. and keep the change. The low-level gang players change from week to week and month to month, but the leaders don't. We want the top of that food chain, not the bottom. It's a real old-boy club, so going undercover won't work. If you weren't in the homeboy military with these crooks, you'll never get to first base in their gang."

Sizemore nodded emphatically. "The Colombian gang I put away was all ex-military, wise to technology, and brutal to the bone. Hardest people I ever came across in my . . ."

. . . *thirty-odd years with the Bureau,* Sam said silently, speaking Sizemore's sentences before the older man could. *Nothing has changed since I set up my own security business. I tell you, don't underestimate these assholes. You'll be . . .*

". . . dead before you know what hit you," Sizemore finished. He banged his empty beer bottle on the table for emphasis.

Warm tap water was sounding really good to Sam, but he knew if he walked out on Sizemore, Kennedy would get even.

It wouldn't be the first time. If Sam stayed long enough in the Bureau, he'd end up in Fargo, North Dakota, the FBI's graveyard for special agents who had pissed off their SSAs. But he was sixteen years into his twenty and figured if it came to that, he could do his last four in Fargo.

Hell, men survived in prison longer, right?

"Any of the metro PDs have anything to report?" Kennedy asked, looking around the room with pale blue eyes.

"Nothing yet," Mario said. "A pawnshop and a 7-Eleven were robbed by Hispanics, but none of the gem shipments that are coming in for the show have been touched. At least I assume they're coming in?" He looked at Sizemore for confirmation.

"Several times a day," Sizemore said. "Right, Sharon?"

"Next one is due in Sky Harbor Airport this afternoon, via Mandel, Inc., a courier service," Sharon said crisply. "The courier's identity and flight haven't been released for security reasons, but if required, we will advise Mandel, Inc. to cooperate with the FBI."

"Damn straight," Sizemore said. He leaned sideways, snagged another beer, and twisted the top off the bottle. "These South Americans have spies and informers everywhere. Toughest, smartest bunch of . . ."

Sam tuned out and hoped what he was thinking didn't show, but he doubted it. He'd had three months to listen to Sizemore hark back to the good old days when he'd become the Legend by overseeing the crime strike force that dismantled three South American gangs that had been operating out of Miami, Manhattan, and Chicago. Murder, mayhem, robbery, rape—the gangs were good for all of them.

And Sizemore would be happy to talk about all of it for hours. An agent's glory days were hard to leave behind.

"You have something you want to say?" Sizemore challenged Sam.

"Bringing those gangs down was a fine piece of investigative work, no doubt about it," Sam said. He knew he should stop there. He didn't. "But that was what—fifteen years ago? The world has changed."

"Crooks don't change," Sizemore said, pinning Sam with cold brown eyes. "Crooks were assholes then and they're assholes now."

"Right," Sam said easily. "All that changes are the names and countries of the players. We've got a smorgasbord of nationalities to choose from. If we concentrate only on the South Americans, then we run the risk of overlooking—"

"Oh, Jesus," Kennedy cut in, "you're not off on your wild-assed Teflon gang theory again, are you?"

"I call them the Teflon gang because nothing sticks to them, not even blood," Sam said neutrally. "They're cold enough to kill and smart enough to stay off our radar."

"Bullshit," Sizemore said roughly. "No one's heard anything solid about a new gang that concentrates on couriers, and we've all heard a hell of a lot about the South Americans."

"The number of robberies has gone way up in the past few years, but the hits that street talk pins on the South Americans has stayed about the same," Sam said. "Plus, the couriers carrying unique goods are being hit. That's what made me think a new gang was at work. When I started comparing—"

"Like you can believe mutts on the street to tell the truth," Kennedy cut in sarcastically. "Stop wasting the taxpayer's time. I need more evidence than gossip and an agent with a wild hair."

"If we're not looking, we'll never find more evidence," Sam said. "Sir."

"We're not looking," Sizemore said, "because there's sweet fuck all to find except South Americans."

Doug caught Sam's eye.

Sam thought about the career opportunities in Fargo, ND.

Kennedy went back to his agenda. "Doug will give you your assignments. For the next week, most of you will be checking hotels for gang members known to the strike force, with special attention to the Royale. Mario and Mendoza will interview the hotel's workers from the floor managers on down."

"Don't mention immigration status," the LAPD cop said. "If the illegals run, there won't be a maid or gardener left in Scottsdale."

"And all of you," Kennedy said over the laughter, "take a good look at the information Ted brought with him. The more you know the big gem dealers and their staff, the faster you'll be able to catch somebody who doesn't belong, somebody who's *wrong*."

"Like the woman Sam collared just before the meeting?" Bill Colton asked.

Sam looked at the SA from his own Phoenix office and wished he liked the man. Hell, he'd settle for not despising the bastard. Colton used ass-kissing rather than good fieldwork to get ahead.

Problem was, it worked.

"False alarm," Sam said.

"What's this?" Kennedy asked.

Colton grinned and grabbed the opportunity to undermine Sam. "Our fearless special agent must have been bored holding up the wall in the gem room. He found himself a classy piece of ass and dragged her out into the lobby for some face-to-face. Nice clothes, nice body, black hair, and dark eyes that could bore holes in even his thick hide. Whatever he was selling, she wasn't buying."

"South American?" Kennedy asked.

"Why wasn't I told?" Sizemore demanded.

Sam looked at a point between the two men and said, "About half an hour ago I noticed a Caucasian female, probably early thirties, well dressed, walk into the conference room that some of the second-tier dealers have rented just off the lobby. Despite her clothes and confidence, something was wrong about her. I took up a position close to the Purcell booth, where she had engaged Mr. Purcell in a business conversation that could also have been a flirtation."

"Nobody would flirt with that slimeball unless money was on the table," Sizemore said.

"My impression was the same, which was why I watched her," Sam said neutrally. "She flashed some skin, Purcell lost focus, and she switched gems on him."

"Big deal," Sizemore said. "Gem shows draw con artists the way fresh shit draws flies. You get her name?"

"Natalie Harrison Cutter. No ID to back it up and I didn't have the authority to push it. Last time I checked, a shell game isn't a federal crime."

"You turn her over to the locals?" Kennedy asked.

"The gem I caught her with was a lab job," Sam said. "I haven't had time to verify if the blue sapphire she left with Purcell is real or not."

"You nailed her too soon," Colton said, shaking his head in false sympathy at Sam's mistake. "She hadn't pulled the switch yet. Patience, boy. How many times do I have to tell you?"

Sam bit back his first answer, looked at Kennedy, and said, "She pulled the switch. I'd swear to it in court."

Kennedy shut up. However much SA Sam Groves chapped Kennedy's Boston ass, he knew that Groves was one of the best sheer investigators in the Bureau. Great eyes. Great instincts.

And too damn smart for his own good.

Sizemore tapped one index finger on his chin and stared into the middle distance. Then he looked at Kennedy. "Anything that weird should be investigated. All my men are tied up in security for this convention."

"Jesus," Kennedy muttered. "Another joker. I have more of them than real cards." He pointed at Sam. "Run her and tell Sizemore what you find. If it still doesn't fit, keep after her."

What Sam thought of the assignment didn't show. It didn't have to.

Everyone in the room knew that he'd just been given more of a slap than an assignment.

Chapter 9

Los Angeles
Noon Tuesday

Eduardo Pedro Selva de los Santos walked up and down the narrow aisles of Hall Import and Specialty Gem Cutting, which for all its fine name was in the basement of Hall Jewelry International along with the heating, cooling, and plumbing systems. Eduardo didn't particularly notice the piercing clamor of cutting machines and the bent backs of the cutters from Ecuador who tended their geriatric equipment the way they had once tended crops.

The air tasted of powdered stone and petroleum-based lubricants.

He no more noticed the gritty air than the immigrants at bus stops noticed smog or bodies that ached before their time. *Ni modo.* It didn't matter. What counted was the cash money to be earned, the kind of wealth that was impossible to find in the jungles and mountains of Ecuador.

Even after forty years in America, Eduardo mailed half his money to his family back home, to his mother and wife and sisters and daughters. While their men worked in the golden north, the women raised children who were the result of the men's seasonal Christmas visits. A lonely way to raise a family, but better than being poorer than dirt, generation after generation, world without end.

With the miraculous American dollars that flowed from the north, the women bought chickens and wool yarn, calves and seed and even the most precious thing of all: land.

"*Hola, Manolito,*" Eduardo said. "*¿Cómo estas?*"

A teenager young enough to be Eduardo's grandson looked up from the machine that noisily, relentlessly ground away to reshape the gem from an older, less beautiful, or more recognizable stone into a new, anonymous one. The young man smiled and nodded eagerly but didn't speak. Eduardo was el Patron, el Jefe, the man who made or broke an immigrant's chances with a single gesture. Manolito's extended family had pinched and saved for three years to pay the smuggler who brought him to the U.S. To be sent home would be a catastrophe for his whole family.

With an expert eye Eduardo squinted at the settings on the machine, measured the angle of the rough being cut, and patted the boy approvingly on the shoulder. "*Bueno, chico. Bueno.*"

Leaving the grinning, relieved boy behind, Eduardo went to the man who oversaw a series of faceting machines. A few quick words, a friendly whack on the arm, and el Patron moved on.

The cell phone in his pocket vibrated. He retreated to a fairly quiet corner of the barnlike building and answered the phone mostly in English, which even if overheard by the workers wouldn't make any sense to them. "*Bueno,* Eduardo speaks."

"There's a shipment leaving Long Beach Harbor. Be ready to mix it with the lot that came in last week."

"Of course, *señor,*" he said, recognizing the voice of Peyton Hall, the COO of Hall Jewelry International.

"Don't get greedy, *chico.*"

"Never, *señor.*"

Silently, Eduardo hoped that one of the lots would have a nice stone or three that wouldn't be missed. That was where his real profit came from—skimming goods that weren't well documented. Who was to know whether a ten-carat stone was reworked into one or three stones, or perhaps ruined entirely and worth nothing at all? Only Eduardo knew, and he wasn't talking.

Then there were the gems that came to him from his country-men by means he never questioned. Profitable, very profitable. It was good to have family that others feared, family that would never betray him, not even for a sapphire bigger than his thumb.

Without realizing it, Eduardo smiled.

He'd sweated for two weeks before deciding that he simply couldn't risk destroying the beautiful stone by reworking it. He'd taken it to a gem trader he knew by reputation only. The man had looked and looked again. And again. Then he gave Eduardo ten thousand American dollars, no questions asked.

Eduardo had been so grateful he'd paid to have a new altar made for the village church.

Humming softly, he dreamed of the next shipment coming in. Three more, that was all. Then he would take his cache of stones and retire to Ecuador to sit and smoke cigars and dream in the hot sun.

Chapter 10

Warily, Kate Chandler stood just outside the bank of elevators and checked the lobby. A lot of men milled about, some of them in jeans and sports coats, but none of them was Special Agent Sam Groves. She was certain of it. She had a vivid memory of him burned into her mind—short, dark brown hair with a flash of silver at the temples. Eyes as hard and blue as the missing sapphires. Way too intelligent. Way too male.

He was an armed chameleon who could be easygoing one instant and rough as a brick the next. She would be a long time forgetting the hand that came out of nowhere, the eyes that saw too much, the contempt in his voice. No, she wouldn't have any trouble picking him out of a crowd.

What she had trouble doing was getting him out of her mind.

Kate rubbed her arms briskly. Even after going home for a shower and a change of clothes, she could still feel his grip and the clammy panic that had swept through her, followed by a flood of adrenaline that even hours later made her skin prickle in memory. It had been so quick, so easy for him to grab her. No warning. No sound. Nothing but a hand out of nowhere clamping around her fingers and the certainty that she was doomed.

It was somehow worse than the phone message that had threatened death in eerie mechanical tones. That had scared her, but not like Sam Groves. With him, between one instant and the next, the world had changed. For the worse.

Is that what Lee felt? Everything fine and then SLAM and it all goes to hell?

A shiver went through her. She ignored it. *Thinking about what happened or might have happened or will happen won't do any good. FBI agent Sam Groves is smart and quick. So what? I'm smarter and quicker. I got away from him.*

Didn't I?

All right. So he let me go. So what?

So I'll look around very carefully before I try any other switches.

No problem with that. She hadn't found another of the Seven Sins, and those were the only stones that were worth the risk involved in switching. Those were the only stones that could lead her to the truth about her missing brother.

Don't think about Lee either. Not now. Crying or being afraid will tank your act. Suck it up.

With a brisk tug Kate straightened her lightweight brown leather jacket over her pink shirt and faded blue jeans. A casual dark plastic clip kept her hair out of her face but let the waves of black tumble freely down her back to her shoulder blades. Simple sneakers replaced the expensive leather shoes she'd worn earlier.

Sam will never recognize me.

Yeah, and I can leap over tall buildings.

But none of that mattered. She wouldn't find any clues to Lee's disappearance hiding in her home.

"Katie? What are you doing here?"

Her stomach clenched in the instant before she recognized Gavin Greenfield, Lee's godfather and lifelong friend of her father. In the months after Lee's disappearance, Gavin and his wife, Mary, had been a blessing to the Mandels. Gavin's younger brother had been a deputy sheriff before he retired, so Gavin had handled a lot of the official details, sparing the Mandels.

"Hello, Uncle Gavin," she said, smiling and opening her arms to her honorary uncle. "What brings you to Scottsdale? Why didn't you call and tell me you'd be here?"

"Because it's all business from early breakfast to midnight drinks. Not a second to myself. Summit meeting of furniture manufacturers. A few days and then I'm right back to Florida to help Mary. Her bad ankle is giving her fits." He gave Kate a big hug. "How about you? Last time we talked, you were up to your eyebrows in new things to cut."

"Oh, I decided that it was time to pull my nose away from the grindstone and see if there was anything new in the gem trade."

Gavin's eyes didn't miss the lines of sadness and tension that hadn't been on Kate's face before Lee disappeared. "Good idea. You need to get out more. Fine young woman like you, I'll never understand why you haven't married and given your parents grandchildren."

Two men yapping into cell phones stepped out of the elevator and nearly ran over Gavin, which saved Kate from having to make her usual reply—*They just don't make them like you anymore.*

Gavin stepped out of the way of the men and said, "Damn things should be banned."

"Cell phones?" Kate asked, hiding a smile.

"Curse of the twenty-first century."

"You still don't have one, do you?"

"No, and I never will."

Kate didn't doubt it. "What's the summit meeting about?"

"Furniture-making is going overseas, like so much else." Gavin shook his bald head. "It's my sad job to inform my colleagues that the Chinese make pretty damn good furniture for a third what it costs if it's made here."

"Better wear armor."

He sighed and changed the subject. "How's your gem-cutting business going? You being driven out by machines or foreigners yet?"

"So far, so good."

"You ever finish that job Lee mentioned you were so excited about?"

Kate tried to ignore the wave of sadness that tightened her throat and made her eyes burn. "Yes, I finished it. Have the police—" Like Gavin earlier, she broke off in midsentence.

"Nothing new," Gavin said. He hesitated, breathed deeply, and told Katie what her parents should have told her months ago. "And there won't be. Lee was a grown man with his own way of looking at the world. For whatever reasons, he disappeared with a packet of goods valuable enough to require a courier." Gavin put his well-manicured hand under her chin. "You've got to let go of it, Katie," he said sadly.

"Has anyone?"

"Your parents are getting better at it every day that goes by without a call or a card or an e-mail from Lee. It's time for all of us to pull our lives together again."

Damn it, Uncle Gavin. Can't you see that Lee wouldn't ever do this to the people who love him? But all Kate said was, "You've been talking to my mother."

"Your dad's worried about you too."

"I've been living on my own since I was twenty. I'm thirty-three now. While I appreciate everyone's concern . . ." She shrugged.

"We all should butt out, is that it?"

Instead of answering, she hugged him hard. "I never should have encouraged Lee to become a courier."

"Aw, honey, that's just pure, double-dyed crap. Lee was happy to find work that paid decent, sent him all over, and didn't bore him."

Kate just burrowed closer and smelled the familiar scents of tobacco and aftershave. Then she stepped back. "Does Aunt Mary know you haven't stopped smoking?"

"I don't smoke unless I'm on the road."

"Better wash everything before you go back."

"That bad?"

"She loves you anyway."

Gavin grinned. "And that's a fact. You have time for some pie and coffee? I can be a little late to the meeting."

Kate was just starting to say yes when she saw someone she didn't want to see get out of an elevator not six feet away. Quickly she moved around Gavin until he was between her and Sam, the FBI man.

"I'd love to, but I've got an appointment I'm late for," she said, watching the nearby bank of elevators rather desperately.

One of the doors opened. Kate didn't look to see if the elevator was going up, down, or sideways. She just took it and hit the button that closed the door. Then she leaned against the steel wall and practiced breathing.

It was something she'd done a lot of since she'd met Special Agent Sam Groves.

Chapter 11

Scottsdale
Tuesday
1:05 P.M.

Sam saw the sexy con artist slide into a handy elevator, thought about following her, and decided against it. Instead, he memorized the name on the bald man's conference ID tag and mentally filed it. Sweet Natalie was jumpy enough that she might rabbit if he started questioning her buddies. He didn't want that to happen until he knew more about her. Enough to find her, for instance.

He checked the window of his cell phone. Still blank. No missed calls. No messages.

C'mon, boys and girls. How long can it take to run a name like Natalie Harrison Cutter through our databases?

"Problems?" Mario asked from behind Sam.

"Slow response from records," Sam said.

"You running that woman—Natalie Whatshername?"

"Cutter. Yeah. Figured I'd try our records first."

"Want me to run her name through Arizona's databases?"

"Thanks, but until I know where she's from, or until Kennedy upgrades her from my punishment to a viable lead, I don't want to waste anyone's time except my own."

"Leave wasting time for Sizemore, right?"

Sam grimaced. "You said it, I didn't."

"Sizemore doesn't work for Phoenix PD." Mario flashed a grin that made him look like a teenager.

"Don't push it," Sam said quietly, looking around the lobby. "Sizemore is a bona fide member of the federal old-boy club."

Mario gave a fluid shrug. "Every law-enforcement operation has a club like that. Cops don't retire—they just hang with one another and talk shop. Hell, I'm not even saying that Sizemore is wrong. I've seen the files on the South American gangs. They're really busy, really bad boys."

"The MOs aren't the same in all the courier robberies."

"Different gangs."

"So Sizemore says. All South American."

Mario gave Sam a sideways look. "The Teflon gang? I ran the name and got nothing."

"That's because it's my personal name for the gang. Since my 'wild speculations' never got past my SAC or SSA into a file, it's not surprising you never heard the name. You get any hits with the maids or bellmen yet?"

"*Nada.*"

"What does your gut say?"

"The help doesn't like talking to cops because no one wants to be shipped south if their illegal status is discovered. So they're nervous. Big surprise. No one I've questioned is from Colombia, Peru, or Ecuador. Some Guatemalans. A lot of Mexicans."

"Mendoza do any better?"

"If he has, he's not sharing," Mario said.

"Then he hasn't. He's not a glory hog."

"So what did you find about our gem switcher, the one that leaves good stuff and keeps the bad? You sure she isn't a blonde?"

"Haven't you heard?" Sam asked. "Blonde jokes are out. Demeaning to groups like Blondes Demanding Respect."

Mario did a double take. "There's no such group."

"Prove it."

The cop gave a bark of laughter and headed for the bell captain's desk, shaking his head.

Sam checked his cell phone, saw the terse message—NO HITS—and swore silently. No female Caucasian between the ages of twenty-five and forty using the name Natalie Harrison Cutter, under any spelling variation, had been arrested, fingerprinted for any job, or otherwise entered into the FBI databases.

Either she was innocent or she'd been using an alias. All in all he was betting on the alias, which meant that subtle wasn't going to get this job done.

He went to the registration desk, showed his badge, and requested the on-duty manager. Very quickly he was in an office with the door closed behind him. Hotels really didn't want to make their clients nervous.

Cops made people nervous.

"How can I help you?" the day manager asked. "There hasn't been any trouble with the security arrangements for the gem trade show, has there?"

Sam smiled easily. The manager was blonde and sleek and not stupid. If Blondes Demanding Respect ever came into being, she would be a charter member and first president.

"Your staff has been very helpful," he said, hoping it was the truth. "We just want to know if you have a Natalie Cutter registered here." He used the Bureau's royal "we" because it worked better than "I." No one gave a crap about what Sam Groves wanted, but people jumped for the FBI.

"That's Natalie with a 'y' or an 'ie' or something else?"

"Check all variations," Sam interrupted. "Same for Cutter."

The manager's elegant eyebrows rose, but she started tapping on the computer keyboard. After a few moments she frowned and typed again. Then again.

Sam waited. He was good at it. As far as he was concerned, being a successful investigator was sixty percent patience, thirty percent luck, and ten percent brains.

And if you were lucky, you could throw patience and brains out the window.

"I'm sorry, sir," the manager said finally. "We don't show anyone with that name registered here, either in the past few weeks or pre-registered for any of our conferences or conventions in the next month."

"Maybe she's at another hotel." *Or more likely she lied to me.* Either way, he wasn't worried. Sometimes lies told him more than truth.

"Another hotel." The manager brightened at the idea that someone who was on the FBI's scope wasn't on her client list. "I'm sure that's the case. Is there anything else?"

"Gavin M. Greenfield. Normal spelling on both names. If that doesn't work, get creative."

Her fingers skimmed over the keyboard. "Normal spelling works. He's with the furniture convention. Room ten-thirty-three. Would you like me to ring the room?"

"No, thanks. Could I talk to your day security chief?"

"Of course."

Sam went to the security office, shook hands with the security man, flashed the badge a few times, watched another hour go down the drain, and finally came away with ten copies of a picture of "Natalie Cutter" taken from the lobby security tape. He went back to the manager's office.

"Thanks," Sam said to her. "Could you ring ten-thirty-three for me? If Greenfield answers, just tell him someone from the front desk is bringing up an urgent fax for him."

"If he doesn't answer?" the manager asked.

"Hang up. I'll try later." And he'd do it in person.

The manager rang the room. And rang it. And rang it.

"I'm sorry, sir," she said finally. "No one answers."

Sam thanked her and headed for the motor coach that was the task force's home away from home. As he walked, he kept glancing at the photo, wondering if it was going to be more help than the name had been. The photo wasn't a great likeness of "Natalie," but

Sam figured that a bald man who was hugging-close to the con artist would recognize her quick enough.

As for Kennedy and Sizemore, they could use a magnifying glass on their copies of the photo and then shove the works up where the sun didn't shine.

Chapter 12

Los Angeles
Tuesday
3:00 P.M.

The headquarters of Hall Jewelry International was in an old building, where a four billion dollar boondoggle—also known as a subway four miles long—had been built to bring thousands of people to the aging central downtown area. But building a subway on top of the complex San Andreas fault system hadn't been a good idea. Eventually politics gave way to reality and L.A. returned to buses and cars as usual, leaving the old downtown stranded well away from the wealth and new buildings of the Miracle Mile.

From the outside, Hall Jewelry International was a modest six stories with a rooftop cornice and false columns that harkened back to slower, kinder times. Inside, it was modern hustle and security. Contrary to the usual practice of outsourcing everything to Asia or India, it was a point of pride with the company that some of Hall's gemstones were cut and polished in the barnlike basement with open plumbing overhead and coded locks on the doors. The first floor was the flagship jewelry store. The second floor was taken up by offices and visiting salesmen hawking everything from synthetic turquoise to the latest patterns in ten-carat gold chains. The rest of the floors were given over to assembling jewelry from various international pieces—chains from Italy, gems from Thailand and Brazil, catches and pins from Mexico. The result was inexpensive jewelry for America's endless malls, nearly all of which had a Hall Jewelry store somewhere in their air-conditioned expanse.

Peyton Hall, the heir apparent to the whole operation, was doing an unannounced check of the cleanliness and appeal of the flagship store's displays when the manager spotted him and rushed over.

"Mr. Hall, how nice to see you," she said. "If we'd expected you, I would have had coffee and pastries brought in."

"No need," he said, shaking her hand. "I have to catch a plane soon. I just wanted a final look at our summer and fall offerings before I go to Scottsdale. Has my uncle arrived?"

"Not yet. He—"

"I'm right behind you," a male voice cut in. Geraldo de Selva shared his sister's dark coloring and confidence. "I was just going over the books with your mother."

The dark hair and confidence of the Selva family had been passed on to Peyton, with the addition of his father's hazel eyes and relentless sex drive. The result was a shrewd businessman and married womanizer with two children. Though Peyton was impatient to run the family business, he was smart enough not to piss off his mother's younger brother, who was in charge until his mother said otherwise.

And that was the problem. Geraldo was only eight years older than Peyton. By the time his uncle was ready to retire as CEO, Peyton would be lucky to be alive. The Selva clan members routinely lived to be a hundred.

Peyton's daddy had checked out at fifty-three. Peyton didn't figure he'd see seventy. As he was forty-nine now, that didn't leave a whole lot of time to make his own personal fortune so that he could spend his last decadent decades chasing young foreign women and drinking expensive old booze.

Geraldo gave his nephew a hard hug. "We're proud of you, *chico*. You're one shrewd buyer. Since you've taken over the estate gems and import end of the business, profits are up forty-seven percent."

Peyton grinned. He got half of all increased profits in the portions of the business he ran, which meant a nice bonus by the end of the year. About a million dollars, as a matter of fact.

"Thanks," Peyton said, returning the hug. He stepped back and smiled at the manager, who was still hovering. "I know how busy you are with the Mother's Day promotions. Don't waste time with us."

The woman smiled a bit uncertainly and withdrew.

The two men began walking down a side aisle of the jewelry store. Geraldo glanced down at the "school sweethearts" display—delicate silver or ten-carat gold chains with two paper-thin hearts joined at the point and two tiny faceted stones, one for each heart. All for under twenty-five dollars.

"We sell a buttload of that junk," Geraldo said.

"Sometimes I think every girl over five owns one or two of them," Peyton agreed. "The real money is in replacing them," he added. "Wear one a few times and wear it out. Costs more to repair than it's worth, so you whine and pine until the parental units buy more jewelry for their precious kids."

"Cheaper to buy a good one in the first place."

"If you had the money, sure. They don't. That's why they buy cheap first, second, and third."

"At least we can offer pretty good value in the estate jewelry boutiques," Geraldo said. "That was a great idea."

Peyton smiled. The best idea of all had been pulling out the real stones and putting in something less valuable. Zircon for diamond, spinel for ruby, synthetic for real, bad quality for good. No one noticed except the accountants, who approved of the fattened bottom line.

Sometimes he wondered if his mother suspected, or if she really believed her son was a frigging business genius who still couldn't be trusted to run the family stores without constant oversight. It really pissed him off that he wasn't allowed to buy a pair of underwear without ten minutes of maternal advice.

Relax, Peyton told himself. *Don't be like your old man and pop a vein in the middle of an argument. Just keep slamming away the*

*money and in a year—three max—you'll be toasting your butt in Rio
de Janeiro with four underage sweeties to keep you happy.*

He took several relaxing breaths and concentrated on his own
personal vision of Paradise: young women in his bed and his safe-
deposit boxes brimming with the best of the gems that the South
American gangs brought to him.

And if the gangs roughed up a few couriers along the way, hey,
life was tough all over.

Chapter 13

Scottsdale
Tuesday
8:00 P.M.

Sharon Sizemore shook back her artfully sun-streaked brown hair, adjusted a pair of thin-rimmed, rectangular black reading glasses, and skimmed the room-service menu. Nothing had changed since yesterday. She could have the scampi on fettuccine or she could just cut to the chase and order a cold pasta and shrimp salad.

Because whatever she ordered, it would be cold by the time it got to her room.

"Make mine rare," Peyton Hall said from the suite's bathroom.

"Cabernet or zinfandel?" she asked, understanding his unspoken request for filet mignon, rare, with baked potato, double sour cream and chives, extra butter.

"I'll try the zin this time." Smiling, dripping water from his shower, Peyton stood in the bathroom door and watched her order their dinner. This was as close as he would get to having a naked secretary, which had been a favorite fantasy since he'd gotten his first executive office. He'd tried it once with a call girl. It just wasn't the same. "Tell them not to hurry."

"You do want dinner this month, don't you?"

"You're too hard on the staff."

"Someone has to be," she muttered. "Once, just *once* I'd like to lift the lid on a room-service dish and see steam rise. Maybe if I ordered shrimp on dry ice . . . ?"

Peyton tied the hotel robe around his thick middle and grabbed the TV remote. He and Sharon had been fairly regular lovers for six years, long enough for him to know that he wasn't going to get lucky again before dinner.

"Hey, they're showing *Blue Velvet*," he said.

Sharon shrugged. "Just because it has dialogue doesn't mean it isn't a fuck flick."

He sighed. She really was out of the mood. "Maybe we should cancel room service and eat out."

She scrolled through the notes she'd been making on various items that should be called to her father's attention. "Why? I thought you wanted to be alone."

"I did. I am."

She looked up, confused.

"You barely stopped working long enough for a quickie," he said.

With a muffled sound of impatience, she set aside her tiny laptop. "Sorry, darling. The more Dad drinks, the more details I have to chase."

"I know. I'm buried too. We're trying to outguess the economy and lock in Christmas gem orders for all the stores. Then the South Americans clobbered one of my couriers last week and my insurance rates are already so high I get a nosebleed just okaying the checks." Not true—the courier's company took the gaff—but Peyton was working on the sympathy vote.

"Poor baby. Come here and let mama make it all go away."

She didn't have to offer twice. Tugging at his bathrobe, he started toward her.

The phone rang.

"You better answer it," she said. "Your calls are being forwarded to my room tonight. No one who calls me will be surprised to hear a man's voice. I don't think Marjorie would be happy to hear mine."

He swore and picked up the phone as his bathrobe hit the floor. "Yeah?" he said roughly.

The change that came over him told Sharon that it was indeed Marjorie calling.

"You got a note from Timmy's teacher?" he asked.

Without missing a beat Sharon picked up her computer and went to the bedroom. Experience told her that Peyton's wife was about to unload a day of single parenthood on her husband's head. No need for Sharon to hang around, listening to Timmy's latest screwup and Tiffany's endless need for expensive clothes, dance lessons, and the car she simply *had* to have for her upcoming sixteenth birthday. As Ted Sizemore had often pointed out to Sharon and her brother, Sonny, kids were an expensive pain in the ass.

Even so, when she was younger, she'd wanted to have children. After forty set fire to her birthday cake a few years ago, she'd decided to forget it. Years of watching Peyton struggle with his demanding wife and spoiled children had made Sharon relatively happy about being the no-strings woman in his life.

There was a lot to be said for consenting adults.

She flipped open her computer and turned to the list of incoming couriers for the Scottsdale Gem Show. Not all of them came under Sizemore's advance—and expensive—security arrangements, but many did. At this, the delivery end, the trick was to keep the shipment secure until a representative or the dealer himself signed for it. After that, it was somebody else's problem.

She began double-checking the arrangements for delivery. When she reached the Carter gems, she frowned.

In the other room the telephone receiver hit the cradle with emphasis. A few seconds later Peyton appeared in the bedroom doorway.

"Something wrong?" he asked, yanking on his robe.

Sharon looked up, saw that his interest in sex had wilted, and said, "Simon Carter had a family emergency. He won't arrive for two more days, but the courier arrives tomorrow with the best gemstones. I'll have to sign for them."

"Carter, huh? Word is he has some choice black opals. The last of the really good stones from the glory days of Lightning Ridge."

"So I hear."

"You hear any prices?"

"He wants a million for the opal that's green-blue on one side and fiery red on the other. A guaranteed natural, not a doublet."

Peyton whistled. "Any collectors lining up?"

"Not until they see for themselves that the stone is as advertised."

"You think he'll get it?"

"I think he likes the stone too well to sell it at any price."

"Bragging rights?"

"Just one more way for the boys to play 'my package is bigger than yours,'" Sharon agreed, scrolling down her screen.

"Wonder how much the opal would bring if it was cut down into earrings and necklace?"

"For your mall stores, it would be a waste of time, money, and material. The people who come to Hall Jewelry wouldn't know a world-class gem if it jumped up and called them by their first and middle names."

"I was thinking of opening a handful of boutique stores," Peyton said, "the kind that would go after Tiffany and Cartier customers. I could offer them more bang for their buck."

"The people who shop high-end stores don't want bang. They want validation. Buying expensive stones from the biggest mall jeweler in the United States won't make those buyers feel special."

"You don't like the boutique idea?"

Sharon rubbed the back of her neck and rolled her head from side to side. "You'd have to change the name, find a big celebrity to front for you, build up an expensive collection of important stones and designs, bid and win outstanding stones at public auctions, the whole enchilada. That's a lot of cash out of your pocket, especially at a time when demand for luxury goods is thirteen percent less than it was last year." She sighed and rolled her head again. "Everyone in the gem business is being squeezed, from wholesale to retail, miners to cutters. Even people who provide security have had to slash prices to stay afloat. In all, this is a bitch of a time to open a high-end jewelry chain."

"That's what I told Marjorie," Peyton said, lying easily because it came naturally to him. It had been his own idea, a way of justifying buying high-end stones to line his retirement accounts.

Sharon dropped her hand. "Since when has your wife become interested in the business?"

"Since she decided that mall jewelry was too downscale for her and the kids."

"*Merde.*"

"I said the same thing in English. Reselling old estate jewelry is one thing. Making modern high-end stuff is another." Which was true. It just wasn't a truth he embraced.

After a sigh and a roll of her head on her neck, Sharon went back to staring at the computer screen. Peyton crossed the room and began rubbing her neck, looking over her shoulder at the computer screen as he dug at tense muscles.

"What's that?" he asked. "Captiva Island and sapphires?"

"Dad has me keep track of all courier murders and/or gem heists. Technically, the Captiva one was a disappearance. Guy skipped with a blonde and at least a million, wholesale, in goods. At least, according to the insurance reports the goods were worth that much." She shrugged. "You know how that goes. Anyway, some relative was trying to track him down."

Peyton's fingers dug into tight shoulder muscles. "Why? Were the gems a family affair?"

"No. Personally, I think the relative is a nutcase. Can't believe her little half brother is a crook, yada yada yada. For a while she made a big enough stink that the FBI file was updated—new interviews, recent gossip, that sort of thing—pretty regularly. When it's updated it shows on the screen."

"So what's new?"

"Nothing. My orders are to check every few days to see if the file pops up with new info."

"Old-boy network. Man, your father's still really wired in to the Bureau, isn't he?"

"You better believe it. Sometimes I feel like I never left the FBI. The pay is the same and the hours are worse." She rolled her head again, trying to release the same tension that Peyton's fingers were working on. Then she sighed and went back to looking at the computer.

Peyton kept reading over her shoulder while his hands slid farther down her collarbone. "I didn't know you were doing off-site security for Branson and Sons."

"New client." Her breath hitched as his fingers curled around her nipples. "This is our third run for them."

"Rough or polished goods?"

"Both."

"Nice catch," he said, tugging at her nipples and memorizing the courier's arrival time.

Smiling, Sharon closed the computer and set it aside. "Speaking of nice catch . . ."

"Hmmm?" He nibbled at her neck.

"You feeling like pitching?"

He pulled her hand inside his robe. "What do you think?"

"Hardball." She smiled slyly. "My favorite."

Chapter 14

Scottsdale
Tuesday
10:30 P.M.

Sam watched while Gavin Greenfield entered the lobby of the hotel with three other mildly drunk conventioneers.

Finally. I was beginning to think he went with the guys to a whorehouse for an all-nighter.

When the men headed for the elevators, Sam put away his newspaper and followed. Two of the men got off on the eighth floor and one on the ninth, leaving Sam and Gavin alone in the elevator. When the doors opened onto the tenth floor, both men stepped out.

"Gavin Greenfield?" Sam asked as soon as the doors closed behind them.

"Yes?"

Sam pulled out his credentials. "FBI Special Agent Sam Groves."

Gavin looked curious rather than alarmed when he saw the gold badge. "What's this about?"

A photo appeared in Sam's other hand. "Do you recognize this woman?"

"Sure. That's Katie." For the first time Gavin looked anxious. "Is she all right? Has anything happened to her?"

"She's fine. Do you have a last and middle name for Katie?"

"Her full name is Katherine Jessica Chandler. Katie to her family. Kate to everyone else. Look, what's this—"

"Excuse me, sir," Sam interrupted without raising his voice. "How long have you known her?"

"Since she was eight. I'm an honorary uncle. Why are you asking about her?"

"Just routine," Sam lied easily. "Her photo came up in connection with a background investigation we were running. We needed to match it with a name. You're sure about the identity?"

"Absolutely."

"Do you have an address and telephone number for Ms. Chandler?"

Gavin hesitated, looked again at the badge on Sam's palm, and gave him the information.

"Local address," Sam said, recognizing the name of a nearby bedroom community. "Is she staying at the hotel?"

"I don't think so. It's only a short drive from her house and the rooms here are pricey."

"Thank you, sir. If we need anything else, I'll be in touch."

Leaving a bemused Gavin behind, Sam got on the elevator and went back to the front desk. Ten minutes later he found out that no Kate or Katie Jessica Chandler was registered under any variation of the name. He looked at his watch and decided it was never too late to catch a con artist at home.

And this time he wouldn't take no for an answer.

Chapter 15

Glendale
Late Tuesday night

Kate heard her doorbell ring, looked at the clock above her workbench, and shot to her feet.

Lee!

Even as the thought came, she tried to control the wild rising of hope inside her. She had a lot of business associates in the immediate area. It wouldn't be the first time that someone with a handful of good rough gems was too impatient to wait for normal business hours to talk to her. It was one of the downsides of working and living in the same place.

With a caution that came from handling small, very valuable, easily portable goods, Kate looked out the expensive peephole in her sturdy front door.

Not Lee.

The Fed.

How did he find me?

Kate flipped on the intercom and left the locks as they were. "Sorry, wrong number."

"Not according to Gavin Greenfield," Sam said.

"What—how—is he all right?"

Sam found it interesting that both of them were so concerned about the other. Family friend and stepdaughter of family. Maybe Gavin was part of the scam, whatever it was.

"He was fine when I left him half an hour ago," Sam said. "Do you remember my name and serial number, or should I entertain your nosy neighbor across the street by dangling my badge beneath your porch light?"

"What do you want?"

"To talk."

"You mean you want to grill me like a cheese sandwich."

Sam's mouth kicked up at the left corner. "I have better manners than that. You going to let me in or do you want to do this the hard way?"

Kate stared at the unexpected smile for an instant. She started to ask him what *the hard way* was, thought better of it, and began opening the unusually strong bolts and locks that secured every door in the house.

"Don't faint if you see my handgun," she said. "And don't bother to ask to see my permit. Arizona has an—"

"Open carry law," Sam cut in. "It's just one of the things that make this such an interesting state to work in."

The door opened. A single look told Sam that the door had a magnetic contact on it. If it was opened after the alarm system was armed, bells would ring somewhere. The door also had a steel plate embedded in it and extralong bolts on the lock. Once that puppy was shut and bolted down, it would take a shaped charge to open it. He went to a window and saw that it was wired into the house alarm system.

Either the lady was paranoid or she had a lot to protect.

Sam turned from the window to the woman who was watching him warily, a woman whose hands were smudged with something fine and dark, like soot.

"You have more security than Fort Knox," he said.

"I doubt it."

"Any particular reason, or are you just paranoid?"

"For doubting you?"

"For the security," he said. "The neighborhood isn't rich enough or poor enough to need it."

"Then I must be paranoid."

Sam shook his head slightly. "Try again."

"Why should I?"

"Why shouldn't you?" he asked, smiling.

Kate stared at him and wondered how many people he'd questioned with that same combination of easy patience, professionally genial smile, and hard-eyed intelligence. "What do you want from me?"

"The truth about you and that sapphire you switched."

She tilted her head to one side and studied him in silence. Hair slid out from the clip that was casually anchored on top of her head. She ignored it.

Sam's eyes followed the slide and bounce of the strand of glossy hair. Hair like that had to be natural. None of the dyes were good enough to put that kind of richness and sheen into the hair shafts. No matter how costly the salon job, sooner or later dyed hair looked like what it was. Fake. And if he had any remaining doubt about the naturalness of her color, all he had to do was stand close enough to verify that the random flashing threads of light in the black were silver rather than gold.

So he stood that close.

"What are you doing?" she asked, stepping back.

He noted that she was fussy about her private space, which must have made flirting with Purcell hard work. "I'm looking at your gray hair. Most women would hide it."

"My father was completely gray when he was forty. I've had thirty-three years to get used to the idea of my follicle destiny."

Sam's smile was different this time, real, like his laughter. "You really don't add up, do you?"

All she said was, "You should laugh more."

"Why?"

"It changes your eyes from hard blue to the kind of shimmer you only get from fine, untreated Burmese blues. Sapphires."

His smile shifted to that of a male who has become intensely physically aware of an interesting female. The resulting expression wasn't quite predatory, but it was a long way from safe.

Sam cursed the quickening of his body and concentrated on business, "You sound like you know a lot about sapphires."

She nodded.

"You're going to make this like pulling teeth, aren't you?" he asked.

Kate didn't answer. She was still stunned by the jolt of sheer physical awareness that had arced between her and the irritating FBI agent. She rubbed her work-grimed hands on her jeans, scrubbing away the residual tingling in her palms.

"I—" She stuck her hands in her pockets. "I'm not used to midnight visits by strange men with badges."

"It's not midnight yet and you've met me before."

"That still makes you a strange man with a badge."

"Do cops make you nervous?"

"Do you ever stop asking questions?"

"Sure. As soon as I have the answers." Sam looked at the hands bunched in her front pockets, stretching her jeans over a good-looking butt and long thighs. "Most women don't garden at night."

"We've already established that I'm not most women."

"Were you digging in the backyard?"

"No."

Sam waited, letting the silence expand with each heartbeat until it was pressing against Kate from all sides like a vise.

"I was working," she said.

At last. A small crack in her verbal defenses.

And they both knew it.

"Doing what?" he asked gently.

"I work for myself."

Sam went back to silence and the sense of a vise squeezing air out of everything.

"I'm a gem cutter," she said.

Bingo.

"Have you done any big emerald-cut blue sapphires lately?" he asked.

Kate's breath wedged in her throat. If she'd had any hope that the man with changeable blue eyes was slow on the uptake, she knew better now. She watched him intently, seeking any shift in his expression when she said, "Not in the last five months."

He didn't miss the faint emphasis on the "five months" or the intensity of her stare. She was expecting him to react.

He was sorry to disappoint both of them.

"Is that supposed to mean something to me?" Sam asked.

"Why should it? It didn't mean a damn thing to the rest of the FBI."

"Try me."

"Oh, sure. You're different. It says so right below the number on your gold-plated badge."

"What do you have to lose?" he asked reasonably.

"My time and my temper," she shot back. "I really hate being treated like I bark at airplanes."

Sam fought it, then gave up and just laughed. "You nailed it. Nobody does high snot like the FBI."

She tried not to grin but couldn't help it. " 'High snot.' Oh, God, doesn't that just describe it." Laughing, she decided that Special Agent Sam Groves might possibly be different from the federal robots who'd interviewed her several times in Florida. Not that the agents had wanted to talk to her after the first time, but she'd made their lives miserable by insisting that she had a lead on a kidnapping between Fort Myers and Captiva Island. And then she went to a local newspaper with the same story, forcing the FBI to at least pretend to listen to her.

She'd paid for it too. That was when the call had come telling her to back off or die.

"Who'd you tangle with?" Sam asked.

"Whoever was on nutcase duty in Miami in November of last year. I forget the names. Dumb and Dumber is how I thought of them." As Kate spoke, she took her hands out of her pockets and decided she had to do something with them besides fidget. "Want a cup of coffee?"

"I'd appreciate it."

"Long hours and less sleep?" she asked, heading for the kitchen.

"That about sums it up." He followed her into a kitchen that wasn't big or small. The appliances were into their third decade. If she made money scamming, she sure didn't put it back into her house.

Kate reached for the bag of ground coffee.

"You going to wash your hands?" he asked.

She looked at her hands and the dark smudges that came from the various fine grits she'd been using to polish a rather nice orange topaz. "What are you worried about? Strychnine is white."

He grinned and wished they had met some other way. But they hadn't, and wishing wouldn't change it.

Kate washed her hands at the sink, wiped them on a small towel, and went back to making coffee.

Sam leaned against a kitchen counter and watched. She moved quickly yet smoothly, no jerks or jumps or stumbles. Good balance. Great hands. The confidence that came of being in a familiar place.

Sexy too. Way too sexy.

Very soon he had a mug of rich, dark coffee steaming underneath his nose. He sipped, sighed, and sipped again. Then he settled back in a kitchen chair and wondered if he really would have to grill Katherine Jessica Chandler like a cheese sandwich to get any information.

The telephone rang before he could decide.

As Kate reached for it, she asked Sam, "Does the name Lee Mandel ring any bells for you?"

The mug stopped halfway to Sam's mouth.

Chapter 16

Scottsdale Royale
Midnight Tuesday

Ted Sizemore's voice cut through the fog of smoke and alcohol chatter at the hotel bar like a brass buzz saw.

"Hey, if it isn't Jack Kirby! You old son of a bitch, what are you doing here? I haven't seen you in years."

Kirby turned, spotted Sizemore, and held out his hand. "I'm working, what else?"

"Still skip-chasing?" Sizemore asked, pumping the former Drug Enforcement Administration agent's hand vigorously. He and Kirby had worked on the crime strike force that had made Ted Sizemore a legend.

"Along with background checks, divorces, child custody, and lost cousins. The usual PI stuff." And some other things that weren't usual, but sure paid well. Not that he was going to talk about that part of his business with old "Straight and Narrow" Sizemore.

"You look like you're doing all right," Sizemore said. He knew Kirby was nine years younger and had a full head of close-cropped gray-brown hair, but that wasn't the real difference between them. Kirby was fit in the lean way that was genetics as much as hard work.

"Nothing big," Kirby said. "Nothing fancy like you. But being a private investigator pays the bills with a little left over to put a few bucks on the ponies when I'm bored. But don't tell my ex-wives. They think I should be eating dog food in a slum."

Sizemore snickered. "Sit down. I just finished an interview with one of the local reporters."

"The media always did love you," Kirby said. And vice versa.

"I sell papers," Sizemore said as he signaled the bartender. "What are you drinking these days?"

"Gin and tonic. Thanks." Kirby settled onto the bar stool and looked around the room with the eyes of a former cop gone private. Nothing to worry about here. Just a gathering of conventioneers and good old boys. He gave Sizemore his full attention. "How are Sharon and Sonny?"

"Pain in the ass, that's how." Sizemore took a long swallow of beer. "Gotta watch Sharon like a frigging hawk or she'll 'forget' to ask me and just run the damn show herself."

"She always was a pistol."

"And Sonny always was a blank round," Sizemore said.

"You're too hard on the boy."

"Yeah yeah," Sizemore said without interest. "I hear that from Sharon twice a week. How are your kids?"

"Grown and gone, like the last two wives."

Sizemore shrugged. "Same shit, different day. What brings you to Scottsdale?"

"A cheating, lying, no good son of a bitch husband."

Sizemore snickered and finished the beer. He rapped the bottle smartly on the bar. "How much is he worth?"

"To me or to his wife?"

"Fuck the wife, she's probably doing the gardener."

Kirby laughed. Even when Sizemore's tongue was thick with alcohol, his mind was still quicker than most. "That bad-boy husband is worth a couple hundred a day and expenses to me. What brings you out of L.A.?"

"Business. I'm security advisor/coordinator for the National Co-alition of Gem and Jewelry Traders."

"So, you tuck them in bed when they're drunk?" Kirby said, ges-turing with his glass to a table of rowdy conventioneers.

Sizemore snorted. "I'm not their nanny. And those guys aren't mine. They're furniture types. My boys are having a convention here in a few days, but most of the high-end trading gets done in the days before the official opening. Private showings in their rooms. I make sure the doors are locked and everyone who leaves with more than he came with has a sales receipt, that sort of thing."

Nodding, Kirby sipped his drink. "Your job sounds about as excit-ing as mine."

"It will be real dull if I can keep the South American gangs out of my clients' hair. You want excitement, you chase one of those bad boys."

"Yeah, I busted my share of them working undercover. That task force you ran still takes the prize for sheer number of arrests." Kirby saluted Sizemore with his glass. "The South Americans were doing drugs, then. Still are, I guess. I've kind of lost touch. I'm all over the country now." He smiled slightly. "Pay might not be much, but the travel can't be beat. It keeps me young."

"You ever miss the DEA?"

Kirby narrowed his eyes and looked at the moisture beading on the gin-and-tonic glass. "Sometimes. A badge opens more doors than a handful of papers. But I can't say I miss living undercover with twenty-two-year-old assholes holding more cash than a work-ing stiff like me would make in a lifetime. That really used to piss me off, especially around April fifteenth."

"Tax time." Sizemore shook his head and picked up the fresh beer the bartender had put in front of him. "Yeah, I hear you."

"How about you?" Kirby asked. "Do you miss the bad old days?"

"What's to miss? I still work closely with the Bureau, but I can do things as a civilian that would get me bounced if I was carrying FBI creds. Best part is I don't have to worry about fancy lawyers fucking up my fieldwork."

Kirby grinned. "Neither do I." He clinked glass against bottle. "To life without badges."

"I'll drink to that."

Chapter 17

Glendale
Wednesday
12:05 A.M.

Sam leaned against the kitchen doorway, sipping coffee and listening to Kate's half of the conversation. He'd guessed after the first few moments that it was good old honorary Uncle Gavin calling to tell Kate that the Feds were sniffing after her.

"No, really, it's all right," she said for the third time. "I'd have done the same thing." *Before Lee disappeared, but not after.* "Sure. Give Missy a kiss for me when you get home. And stop worrying. I'm fine."

She hung up and gave Sam a look that could have been amused or irritated or both. Underneath those emotions was the sadness that had begun five months ago and the fear that had started with the blind phone call threatening death unless she stopped asking questions.

She hadn't stopped, but she'd been a lot more careful about who and what she asked.

"Have fun listening?" she said.

"Yeah. It was a stitch and a half. I take it Gavin Greenfield lay awake thinking about our chat and finally just had to call you."

"He's a good, decent man."

"Damn few of us left," Sam said, watching her over the rim of his mug. "What relation is he to Lee Mandel?"

"Gavin is Lee's godfather."

"Are they close?"

"Not for the last five months." Kate clenched her hands together, then forced herself to let go. "You recognized Lee's name."

Sam didn't hesitate. He'd already decided what he'd tell her and what he wouldn't. Not that there was much to tell. The Bureau grapevine had already tagged the McCloud case as a career disaster that no one wanted to touch, much less request the file and go on record as having read all about it. Sam had done his best to duck that whole aspect of the crime strike force's brief—he was afraid Kennedy would tie the McCloud case to Sam's career and sink him without a trace.

"Lee Mandel," Sam said, "is a courier who went missing with a package that cost Mandel Inc.'s insurer seven figures to make good."

Lee was also the final straw that had set the crime strike force into being a few months later. Arthur McCloud, the man who'd lost the sapphires, was a friend of the governor of Florida and a brother-in-law of the president of the United States, but Sam didn't figure Kate needed to know that. Neither did she need to know that the McCloud case had been a woofer for everyone involved. Once Kennedy had seen where it was going, he delegated the case to the Miami office and ran away like the politically savvy coyote he was. By then, the crime strike force had developed a momentum of its own independent of McCloud.

Thank God.

Not that the president's wife didn't make inquiries from time to time, scaring the hell out of the Bureau director. It would have been funny if the director hadn't passed the fear down the line as fast as he could. Even the name McCloud could make grown men turn pale.

"What's your connection to Mandel Inc.?" Sam asked.

Kate didn't answer. She was too busy telling herself that Sam wasn't the kind of man that appealed to her. He was too cold, too controlled, just one more federal robot mucking up her life. Yes, he was intelligent, but she needed more than that. She demanded a sense of humor in a man. She doubted if Sam had one worth mentioning.

He gave her a long look. "Anything that's public knowledge about you—and a lot that isn't—will be mine before the sun rises. Same for Mandel Inc. Save your energy for a fight you can win."

"My stepfather owns Mandel Inc."

"There. That didn't hurt, did it?"

She gave Sam a look that could have blistered paint.

He smiled thinly. "You're not stupid, Ms. Chandler. Don't act like it and I won't act like you are." He took a sip of his cooling coffee. "Lee Mandel, son of your stepfather and your mother . . ." He waited, silently asking a question.

"Yes," Kate said tightly. "He's my brother. Half brother, actually, but Mom was helping Dad begin Mandel Inc., so I practically raised him. He was such a fun baby, always laughing and making sweet sounds."

"How old were you?"

"Eight when he was born."

Sam nodded, trying to think of a gentle way to tell Kate that her sweet little half brother had grown up into something sour.

To hell with it. There isn't a kind and gentle way to say it.

"From what I remember of the file," Sam said, "Lee Mandel is believed to be living the high life in Aruba with his big-boobed blonde squeeze."

Kate's face tightened until she looked like she felt—hard and angry. "So the FBI says. I don't believe it. I know him. He wouldn't do that to his family!"

"Local law enforcement disagrees."

"Local law enforcement couldn't find a clue unless it was in a box of doughnuts."

"Ouch. You're really down on cops, aren't you?"

"For good reason."

"I'm listening."

"Why?" she asked bitterly. "They didn't."

"They didn't see you make a switch under a lecher's twitching nose."

She laughed without meaning to. "It did twitch, didn't it?"

"Like a rabbit's."

Her smiled faded. "Even if Lee has some issues with Dad—and what son doesn't?—Lee and I are very close. He'd never just disappear without saying anything to me. He'd call or write or e-mail or—something."

"Has he?"

"No."

"What do you think happened?"

She closed her eyes and said in a raw voice what she really didn't want to believe. "I'm afraid Lee's dead."

"Robbery?"

She nodded jerkily.

"Then why was his rental car turned in at the airport?" Sam asked.

"If the keys and the papers were in it, anybody could have turned it in instead of him. You've seen the lines of cars waiting to be checked in. Lots of people leave the keys and the rental contract, and run for their planes without the check-in drones ever seeing their face."

"Okay," Sam said, watching her intently, "someone else could have turned in Lee's rental. Why would they?"

"To frame him and throw everyone off the trail. And it sure did the job. No one is really working on the case. Everyone believes Lee is a crook who got away with it. End of story."

Carefully, Sam took a sip of coffee. The stubborn look on Kate's face was at odds with her tousled hair, but he didn't doubt her determination. *Tread carefully, boy, or you'll blow every bit of the progress you've made.*

But tiptoeing around things was also a good way to blow a case. People revealed more when they were off balance than when they were relaxed.

"Assuming a frame job and murder, where is Lee's body?" Sam asked neutrally.

"Have you ever been to Sanibel Island?" Kate asked. "It's on the way to Captiva, one of Lee's favorite places. If he stopped anywhere, he stopped there."

"I don't know either island, but I've done time in Florida."

"Most of Sanibel is a mangrove wildlife preserve. It wouldn't be hard to . . ." She gestured futilely.

"Hide a body?" Sam finished.

Kate flinched but didn't disagree. "At low tide a lot of Sanibel is a maze of mangrove roots sticking up from the mudflats and branches coming down. It looks like small caves made of twisted wood. If someone anchored a . . . body out of sight, the crabs would take care of the rest. Or the alligators in the swamps. Or chain and weights wrapped around the body. Or . . . hell, you're the federal cop. Fill in your own blanks."

"So, we have a returned rental car and a missing, possibly murdered, Mandel Inc. courier who was carrying something valuable and portable. Go on."

She grimaced. "There's no place to go."

"How close were you and Lee?"

"As close as siblings can get. Maybe closer. I really was more like a mother to him than a sister, especially when he became an obnoxious teenage male."

Sam hesitated, sipped coffee, and asked, "Half siblings have been known to be sexually involved."

Kate stared at him. "Do they teach you to be revolting or is it a natural talent?"

"I'll take that as a no."

"Take it as a hell no!"

"Okay, you were his half sister and semi-mother. Kids hide stuff from their family all the time. What makes you so sure Lee didn't take off to Aruba with the loot and a blonde?"

"The blonde with the famous boobs?"

"Yeah."

Kate hesitated, laced her fingers together, freed them, and said, "I don't want to do this. If Lee is still alive, he'll be furious."

"Do you think he's still alive?"

Tears shimmered and didn't fall. "No," she whispered. "He would have gotten in touch. Even if he didn't want to talk to Mom or Dad, he'd talk to me." *Or to Norm.*

"Maybe Lee didn't want you to know about the blonde. Brothers don't want sisters to know how bad their taste is when they're thinking with their dicks."

Kate smiled wanly. "Lee is gay. No blonde women in his bed."

Sam's left eyebrow lifted. "Nothing about that was in the report."

"The cops didn't ask me."

"And you didn't offer."

"I'd promised Lee."

"No one else close to Lee mentioned it either."

"He didn't tell our parents," Kate said. "He didn't want to hurt them. He never told anybody from his childhood but me."

"How about the people he worked with?"

"Mandel Inc. wouldn't have cared, once Dad got past the shock of his only son being gay. Unfortunately, I can't say the same for some of the other courier services he freelanced for, especially Ted Sizemore's operation. Sizemore has the reputation of wanting only heterosexual white males and just enough ethnic females to keep the government off his back. So does Global Runner, for that matter, and Lee also did a lot of work for them."

"So, other than anonymous lovers, you're the only one in the world who knew that Lee was gay?"

Her eyes narrowed at the neutral expression Sam wore and the cynicism in his cold blue eyes. "You don't believe me."

"I'm trying to figure out why Lee told you his deepest secret. You have any guesses?"

She hesitated, then decided it probably wouldn't matter; Lee needed justice, not old secrets. "I knew before he did. Girls loved him, and he loved them, but it was the same way he loved me. Affection. No sparks. The night he came back from the senior prom, I was there because I'd come home for Lee's graduation."

When Kate hesitated, Sam sipped coffee and waited.

She closed her eyes, remembering. And in remembering, knowing all over again how much she loved and missed her baby brother. Since she couldn't pace in the small kitchen, she began making a sandwich even though she wasn't hungry.

"Lee tapped on my door and asked if we could talk," Kate said as she opened the refrigerator. "The moment he came in the room I could tell he'd been drinking. He sat on the floor by my bed and started talking about his girlfriend. He'd broken up with her."

"Why?"

"She wanted sex. He couldn't. Not with her. Her brother, however, turned Lee on big time, but he couldn't say that to her, didn't even want to admit it to himself." Tears magnified Kate's dark eyes. "Lee said he'd tried to kill himself on the way home but yanked the wheel aside at the last instant. He sat on the floor and sobbed about how worthless he was, what a disappointment to his father."

The refrigerator door slammed. Blindly, Kate went to work slicing the leftover turkey she'd found.

"I grabbed him and hugged him and told him that he wasn't worthless," she said, "that he was bright and funny and handsome and kind and an all-around wonderful pain in the ass, and if he ever tried anything so stupid again I'd kill him myself."

Sam would have smiled but the pain Kate was feeling was too real.

"We talked for a long time, long enough for him to get sober. He said if I promised not to tell anyone that he was gay, he wouldn't try killing himself ever again." She ignored the tears sliding down her cheeks. "I promised. He went away to college and neither of us mentioned that night again. But he never dated. Women, that is."

Sam watched Kate slice turkey and then tomatoes with a knife he could have used for shaving.

"The report I read was real specific about the blonde," Sam said neutrally. "She wasn't the first either. The impression from observers and acquaintances and family is that Lee likes women."

"He does. He just doesn't want sex with them. He is everyone's best friend and nobody's lover. Female, that is." Kate stacked a second piece of bread on the sandwich and sliced through with a slashing motion of the blade. "He is a good, kind, loving man. He had a lot to offer someone, and he'd finally found a man he wanted to settle down with and—damn!"

With the back of her right hand, Kate swiped at the tears that wouldn't stop. The knife blade flashed near her face. She ignored it.

Sam gently pried the wicked blade free. "Easy, now. That thing could shave steel."

Her fist hit the counter. "I hate sniveling."

"So do I. You're crying because you've lost someone you love. Big difference."

She shuddered and fought for control. "Then you believe me?"

"Yes." *Until I catch you lying.*

"They didn't."

"Who?"

"The damned FBI agents I went back to again and again whenever I turned up something I thought would make them take an interest in going to work on Lee's disappearance."

"Did they?"

She made a disgusted sound. "They patted me on the head, said something about giving false information to federal agents, and sent me out the door."

Sam's eyebrow went up. That too hadn't been in the report. "Yeah, well, the stuff that doesn't agree with official theories often gets left out. Simple fact of bureaucratic life."

Kate watched him with tear-drenched, determined eyes. "Voice of experience?"

He smiled sardonically and wondered why he felt more kinship with this sad little con artist than he did with ninety-five percent of the people he worked with.

"Do you know what car rental agency Lee preferred?" Sam asked.

"FirstCall. My father's company has a deal with them."

"Which airport would Lee have used that day?"

"Fort Myers. He liked to go shelling when business took him to Sanibel or anywhere else with a beach. Instead of spending time on the road driving down from the Tampa airport, he flew in through Fort Myers and used the extra time for picking up shells."

"Did he have a lot of business on Sanibel or Captiva?"

"Too much, apparently," she said, her voice rough.

"What do you mean?"

"Predictability. It's a problem for couriers. Especially with the South American gangs."

"Everybody's favorite bad boys," Sam said.

"You have a better candidate for what happened to Lee?"

"I was hoping you would."

She shook her head and gestured to the sandwich. "You hungry?"

"Thanks. What about you?" Sam asked, picking up half of the sandwich.

"No."

"Not hungry and not dressed for bed. Not watching television. Not drinking."

"How do you know?"

"TV in the corner is off. So are the lights. No open books or magazines around. Your breath smells of coffee, not alcohol. What were you doing this late at night that required coffee instead of sleep?"

Kate realized all over again that no matter how relaxed and easygoing Sam appeared, he didn't miss anything important.

"You'd never guess," she said.

"Then save us both time. Tell me."

"Cutting stones."

"Sapphires?"

"Among other colored stones. I don't do diamonds."

He looked at her for a long moment, remembering how she'd seemed pleased when the big sapphire's cut was praised by someone who ought to know.

"You cut that fake—"

"Synthetic," Kate corrected automatically.

"—sapphire, didn't you," he finished, ignoring her interruption.

"Yes."

"What does that have to do with Lee Mandel?"

"I cut the gems that he supposedly disappeared with."

"What were they?"

"Seven sapphires cut from an enormous piece of Burmese rough that a collector's family had held on to for more than one hundred years. There were too many problems with trying to cut a single huge stone from the rough, so no one had done anything with it. After I studied the rough and reported to McCloud, he decided that he wanted seven different gems. He called them the Seven Sins because he spent a sinful amount of money on them."

"He didn't use that name with the FBI. Nothing like that appeared in the file."

"Maybe McCloud didn't think the Bureau had a sense of humor," Kate said.

"He wouldn't be the first. Go on."

"Not until I have some assurance that what I'm saying will be kept confidential. Out of any open files."

"Why?"

"The last time I told the FBI anything, I was told if I kept pushing, I would die."

Sam went still. "The FBI told you *what*?"

"It wasn't the FBI. At least I don't think it was." Kate shrugged. "Hell, it could have been. They sure were tired of hearing from me."

"How, precisely, did you get the death threat?" Sam asked distinctly.

"On my voice mail. I have a tape backup so I can have a record of client requests."

"Do you still have the message?"

"Sure, but it won't do you any good."

"Why?"

"They used a voice distorter."

"I'd like to send the message to the lab."

She hesitated, then went to a filing cabinet. A minute later she handed him a small cassette tape that had been sealed into an envelope with her business logo on the outside.

"You're sure the voice was distorted?" Sam asked, pocketing the tape.

"Yes. I could hardly understand the words. Then I wished I hadn't."

"You could hardly understand, yet you assumed the caller was somehow connected with the FBI?"

"No. I assumed that whoever sent the message knew that I'd been to the FBI again. It could have been the local cops. That's possible, isn't it?"

"If this someone has access to FBI files, or local police files, and somehow knew that the Lee Mandel file had been updated, yes, it's possible. Just."

"You don't believe me."

"Ms. Chandler—"

"Never mind," she cut in. "You won't believe me even after you file your report and Lee's file is updated and I'm found with my throat slit in my own house. Suicide, no doubt."

The sarcasm didn't move Sam, but the edgy fear in Kate's eyes did. Whatever he believed or didn't believe about the quick, sexy con artist, she was sure her life was at risk if she kept trying to solve the mystery of Lee Mandel's disappearance.

"You're going to keep pushing anyway," Sam said.

"Until I have answers, yes."

"Or you die."

She bit the corner of her mouth and said nothing.

Sam decided quickly, going with his gut rather than with FBI procedure. Trusting his own judgment was just one of the many things he'd been in trouble for over the years.

"Ms. Chandler, do you know what a confidential informant is?"

Chapter 18

Scottsdale
Early Wednesday morning

Kirby grabbed his digital phone off the bedside, looked at the incoming number window, and swore. The number was blocked.

"If this is a six A.M. telemarketer from Nebraska," he muttered to himself, "I'm going to find the asshole and make his headset a permanent part of his equipment."

Kirby answered the phone anyway, but only after he started the built-in digital recorder. The person he knew only as "the Voice" used the digital phone to send him new information. He—or even she, who could tell?—used a voice distorter. The meaning of the conversation was always clear though. Every call put Kirby onto a courier who was carrying portable, anonymous wealth. Gems. Rolex watches. Bearer bonds. Even cash. Kirby had several sources, but the Voice was the best. He didn't mind putting half of the take in an offshore account, even though he couldn't trace the money's ultimate destination.

And he had tried. He wanted to know who his informant was. More important, he wanted to know how the caller had gotten the information to blackmail Kirby into working for him in the first place.

"Yeah?" he said roughly.

"Mike Purcell. Clean him out and give him a Colombian necktie."

Adrenaline kicked as Kirby recognized the Voice. "That'll cost more."

"I won't expect a split on this one. It's all yours. Should be worth at least a hundred thousand to you, maybe more."

"And if it isn't?"

"Have I ever cheated you?"

"No." It was the sole reason Kirby put up with taking orders from a ghost. The Voice was smart, thorough, and wired into the gem trade. Since the Voice had started calling three years ago, Kirby's overseas accounts had fattened into six figures, heading toward seven. "When do you want it done?"

"ASAP. Purcell is sleeping in a motor home parked in the Royale's employee lot. An old Winnebago. Security is battery operated. Pull the leads in the service panel."

"He's not using the hotel safe for his goods?"

"He doesn't trust anyone."

"Smart," Kirby said. "Dumb too."

"Make sure you get the big sapphire. Size of your big toenail, emerald cut."

Kirby smiled. "Where'd a crud like Purcell get that?"

"Who cares? Just be sure that nothing weighs more than four carats when it goes back into the market. Don't use Hall. At least one of his cutters is unreliable."

"Which one?" Kirby asked.

The Voice ignored his question and asked another. "You have enough men for another job at the same time?"

"Depends on the work."

"Standard hijack."

"Scottsdale?"

"Yes. Incoming from L.A., usually stops for fuel in Quartzite and at McDonald's for a clean john. Beige rental car, Taurus, Arizona license . . ."

Kirby was already writing on the pad he kept beside the bed. "Electronic key?"

"Yes, but use a crowbar anyway. Rough up the courier. Have one of your boys drop some gutter Spanish."

"*Sí. ¿Cómo no?*"

Eerie mechanical sounds came over the line. Kirby assumed it was laughter.

Hoped.

He wasn't a pussy, but sometimes the Voice creeped him out.

"Be ready to do it again a few days later," the Voice continued. "They'll have to send in more gems for the show. I'll tell you when. The second lot should be the best."

"Usual split on that one?"

"Fifty-fifty."

The connection went dead.

"Fucking-A," Kirby said, grinning and counting money in his head. Even if he gave half of his half to one of his men, it was still a good score.

He turned off the phone, stretched his wiry body, scratched his crotch, farted, and walked naked to the bathroom. While he emptied his bladder, he went through his various gem-cutting connections in his mind. Mexico had a few cutters, but like a lot of black-market workmen, they tended to skim the cream off incoming shipments and resell on the side. If the Voice didn't want anything bigger than four carats out there, Mexico wasn't a good bet. Maybe Burma. Tricky though. His connection there had pissed off some drug warlords and was still in the hospital.

"Hell," he muttered, shaking off the last drop. "Gotta be Pakistan or Afghanistan. Wonder if Abdul is still alive."

A few phone calls, a little patience, and the news came back that Abdul was alive and well in Karachi.

Kirby looked at his watch. Too late to do anything about Purcell. That left the courier. Only question was, Who to call? Murphy was in New York following some merchandise. Rodrigo was in Texas, but he had a new baby and was taking some time off. Sumner was making noises like he wanted out of the game, which made Kirby nervous about assigning him anything physical; if he was caught, he'd roll over in a New York minute.

Time to check through the files of unhappy ex-agents and soldiers again. Someone is bound to be interested in a little adrenaline and cash.

Unfortunately, he needed someone now. Someone reliable. Or mostly reliable, which was how John "Tex" White was becoming.

What makes him think he can do drugs and not turn into a mutt? Stupid bastard.

Shaking his head, Kirby punched in a number. It was picked up on the forth ring.

"Yah," said a man's voice, yawning.

"'Morning, Tex. You ready to rock and roll?"

Chapter 19

Scottsdale
Noon Wednesday

Sam's stomach growled as he climbed up the steps to the strike force's big motor coach. He was carrying a plastic bag from a nearby minimart and thinking wistfully of the *taqueria* three miles away. Then he pulled a soda and two packages of peanut butter and cheese crackers from the bag, wadded the plastic into a ball, and fired it toward the first trash basket he came to.

It missed, but so had a lot of other trash.

With a nod of greeting to the men and women whose attention was buried in the array of electronics that were crammed into the coach, Sam popped open the soft drink and went toward the SAC's office. The door was open, so he walked in.

"'Morning. Oh, wait, it's lunchtime." Sam saluted Doug Smith with a package of crackers. "Good afternoon."

"Close the door."

As Sam did, he braced himself for whatever came next. He wasn't sure how he'd pissed off his immediate superior, but he was sure he had. If he'd had any doubts, the fact that Doug didn't ask him to sit down was another bad sign. With a sigh, Sam stuffed the crackers into the pocket of his casual jacket and waited for his boss to drill him a new asshole.

He didn't have to wait long.

"What in hell were you thinking?" Doug snarled.

Since Sam didn't know why he was being reamed, he didn't answer.

"Well?" Doug shoved back his chair and gestured to a slender file that lay on his desk like an accusation.

Sam had long since perfected the art of reading upside down. The file's jacket said it all: Lee Andrew Mandel. Well, Sam had been prepared for that. He just hadn't expected it to hit the fan so fast.

"If you discovered anything about the Cutter woman, you were supposed to tell Sizemore," Doug said. "Direct order from Kennedy. Simple to follow. And you fucked it up."

"I'm sorry, sir." Sam worked very hard at sounding contrite. "I was following a CI's leads. There could be some intersection with the woman Natalie Cutter. Even so, Bureau policy has always been that an agent's confidential informants aren't given to anyone in the Bureau without overwhelming reason, much less to a civilian like Sizemore, who is no longer with the Bureau. A civilian, I might add, who knows more than we do about some aspects of the crime strike force's objectives and keeps that information to himself. His privilege. He's a private citizen. A CI is an agent's privilege."

Doug blew out one long breath, then another, before he said neutrally, "You have a CI."

"Yes, sir."

"So instead of working with Sizemore as directed by SSA Kennedy, you're following leads from a CI you've turned up somewhere, somehow, all on your own."

"Yes, sir."

"Leads that made you curious about a five-month-old case that has career suicide written all over it?"

"Yes, sir."

"Leads that were so red fucking hot that you just had to put highest priority on your requests?"

"Yes, sir."

"Do you have any idea how many man hours it could take to trace a rental car after five months?"

"No, sir."

"Confidential informant," Doug said with a bitter twist to his mouth, as though the words tasted bad.

Sam didn't answer. It wasn't a question.

Doug picked up the file. "I'll cover you with Kennedy as long as I can. Again." He threw the file at Sam, who caught it without flinching. "You better come out smelling like a rose garden or you'll finish your twenty in Fargo and I'll laugh out loud when I sign the orders."

"Yes, sir."

"Get your smart ass out of my sight."

Sam was shutting the door behind himself before Doug finished his sentence.

Chapter 20

Quartzite, AZ
Wednesday afternoon

Tex White acquired his target just where he'd been told she would park: the McDonald's in Quartzite. He watched her make a short call on her cell phone—probably checking in with her boss. Then she got out, locked the car with a remote-control key, and stretched like she hadn't been out of the vehicle since L.A.

Probably she hadn't. Couriers didn't take many breaks, because they knew that was when they were the most vulnerable.

He moved his white van into the parking space next to hers, near her left front door, but he allowed her plenty of room to open her door. He didn't want her to feel so crowded that she got smart and went around to the passenger side to get in.

The van's windows were very dark, even on the driver and passenger doors. The windshield was just light enough to get past the law in California. Quickly, White unfolded a wide sunscreen on the inside of the windshield. Not only would it keep heat out, it would give him complete privacy.

He got in the back of the van, cracked the side door so that the courier wouldn't hear it open, and pulled on a ski mask. He reached for the exam gloves he'd stashed in a grocery bag. He pulled on the gloves, flexed his hands, and examined the gloves for flaws. The damn things came apart quicker than a rubber. Satisfied, he pulled a spring-loaded sap from his rear pocket.

Ready to rock and roll.

With the patience of a trained hunter, he crouched in back and waited for the courier to use the john, pick up her order, and come back to her car.

Sweat seeped into his ski mask.

He ignored it.

There weren't many people around the parking lot. The snow-birds had mostly pulled up stakes and headed north again, following the melting ice. Nothing was going on in Quartzite this week, so there weren't thousands of people crammed onto the dry, dusty grounds of the annual gem and mineral show. It was too late for lunch and too soon for dinner. Only people traveling between L.A. and Phoenix stopped here for a break.

Not that the nearly deserted parking lot mattered to White one way or the other. He'd taken people out of theater lines with no one the wiser.

The glass door to McDonald's opened and the courier came out. Middle-aged, dyed brown hair, lightweight slacks and T-shirt for the hundred-degree heat. Her purse was as unremarkable as she was. She already had the key to the car in her hand. She punched the button that opened the driver-side lock and opened the door.

White went out of the van like a hundred-and-seventy-pound cat. His lead-filled sap hit the base of her skull with a meaty sound. As she slumped forward, he grabbed the key from her hand and used her momentum to dump her over the car's center console and into the passenger foot well. He ripped off the ski mask and threw it on the seat. Then he turned and closed his van's side door.

Five seconds after the courier had unlocked the door to her car, White slid into the driver's seat, shut the door, and started the car. He drove to an empty stretch where desert and town overlapped right next to a motel that was barely clinging to survival. Most of the action here was at night, when girls took their customers for a fifteen-minute spin. In the daytime, the place was a ghost motel.

He drove around to the back, parked next to the big trash bin, and dropped his pants. Gritting his teeth, he ripped off the tape holding a steel bar to his right calf.

After a quick look around to assure himself that nobody was watching, he went to the trunk, wedged the bar beneath the rim, and gave a brutal yank. The trunk of the little car popped open. He saw a suitcase and a package with brown paper wrapping closed by various security seals. He stuffed the package under his shirt and closed the trunk. Because it had been forced, the lid didn't shut completely, but it was close enough to look good from across the lot.

Again he glanced around without seeming to. Still alone. He started to walk back to his van, then remembered the rest of his instructions.

Rough up the courier.

He pulled on black leather gloves with lead inserts in the back of the fingers and opened the passenger door of the white car.

Chapter 21

Glendale
Wednesday evening

Why hasn't he called? *Did he tell his boss about me and now he doesn't want to face me?*

Kate paced her workshop, wondering if by trusting Special Agent Sam Groves she'd effectively signed her own death warrant.

Don't be silly. No one has called to threaten me.

Maybe that's because they won't threaten this time. They'll just kill me and be done with it.

Automatically, she glanced at the bolts securing the doors to her home workshop. Still locked. Status lights on the security system were still green. She wished it made her feel better, but it didn't. She was smart enough to know that all the locks and alarms in the world wouldn't keep out someone who was really determined.

The knock on the front door made Kate jump. Heart racing, she went to the nearest intercom, flipped the switch, and said curtly, "Yes?"

"Sam Groves."

"Are you alone?"

"I keep my promises, Ms. Chandler."

"I'll be right there."

What she didn't say was that she'd be praying every step of the way.

Sam waited with barely leashed impatience while Kate went through the ritual of peering through the spy hole and undoing the heavy-duty locks and bolts. An afternoon spent memorizing a career-breaking file and making calls to agents who blew him off was just the thing to put a fine edge on his temper.

When the door finally opened, Sam stepped through fast, making sure she didn't change her mind about talking to him.

"Did those locks come before or after Lee died?" he asked bluntly.

"Before," she said, shooting the bolt.

"Why? Do you get a lot of death threats in your business?"

"No, just hijackers. Some of the rough I cut is quite valuable even before it's worked."

"Like the Seven Sins?" he asked.

"Yes. They were far and away the best quality rough I've done." She walked three steps and armed the security system again.

Sam remembered what the dealer had said about the big synthetic sapphire. "So the rough had great color, clarity, and rarity?"

"All three to the max." Kate pushed a wave of black hair away from her face as she turned toward Sam. "It was the most beautiful rough I've ever worked. Even better, it was one hundred percent natural."

"As opposed to synthetic?"

"You really want to know?"

"That's why I asked."

She sighed. "It's tricky. I mean, lab gems are synthetic through and through. Everyone agrees on that. But at what point does a natural stone become so enhanced by man that you can hardly call it natural anymore?"

"You got me."

"Daunting thought." The corners of her mouth twitched upward. "Every gem association in the world has long, tedious, occasionally short-tempered meetings about where to draw the line between acceptable enhancement of a gem and treatments that are so extensive that they effectively make the stone not natural."

"Unnatural translates into less valuable?"

"Every time."

"The rarity thing?"

She nodded, swiped hair away from her face again, and said, "I've got a hair clip in my workroom. You need anything from the kitchen first?"

"No thanks. There's a great taco place only a mile from here."

"Pedro's Burrito Gordo?" she asked.

"That's the one. Nuclear hot sauce. I had to order milk to put out the fire."

"I noticed."

Sam licked his upper lip and felt the roughness of dried milk. He rubbed at it with his hand. "Well, damn. It's hard to have command presence with milk on my manly mug."

She snickered and felt the tension ease. If she had to have a cop hanging around, she'd take one with a milk mustache and a bent sense of humor. *Watch it, girl,* she told herself. *He's not supposed to have a sense of humor. He's too damn appealing already.*

"So you don't have motion sensors in your alarm system?" Sam said, looking at the status lights.

"No. When the system was installed I had a cat. It came with the house, sort of a package deal. But no matter how the security guys tinkered to give me a pet zone, I still had too many false alarms. I got tired of paying for the call-outs, so I canceled the motion sensor."

Sam looked around. No sign of a pet anywhere. "What happened to the cat?"

"Gone. She liked the neighbors better."

Enjoying the female sway of hips beneath butt-hugging jeans, Sam followed Kate toward her workroom. He started to tell her that she didn't need to clip her hair in place as far as he was concerned but decided that was the kind of unprofessional remark he should avoid. Just like he should avoid noticing her long legs and fine ass and the citrus fragrance that floated from her skin if he stood close enough.

And while he was at it, he should sign up for sainthood.

"So," he said, "except for cutting and polishing, you aren't supposed to do anything to gemstones?"

"That's the ideal." She opened the door to her workroom and started looking for her hair clip.

"We're talking human beings here, not saints," Sam said dryly.

"Ya think?" She found the clip on the first worktable with a set of dop sticks and began taming her hair. "Some treatments are so old that they've become acceptable. It's the newer treatments that are a problem."

"Sort of a grandfather clause? If your grandfather did it, that's okay, but you can't do anything new?"

She nodded, felt her thick hair come loose, and started all over again with the clip. "Actually, you can do anything you want as long as you tell the buyer what has been done, particularly if the treatments aren't permanent or don't need special handling to keep their glow."

"But if you tell the buyer," Sam said, "he might not want to pay top dollar."

"Bingo. All treatments are supposed to be disclosed to the buyer, but too many mall jewelers—and some upscale ones as well—figure if the buyer doesn't ask, the buyer doesn't care, because *everyone* knows that gems are treated somewhere between being mined and being set in precious metal."

Sam's left eyebrow rose. "I consider myself a fairly well-educated dude, but I don't know squat about the difference between a treated and an untreated stone."

"Neither do ninety-nine percent of mall shoppers, which is why disclosure is so important." She spoke fast, telling herself that the fact that he could raise one eyebrow wasn't sexy and neither was the width of his shoulders. "Some gemological societies boot out members who sell treated stones and don't mention it, especially if the treatments aren't permanent."

"So some folks dick with the stone and make it a better-looking gem and sell it without comment."

She looked away from his intense sapphire-blue eyes. *He's not sexy. He's a federal robot. Remember that.* "Emeralds have been oiled to deepen the color for hundreds of years. Rubies and sapphires have been heated for the same reason for thousands of years. Take corundum that's too light or too orange or too purple or whatever, add controlled heat, and you end up with better color in your gems. For every gem in creation, there's a way—usually several ways—to enhance it."

He leaned against a table and told himself he couldn't smell her citrus scent. Really. "So why the fuss? If everyone does it, who cares?"

"Rarity. Rarity. Rarity. A synthetic gem is the bottom of the barrel. We can make them by the container load. A treated stone is more valuable because naturally occurring gems of any color or clarity are, by their very nature, relatively rare."

"What you're saying is synthetics suck bad water."

The corners of her mouth curled upward and she admitted that the man was getting to her. "Yeah. Treated stones are naturals that weren't up to par. All treatments I know about can be detected if you and your tools are good enough. Heat treatments leave traces that any expert should recognize. Despite that, a treated stone of fine color will almost always cost more than a natural stone of inferior color, and a synthetic of any color is just plain dismissed."

"Okay." He leaned slightly toward her, breathed in. Lemony and warm. Definitely. "So what kind of premium does a natural stone get?"

Kate's hair slithered out of its coil. With a muttered word she gave up trying to look professional and clipped it all at her neck.

"Say you have two blue sapphires of equal weight and extra fine color," she said, tugging at the clip. It held. "One is heat treated.

One isn't. The stone that hasn't been treated is priced at least a third higher—sometimes a lot more, depending on size—than a treated stone of equal weight and color. When you're talking natural, untreated gems, you're talking about the best of the best."

"So when Lee disappeared, you started looking for the natural, fine, very rare blue sapphires he'd been carrying."

She blinked and reminded herself that a half rubbed-off milk mustache didn't make the man slow or stupid. "I hoped I could backtrack one or all of the Seven Sins and find out where it came from."

"You must have had some luck."

"Why do you say that?"

"Someone offered to kill you."

"But it didn't make any sense." Kate threw up her hands and looked away from Sam's vivid blue eyes. "Sure, I'd been bugging the FBI and the local cops and putting pictures of the missing stones on-line so that I'd be notified if any of them turned up, but nothing—"

"Hold it," Sam cut in. "You have photos of the McCloud sapphires?"

"Both the Seven Sins and the synthetic ones I cut while I was deciding how best to work the rough."

He shook his head like a dog coming out of water. "Back up. You cut *synthetic* sapphires?"

"Of course."

Sam told himself to be patient. "Why?"

"Burmese rough as valuable as McCloud's doesn't come along every year or even every fifty years. Take my word for it," she said quickly, heading off another question. "The Thai dealers who control sapphire and ruby rough have a stranglehold on mines, miners, and smugglers. Everything is treated. McCloud's rough had been mined more than a hundred years ago, before every last gem was cooked, filled, oiled, pressure diffused, and in general dicked with."

"Got it. Rarity, rarity, rarity."

"Right. So when I saw the McCloud rough, I did what a lot of high-end cutters do. I bought a synthetic version of the rough and practiced on it, trying out various cuts and sizes so that I would get the most valuable finished stones possible out of the natural rough."

"Isn't that work computerized now?"

"A lot of it is, especially at the lower end of the trade. And some high-end gem cutters are enthusiastic about the computer-aided design programs they use on their computer when it comes to deciding how to cut rough, but I'm not convinced." She shrugged. "For me, nothing works as well as hands-on experience."

"Well, that explains it."

"What?"

Sam rubbed his short, almost spiky hair. "Why you didn't have to chase around and hustle up a big blue stone to run the con on Purcell. You already had one right at hand. I thought maybe you went to him the first time to size up the stone, then came back with the fake the next day."

"You talked with Purcell again?"

"His wife. She remembered you."

"What a harridan."

"She loves you too."

Kate grimaced and began fiddling with one of the dops that had been next to her hair clip.

"What's that?" Sam asked, eyeing the slender rod rather warily.

"A dop. A cutter's tool used to hold the stone against the lap." She brightened. "You want a tour of my workshop?"

"Right after you tell me why you switched stones on Purcell. Twice."

She bit the corner of her mouth. "You're really quick, Special Agent Sam Groves."

He could have said the same about her, but he didn't; if he was talking, she wasn't, so he waited for her to speak. It wasn't a hardship. It gave him an excuse to study her dark brown eyes and wide, tempting mouth.

Trying to ignore Sam, Kate leaned her hips against the worktable, crossed her arms, and tried to decide how much she could safely tell him.

"All of it," he said.

She gave him a startled glance. "Are you a mind reader?"

"No more than any other cop. Don't hold out on me, Ms. Chandler. You won't like what happens."

"Call me Kate," she retorted. "The other guy who threatened me did."

Sam filed that away for future reference and waited for silence to do its trick of opening Kate's mouth.

"All right." She braced her hands on the table and crossed her ankles. "I'd been looking for the Seven Sins, using my photos of the finished stones."

"Any luck?"

"Everybody I asked said some variation of 'Nice stones' and 'Sure, babe, I'll let you know if I see them.' I waited for calls. The only one that came was a death threat. So I started going to high-end gem shows and not telling anyone my name or connection to Lee. I was about to give up when I saw Purcell's sapphire. I asked about it and he gave me a load of bullshit."

"So you rushed home, got the twin stone, and switched them the next day."

"Yes."

"That took balls."

"So to speak."

He grinned.

So did she. "When I was younger, I used to do magic tricks. I earned money at kids' birthday parties and even thought about magic as a career. Then I realized that the only women I saw in magic acts were centerfolds that were cut in half while wearing glittery underwear. One look in my bathroom mirror, plus a love of gemstones, saved me from the stage."

Sam's eyes gleamed with humor at the thought of a younger Kate dazzling her friends by pulling coins or bunnies out of their ears. "Okay, so you did the switch on Purcell. Then what?"

"I brought Purcell's sapphire home and photographed it from all angles and compared the photos with the original photos of

McCloud's stones. There's no doubt about it. Purcell's stone is one of the Seven Sins."

"So after you verified the identity of the stone, you switched it back."

"That's when we met." Kate's humor vanished. Sam hadn't come here to swap smiles with her. He'd come as a cop.

"Why did you go back to Purcell with the synthetic sapphire? What was the point of the risk?"

"I wasn't swapping the stones for fun and profit," she said, her voice curt. "I figured that if I had proof that the stones were the same, Purcell would have to talk to me about where it came from. And if he wouldn't talk to me, the FBI might help him change his mind. Either way, I'd be closer to what really happened to Lee between Fort Myers, where he last called in, and Captiva Island, which was his final destination."

"So you're not sure where Lee went missing?" Sam asked.

"No. I concentrated on McCloud first, but he never heard from Lee. At that point I worked with the assumption that Lee stopped on Sanibel for lunch at his favorite café."

Sam remembered one of the entries in the folder he'd spent most of the afternoon memorizing. "McCloud lives on Captiva."

She nodded. "Lee was taking the finished stones back to him."

"Seven Sins. Were they all alike?"

"No. Each had a different cut, a different weight. It was a real challenge to maximize the rough and at the same time follow McCloud's desire for seven sapphires of different shapes and the same extraordinary color."

"Wonder why he wanted them."

"He's a collector. The point of collecting is to have something no one else has. The Seven Sins were just that—the rarest of the rare."

"Worth killing for."

"Somebody did." Her voice, like her expression, was unhappy.

"Can you make up a list of collectors who would have wanted those gems?"

"Everyone."

"Not everyone would kill for them," Sam pointed out. *I hope.*

Kate fiddled with the dop on the table. "You have more faith in human nature than I do." She released the rod. It rolled against another dop with a metallic sound. "The point is, who knew Lee had the stones *and* would kill for the Seven Sins?"

"When the FBI interviewed McCloud, he said he hadn't told anyone about the stones."

"What would you expect him to say, that he called every collector he could think of and crowed over his incoming goodies?"

"Is that what you think he did?"

"I don't know, but I'm damn sure *I* didn't tell anyone except Lee about the sapphires."

"Who would Lee have told that he was carrying the Seven Sins?"

She started to say no one, then stopped. "He might have told his lover. I don't know. Norm didn't say anything about it when he called to tell me that Lee hadn't come back to L.A. and hadn't phoned to say where he was, or why."

"Are you still in touch with Norm? Does he have a last name?"

"Norman Gallagher. He was so hurt when Lee just disappeared without a word. We both agreed to call the other if we heard anything."

"Did Norm call again?"

"Just to talk. Not with news."

"Where does Norm live?" Sam asked.

"Los Angeles. I'll give you his address and phone, but it's a waste of time. Norm knows less than I do about why Lee vanished."

Sam wished he thought she was lying, but he didn't. "Is it possible that Lee found another lover and just blew off the rest of his life?"

"Anything is possible. But probable? No. That would be against everything that Lee is." Her eyes filled. "Was. If he's dead, and I'm so afraid he is. Damn it." She swiped at her tears with the back of her hand. "How long does it take before it stops hurting?"

"It never stops. You just get used to it."

"God, you're a fountain of human cheer."

"You'll get used to that too."

Chapter 22

"You don't know?" Ted Sizemore stalked around his daughter's hotel room, which was on the same floor as her lover's—and that really pissed him off. "What the hell does that mean, 'You don't know'?"

Covertly, Sharon examined her nail polish. The right index finger was still chipped. She really had to do some touchup before she went out tonight. Like Sizemore, Peyton noticed every flaw in her appearance, no matter how small. It was like being in the frigging FBI again.

"Well?" Sizemore demanded.

"It means I don't know." She met her father's furious temper. Or maybe it was alcohol rather than anger that had brought the flush to his cheeks. Either way, she was tired of being the target of his scream-and-stomp-around management style. "The courier was supposed to check in with us two hours ago. She hasn't called. I don't know why. I do know that she isn't answering her cell."

"Well, by God, find her!"

"The patrol put out a statewide alert for her car. Phoenix PD is checking parking lots at the stadium and airport and other large public areas where a car could be dumped and not noticed for a few hours or days. Arizona Department of Public Safety has run all the traffic accidents since the courier last checked in. Her car wasn't in any of those accidents. I've called hospitals and urgent care centers between here and Quartzite, where she last called in. Short of opening the window and yelling 'Yoo hoo, where are you?' I've done everything you suggested." *And I did it before you suggested it, but you won't mention that and I know better than to bring it up.* "No one with her name or ID has been admitted for treatment. No one with her name or ID has been involved in a traffic accident anywhere in the state. No one—"

"Don't tell me your problems. Give me solutions!"

"As soon as I have one, sir, you'll be the first to know."

"Well, don't sit on your ass waiting for something to drop out of the sky. Go make it happen!"

Before Sharon could tell her father what a useless boss he was, her cell phone rang. She answered it, listened, and disconnected.

"They found the courier in a motel parking lot in Quartzite," Sharon said. "An ER doctor is picking pieces of skull out of her brain right now. Even if she wakes up, she won't be any help. Concussions like that take away short-term memory."

Sizemore grunted. "Standard operating procedure for the South American gangs. Beat the crap out of the victims, even if you don't have to. What about her package?"

What do you think? But all Sharon said was, "Branson and Sons will be spending a lot of time with their insurers, as they were using one of their own couriers." She waited. "Don't you want to know the courier's chances for survival?"

"The only survival I'm interested in is my own. If we don't get a handle on those South Americans real quick, I'll start losing customers. I can't afford that. And if you want to keep working for me, neither can you."

Sharon kept her mouth closed. She knew more about the company's finances than her father did.

And he was right.

Chapter 23

Glendale
Wednesday night

Sam looked up from the mug of coffee Kate had poured for him. Lee Mandel's file lay open on the worktable next to the tool she called a dop.

"Okay," he said. "The Bureau and the local cops agree that the rental car was returned late but intact. No popped trunk. No broken locks. Security system in working order." He looked up. "None of the cars I've rented have security systems. Most of them don't even have remote-controlled locks."

"Try upgrading."

"Try living on the government's per diem for travel."

"Just because the trunk lock wasn't broken doesn't mean Lee is a thief," Kate said harshly. "The attacker or attackers could have taken the key from him."

"Nobody reported a scuffle involving a man of Lee's description and a white rental car."

"Did anyone ask?"

Sam's mouth flattened. "Look. We didn't know where between the airport and Captiva Island the hijacking took place. *If* it took place. None of the locals were interested in having a hijacking reported in their tourist paradise. Our men covered the bases, but it was uphill work. No one saw or heard, or wanted to. To be fair, no matter what happened, it was a long shot that anyone would have seen it, always assuming there was something to see in the first place."

"That's crap." Kate's own coffee mug slammed down on the table. "A man doesn't just vanish into thin air between Fort Myers airport and Captiva Island."

"You'd be surprised," Sam said. "It's easier than you want to believe, Kate. People with things to hide do it all the time."

Her chin came up. Her mouth settled into a stubborn line. "You sound just like the other agents."

"You want me to lie to you?"

"I want you to give me some credit for not being an idiot. Lee wouldn't have done this to the people who love him. Period. If you start from there, maybe you'll find different *useful* questions to ask."

Sam opened his mouth, closed it, and nodded. "Point taken."

She was too astonished to say anything.

It was very quiet while he drank coffee and tried to put himself in the shoes of a courier who knew he was carrying a million bucks, wholesale, in his palm.

Kate watched Sam curiously. Every time she thought she had him pigeonholed, he surprised her. Behind those startling blue eyes there was a first-class brain. Behind the hard line of his mouth there was a sense of humor. Behind his cop arrogance there was a willingness to learn.

It knocked her off balance.

He knocked her off balance.

"What are you thinking?" he asked quietly.

"Um . . ." She didn't know what to say. She sure wasn't going to say that he appealed to her as a man.

"It's a prosecutable offense to lie to an FBI officer."

"Then you must be a real busy man."

He grinned. "And while we're on the subject, you can't caper while you're a CI."

"Caper?"

"Switch more stones, if that's what was going on in your head."

She looked startled. "Would it help if I did?"

"I'll let you know if it ever comes up."

And he would make sure it didn't.

He turned over some pages in the report. The silence made the rustling of the paper seem loud.

"Are trunks always forced in courier heists?" she asked after a few minutes.

He blinked, followed her train of thought, and said, "The South Americans do a lot of trunk popping. And sometimes they beat the crap out of a courier who doesn't give up the goods quick enough."

"Maybe that's what happened with Lee. Maybe they beat him and hid the . . . result."

"Their usual method is to leave the body as a warning to the next guy not to be a hero."

"Lovely."

"Yeah, they're real sweethearts." Sam flipped over another piece of paper, frowned, and shook his head.

"What?" she asked.

"You said something about Lee having a favorite stop on Sanibel. A café."

"The SoupOr Shrimp. Best shrimp on Sanibel. And they had a server there with a great butt—or so Lee said. I never checked him out myself."

"Did you tell the cops about the café?"

"Several times," she said. "Why?"

"I don't see any follow-up," Sam said.

"Like what?"

"Like interviewing the staff at SoupOr Shrimp to find out if Lee was there, and if so, when, and was he alone. Simple stuff. Basic stuff." As Sam spoke, he thumbed rapidly through the slim file. "Nope. Maybe the cops didn't give it to us."

"Maybe they didn't bother in the first place," she said acidly.

He pulled out a narrow spiral-bound notebook and wrote in it. "We'll find out."

"I'd rather you find out what Purcell knows."

Sam looked at his watch. "Too late. They've already folded their tables, locked up the pretties, and are well into their second or third drink."

"So go to his room."

"He's not registered at the hotel. Just picks up his messages at the desk three times a day."

Kate made an impatient sound.

Sam smiled. "You can't wait to see the look on his face when I drop my badge on him."

She bit her lip but had to laugh anyway. "You're so right. Payback for all his leers and nose twitching."

Sam liked seeing her laugh way too much. It made him wonder if she tasted as tempting as she smelled.

Don't go there.

He flipped to a new page in his notebook. "So Lee always ate at this SoupOr Shrimp place?"

"As far as I know."

"Most couriers are careful not to have a pattern."

"If you look hard enough, there's always a pattern."

He lifted his left eyebrow. "You sound certain."

"I am. It's what gives me the courage to take a million dollars in rough and transform it into at least double that value in cut and polished gems. Because if I miss the pattern, I get a handful of garbage and my client gets to explain to his backers where the million in rough went."

"So cutting is just a matter of seeing the pattern?"

"And the guts to throw away what doesn't fit."

Sam thought about that for a few moments. Then he pushed the file toward her. "Read this. Tell me if there's something that doesn't fit."

Chapter 24

Scottsdale
Very early Thursday morning

While Kirby snapped on exam gloves, he watched the golf cart with the Royale logo move slowly through the employee parking lot. The speed didn't have anything to do with the guard's alertness. The cart simply didn't go much faster. A cigarette flared briefly, giving the guard's face a ruddy glow against the sodium vapor lights that flooded the lot with an odd yellow color.

Now there's a real sentry, Kirby thought in disgust. *Just in case a sniper couldn't find him driving under the lights, he sticks a cigarette in his mouth like a frigging laser tracker.*

Even worse, the guard was as predictable as an atomic clock. Every twenty-four minutes he made another tour of the employee lot. And every twenty-four minutes he found the same thing—a two-thirds empty lot with small cars and light trucks crowded close to the nearest hotel employee entrance, and a handful of motor homes and travel trailers parked wherever a newly transplanted tree offered thin shade against the heat of day.

Purcell's road-weary home on wheels was huddled next to a palm tree like a fat man trying to hide behind a telephone pole. Kirby glanced from the motor home to the FBI's rolling strike force headquarters parked less than a hundred feet away. He wasn't worried about the agents noticing him, because they would stay locked inside until their shift change, which wasn't for two more hours. As for sound alerting anyone, it would take a really loud noise, like a grenade or an unmuffled gunshot, to pull the agents' attention from their earphones, computers, and official radios.

Kirby wasn't going to make any loud noises.

As soon as the guard disappeared in the direction of the public parking lots, Kirby grabbed the small duffel bag from the passenger seat of his rental car, got quietly out, and went to Purcell's motor home. It took less than a minute to open the service panel and disconnect the electrical leads from the big batteries.

The side door of the motor home was away from the parking lot light, which put the doorway in deep shadow. Kirby almost smiled, but he was too much of a pro to get overconfident. Opening the side door took a little longer than the service panel because Purcell hadn't bothered to oil the lock. Even so, Kirby was well under the five minutes he'd given himself when he eased inside and shut the door.

The place smelled like stale hamburger, onions, and beer. Rhythmic snores came from the bedroom down the narrow hall to Kirby's left. To his right was the passenger's swivel chair and the driver's butt-sprung armchair. Like everyone else camping in the desert, the Purcells had blacked out the wide windshield with a sunscreen that turned away heat during the day and gave privacy at night. The curtains between the driving compartment and the living area were partially closed.

No one on the outside could see anything of the interior.

Kirby waited and listened. There wasn't any rush. Now that he was inside, he had all the time in the world or until dawn, whichever came first.

He didn't think breaking Purcell would use up many minutes.

While Kirby's eyes adjusted to the near-darkness, he listened to the snoring of two people. Twenty years ago it wouldn't have taken this long for his eyesight to sharpen, but the older he got the longer he had to wait for his body to do what he'd once taken for granted.

Twenty years chasing assholes who shoved hundred-dollar bills up their nose. Twenty years watching them live high—best food, best booze, best pussy money could buy. Twenty years of eating shit. And for what? Assholes still shove hundred-dollar bills up their nose and I have a pension that wouldn't keep a cockroach in crumbs. Especially after I pay the two ex-wives their share. Their "share." What a crock. Like the two dumb bitches earned it by sitting at home watching soaps and whining for more money while I risked my butt as an undercover.

Half of the snoring stopped. After a moment it resumed in a slightly different pattern.

He smiled at the familiar spike of adrenaline that had flashed through his body when the snoring changed, as though someone had awakened. In his more honest moments, Kirby knew that this, not money, was why he'd gone from retired cop to practicing crook. It was the rush of adrenaline telling him he was alive. It was the same rush that came to a gambler placing a bet, a drinker opening a fresh bottle, or a crackhead setting up a pipe.

Now Kirby's eyes could pick out the shape of the dinette table half surrounded by a padded booth, a tiny kitchen with pots and pans still on the stove, and a sink that couldn't hold any more dirty dishes. Where a small living room should have been, broad cabinets with narrow drawers were bolted to the floor. A calculator and a cash box sat on the dinette table next to a tablet and pen. Apparently, Purcell hadn't gotten around to computerizing his business.

Kirby set down his duffel. He took out paper booties like those worn by surgeons and covered his shoes. Then he pulled out a roll of duct tape and a small penlight. Following the narrow beam, he walked softly over to the cabinets. There were no obvious alarm wires and no worries in any case—the electricity to run any alarms was history.

Ghostlike, he moved toward the sound of the snores. The closer he got, the more adrenaline and anticipation lit up his blood. He didn't know when he'd started liking to hurt people. He only knew that he had.

The bedroom door was open. Even so, the smell of stale beer rising from the two sleepers was thick enough to walk on.

This is too easy.

With a vague feeling of disappointment, he went to Purcell, put his thumbs in the man's neck, and shut down his carotid arteries. Purcell twitched and went slack without ever waking up. Kirby taped the man's feet and hands together behind his back and taped his mouth closed. Then he went to work on the wife. He did the same to her and added a swath of tape around her head, covering her eyes.

Although if the sound of her clogged nose was any indication, even if he left her eyes uncovered, she likely wouldn't survive long enough to identify him. Breathing through duct tape was a pretty quick way to die.

A change in the tension of Purcell's body told Kirby that the man was awake. Kirby shifted the penlight so that it shined in his victim's eyes. They were wide and bugged out with fear. Kirby smiled and began speaking with the accents and rhythms of the border creole he'd learned so well in Miami.

"*Buenos dias,* Miguel. You and me, we talk. But first I hurt you so you no lie to me."

Kirby yanked down Purcell's underwear, grabbed his genitals, and dug in. When he finally released Purcell, the man's body was slick with sweat and the feral smell of his fear had blotted out that of stale beer. Kirby judged his victim, gave him a final shot to the balls, and waited until he stopped whimpering.

"*Señor,* you hear me, yes?" Kirby whispered.

Purcell nodded frantically.

"*Bueno.* You move jus' once and I rip off you cock and shove it up you fat ass."

Purcell lay on the bed and tried to be absolutely still, but he couldn't control the shivers of fear racking his body.

Sure that the man wouldn't give him any trouble, Kirby went back to the cabinets in the other room. He pulled a crowbar from the duffel and systematically broke the locks on the cabinets. Moving quickly, he flashed the penlight around in each drawer before he emptied the contents into his duffel. There was a lot of satisfying shine and glitter in the drawers, but nothing that matched the sapphire he'd been told to take. He went back to the bedroom, bent over Purcell, and whispered in his ear.

The smell of urine overwhelmed the other odors in the room.

Kirby ripped off just enough of the tape for Purcell to gasp out, "Milk—in—fridge."

Kirby taped his victim's mouth shut again, patted him on his bald head, and went to the kitchen. He opened the surprisingly large refrigerator. There were three cartons of milk inside. One of them had been handled so much that the carton's cheerful black-and-white cow was mostly rubbed away. Purcell might as well have pinned a sign on his hiding place.

Taking the carton, Kirby went to the sink, put in the stopper, and poured out the white fluid. Five gemstones emerged, shining through the milk. He picked them up, rinsed them, and put all but the sapphire in his duffel. He didn't know yet why the sapphire was important to the Voice, but he was sure it was.

That made it important to Kirby.

From the first time the Voice had called out of the blue and recited chapter and verse of Kirby's criminal life, he hadn't been his own man. He'd been well paid, and the jobs had been well planned out, but it just wasn't the same as being his own boss. Maybe the sapphire would be the key to his freedom. Maybe it wouldn't.

Either way, he was keeping it.

He pulled a pearl-handled knife out of his jeans. He'd taken the knife off a Colombian smuggler years ago. Mostly, Kirby used it to clean his fingernails. Occasionally, he put it to heavier work.

Adrenaline and anticipation hummed through him as he walked back into the bedroom and bent over Purcell.

Moments later, the smell of blood overwhelmed the odor of urine.

Chapter 25

Scottsdale
Thursday morning

When Sam slid in and shut the door behind him at three minutes after nine, Ted Sizemore's suite was packed with crime strike force personnel. Sam looked at the assembled people with tired blue eyes and an expressionless face. At least he hoped it was expressionless. *Mother of all clusterfucks* wasn't an observation his SAC or SSA would appreciate.

As for Sizemore, he was a bomb looking for an excuse to explode. *Screw him,* Sam thought.

The fact that Sam had spent the hours just after dawn reviewing the bloody crime scene might have had something to do with his impatience. Of all the others in the room, only Mario had been to see the trailer. No one else had been interested in the murder of a third-rate gem dealer and his shrew of a wife. The beating and robbery of a gem courier had drawn a lot more strike force attention.

But then, Sam was the only one who had a gut certainty that the Purcell deaths were linked to the disappearance of a courier five months ago in Florida.

A ringing telephone punctuated conversations erupting around the room. No one picked up the phone. Everyone knew what would be on the other end—the media yammering for interviews with anyone who wanted the cheap fame of a sound bite on the six o'clock news. Normally, Ted Sizemore would have leaped to line up an interview, and the free advertising, but this wasn't one of those times when Sizemore Security Consulting wanted to be linked to a sensational crime. Sam knew why Sizemore was being coy this time. The Purcell murders had unsolvable written all over them. No glory there.

"All right," Kennedy said in a loud voice.

Everyone shut up.

The telephone rang.

"Yank that mother out of the wall," someone muttered.

Kennedy ignored everything but the agenda in his mind: Cover Your Ass.

"For those of you who just came in," Kennedy said with a slicing look at Sam, "I'll summarize."

Sam hoped the look was because he'd been three minutes late, not because he hadn't had time to shave.

Kennedy flipped through his notes. "Yesterday one of the Mandel Inc. couriers was waylaid in Quartzite. She was delivering a package to Branson and Sons. We should have a complete list of the missing items in a few hours."

Kennedy lit a cigarette.

Sizemore got up, bummed a smoke, and sat down again. Usually he preferred cigars but knew better than to choke up the motor coach that way.

The NYPD cop whose marriage had just ended looked grateful and lit up her own cigarette.

Sam gave the room five minutes before it became uninhabitable.

The phone stopped ringing. The message light blinked urgent red. Nothing new there. It had been blinking since dawn. Ditto for the phone in the other room, the one with a supposedly private number.

"The courier hasn't regained consciousness after the surgery to remove bone fragments from her brain," Kennedy said. "She won't be any use to us until she wakes up. Probably not even then."

A few murmurs around the room made it plain that none of the cops figured the courier would be good for anything in the way of information, or anything else, after that kind of brain trauma.

"The MO was pretty much same old same old," Kennedy said, exhaling heavily. "She was intercepted at an obvious stop and—"

"What was she doing being so careless?" the NYPD cop asked.

Mario said from the back of the room, "This isn't Manhattan. If you're driving from L.A., stopping in Quartzite isn't a choice, it's common sense. You've been through hours and miles of empty desert. The car needs gas to get to Phoenix. If you don't do it in Quartzite, you have more hours and a lot more empty desert before you get to another gas stop. Only an idiot drives out of Quartzite without water and a gas tank at least three-quarters full."

"Who'd want to live like that?" the NYPD cop muttered.

"After the thief intercepted the courier," Kennedy said, "he drove or forced her to drive to a deserted place. Then he beat her unconscious, stole the package, and left."

"How did he leave the scene?" Sharon Sizemore asked.

The telephone started ringing again.

Everyone ignored it.

"Either the robber had a confederate who followed the courier's car and picked him up or he simply walked to another car he'd parked nearby. I get the impression," Kennedy said, looking around the room for confirmation, "that Quartzite isn't real big."

"Not unless it's January," Mario said. "Then you have a few hundred thousand swap-meet fanatics dry-camping everywhere."

The phone rang in the second room.

"Dry-camping?" the NYPD woman asked.

"No water but what you bring in yourself," Sam explained.

"What about toilets?" she asked.

"Bring your own shovel."

"Jesus." She shook her head and shuddered. "Give me a crack house any time."

The phones kept ringing.

"Okay," Kennedy said, speaking loudly. "The point is that the heist was easy because everybody stops in Quartzite and it's a damn small place."

"He could have followed her from L.A.," Sizemore said, looking at the burning end of his cigarette. "The desert is empty but the Interstate isn't. That way he would know exactly where the courier stopped. He parks his car, waits for her to finish whatever she was doing, takes her, and drives her somewhere close by where they won't be noticed."

Kennedy nodded. "Chances are, that's just what happened."

"What about inside information?" Sam asked.

One of the phones quit ringing. The other didn't.

Kennedy gave him a look that was anything but encouraging. "So, has your fancy confidential informant given you information that Branson and Sons is a front for the South Americans?"

"Nothing like that, sir," Sam said, keeping his voice even. "I'm simply pointing out that a variety of people had access to the courier's schedule—Sizemore Security, hotel security, Branson and Sons, plus everyone on the strike force who reviewed the schedule of incoming couriers."

"Do we look like South Americans?" Sizemore asked sarcastically.

"My college roommate married a Hungarian gypsy," Mario said. "Does that count?"

Muffled laughter went around the room, but everyone was careful not to be caught at it because Kennedy wasn't even smiling.

The SAC took his balls in his hand and stepped up. "Special Agent Groves has a point," Doug said. "If we assume too much, we risk missing something."

The phone rang.

"She-*it*," Sizemore said. "What do you want, a fucking business card left at the scene by the South American gangs?"

"Naturally, we'll look at every possibility," Kennedy said curtly to Doug, "but I can't allocate resources on the basis of a wild-ass theory. I have to stick with what's most likely according to past and present information." He looked at Sam. "Any questions?"

"No. Sir."

Kennedy gave Sam a look that had Fargo, North Dakota, written all over it.

The phone shut up.

"Next on the list," Kennedy said grimly, "are the murders of Mike and Lois Purcell in the employee parking lot of the Royale, about ninety feet from the strike force's headquarters."

A murmuring went through the room.

"Yeah. Really sweet." Kennedy's voice was ripe with disgust. "It's not anyone's fault. We weren't supposed to be guarding the gypsy brigade camped out all over the lot. But since the media picked up on our proximity to the murders, we're going to spend too much time covering our asses and not enough time investigating. I want the murderer or murderers busted before we look like fools on the network feeds." He paused to glare around the room. "Now, I know that everyone here has media favorites. I have a piece of advice for dealing with the media that I don't want to have to repeat: shut the fuck up." He waited for a long three count. "Any questions about how to handle the media?"

No one spoke.

The telephone started ringing again.

Kennedy leaned over, picked it up, and hung it up an instant later. "Here's what we have on the murders so far."

Everyone leaned forward a bit, not wanting to look inattentive. Kennedy was in a pisser of a mood.

The phone rang.

Sharon Sizemore picked it up, put the line on hold, and hung up without a word.

"Thank you," Kennedy muttered.

"My pleasure, sir."

The phone in the second room started in.

"I'll take care of it," Sharon said, standing up.

He nodded at her, then went back to his notes. "We can't be sure at this point, but from the evidence gathered so far, it looks like a one-man job. Any more and they'd be tripping over each other, the motor home was that small. The perp was a pro. He opened the service bay on the motor home, took out the electricity, which took out the alarm, and picked the lock on the motor home door."

"No other sign of forced entry?" one of the Phoenix cops asked.

"None. Just scratches consistent with what you'd expect from rakes and picks working a lock," Doug Smith said.

Sharon came back to the room and sat down.

"We're taking fingerprints throughout," Kennedy said, "but we don't expect anything to come of it. Like I said, a pro. He would have worn gloves. He was in the motor home with the door shut behind him long before anyone had a chance to spot him."

"What about the Royale's roving night security?" Sizemore asked.

"Never saw anything," Doug Smith said. "My guess is he made predictable rounds and the murderer knew it."

"When I had my conference with all the employees, I emphasized that the security personnel shouldn't be predictable. Did they listen? Shit." Sizemore took a final drag and crushed his cigarette out on a plate that had once held fried eggs and sausage and still held the fresh fruit that he hadn't touched. "The hotel security is a bunch of square badges, dumb as they come."

Snickers rippled through the cops. "Square badges" was the ultimate insult. Real law-enforcement officers had oval shields.

"You get what you pay for," Sam said. "Your breakfast probably cost twice what that poor security slob makes per hour."

"Square badges" was all Sizemore said.

"Once the murderer got inside," Kennedy said, "he went to the bedroom and tied and gagged the victims with garden-variety duct tape. No leads there. We don't have the autopsies yet, but from the beer cans piled around, it looks like the Purcells took on a load of brew and passed out in bed. No sign of struggle. The wife's eyes were covered with tape, but not Purcell's."

"He was the target," Sizemore said. "Guy didn't care if Purcell saw him. Dead men don't give descriptions."

Kennedy put out his cigarette. "That's our thinking too. From the evidence of trauma to the victim's genitals, we assume he was tortured before he died. Either that or his wife was into really kinky sex."

Someone laughed.

"Was there a safe?" someone asked.

"Just locked specimen cabinets," Sizemore said. "The murderer opened them with a master key."

Smiles went around the room. "Master key" was cop slang for a crowbar.

"So there was no reason to torture the victim?" Sam asked. "Nothing to gain by getting a bigger haul?"

"The murderer was a South American thug sending a message," Sizemore said. "When he was finished, he slit Purcell's throat, reached in, and pulled down his tongue so that it came through the opening."

"Colombian necktie," Mario said. "Haven't seen one of those in a while. Nowadays they mostly just cut the genitals off and stuff them in the victim's mouth."

"Ah, progress," Sam muttered. "Ain't it grand?"

"All the evidence we have now points to the idea that Mr. Purcell pissed off some South Americans," Kennedy said, "and they made an example of him."

"What about the wife?" Sharon asked. "What killed her?"

Kennedy flipped to the next page. "Bad sinuses. She suffocated before she was found."

"Yikes." Sharon grimaced. "Well, it was probably better than waking up in a blood-soaked bed and seeing her husband's tongue sticking out of his throat."

Kennedy smiled slightly. "If I ever see her in heaven, I'll ask. But the murderer bled Purcell out pretty well before he cut his throat, so the place wasn't wallpapered with blood and neither was the perp."

Sam nodded to himself. A pro wouldn't get so messy he'd stand out on the street.

"As for the wife," Kennedy said, "there was no rape, no skin under her fingernails or her husband's, nothing indicating a defensive struggle of any kind. From blood traces in the kitchen sink, we're assuming he washed off there before he left."

"Did Purcell have an inventory of his stones?" Sam asked.

"If it was in the trailer, it's gone," Kennedy said. "After the perp did the magic trick with Purcell's tongue, he ransacked the place. Even trashed the stuff in the refrigerator. Only one set of tracks in the mess. Guy wears a size ten shoe and had on clean room boots over them."

"Did any wear pattern show through the paper boots?" Sam asked.

Doug shook his head. "Shoes were new. We're trying to match treads now, but the boots are making it hard."

"Well," Sizemore said, "he sure didn't leave much for us."

"We're going over the motor home for hair and fiber," Kennedy said. "Since Purcell used the place to meet clients and other traders, we aren't pinning our hopes on making the case that way."

Nobody argued. Lab work was very useful in convicting people, but it wasn't much good at helping cops to make up a list of suspects. Having DNA was one thing. Matching it to a perp was another thing entirely.

"Who found the bodies?" Sam asked.

"Some local dealer who was coming to see if Purcell felt like swapping some inventory," Kennedy said.

"What kind of inventory?" Sam asked.

"Gems, what else?" Sizemore said sarcastically. "Where you been, boy."

"Most of these dealers specialize," Sam said to Kennedy. "Did Purcell?"

"That will be your job," Kennedy said with a cold smile. "Find out everyone who was Purcell's client and interview them. Divide it up with Mario. You're homeboys, so you handle the local media. The rest of us will stumble along on the main job without you two."

Several of the cops shifted uncomfortably. Everyone in the room had enough experience to know that the chances of a quick solution to a professional hit were very small.

Kennedy had just selected Sam and Mario to take the fall when the case wasn't solved in time for the six o'clock news.

Chapter 26

Royale parking lot
Noon Thursday

Sam had more experience with the media than Mario. When the on-scene director called for yet another makeup break, Sam didn't even shift his feet.

Mario tugged at his tie and said out of the side of his mouth, "I thought this was 'live' television news."

"We're breathing, aren't we?"

"I won't be much longer if that reporter's perfume doesn't lighten up." Mario sneezed for the fifth time in as many minutes. "Does she swim in it before she goes on camera?"

The corner of Sam's mouth kicked up. "Nobody told her that TV may stink but it doesn't smell."

Someone straightened the TV reporter's suit collar, powdered her nose, and tucked in some stray blonde hair. The reporter swapped sexist jokes with one of the technicians until the director gave the signal. Instantly, grave concern replaced the humorous leer on the reporter's face. She checked her notes and faced the camera squarely.

"This is Tawny Dawn reporting live from the parking lot of one of Scottsdale's most exclusive hotels, where a shocking double murder has just taken place. The terrible details are still unfolding, but we're here to bring you what we've learned by questioning people close to the case."

She turned to Sam. "You're Special Agent Sam Groves with the FBI."

"Yes, ma'am."

Then to Mario, "And you're Mario Hernandez, a detective with the Phoenix PD."

"Yes, ma'am."

Behind the camera, the director sighed but didn't interrupt. There was plenty of time to edit out overlaps with the other "live" interviews she'd done with the two cops.

"You're both part of the crime strike force that is gathering evidence against the gangs who target couriers," Tawny said.

Both men nodded and wondered why in hell their boss had decided to spread that fact all over the TV news. Maybe Kennedy was angling for a segment on *America's Most Wanted*.

"Were these murders part of your investigation?" Tawny asked.

Mario struggled not to laugh at the badly worded question—*Yes, ma'am. We always kill people in the course of our investigation. That's why we're called a crime strike force.*

Sam didn't crack a smile or miss a beat as he fed meaningless phrases to the TV reporter. "We can't be certain. We're investigating all possibilities."

Holding the mike between herself and the two men, Tawny leaned closer and tipped her face up to them earnestly. "Mr. Groves, what can you tell us about this tragic double murder?"

Sam didn't even flinch at being reduced to a civilian mister. He'd learned long ago that TV was a prime example of "their marbles, their schoolyard, their rules." He and Mario were sacrificial goats for the titillation of breaking-news junkies. Screw facts. Sensation was all that mattered.

"We're still gathering evidence, ma'am," Sam said. "It would be premature for me to divulge any details of the investigation at this time."

"What were the names of the victims?"

"The names of the victims are being withheld pending notification of next of kin," Sam said.

Mario sneezed.

"Keep going," the director said. "If he sneezes again, make it a close two-shot with Tawny and the other one. We'll clean up the sound later."

Mario's sideways look at Sam said, *Live, huh?*

Sam's look said he'd done it all before.

"But surely you've arrived at some conclusions as to the manner of death?" Tawny asked.

"Unexpected," Sam said without inflection.

Mario turned a laugh into a sneeze.

Tawny's eyes narrowed. "Have you any explanation as to why the FBI agents who were less than a hundred feet away didn't hear anything?"

"The crime strike force motor coach is heavily soundproofed."

"But still, less than a hundred feet! Surely the victims screamed for help?"

Not with duct tape over their mouths. "We're questioning other people who might have been nearby," Sam said.

"Did anyone hear anything?"

"Not so far as we know."

"Was robbery the motivation?" she asked.

"We're investigating that possibility very closely," Sam said with a total lack of emphasis.

"Was anything missing?"

"We're investigating that too."

With her back to the camera, Tawny rolled her eyes. This agent was about as interesting to interview as a dead fish. At this rate she'd be lucky to get twenty seconds in a network feed.

"They're bringing out the bodies," one of the techs called.

Instantly, the camera swung toward the two slack sacked up corpses being hauled out on stretchers and then put on gurneys for the short ride to the waiting ambulance.

"Do your intro again," the director said.

Without being told, Tawny stepped away from the two cops so that the first camera could shoot the scene behind her while the second one would keep her in a close-up.

"This is Tawny Dawn, reporting live from the parking lot of . . ."

Sam yanked off his tie and walked away to question the crime techs who were still in the trailer. If sweet Tawny needed anything from him, she'd have to splice it together from the first five interviews.

Chapter 27

Glendale
Thursday night

Kate glanced out the peephole of her front door, then started opening locks to let Sam in.

"You look like hell," she said.

"Comes from interviewing clients of recent corpses."

"The Purcells?"

Sam shut the door behind him with his heel and shot the bolts before the thirty-second grace period on Kate's alarm system ran out. "How did you know?"

She waved toward the TV set in the living room.

Though the sound was muted, Sam didn't have any trouble placing the scene. Beneath a pitiless sun in an unshaded parking lot, two sacked up bodies were being loaded into an ambulance. The camera zoomed in for a close-up, saw no blood, and drew back to focus on the immaculately painted, suitably solemn face of a young blonde female who looked like she'd started life as a Barbie doll and would end it as a cosmetic surgeon's wife. Her well-painted lips moved. Words crawled across the bottom of the screen.

Sam and Mario, freshly shaved, wearing suit and tie and white shirt, were standing behind the reporter, looking officially impassive. It had been a hard act to pull off while explaining how a motor coach full of FBI agents hadn't tumbled to two murders going down a stone's throw away.

"She pronounced Mario's name like a native Spanish speaker," Sam said. "Is her name really Tawny Dawn?"

Kate shrugged. "You're the one who talked to her."

"Like I had a choice." He gritted his teeth against a yawn.

"What really happened?" Kate said. "And don't give me the same line of condescending bullshit you gave to Tawny baby."

"Mike Purcell was bound with duct tape, carved up some around the genitals, thighs, and neck, and then murdered. Apparently, the wife was an accident. Couldn't breathe much through her nose and couldn't open her mouth because of the duct tape wrapped around it. It took a while, but she suffocated. Probably after her husband bled out next to her in bed."

Kate ran her hands up and down her arms.

"Chilly?" he asked sardonically. "Turn off the air conditioner."

Her head came up. She started to take a chunk out of him for being cold enough to freeze a stadium, then saw all over again how weary he looked.

Interviewing corpses.

"Your job sucks," she said.

"It has its moments," he agreed. "You got any coffee?"

"Is that what CIs do?" she asked lightly, trying to shift the mood. "Keep their agents in coffee?"

Instead of smiling at her joke, he turned back toward the front door. "Forget it. I'll—"

"Of course I have coffee," she cut in, putting her hand on his arm to hold him back from the door. "There's a pot in my workroom, if you don't mind using my cup. The dishwasher is full and I haven't—"

"Right now, I'd drink coffee out of a dirty shoe."

She didn't have to lead him to the workroom; he knew exactly where it was. Another muted television was on in that room. Interviews with people who had walked through the employee parking lot last night seemed to be a specialty. Tawny was flogging it hard to lead the six o'clock news.

Sam glanced away and hoped that tomorrow wasn't another slow news day. He really hated talking to earnest young things who were trained to look horrified one moment and segue into a chirpy sign-off the next.

He poured himself a cup of coffee, drank it down in two long gulps, and poured another, trying to wash away the taste of the bloody crime scene.

"Sit down before you fall down," Kate said, shoving one of her rolling work chairs at him.

"Thanks." He sat heavily and finished off the second cup of coffee. "Sure tastes better than the crime scene or the morgue."

She stood close to him, uncertain of what to do. This was a side of Special Agent Sam Groves she hadn't suspected existed. Worn. Haunted.

Way too human.

"Have you eaten anything today?" Kate asked.

"More than I wanted." He finished the coffee, rubbed his eyes briskly, and shook his head like a dog coming out of water. He pinned her with hard blue eyes. "I need everything you can tell me about Mike Purcell, especially any clients he had who might be happy to dance on his grave."

She stared at him.

He waited.

"Like a light switch," she said finally.

"What?"

"Off with the tired human being. On with the cop."

"Two sides of the same coin. The cop's tired too. What about Purcell?"

"I didn't know him any better than I had to."

"What did you hear about him?"

Kate took the empty coffee cup, filled it, and drank. "He was the kind of dealer that gives the business a bad reputation."

"Meaning?"

"Under a different name, he and his wife ran an Internet site that was a scam. Murphy's Law of Gems. Colored stones for investments. A hedge against inflation, deflation, war, drought, and hemorrhoids."

"Interesting," Sam said, pulling out his notebook. "Nobody else mentioned that."

"That's because the site was designed to be a lure for absolute gem amateurs and virgin investors. Then I noticed that the PO box listed at the site was the same as Purcell's. No one in the gem trade would give the site a second look. The only reason I did was that I searched *every* site on the Internet for sapphires, even the web pages that were set up for gem novices."

"So he ran a site for amateurs?"

"Worse than karaoke."

"You're saying that none of Purcell's clients in Phoenix at the moment are novices, so they wouldn't associate Murphy's Law of Gems with Purcell."

She looked amused. " 'Not novices' is a gentle way of putting it. A lot of Purcell's clients and fellow dealers are as, um, generous in their descriptions of their own stones as he is."

"And as careless about detailed sales receipts."

"What do you mean?"

He flipped through his notes. "Two thousand carats of mixed Sri Lankan stones, Indian cut. Three kilos of mixed Brazilian rough."

"Invoices like that aren't especially unusual." As she spoke, she pulled a mother-of-pearl clip out of her hair and rubbed her scalp. "Most people think of gems as being scarce and tiny and very valuable. Not necessarily so. Sri Lanka exports zircons and topaz as well as rubies and sapphires. Brazil ships *tons* of colored stones from the Minas Gerais district."

"Like?"

"Tourmaline, amethyst, smoky quartz, to name just a few. They're the kinds of stones we used to call semiprecious but now are firmly encouraged to describe as 'colored gems.' In the jewelry trade, they're entry-level goods."

"So Purcell's record-keeping was no more slipshod than the next guy?"

"Oh, I wouldn't go that far," she said, shaking out her hair again and rubbing her scalp where it prickled from the clip's teeth. "Anyone who sells heated, filled, doubled, tripled, glued, diffused, oiled, and otherwise treated stones and doesn't mention it to the naive customer might be deliberately careless in other ways."

"Stop, you're killing me."

She blinked. "Excuse me?"

"Running your fingers through your hair and looking all sleepy-eyed and sexy like you're thinking of bed."

Kate's jaw dropped.

"Was Purcell noted for an emerald specialty?" Sam asked, but what he wanted to do was slide his fingers into her black hair and feel the heat of her scalp beneath his palms.

She closed her mouth, opened it, and closed it again.

"Sorry about that," he said, taking the cup of coffee from her. "When I'm tired and disgusted with my fellow man, my human side overtakes the cop. But don't worry. I'm not going to jump your bones."

She watched him drink from her cup and wondered if he tasted her on the rim. Just as she started to ask him, she caught herself. *Whoa, babe. Unless you plan on tearing up the sheets with SA Sam Groves, you better think before you speak.*

What really worried her was that the idea of grabbing him and dragging him into the bedroom made her heart kick hard and her blood light up like a Fourth of July sky. She wasn't used to having that reaction when it came to men.

It made her edgy.

"Um . . ." She let out a breath she hadn't been aware of holding. "What was the question?"

His smile was slow, very male, and said that he liked knowing he tempted her. "Emeralds."

"Oh, yeah. Emeralds." She started to drag her fingers through her hair, stopped, and wondered what his hair would feel like. "What?"

"Emeralds," he repeated. "Or sex. Your choice."

"Sheesh, you really know how to sweet-talk a girl."

Sam laughed, then looked at Kate straight on. "You're a woman, not a girl. Quite a woman. The FBI turned loose its finest on you and came up with a profile of a person who is too honest and intelligent for her own good, fiercely loyal to the people she loves, a gem cutter of great skill and growing reputation, and stubborn enough to get herself killed investigating a half brother's disappearance."

"Disappearance? I think he was murder—" She broke off when the rest of Sam's words hit. "The FBI investigated *me*?"

"Yes."

"To which, Lee's murder or investigating me?"

"Both."

Kate went still. For the first time, Sam wasn't backing away from the idea of Lee as a victim rather than a crook. It should have made her feel better. Instead, she felt hollow all the way to her soul.

She really had wanted Lee to be alive.

She really had been afraid he wasn't.

For the first time she asked herself if she would feel better knowing, dead or alive.

She didn't have an answer. All she had was the gnawing certainty that she couldn't live without knowing. Maybe that was the answer after all. Knowing was better than fearing.

And right now she was afraid.

"What convinced you about Lee?" she asked finally.

"Purcell's murder."

"Why?"

"First we go back to the emeralds. I want to be sure of a few things before I . . ." He hesitated. *Before I drag you into a situation that's more dangerous than the one you're in right now* wasn't the sort of thing an agent dropped in the lap of an informant. "Were emeralds Purcell's passion or specialty?"

"Not that I've heard."

"Would you have heard?"

"After I found one of the Seven Sins in Purcell's case," Kate said, hitching herself up onto a nearby worktable and letting her legs dangle, "I asked around about Mike and Lois Purcell. No one mentioned emeralds. Quite a few mentioned the gray market in Thailand. A lot of colored gems come out of there, but damn few emeralds."

Shit. Sam rubbed the stubble that had already layered over his late afternoon shave. If it wasn't for his job, he'd have given up shaving twice a day and grown a beard.

"For once I'd rather have been wrong," he said heavily.

"About what?"

"A South American connection." He gave up fighting against a yawn.

"I'd offer you more coffee," Kate said, "but the pot's empty and you've had too much anyway."

"Worried about me?"

"You bet. Even if I don't like it, you're the only one besides me who believes Lee was murdered." She hesitated and then asked almost violently, *"Why do you believe it?"*

"You'd make a good interrogator," he said.

"I learned at the feet of a master. Your turn."

"What master?"

"You." With that, Kate shut up.

And waited.

Sam held his hands up in surrender. "Before I tell all, ask yourself if you really want to know any more than 'condescending bullshit.' A lot of what's going down around this isn't pretty."

She remembered his blunt description of the Purcell deaths. Then she thought of Lee, out in a mangrove swamp feeding crabs. She wanted to cry.

But even more, she wanted to make the person who had hurt Lee cry. The savagery of her need would have surprised her if she'd noticed it, but she didn't. She was too intent on Sam.

"I can take it," she said.

He let out a long breath. "Good. It's hard to protect someone who believes that ignorance is bliss. You sure there isn't any more coffee?"

"Protect? What are you talking about?"

He didn't answer.

She handed him the pot from the automatic maker. There was about a tablespoon of thick black liquid cooling in the bottom.

He drank it.

She kept waiting. Silently.

A corner of his mouth kicked up. "Okay. The preliminary background we have on Purcell sounds just like what you found out. He's probably not a through-and-through crook, but he sure traded gems with some of them. He didn't ask them any questions and they didn't tell him any answers. He was questioned a few times by various law-enforcement agencies in regard to missing or laundered gems but never even arrested, much less charged."

Sam looked regretfully at the empty pot.

Kate didn't take the hint.

He unplugged the whole unit and walked to the kitchen with it. She was right on his heels. He went to the correct cupboards, pulled out filter and coffee, opened the drawer that held the coffee measurer, and went to work.

"You have quite a memory," she said, impressed that he knew where everything was after watching her make coffee. Once.

"It comes in handy in my line of work," he said. "And everything I tell you from here on out is privileged information. You don't talk to anybody about it but me. Okay?"

"Like I have Tawny's home number?" Kate asked sarcastically. Then she waved her hand. "Of course I won't talk to anybody but you."

Sam filled the top of the coffeemaker with water and plugged the unit in. Then he pulled a dirty coffee cup out of the dishwasher. He didn't bother to rinse the cup before he put it on the counter. He'd drunk out of much worse containers at headquarters, and in his own office for that matter.

Kate went to the refrigerator and began pulling out food. She knew from experience that too much coffee was hell on the stomach. She piled cheese, fruit, crackers, and some brownies she'd been resisting since yesterday on a plate and put it in front of Sam.

Ignoring the food, he leaned against the counter, crossed his arms across his lightweight jacket, and began talking. "Usually the goods Purcell traded and sold weren't high end. The other dealers he rented the conference room with wouldn't have let him in at all, except that he had four quite good gems and one very fine one, and they needed help on the Royale's stiff rent."

"The best stone was the blue sapphire," Kate said without hesitation.

"Yeah. None of the other good ones was an emerald. None of them came from South America. Thai stuff all the way."

"So it wasn't a South American gang that killed Purcell?"

"Doubt it," Sam said, yawning. "The Colombian necktie appeared years ago as a warning to snitches and turncoats in the drug trade. If Purcell didn't have regular deals with South Americans, they didn't have any reason to slice him up and hang him out to dry."

She winced and reminded herself that she'd asked for it. And she would *not* let herself think about Lee undergoing the same torment. She'd mourned his death in her dreams for months.

Now it was payback time.

"Right," she said flatly. "So where does that leave us?"

"Lip-deep in shit."

"Any particular reason?"

"Think about it. Purcell has led a long and murky life as a gem dealer. During all that time he never was big enough or greedy enough or dumb enough to attract attention on either side of the law."

She nodded.

"Is it fair to assume," Sam said, "that he owned the blue sapphire for more than a few days or even a few weeks?"

"He must have owned it for at least two months."

"Why?"

"You needed that much advance time to rent space at the Royale for the gem show. I know. Dad barely made it in under the deadline. He wanted a small booth next to the exit, so people would think of Mandel Inc. as a safe way to get their goodies home." Kate watched the coffeepot as she spoke. It wasn't quite time to steal the first cup while the rest was still dripping. "And if the other dealers wouldn't normally have set up shop next to Purcell, but were persuaded by the fine blue sapphire to ask him into the club, then—"

"He must have had the stone at least two months ago," Sam finished. He smiled wearily. "It fits, damn it."

"What does?"

"Purcell was killed to close off inquiries about the source of that sapphire."

"But if . . ." she began. Then her voice died.

"Yeah. If someone was going to get his dick in a knot over Purcell's sapphire, it should have happened at the first gem show he attended with it, not the third or fourth. Unless he didn't flash it around at the Kansas or Chicago shows?"

"I'll ask some dealers if—"

"No," Sam cut flatly. "I'll do it."

"People get nervous talking to the FBI. Especially the people who hang out with Purcell. They're much more likely to talk to me."

She was right, but he really didn't want to do it that way. She had no idea how much at risk she was.

"I'll get around them," he said easily. "Just one of the things I'm paid to do."

"Why bother?" Kate asked. "People are used to me asking about stones. I'm a cutter. I'm always looking for good rough or badly cut Indian gems to rework. I don't need an excuse to talk about fine stones with other professionals. And I sure won't make them nervous. Dealers and traders love to talk shop with another insider."

Sam grabbed the glass carafe that held a thin layer of just-brewed coffee. Ignoring the hiss and burn of coffee dripping onto the hot plate, he dumped scalding coffee into the cup. Barely two-thirds full. He shoved the carafe back into place under the dripping coffee and said roughly, "You're not thinking too well, Kate."

She raised her eyebrows, took his coffee, sipped. "I'm sure you'll tell me what I'm missing."

"Pretty simple. If Purcell had the big sapphire for months and nobody gave a damn, why was he killed now? What's different about *this* show?"

Kate gave back the coffee with a hand that wasn't as steady as it had been. She didn't like the direction the conversation was taking. "I saw the blue sapphire. I asked questions."

"And got caught switching stones by SA Sam Groves, a fact that's no secret, thanks to SA Bill Colton," he added with disgust. "Pretty quick after that, a pro shuts up Purcell and takes the sapphire. End of the first promising evidence trail that might have led to discovering what really happened to Lee Mandel. The only good news in this Mongolian goat roping is that I'm the only one who can connect your name to Purcell and to one of the Seven Sins."

"You just said that it wasn't a secret."

"The stone swap isn't, but nobody except the two of us knows that Natalie Cutter is Kate Chandler."

Her eyes widened as she understood what he wasn't saying. "Are you telling me that—"

"Someone in the crime strike force is talking out of school," he cut in. "Not the first time. Won't be the last."

"You mean you can't trust them?"

"With a whole lot of things, yes. But I can't take the chance that one of the ambitious cops will whisper the wrong thing in the media's ear, and next thing we know your name is headlined with Natalie Cutter's."

"I can take the embarrassment."

"You wouldn't have to for long."

"Why?"

"You'd be dead."

Chapter 28

Glendale
Friday
5:00 A.M.

Sam's cell phone woke him up. He grabbed it and checked the window. Then he punched the button.

"Hello, Hansen. What do you have?"

"We sound a little sleepy," came the lab tech's bright reply.

"*We* are in Arizona, not on the East Coast."

"Just getting even for all the times you and your kind have dragged me out of bed or made me work overtime. Last Wednesday, for example, when you lit a fire under someone and they passed the burn on to me. Then there's the five-months-later rental car. But, hey, who's counting? Not me. Especially as we got lucky right off with the car."

With one big hand, Sam rubbed his eyes and looked around, wondering where in hell he was. Even before the thought registered, he knew: Kate's house. The couch in her workroom, to be exact. Someone had taken off his shoes, stuffed a pillow under his head, and thrown a blanket over him.

Too bad she hadn't taken off his gun harness while she was at it. His ribs felt like they'd been kicked.

"Okay, we're even," Sam said. "Talk to me."

"Even? Hell, you owe me on this one. The trunk liner on that rental car showed traces of blood and feces. The liner had been shampooed but there was enough blood residue to glow in the dark, once we added Luminol. We started DNA sequencing on the samples using a new technique. Should have the results any time now."

Sam knew that *any time now* wasn't necessarily fast. Usually, but not always. "Was the blood human?"

"Yeah. O positive. I can break it down further into subgroups if—"

"Do it," Sam interrupted. "I won't update the file until I have the DNA report. You find anything else?"

"Dirt and sand," Hansen said cheerfully. "A lot of it. Most of it is typical for the west coast of Florida. There was some central and east coast debris too."

"Don't those rental companies ever vacuum their cars?"

"Not like we do."

"What about fingerprints?" Sam asked. "You get any?"

"It's a rental car, for Chrissake. Of course we got fingerprints."

"Run them, including partials."

Hansen made a strangled sound. "Do you have any idea how many—"

"Just do it," Sam interrupted. "Strike force priority. That should come in front of everything but suicide bombers at the White House."

He disconnected before Hansen could say just how much he loved him, and why. Then Sam shook his head to send away the last cobwebs of sleep, spotted a half full mug of old coffee, and slugged it down while he punched in the number of the Miami office and asked for Special Agent Mecklin.

"Special Agent Sam Groves," he said when Mecklin picked up the phone. "Following up my request for an interview with the—"

"Yeah, yeah, I did it," Mecklin interrupted. "File's right on my desk."

"And?"

"The kid—Bruce Conner, twenty-two, Caucasian, nothing but a

speeding ticket on his record—has worked at SoupOr Shrimp for five years. Big favorite with the regulars. Boss loves him. Maybe a little too much. Did I mention it's a gay hangout?"

"No."

"Well, it is."

"Last time I checked, that wasn't a federal crime. What else?"

"Bruce remembers Lee Mandel. They weren't on a first-name basis, much less asshole buddies, but Bruce remembers the good tippers. He always gave the guy some extra doggie bags. Mandel didn't say what they were for and Bruce didn't ask. Like I said, the guy tipped good."

Sam settled back to listen. He didn't know SA Mecklin, but it was obvious he had conducted a real interview rather than blowing off Sam's request.

"So, has Lee been back to the place since, say, December?" Sam asked.

"Nope. Bruce is worried about that. Wonders if he somehow pissed the guy off."

"Why?"

"Because Mandel left without waiting for his meal to arrive and never came back. He even left the doggie bags behind."

Sam almost purred at the familiar jolt of adrenaline that came as he sensed pieces of a case falling into place. "Was that the same day he was supposed to turn in his rental car at the airport?"

"Yeah."

"So Bruce is the last one to see Lee?"

"Yeah. But like I said, the kid is clean."

"How did he react to being questioned by the FBI?" Sam asked.

"He wasn't nervous, if that's what you mean. He met my eyes, didn't fidget, was curious about why I was there but accepted the standard explanation."

"Background check?"

"Yeah."

"Okay. Thanks."

"Wait," Mecklin said quickly. "Have you reopened the Mandel case?"

"No," Sam lied.

"Then what's all this about?"

"Just asking questions that should have been asked five months ago."

Chapter 29

Scottsdale
Friday
7:45 A.M.

Sharon rolled over in bed, caught sight of the radio alarm clock, and swore. She'd have to move like a racehorse to be on time for her father's morning pep talk to his security crew.

I knew we should have gone to my room last night. Peyton can't set an alarm clock without his secretary to cheer him on.

Peyton gave off sleepy noises and burrowed deeper into the blankets.

Sharon gave him an impatient shake. Sometimes she felt like a juggler with all the little boys she had to keep dumb and smiling, thinking they were running everything just fine.

"Mmph" was all Peyton had to say.

"You told me you had an eight o'clock breakfast with a dealer," Sharon said, getting out of bed. "It's seven forty-five."

"Can't be," he mumbled. "I set it for six-thirty."

She dragged the radio alarm clock to the full extent of its cord. "Read it and weep."

She dropped the clock near him and started pulling on clothes, grateful that they hadn't gone out last night. If she'd strolled in late for a meeting dressed for yesterday's cocktail hour, her father would have the coronary his doctor kept warning him about and Sizemore kept brushing off.

Only the good die young. Now get me a frigging beer.

There were times Sharon thought of having someone make a T-shirt emblazoned with those words. It would be worth it, just to see her father's tomato-red face. The early meetings were a load of crap, but God help anyone who didn't show up to listen to Sizemore's words of wisdom.

Thanks to her late start, she only had enough time to brush her teeth, sleek down her hair, and run for the elevator. Two other people were waiting. She nodded politely at them and kept the unstated social distance away.

Her cell phone rang just as the elevator arrived. She looked at the window, sighed, and opened the connection.

"Hello, Sonny," she said in a low voice. "What's gone wrong now?"

"Dad just finished chewing me up one side and down the other."

So what else is new? Sharon stepped into the elevator car and punched in the floor she wanted. "He chews on everyone, but you're his favorite flavor. What lame excuse did he use this time?"

"He's blaming me for everything from the beat-up courier to the murders in the parking lot, and I'm here in L.A., for Chrissake. What the hell am I supposed to do? I'm a salesman, not a gun-toting agent."

She looked at her watch. Three minutes to spare. If the elevator didn't stop at every floor, she'd make it on time. "He blames everyone. You can't take it personally."

"You always say that. Then you tell me to find another job."

"You're a very good salesman. You could sell sand in the Sahara. A different employer would appreciate that. Dad never will."

"But last year I increased the business by—"

"Give it up," she cut in impatiently. She turned her back on the other two people in the elevator and spoke in more discreet tones. "I know you're all that kept us afloat last year. Dad may or may not know, but he won't say either way. You should have had my pragmatism or I should have been born with your hang-downs. But you don't and I wasn't, and Dad can't get over either one. He'll go to the grave disappointed in his children. I can live with that. You can't. That's why you should get out."

"Can you live with it?" Sonny asked unexpectedly. "I mean *really*? Are you sure you aren't trying to make up for failing him by being booted out of the Bureau?"

"I resigned," she muttered as the elevator slowed to a stop at her floor.

"Oh, come on. Don't split hairs with me. You didn't have a choice about resigning and everyone knows it."

"Sure I did. I could have sued the bastards for sex discrimination for not making my SAC resign along with me."

Sharon stepped through the open elevator doors, dodged someone who was desperately trying to make the elevator before the doors closed, and started toward the Sizemore Security Consulting suite. It was actually adjoining rooms, but God help anyone who pointed that out. Her father was still pissed off at not getting his deposit in on time. Her fault, of course.

Everything was.

"But you didn't sue anyone," Sonny pointed out. "You came home with your tail tucked between your legs and took the job Daddy offered."

"Man, Dad must have really given your ego a going-over," she said in a low, fierce voice. "Don't take it out on me. You know damn well I spent six months applying for other jobs before I came home." *And during each of those six months had to look at the leers from every other law-enforcement agency type who had heard what really happened. And they all had heard.* "The pay was the same working for Sizemore Security Consulting and I don't have to suck anyone off to keep my job. Just one of the perks of working for my daddy."

Sonny blew a long breath over the receiver. "Sorry, sis. I didn't mean it. I was feeling raw and . . . I'm sorry."

"Don't worry. Dad's given me a lot worse. Did he chew on the whole L.A. staff or just you?"

"He was pretty rough on Jason."

"Okay, I'll call him. We can't afford to lose Jason. He's the best connection we have to the jewelry trade in general and exclusive collectors in particular. He and his brother know where all the bodies are buried, who's buying, and who's lying."

"I tried to smooth it over, but Jason needs to hear it from you too. Everyone knows that for all Dad's shouting, you're the glue that holds it all together."

"First insults, now flattery."

"Not flattery. Truth."

"Yeah, well, I'll tell Jason the seagull manager joke."

"What's that?" Sonny asked.

"A seagull manager is one that flies in from nowhere, squawks a lot, craps on everything, and flies off."

Sonny snickered. "You just described Dad."

"Ya think?" she asked sardonically. "Listen, I'll call you later. I've got to go or I'll be late for Dad's coffee pep talk to the staff here."

"Better you than me. Thanks, sis. Since Mom's been gone, I don't know what we'd do without you."

"Don't thank me. Just go out and hustle more business. We're going to need it when news gets out about the courier. That's three in the last three months we've lost."

"Four. Brady backed out of the deal this morning. We're looking for another courier now."

"Jesus. Did you tell Dad?"

"Uh, no. I thought I'd leave it to you."

"Sweet. Really sweet."

Sharon punched the disconnect, squared her shoulders, and headed in for the morning squawk from her seagull manager.

Chapter 30

Peyton was in his bathrobe when he opened the door for Jack Kirby.

"Late night?" Kirby asked.

As usual, Kirby was wearing the kind of slacks and shirt that could be dressed up or down as the occasion required. When you were following a subject, you never knew where he would go next. The paper bag dangling heavily from his left hand had the logo of a local coffee and bagel shop.

"Late enough." Peyton closed the door quickly. Even though Kirby was carried on Hall Jewelry's payroll as a personnel specialist, Peyton would just as soon not be seen with the man too often.

"Got any coffee?" Kirby asked.

Peyton looked at the paper bag in Kirby's hand. "Over there." Peyton pointed to a low table. "Extra cream is in the bar fridge. Room service should arrive with the food any minute."

"Great. I haven't had a chance to eat yet. Place is crazy since the Purcells were murdered. Suddenly everyone wants a rush background check on their great-aunt Tillie." Kirby laughed. "Glad I'm not one of those crime strike force boys. Eating shit on the six o'clock news was the worst thing about being a government agent."

"Awful thing, those murders," Peyton said, frowning. "With all the good stuff floating around the Royale right now, why murder the Purcells for a handful of second-rate gems? And the FBI was in the frigging parking lot while the murders went down. That's just nuts. Must be some psycho."

"Probably." Kirby sighed and shook his head. "I gave up trying to figure out people the first time I saw a ten-year-old crack whore turning tricks for his mother, who was also a crack whore but too pregnant to be much good on her back or even on her knees. After that, something like a middle-aged man with a Colombian necktie and a dead wife in bed with him doesn't even make me look twice."

"Jesus. Is that what they did to him?"

Kirby shrugged. "So I hear."

With a grimace Peyton poured coffee. "Do you mind changing the subject? I'm going to be eating breakfast soon."

Kirby bit back a smile. He just loved Peyton's pussy reactions to the facts of life. "Sorry. I brought something that should put you in a real good mood."

"Did some shipments come in?"

"Fresh from my Thai connection," Kirby lied easily, taking the coffee cup Peyton handed to him. "Second-tier stones, Asian cut for carat weight rather than shine."

"Just the way I like them."

"That's why I thought of you." Kirby started to open the paper bag he'd brought with him.

"Wait until room service comes," Peyton said quickly.

"Oh. Sure." Kirby struggled not to smile at Peyton's nervousness. *What a girly. Everybody and his brother is showing gems around and he's afraid to be caught looking at them by the Mexican help.* "Does your company have any finished Thai merchandise in the pipeline?"

Peyton went to his own computer, entered a password, then entered another password and a string of numbers. A block of the computer's hard drive that wasn't listed in the directory opened obediently.

There was a knock on the door and a call, "Room service."

Peyton tucked the computer under his arm, opened the door, and signed for the meal.

While the food was being set out on a linen tablecloth in the next room, Kirby and Peyton talked about sports. As soon as the guy finished arranging plates and left, Kirby pulled a package out of the paper bag.

"Let's sit down while it's still warm," Peyton said, heading toward the food. "I'm starved."

"Sure. For once, that stuff smells good enough to eat."

Kirby pulled a chair out and sat at the small dinette table. Peyton lifted a small vase of fresh flowers out of the way, put his computer next to his plate, and went to work on breakfast.

"Hey, this is almost hot," Kirby said, biting into a sausage-and-onion omelet. "How do you rate?"

Peyton took a big bite of rare steak. "I tip well. Something Sharon never figured out."

Kirby snickered and wondered if Sharon Sizemore would ever "figure out" that Peyton was using her for more than sex. When she finally got smart, it would be fun to be a fly on the wall. If her temper was anything like her old man's, you could sell tickets to the explosion.

After a few fast bites, Peyton opened his computer and started scrolling down the screen, eating as he worked.

Kirby didn't try to see what was on the screen. No point in peeking. Peyton wasn't Kirby's only source of courier and gem insider information—and vice versa, no doubt. So Kirby just settled in and concentrated on cleaning his plate before the grease got cold enough to write in. He was almost finished when Peyton spoke again.

"We've got several Thai shipments of mixed cut and rough in the pipeline," Peyton said around a mouthful of breakfast. Not that there was much rough, just enough to keep an auditor from wondering where the extra stones came from. Most of the rough ended up where it belonged—in the trash. "Two weeks is the earliest arrival for finished goods." He shoveled in a forkload of eggs and potatoes. "You want to take the gems to Eduardo personally or just send them to the PO box?"

"I'll send them to the usual place." Kirby swallowed and took a gulp of coffee.

"Okay," Peyton said. He entered a note into the file. In a few days Eduardo would pick the stones up and mix them in with the Thai shipment when it arrived. Peyton himself would never be seen handling either shipment. "What kind of stones and how much do they weigh?"

"How should I know? I don't carry a scale."

"Guess."

"Maybe like a half brick of marijuana."

"And that would be . . . ?" Peyton asked impatiently.

"About half a kilo."

"Let's see them."

Kirby shoved his empty plate aside, shook out his napkin, and reached for the bagel bag. He pulled out another smaller bag and poured the contents on the big napkin. Stones the size of confetti spilled across the napkin like a broad multicolored tongue.

"A grab bag," Kirby said. "Maybe eight ounces of blue sapphire, two of ruby, and the rest are topaz, tourmaline, zircon, amethyst, whatever. Hell, I don't know. You're the expert, not me. You want to examine the stuff?"

Peyton looked at the sparkling stones. The pick of the litter was a big pink-orange sapphire, followed closely by a large nearly chartreuse stone that was a hybrid emerald brilliant cut and was probably green garnet. A fine natural star sapphire in an unusual shade of luminous gold caught his eye. Then there was a cushion-cut stone that could have been garnet and would be worth a pile if it was a natural pink ruby.

His eye went back to the brilliant yellow-green stone. The last time he'd seen it, Mike Purcell had been trying to sell it for twenty thousand to a collector who specialized in unusual colors of semi-precious gems.

"Nice enough blue on some of these sapphires," Peyton said, "but they're all small and I guarantee they've been treated up the ass." Some of the lot was probably yellow sapphire, which was in high demand right now. Not that he was going to mention that to Kirby. If the guy didn't know his stones, tough. "What are you asking for the shipment?"

"Two hundred thousand."

Peyton didn't hesitate. "Eight thou."

"A hundred. I got expenses just like you."

Peyton hesitated, saw that there wasn't any give in Kirby, and shrugged. The four good stones would bring that much, easily, even after reworking. Or better yet, he could put them in the vault and be that much closer to retiring.

"If I don't like what I see when these are inventoried," Peyton said, "I'll take it out of your next shipment."

"That's the deal," Kirby agreed.

Peyton looked at the bagel bag. It still bulged.

"I got lucky with another shipment," Kirby said. "Cut stones. Well cut."

Chewing on a bit of steak, Peyton hesitated. "How big?"

"How the hell should I know? The dude said they were real good quality and not small. Top-tier stuff."

"Total weight?"

Kirby hefted the bag. "Maybe a pound."

Peyton turned to his computer again. "Precious or just colored?"

"You tell me."

Kirby rolled up the first batch of stones in his napkin and put it on the other side of the table. He opened the bagel bag and carefully withdrew a fat plastic bag. With a care he hadn't showed for the other stones, he eased the gems out of their package and nudged them over the white tablecloth until he could see individual stones.

Peyton had his game face on. He looked at the blue, red, green, and occasional pink or silver-blue stones—diamonds, likely—without a flicker of expression.

"Blue sapphires, rubies, and emeralds." Kirby drank coffee. "Might be a colored diamond or two."

Peyton gently stirred through the flashing, brilliant stones with his fingertip. Taking tweezers from his bathrobe pocket, he carefully sorted by color. Then he pulled a loupe from his pocket and picked up stones at random to examine them. After a few minutes he put the loupe aside and fiddled with the tweezers. These were nice stones. Really nice. Well cut. Well polished. Except for the diamonds, there was nothing smaller than five carats. Yet no stone was so big it would have been photographed and documented for insurance purposes.

If Peyton had to bet, he'd bet the stones were naturals. And they were big enough to show all those comforting flaws with just a 10x loupe. Even at wholesale prices, he was looking at a nice pile of portable wealth.

"Too bad they aren't Asian cut," Peyton said, sighing.

Kirby shrugged. "I take what I get. You interested?"

Peyton tapped the tweezers on the thick linen, set them off to the side, and reached for his computer.

Kirby watched Peyton's quick hazel eyes scanning through whatever he'd called up from the computer's memory.

"Okay," Peyton said after a few minutes. "We're doing a nationwide loose stone promo in four months. Emphasis on higher-end stones."

"Looks like we're both in luck." Kirby grinned and poured more coffee.

"Maybe." Peyton used the tweezers to sort through the small puddle of green stones. When he was finished, it was divided into two uneven piles. "I can use Brazilian emeralds," he said, indicating the larger pile, which was a darker green with a very faintly bluish tone, "but not Colombian." He pointed at the smaller smoldering green pile, which had no hint of blue.

"Why not?" Kirby asked. "I mean, they're a little lighter than the others, but who the hell could tell?"

"I can." Peyton shrugged. "At the moment, buyers are shying away from the bad press about Colombia, drugs, emeralds, and politics. Traders are staying away because the stuff coming out of the Colombian mines today is treated from beginning to end and some of the treatments aren't permanent."

"These are treated?" Kirby asked.

Peyton grabbed his tweezers, picked one of the Colombian emeralds up, and viewed it from various angles.

"Looks like it's been filled," he said finally. "Can't be sure without more testing, but lately the Colombians have been doing everything to emeralds except making them in a lab." He shrugged again and gestured with the tweezers toward one of the other piles of colored gems. "Blue sapphires are always at the top of the customer list. I'll take everything you've got. Rubies . . ." Peyton shook his head and pointed toward the red stones that glowed like wind-stroked embers. "I'll take these because I value your business, but I can't offer much."

"Why?"

"Like I told you the last time you brought me red stones, even at the mall end of the trade, treated Vietnamese rubies are blowing out the market. Not to mention that anything over four or five carats will have to be reworked. Just too easy to trace, if it's truly top-tier goods."

"So you say."

"I'm the one doing the buying, remember?"

Kirby sighed. He wasn't going to get as much as he wanted from these stones. On the other hand, he hadn't paid anything for them other than White's share, twenty thousand.

"Reworking an already well-cut stone," Peyton said with emphasis, "costs time, money, and a lot of the weight of each stone. It's a very expensive way to do business."

"Not when you get the stones at pennies on the dollar."

Peyton smiled slightly. "Still, I can't give you the same money weight for weight as I would for badly cut stones."

"One hundred thousand."

Peyton's eyebrows shot up. "For sixteen ounces of hot, finished goods I have to rework?"

"Yeah." Kirby smiled thinly. "Trust me. It's a steal."

Chapter 31

Glendale
Friday
9:00 A.M.

Sam leaned on the table and watched Kate working over various pieces of equipment. He was close enough to touch her, but he kept his hands in his pockets.

Her hair gleamed despite being skinned back in a clip to keep it out of her face; he wanted to take the clip off and bury his fingers in all that sleek hair. Her eyelashes were night-black and long enough to cast shadows; he wanted to kiss them. The casual cutoff jeans and faded red T-shirt looked as soft as butter; he wanted to touch them. Despite the curves of breasts and hips, there was a suppleness to each movement she made that looked like muscle tone to him; he wanted to test it with his hands. The economy and ease of her motions told him she was doing familiar tasks; he wanted to be that familiar with her body.

The fact that she didn't even look in his direction told him she wasn't interested.

Damn.

Considering that he'd been enough of a gentleman and a scholar to keep his hands off her when he wanted her so much his palms itched, it rankled him to get the silent treatment. It was just professional irritation, of course. He needed her help.

And if he told himself that often enough, he might believe it.

"What's that?" he finally asked, pointing.

"A dop." She didn't look up.

"No. Not the rod, the machine."

"It's a transfer fixture."

"What does it transfer?"

Kate gave him a brief, sidelong glance. "What's this? Twenty questions?"

"Yeah."

"I don't want to play." Not the truth, but better than saying that the heat in his blue eyes made her clothes feel too tight. She picked up a special torch. "Go away. I've got work to do."

"So do I."

"Then go do it."

"I am." Before she could say anything, Sam kept talking. "Look, right now I'm Joe Schmuck walking in the mall with the old lady and three whiny kids. I see a corner store full of glitter and I know I'm in trouble. Our anniversary is coming up and I've been hearing that 'diamonds are forever' so I go in and buy her fifty bucks' worth of flash and I walk out. That's all I know about the gem trade—what I see in a mall case and on TV ads."

Kate completed the transfer of the stone she was working on, set down the small, handheld torch she had used on the dop wax, and looked at him directly for the first time. The heat was still there. Damped down, but still burning.

So was she.

"And this matters to me how?" she asked sardonically.

"I don't want to be Joe Schmuck," Sam said. "I want to know what happens *before* all the shiny stuff gets into the jewelry case. Where did the stone come from? Who transported them? Who worked them? Who mined them? But most of all I want to know who died and who lied so there could be stores full of flash and glitter."

She put the stick of dop wax aside and looked away from Sam. It was that or lean close enough to taste him. "You're serious."

"As hell. I keep thinking I'm missing something because all I know is cops and robbers. I need some insight into the gem business as a whole, not just the moments of obvious danger when small, anonymous, valuable goods are wrapped up and transferred from point A to point B by a courier."

Kate removed the big clip she used to keep her hair out of her eyes while she was working. She shook her head and sighed in relief. The clip was good at its job, but it wasn't vegan. It had a real taste for flesh.

"I'm not an expert on the whole business," she said, rubbing her unhappy scalp. "Just the cutting end of it."

"You know more than I do about the rest. That's all an expert is. Someone who knows more than I do."

She smiled slightly. "Okay. 'Who died and who lied . . . ' "

Sam watched her intently. She was fiddling with another machine, a piece of equipment she called a lap or something like it. Observation had told him she used it for cutting or polishing a stone. But she wasn't working on anything now.

He'd finally managed to distract her.

Professionally, of course.

"No matter the state of civilization in gem countries like Thailand, Cambodia, Sri Lanka, Brazil, Venezuela, Russia, South Africa, or whatever and wherever in the world you are," Kate said slowly, "most colored stones come from wild places where the twenty-first century is barely a rumor. Men on the moon? Forget it. Never happened. Skinny miners crouch in hand-dug holes in the jungle or crawl through slanting, unstable tunnels that are just barely big enough to take the width of a miner's shoulders. If you're above ground, insects and standing water make your life miserable. If you're below ground, standing water and cave-ins take your miserable life. Is that what you want to know? The age-old connection between death and gems?"

"It's a start." Sam looked away from the distracting sway and shine of her unbound hair. And her hands in her hair, rubbing, sliding, just the way he wanted to do. She was making him nuts and she didn't even notice. "Are the mines you're talking about private or government?"

She rolled her head on her shoulders. "It varies, but in the end it doesn't matter."

Sam looked at the machinery and told himself he was an idiot for being aroused by something as simple as a woman with a headache. But there it was, and he was stuck with it. He wished he'd put his jacket on when he got up earlier—it was long enough to cover the woody he was fighting against. And losing.

"Why doesn't it matter?" he asked.

"Government is always the choke point of trade," Kate said. "In some countries armed soldiers confiscate stones dug by miners and call it taxation. In others, the bandits are running things, which makes them a government of sorts. Then the taxation is direct and brutal. In those countries Joe Schmuck is a man who sweats his balls off year after year in hope of digging out a stone big enough to hide and retire on."

"Does it happen?" Sam asked, looking back at her.

"Sure."

"Often?"

"The odds of finding that big stone are slightly worse than those of winning a big state lottery and then running naked through a gauntlet of thieves and tax collectors to get your prize to the bank."

The corner of Sam's mouth kicked up.

She wanted to lick it, so she looked away.

"Most of the time," she said, rubbing the back of her neck so that she wouldn't reach for him, "the miner just finds a stone big enough to get himself drunk or laid with enough left over to buy food for the next week of gambling. Only instead of going to the corner convenience store to buy another lottery ticket, these Joe Schmucks go back to the mines and gamble in unsafe pits and die young."

"But not without hope."

She sighed and clipped her hair loosely at the base of her neck.

The hair wouldn't stay put that way for long, but the way Sam was watching it—and her—was making her pulse kick.

My problem, not his, Kate told herself bitterly. *Federal robots don't think with their dicks. In fact, I wonder if they even know they have one.*

"You're right," she said. "In nearly all cases this is voluntary rather than slave labor. It's just that I'll never forget the first time I saw mining in Brazil. Or Thailand. It was a real shock for this First World girl. Of course, that was before I really understood the first axiom of buying rough gems."

"What's that?"

"The closer the mine, the more likely you'll buy synthetics."

Sam laughed and wished she hadn't tamed her intriguing hair with the clip. It was making things easier on him, but sometimes easy just wasn't as much fun as hard.

That was something else he wasn't going to think about.

"No joke," Kate said.

Her dark glance drifted over him. Pale shirt with sleeves rolled up. The weapon and harness she'd been afraid to touch when she tucked him into an uncomfortable bed on her couch. Dark jeans that hinted at long legs and bluntly stated that he was male.

And aroused.

Okay, so he's not a robot. So what? Healthy men get hard over toothpaste commercials.

And from where she stood, that was one healthy male.

"At mine sites I found synthetic rough mixed with so-so real rough," Kate said, looking everywhere but at him. "A hundred yards away, I found synthetic locally cut stones mixed with batches of so-so natural locally cut gems. I found buckets of synthetic stuff in local jewelry stores whose owners assured me they carried only natural gems lovingly set in eighteen-carat gold. Yeah. Sure. And I'm the Queen of the Damned."

"So the closer the mine, the better the chance of fraud?"

"That's my experience." She wondered if it was safe to look at him again and then decided it might never be safe. "Someone who goes to the backwaters of any country figuring to score big on a stone purchased directly from 'ignorant' miners or country folk is going to get taken for a real expensive ride."

"Voice of experience?"

"I bought my share of crap," she said wryly. "I think of it as the price of learning a business. Now I buy my rough through reputable wholesalers. I pay them a markup, sure, but travel isn't cheap and neither is experience."

Sam walked over to one of the worktables and stared down at the mysterious equipment. It was that or touch her. That would be a bad move. Really stupid.

Really tempting.

"Okay," he said. "You've bought rough from a reliable source. Then what do you do?"

"Study it."

"For what? You think you're being taken for a ride even after all the precautions?"

"I'm not looking for synthetics in my rough," Kate said. She looked at her hand gripping the edge of the table. Fingers that were grubby from tools and grits. Short nails, no polish. She wondered if Sam would want to have such unfeminine hands on him. Then she remembered the fit of his jeans and knew the answer. Her pulse kicked. "I'm trying to decide which of all the possible shapes will bring out the best in the stone for the least amount of wastage."

Sam made an encouraging sound. At least he hoped it was encouraging rather than the throttled growl of a frustrated male.

"An otherwise good piece of rough might have a cluster of flaws," she said quickly. "If I cut them out, the remaining rough could make me a lot of money. Or it could fall apart and leave me with junk. That's the risk I run. That's why you can buy good wholesale rough at a decent price. No one is certain what the final stone or stones will be worth, if anything."

"Okay, it's a gamble." He stepped closer and told himself he wouldn't remove her hair clip. "You have the rough. You study it. You choose a shape. You start cutting."

"Grinding, actually. I don't so much cut stones as grind away the excess to reveal the natural beauty within." With her fingertip she stroked the metal rod that was holding a gem on its tip with the help of dop wax. "On this one, I've already set the angle that the rough will meet the lap."

"Lap? Like a dog at a dish of water?" *Or a man loving a woman.*

"Um . . ." The sudden intensity of his eyes made her feel like she was on the receiving end of a teasing, tasting lick. *Oh, God, I'm losing it.* Frantically, Kate gathered what was left of her wits. "Think of a lap as a kind of flat, circular sander, like a CD with steel teeth," she said, talking so fast the words almost ran together. "You use the coarsest lap for the basic shaping, then work your way up through to the finest lap and grit for the polish. Along the way, each separate facet of the stone requires another setup on the equipment to ensure that each facet is the correct shape and angle."

"Can't machines do it?" His voice was deeper than usual. Almost husky.

"Sure."

Kate turned away from Sam. His intense blue eyes were making her edgy. Needy. Hungry. It wasn't that he was ignoring her words. He was listening intently.

Too intently. She could almost feel his interest.

"Kate?"

And she knew that the physical attraction electrifying the atmosphere wasn't one-sided. She just didn't know what would be the smart thing to do about it, except talk as though her life depended on it.

"Most of the medium and low-end cutting is done by simple machines run by badly paid workers in the Third World," she said. "Ranks and ranks of cutters hunched over in rooms filled with the scream of stone being ground and a haze of silica dust. Real assembly-line stuff, and lethal to the workers if the air isn't properly filtered."

"Is it?"

"Sometimes. And sometimes . . ." She shook her head. "High-end cutting is different. It's one of a kind. I'm cutting collector stones or designer stones. Each is unique. Preset computer programs are worse than useless for me. The quick and easy way doesn't get the job done for me. Any job."

Sam took the clip out of her black hair and smiled at the results—and at the sudden drawing in of her breath. "What comes next?"

"I wrestle you for my hair clip?" she said, spinning to face him. The look in his eyes made her wonder what sex on a worktable would be like. "Forget I asked," she said quickly.

"Not likely."

"Once the stones are cut," she said, talking over his words, talking fast before she did something really stupid, "in most cases they're sold by the pound or kilo to mass jewelry makers. Again, most of the assembly work is done overseas in India and especially China. Really rare stones are bought as is by collectors or investors or designers. The vast majority of the stones are cut in Asia for use in mall jewelry or hobbyists or— I'm babbling. Stop playing with my hair."

"I'm not touching it."

"You want to," she accused. "You're thinking about it."

"What about you? Are you thinking about it?"

"Sam, help me with this. Or am I wrong about what happens to agents who sleep with their informants?" she asked hopefully.

He closed his eyes. When they opened, they were no longer smoldering with hunger. "No. I'd be sent to Fargo or fired. If the brass could manage it, they'd do both."

She let out a quiet breath and told herself she wasn't disappointed. Really. Feeling like you'd been dropped off a roof didn't count as disappointment.

"A fate worse than death," she said lightly. *Now remember to breathe. Good girl. I knew you could do it.* "We'll just have to make sure it doesn't happen. Right?"

"I'll get back to you on that." Then he sighed. "Right."

Sam allowed himself one more thought about burying his face in her hair and feeling her legs wrap around him as he pushed in deep.

Then he shoved down the human and dragged the agent up to the surface again.

"If you were stealing stuff from couriers," he said, "where in the gem food chain would you start? Overseas?"

Like a light switch. Back to cop mode. Kate told herself she was grateful. Then she told herself again.

"No," she said tightly. "Not overseas."

"Why?"

She let out a long breath and told herself that her pulse was normal. Entirely. Normal. *For a sprinter.* "They haven't heard of Miranda over there and their prisons are shit holes."

"Personal experience?" he asked, surprised.

"Not mine. That doesn't mean it isn't real."

"Oh, it's real," he agreed.

"Personal experience?" she asked dryly.

He didn't answer. He hitched a hip up on the sturdy table and shifted his weapon harness so that it rode comfortably. "So you wouldn't start near the mines. Where would you go next?"

Actually, I'm thinking of pulling out your gun and shooting the cop so that Sam can come out to play. If I'd known I had only one chance, I'd have jumped for it.

All she said aloud was, "I'd go to a big international wholesaler that imports stones into the U.S."

"Why?"

"They move a lot of gems with inventories that read pounds and kilos. It would be easy to mix the stolen and the legal together, as long as you haven't stolen anything outstanding."

"Like the Seven Sins?"

Her nod sent her dark hair slipping and sliding along her neck.

Sam swatted down the human and hung on to the cop.

"For all the expensive advertising," Kate said, "colored gems—especially treated colored gems—aren't *that* rare. Or that unique. A bucket of small blue sapphire rough isn't going to raise your heart rate. Cut and treated, maybe it would make your pulse kick, but only for a few moments." She blew out a long, quiet breath and felt her own pulse slow. Better. Much better. "Then you start seeing the differences in cut and quality and color. There's a lot of junk out there."

Sam tried to imagine a bucket of gems. He couldn't. But that was why he had his own private expert. She could imagine all that and more.

It was what he was imagining that was the problem.

"And if that isn't enough, by the time you've been through an assembly-line cutting and polishing operation," Kate said, "you'll hold a handful of low-end cut gems and all you'll think is what a pain it will be to put all the tiny bits of glitter into a silver necklace or ten-carat gold."

He tried not to, but couldn't help it. He laughed. If nothing else, it eased the claws of desire digging into him.

"It's true," she said.

"I believe you. I was just thinking of childhood dreams of treasure chests and pirates. What would Blackbeard have said?"

"Bluebeard."

"Whatever." Sam's grin said *gotcha*. "So you dreamed too."

"Doesn't every kid?"

His smile faded. "No. Dreaming takes energy, health, hope. Those things are real scarce in some times and places."

Before Kate could ask about the shadows in his eyes—cop or human?—he was talking again.

"Okay, you've picked your wholesaler," he said. "Now what?"

She blinked, accepted the change of subject, and said, "The wholesaler could also be a jewelry maker, a retailer, or a gem trader. All that's required is large quantities of gems coming in, enough so that some extra stuff here and there wouldn't ring alarm bells. Maybe whoever owns the company doesn't even know what's happening. A few corrupt employees would be all it takes."

"What if the stones aren't, uh, ordinary?"

"You cut them again until they are. Or you hide them until the statute of limitations runs out."

"Seems a waste."

"If you paid for the finished stone in the first place, it's a waste to cut them all over again. If not, all you're out is the cutter's time—and the cutter in this case is probably a machine."

"What about the Seven Sins?"

"I'm afraid that six out of seven have already been reworked and reduced to stones weighing between two and five carats." Her voice was bleak. "Maybe, just maybe, a ten-carat stone would sneak past the necessity to be anonymous. Either way . . ." She shook her head. "Something incredibly rare and beautiful has been lost forever. Blue sapphires like the Seven Sins just don't come out of the mines anymore. They probably don't even exist outside of a few private collections and a handful of museums."

The look on Kate's face made Sam wish he hadn't asked. But that was his job—asking questions that had unhappy answers.

"So the gangs knocking off couriers," he said, "wouldn't have any trouble getting rid of the goods in the States, even if it's rough gems rather than Rolex Oysters."

She risked a glance at his eyes. Blue. Intent. Cool. *Full cop mode. That's good. Really.*

Okay, it isn't, but it sure is safer.

"If the gangs couldn't unload their stuff here," she said, "they could do it overseas. Not everyone has my prejudice against foreign prisons."

"But on the whole, you think it would be more likely that the stuff from couriers who get clouted in America ends up in America?" Sam asked.

"Depends on the package." Another long breath. *That's it girl. Heart rate back to normal.* "We have a huge market for entry-level colored stones. Everybody's buying and selling them, including your grandmother on Internet auctions. Given that, why ship stuff to India, which already has its own historic supply lines for colored gems?"

"Could you give me a list of likely outlets for stolen gems?"

Kate hesitated. No doubt about it. He was all cop right now. "Likely as in shady or likely as in having a big enough supply line to bury some extra goods?"

"Both. The Purcells, for instance. From what you know about the business, could they have been a regular outlet for hot goods?"

She bit the corner of her mouth.

"Don't worry," Sam said. "You won't have to swear to anything in court." *Yet.*

"I've heard gossip."

"What kind?"

She started pacing along the edge of the nearest worktable. As she walked, she fiddled with the equipment without changing any of the settings.

"Kate?"

After a moment she turned to face Sam. "I hate gossip."

"I figured that out after the way you kept Lee's secret," Sam said. Then he noticed the change in her expression at her half brother's name. "Did Lee?"

"Did he what?"

"Hate gossip." Sam's voice, like his expression, was neutral and patient.

Kate hesitated, then shook her head unhappily. "It was his one vice."

"What did he tell you?"

She laced her fingers together. "Damn it, Sam, I could open my mouth and ruin some honest dealer's life."

"Or you could keep your mouth closed and shorten your own life," he said bluntly. "Whoever whacked the Purcells wouldn't have pulled a single punch for Saint Teresa and you know it. If you don't, I'm telling you now, loud and clear. Bad guys just love it when you play nice with them. Don't do it, Kate. It will kill you."

For a long time there was only silence.

"All right," she said finally, sighing. "The Purcells had the reputation of not asking too many questions about previous owners if you sold them stones at a really good price."

Sam already knew that, but he nodded to encourage her.

"The outfit called Worldwide Wholesale Estate Gems doesn't have a great reputation," she said reluctantly.

"In what way?"

"It's pretty much common knowledge that more loose stones came out of the company than ever went there set in estate jewelry. Particularly from South American sources."

Sam made a mental note of the name. He'd bet that the corporate headquarters was in Aruba or Panama or some other place where the banks were friendly and the questions nonexistent. The answers too. It took an act of God or a world-class hacker to get information out of those places.

"Some of the importers who supply the hobby trade have uneven reputations," Kate said. "Starr Crystals and Overseas Coral and Gems come to mind."

"Would these outfits be able to handle the kind of high-end stuff that couriers sometimes carry, especially for a gem show like this?"

"Probably not, unless they were spotting for private collectors or lining their own retirement accounts."

"Some of the couriers we lost were carrying Rolex watches and gold coins," Sam said. "Could they go to the same outlet as the rough and loose-cut stones?"

Kate thought about it. "If you have a chain of jewelry stores, maybe. Several such operations follow the gem circuits, because they make their own jewelry and like to keep in touch with what new colored stone is hot in the trade. Peyton Hall's family operation is one. Morgenstern and Sons is another. Heartstone Gems and Jewelry is a third. They're all here in Scottsdale. Then there are the nationwide chains." She shrugged. "There are three other big ones I could name and maybe fifteen in the next tier. Any of them could be an outlet for stolen goods, either at the national level or through a corrupt local manager. Their representatives also follow the gem circuit just to keep a feel for what the trade is doing."

"What about the local pastor?" Sam said wryly.

She laughed. "In other words, I'm giving you too many suspects?"

"Hey, I asked."

Her smile vanished. "I'm sure the courier companies are also suspect. And the couriers themselves."

He nodded.

"Even my stepfather's couriers," she said.

"Yes."

"And my stepfather."

"You know the answer," Sam said.

"My stepfather isn't a crook!"

Sam looked at Kate's fierce eyes and determined chin, and hoped to hell she was right.

For everyone's sake.

"Okay," he said. "You read Lee's file again. Something might jump this time."

"It didn't the first three times."

"When you can recite it chapter and verse, I'll be sympathetic. Until then, I've got some folks to talk to."

"They'd talk better if I was along," Kate said.

"No."

"Why?"

Sam went out the workroom door without answering. He didn't think she would want to know that Lee's file would soon be updated, which put her ass right on the firing line. He sure didn't want to be the one to tell her.

And he knew he would be.

Chapter 32

"Where the hell is Groves?" Kennedy demanded, slamming the hall door of Sizemore's suite behind him.

Doug straightened from the cup of coffee he'd been pouring from Sizemore's ever-cooking urn. At the other end of the room, Sizemore was growling into a phone, reaming someone in his L.A. office for not preventing the sun from rising or setting—Doug was only hearing one side of the conversation, so he wasn't sure which impossible chore the underling had screwed up.

"Special Agent Groves is working on leads from his CI," Doug said. "When he develops anything significant, you'll be the first to know."

"Uh-huh," Kennedy said, unimpressed. "Colton said she was a real hot piece of ass."

"Bill Colton wants to be the next SAC in Phoenix." Doug topped off his cup with lethal black liquid before he turned back to his boss and said, "Groves stands in the way of Colton's ambition. A small matter of seniority and cases cleared."

"Colton is a hard worker."

Doug took a swallow and shuddered. "Colton is a decent agent, a good bureaucrat, and a gifted ass-kisser. None of that should be news to you after working with him for a week."

"You spend too much time protecting that pet hardhead of yours," Kennedy retorted. "I didn't want Groves on the strike force in the first place."

"Groves gets results." *And I hope to hell he gets some on this case real soon.*

"Then tell the son of a bitch to pull his finger out of his ass and get me some results before tomorrow," Kennedy snarled. He grabbed a clean cup and filled it with coffee. Every motion he made radiated anger. "This whole strike force is shaping up to be a real clusterfuck. We're what—three months into it?—and all we've got is more robberies and murders and not one lead. I've got the director himself calling me for updates and all I have to say to him is the same crap Groves serves up on the six o'clock news."

"We're doing everything we can."

"We're looking like idiots."

Doug didn't disagree. Nor did he point out the real reason for Kennedy's temper. All crime strike forces began and ended in politics. So did the careers of supervisory special agents. Arthur Mc-Cloud, who had lost the shipment that had kicked off the crime strike force, was the brother of a sitting president's wife. If Kennedy broke the ring of hijackers, his career was made. And if he didn't, well, he could always take early retirement.

For a man of Kennedy's ambition, retirement was worse than death.

Sizemore slammed the phone back into its cradle and stalked past the coffee urn on the way to the tub of ice and beer. Before two P.M. he drank the light stuff. After that, he went for the gusto.

"Well?" Kennedy asked him.

Sizemore yanked the tab. Foam spewed. "Nothing." He drank. "Not a fucking thing. You?"

"Possible ID on an Ecuadorian that informants say is into drugs, murder, robbery, and gems," Kennedy said. "He came in on a private plane that landed in the Scottsdale airport."

"You nail him?"

"No warrant," Doug said. "No probable cause."

"Give him to me," Sizemore said. "In a few hours I'll have enough probable bullshit to bury a judge."

"There's the small matter of the Constitution," Doug said mildly. "It gets in our way a lot, but we've grown fond of it."

Sizemore snorted and took another hit of the beer.

Kennedy smiled reluctantly. Doug might have a soft spot for hardheads, but he also had a way of defusing anger. With Sizemore around, it was a useful talent.

"So, what's old that might lead to something new?" Sizemore asked.

"We've requested that local law enforcement keep an eye on any couriers in their territory who are known to be driving goods to the show." Kennedy shrugged. "The various agencies will do what they can, but everyone who works for the state or county or city is doing two jobs already to make up for budget shortfalls."

Sizemore grunted. "I've told the traders to foot half the bill for someone to ride shotgun twenty-four-seven with their couriers. I'm paying the other half. Had to hire some square badges to cover everyone, but there wasn't any choice." He grimaced at the thought of resorting to hiring men who had never carried a real law-enforcement shield. "We lose any more shipments and the clients lose confidence. Rentacops are better than nothing. Barely."

Kennedy finished his coffee and dropped into a nearby chair with the heaviness of someone who hasn't been getting enough sleep. "We lose any more shipments and it will be my face on the evening news. The media is baying for blood on this one." He lit a cigarette and blew out a weary stream of smoke. "Bastards don't care who's dead as long as they get a sound bite out of it."

Sizemore lowered himself into his favorite chair—beer on one side and documents stacked on the coffee table in front of him. "It's not like the Purcells were frigging saints," Sizemore said, flipping through a report Sharon had prepared for him. "The background I did reads like a how-to for losers and grifters."

"Yeah?" Kennedy held out his hand. "Let me see. Maybe I can drop some stuff to a media source and get a different spin for today's news. I'm getting sick of hearing about 'slain grandparents of three.'"

So much for not talking to the media, Doug thought without surprise. *What's sauce for the goose definitely isn't sauce for an SSA whose dick is in a wringer.*

"What about Groves's CI?" Sizemore asked.

"He's working every lead he can," Doug said. "Mario is helping."

"What leads?"

"The ones Kennedy told you about."

"He didn't mention any."

Doug looked concerned. "Then I shouldn't."

"Tell him," Kennedy said without looking up from Sizemore's report.

Doug would rather have kept his mouth closed, but he knew better than to dodge a direct order. "There might, just might," he stressed the word lightly, "be some connection between the Purcell murders and Lee Mandel's disappearance five months ago."

Sizemore's eyes narrowed. "Mandel? Refresh my memory."

"The courier who vanished in Sanibel, Florida," Doug said. "I'm sure you have a copy of our file on that somewhere."

Sizemore dug through one pile of papers, then another, until he came up with a file. He went through it with a speed that said beer might be his drink of choice, but his brain wasn't pickled yet.

"Okay. Lee Mandel . . . gone, no trace . . . no contact with family . . . father owns Mandel Inc. courier service . . ." Sizemore grunted. "No credit card or check transactions . . . no cell phone use . . . no description of the missing package or its contents."

"That was Arthur McCloud's choice," Doug said. "He said he had better means of tracking the lost shipment than we did, and the less said the easier it would be to find the lost package. His insurance company agreed."

"But you think it was gems?"

"Given that McCloud is a well-known collector of rare and extraordinary gems," Doug said carefully, "the Bureau is assuming that gems were involved in some manner. McCloud didn't say either way. Nor did his insurance company, other than to put a price of one million U.S. dollars on the missing package."

"Must be nice to be the president's brother-in-law," Sizemore said. "You don't have to say dick if you don't want to."

"McCloud has better wires into the international gem community than we do," Kennedy said, still looking at the Purcell file. "Purcell was a putz. The guy who whacked him did the world a favor."

"If being a putz was a capital crime, there would be about two hundred people left alive on the whole planet," Doug said, relieved to be off the subject of Sam's CI, "and we'd be hunting each other."

"I'd pay to see that." Kennedy grinned and dumped the file back on one of Sizemore's stacks. "I have to make a call. Which do you think sounds better—lecherous grandpa or thieving granny?"

"What did she steal?" Doug asked.

"Their website was a scam."

"Yeah? When were they convicted?" Doug asked. "I didn't see anything in their file."

Sizemore's empty lite-beer can thumped down on the table. "They weren't convicted. Nobody wastes time on Internet grifters unless they're doing kiddy porn." He flipped to another page of the Mandel file.

"Besides," Kennedy said, "since when do reporters care about the fine print? They need sensation to sell ads."

"What about the lawyers?" Doug asked.

"You can't libel a dead man," Kennedy said cheerfully, reaching for the phone.

Chapter 33

Scottsdale
Friday
11:20 A.M.

Peyton adjusted his dark suit jacket and waited impatiently for Eduardo to answer the damn cell phone that Hall Jewelry International paid for.

"*Bueno*, hello!"

Grimacing, Peyton held the cell phone away from his ear. Eduardo was shouting to be heard over the usual noise of the cutters reworking "estate" stones.

"Get to a quieter place," Peyton said loudly. "I'll wait."

"*Sí*, yes, of course. *Momentito*."

Peyton waited until the racket and jabber of the stone-cutting room faded to an irritating background.

"Is more better?" Eduardo asked.

Peyton didn't waste any time with small talk. "In three days you'll pick up a package at the special PO box. About half a kilo. Mix it with the May fourth shipment from Thailand and follow the normal procedures."

"*Sí*. Yes."

"There will be a second package at the same time. Good stuff. Some of it will have to be reworked."

"Yes."

Peyton tucked his tie beneath his jacket. "Eduardo?"

"*Sí, señor?*"

"If you skim more than five percent of the second package, I'll cry at your funeral."

"*Mi primo* is then *muy* unhappy, *señor.*"

"Your *primo* isn't the only one in L.A. with a gun," Peyton retorted. "No more than five percent, understand?"

"I understand. I not cheat you, *señor.* You know that, yes?"

"Saint Eduardo, eh? My ass." Peyton laughed roughly. "Five percent or you're dead."

And after thinking about the goods he'd seen an hour ago, Peyton knew just who he'd call to do the job.

Chapter 34

Worldwide Wholesale Estate Gems had a booth in the same room that the Purcells had recently inhabited. Everything in the room had been shuffled to cover the gap left when the Purcell booth was removed. WWEG had done its part by expanding with another case of "antique" gems.

"A big blue sapphire?" Tom Stafford asked, leaning forward over the heavy glass counter of the booth. "How big?"

Sam put his badge holder in his hip pocket and took out one of Kate's photographs of the emerald-cut blue sapphire. He put the shiny photo faceup on the WWEG counter. "About forty carats, give or take."

Stafford whistled silently. "If that photo's color register is accurate, that's one fine stone."

"You see a stone like this recently?"

Stafford looked uncomfortable. "Uh . . ."

Sam wondered if he should shove his badge up Stafford's uncooperative nose. He certainly was in a mood to do it.

Kate had been right: no one wanted to talk to the FBI, even after a grisly murder in their own gem-studded backyard.

"Think hard, Mr. Stafford," Sam said easily. "Other people have identified the stone from this photograph. It would be a little odd if you, a dealer who had a booth next to the Purcells, never noticed a gem like this."

Stafford shifted his feet, fingered his tie, and drummed fingers on the countertop. "The Purcells had one that might have looked like that," he said finally. "But I can't be certain they're the same stone."

"Oh, so you see a lot of stones like this?" Sam asked, smiling.

It was the kind of smile that made smart people look for the nearest exit.

Stafford cleared his throat and stroked his tie again. "Well, no, not a lot, of course not, but I've heard rumors of a synthetic stone that looked like your photo."

"What rumors?"

Stafford shifted unhappily and glanced toward the booth near the doorway. "I don't know. You know, you hang around with gem traders and you just hear things."

Sam followed the other man's glance. Sam hadn't really expected the helpful gray-haired lady trader to keep such a juicy secret, but it would have been nice.

"Have you seen or heard of either stone since the murder?" Sam asked.

"No." Stafford's face, like his voice, didn't invite more questions.

"And you'd tell us if you did," Sam said cynically, pocketing the photo of the sapphire.

"Of course. Terrible thing. Just terrible."

"The stone?" Sam asked, deadpan.

"The murders," Stafford said, trying to look like a preacher or an undertaker—not part of the inner circle of mourners, but sympathetic all the same. "Just awful. I heard there was blood all over the place. Were you there? Did you see it?"

Jesus, another vulture. "Thank you for your help, Mr. Stafford." Sam pulled out a business card that had the deep blue and shiny gold shield of the FBI on it. "If you think of anything, or hear anything, at any time, please call this number."

"Of course. I know my duty as a citizen."

Sam's smile went no farther than his teeth. "I'm sure you do." He started to turn away, then turned back, as though as an afterthought. "Is a stone like that sapphire unusual?"

"Er . . ." Stafford thought frantically and decided there was no harm in the truth. "If it hasn't been treated, the stone would be very unusual."

"And if it had?"

"Well, the cut is unusual for a blue sapphire, but large treated blue sapphires aren't *that* unusual, if you know what I mean. WWEG sees hundreds of big colored stones every month, especially since the recent turmoil in the Middle East, Pakistan, Afghanistan, Russia, you name it. Those countries were—and are—home to some of the great personal wealth in the world. When times get bad, Grandmother's jewelry hits the market. The settings don't have any value beyond bullion, but the stones do quite well for us."

"What shapes of blue sapphires have you seen that were forty carats and up?"

The other man looked uneasy again. "I'm not sure I understand your question."

Sam smiled.

Stafford looked even more worried. "Uh, do you mean have I seen any other emerald-cut—"

"Shapes. Any and all kinds. Over forty carats."

"Uh, shapes. Over forty."

Sam waited.

Stafford looked more like a man wondering if he was going to step on a land mine than a man trying to do his civic duty. "Uh . . ."

"Forty carats," Sam said helpfully. "That would be about the size of your thumb down to the first knuckle."

"Carat is a measure of weight, not size. Some stones are heavier than others, so forty carats of a heavier stone wouldn't be as big as forty carats of, say, feldspar. In fact—"

"In fact, we're talking blue sapphire," Sam cut in ruthlessly. "Emerald-cut, brilliant-cut, cabochon, heart-shaped, pear-shaped, oval, square, any old shape you can imagine. Over forty carats. Ring-ing any bells yet?"

"Uh . . ."

"Ever hear of the Seven Sins?"

"You mean like sloth and gluttony and—"

"Like this." Sam slapped a photo of all seven blue sapphires down in front of Stafford and watched his eyes pop.

"God. God. God." Stafford swallowed hard. "Are these *real*?"

"Have you seen or heard of anything like these stones?"

Stafford reached for the photo.

Sam pulled it back.

"Did Purcell have all of those?" Stafford asked hoarsely. "My God, where did he get them? Why didn't he—"

"No one said these were Purcell's. Is that what you're saying?"

"No, no, no. It's just that he had one so I assumed he had the rest."

"Is that what everyone assumed?" Sam asked.

"I don't know." Stafford shook his head like he was coming up from deep water. "I only knew about the emerald-cut stone. That's all he showed me. I can't believe he'd keep the rest secret. He loved showing us that one stone, watching us want it. I still can't imagine why it originally was offered to him instead of . . ." Stafford's voice dried up.

"Instead of you?"

Stafford looked hunted.

"You *are* head buyer for WWEG, right?" Sam asked.

"Yes." It was almost a whisper.

"Was Purcell known for spending top dollar?"

Involuntarily, Stafford laughed. "He barely squeezed out bottom dollar."

"Yet he ended up with the big blue prize. Why?"

"Uh . . ."

Sam waited.

Stafford started sweating.

Sam waited some more.

"Look," Stafford said hurriedly. "I can't help you. I'm sorry. Obviously, Mike Purcell had some contacts that I don't have. And I thank God for it. I don't want to end up the way he did, his tongue hanging out of his throat, for God's sake."

Sam went still. "Who told you that?"

"I don't know, I just heard it somewhere. You know, when you hang around with gem—"

"—traders you hear things," Sam cut in, because he'd heard it all before and was damn tired of it. "Yeah, I know. What else have you heard?"

"Nothing," Stafford said desperately. "Look, I'm an honest businessman. I can't help you and you're ruining my business by standing here."

"Why would an FBI agent keep clients away from an honest businessman?"

Stafford groaned.

Sam decided he had better things to do than watch Stafford twist in the wind. At least, Sam hoped he did. He might get something out of Stafford if he spent the rest of the day with him in a locked room. And then again, he might not. All Sam knew for sure was that somebody was talking out of school.

The Colombian necktie hadn't been one of the facts released to the press.

Chapter 35

Glendale
Friday
3:00 P.M.

"You were right," Sam said to Kate as he put a shopping bag on the worktable. He didn't take out the red wig and colored contacts. He'd save those for later, after he'd told her the bad news.

Kate looked up from the transfer machine. "I was right? Can I have that notarized and framed?"

One corner of his mouth lifted in a half smile. "Hey, am I that bad?"

"Worse." Then she smiled. "Actually, you're a lot better than most of the men I deal with."

"Wow. Tanked by faint praise."

"I think the original phrase is 'damned.'"

"That too."

Sam walked down the aisle between two rows of worktables, touching machines and tools without actually moving anything out of whatever alignment she'd put them in. He saw that Lee's file was open in the middle of one table. On the right side of the folder there was a snapshot of Lee grinning out at the world he would soon leave.

Saying nothing, Sam pulled a sealed envelope out of his light-weight jacket. He dropped the fat envelope with the Royale's logo into the folder. He didn't bother to take out the paperwork describing Lee's blood group and major subgroup, plus a VNTR sequence analysis. It was the kind of techno jargon that would have meaning only to a lab tech or a prosecutor looking to nail a perp's ass to the jailhouse wall.

Or someone trying to prove that Lee Mandel's blood had been spilled in the trunk of a rental car five months ago.

Sam didn't have any real doubt, but that didn't add up to a court case. He'd applied for a warrant for Lee's medical records and a search warrant for his apartment, among other things. A few more in a long list of paper chases Sam had set off in the name of a case everyone had wanted to vanish five months ago.

A case that, unlike Lee, wasn't going to go away.

Grimly, Sam wondered how long he had before somebody noticed that the Mandel file was active again. Weeks, if he was lucky. Days, most likely.

And if he was shit out of luck, it would be a matter of hours before alarm bells went off somewhere and Kate got to find out if her electronically distorted caller was bluffing.

The last time I told the FBI anything, I was told if I kept pushing, I would die.

Sam didn't like thinking about that. He kept seeing her on a blood-soaked bed, prisoner of silver duct tape and a sadist with a knife.

Kate looked sideways at Sam. The dark beard was already showing through along his jaw. His eyes were weary, angry, and as beautiful as any gemstones she'd ever seen. But there was more than that. There was the intelligence that both animated and drove him. The emotions that ran deep and swift beneath the lid of his discipline. She sensed all of it, the frustration and the fear, the anger and the intensity.

It was scary, but somehow she knew him well enough to know that he was getting ready to do something he didn't want to do.

"Okay," she said, pushing back from her work. "Drop the other shoe."

"Have I dropped the first one?"

"You're here when you're supposed to be questioning dealers about an emerald-cut blue sapphire, then you put something in Lee's folder and don't say what it is. That's shoe number one."

Sam stopped just short of touching what looked to his eye like a nifty handheld torch that sat to the right of the folder. He gave Kate a sideways look. Her eyes were dark, searching his. The long fingers of her hands were quiet, waiting. There was a strength in her that drew him more deeply than any physical appeal. Looks wore out. Character didn't.

"You know, it's flat-out amazing how much the traders *don't* hear while they're listening for gossip," Sam said. "Everyone I showed the photo to said the equivalent of 'Wow, nice stone.' And that was all they said."

"Did you show them your badge?"

"Yeah."

"And they shut up," she said.

"Oh, they talked. They just didn't say anything. Close as I got was Stafford of WWEG."

Kate pulled out her hair clip and rubbed her scalp. "What did he say?"

"He was surprised WWEG hadn't been approached to buy the sapphire."

"So am I."

"Why?" Sam said, walking over to her, telling himself he wasn't going to touch her. He was just going to get close enough to see if she was still wearing that lemony summer scent. Just close enough to reassure himself that she was warm, alive.

Safe.

"If Lee's gossip was true—big if, by the way," Kate added, "then WWEG would make a great laundry for stolen goods." She rolled her head on her shoulders and rubbed at her unhappy scalp. "In fact, WWEG was one of the first traders I approached after Lee disappeared. It was the Miami show."

"Was it Stafford?" Sam asked, sliding his fingers into her hair, kneading gently.

"What are you—? No, forget I asked." Her hands fell to her side and she almost groaned. "That feels so good it should be illegal. If you ever want another career, I'll recommend you as a masseur to the local health clubs."

The soft breath of his laughter stirred her hair. Sensation rippled through her.

"It wasn't Stafford at the Miami show," she said quickly. "It was a woman. I can look up her name if you like."

What he liked was the feel of Kate's body relaxing beneath his hands. What he'd like better would be to get her tight all over again, differently, and then feel her come apart in his arms.

"If Stafford or WWEG does something that raises a flag," Sam said, "I'll need the woman's name. Otherwise . . ." He leaned over just enough to inhale citrus and summer.

"Otherwise?" Kate asked.

She rolled her head, trying to help him release that tension that owed more to Lee's disappearance than to hours of working over some really nice green sapphire. When she felt his hand pressed between her shoulder and her cheek, she hesitated. Then she sighed again and smoothed her cheek over his skin. His palm cupped her jaw.

"We've got to talk," he said roughly.

But the thumb tracing and retracing her jawline was gentle enough to take her breath away.

"I thought we were," she said.

"We've got two problems."

She moved her chin just enough so that her mouth could reach his thumb. "What's the first?"

His breath hissed in at the brief, hot touch of her tongue on his skin. "This."

"You sure it isn't this?" Her teeth closed around his thumb, she tasted him, then she released him slowly.

"You're killing me."

"Funny, I thought I was seducing you."

He groaned and rested his forehead on her fragrant hair. He wanted her in a way that was new to him. He wanted to take what she wanted to give. He wanted—

But he couldn't. Not until he told her. And after he did, she wouldn't want to give him anything but the back of her hand.

"Kate," he said, not able to let go. "I shouldn't be doing this and neither should you."

"Speak for yourself."

He closed his eyes and fought against what he wanted so much he could taste.

Kate looked at the unhappy lines on his face. Abruptly, she swore and stood up, ending the sweet contact.

"Forget it," she said. "This isn't fair to either of us." Arms crossed over her grit-smudged blue shirt, she met Sam's eyes squarely. "How long do you think it will take for your damn strike force to be finished so you can be seduced by a woman who was once your confidential informant without getting fired?"

Sam opened his mouth, closed it, and shook his head. "I must be certifiable."

"Why?"

"I understood what you said."

She opened her mouth, shook her head, and laughed almost helplessly. "We're a real pair."

"Wild cards," Sam said.

She looked at him curiously.

"That's what my SSA called us. Jokers. Wild cards."

"He knows about me? I thought—"

"Kennedy knows about Natalie Cutter," Sam interrupted, "thanks to a big mouth called Bill Colton."

"Who's he?" she asked.

"A Phoenix-based special agent who would like to cut me off at the knees."

"Any particular reason?"

"The usual," Sam said.

"And that would be?"

"Office politics."

Kate raked a hand through her loose hair. "Okay, so your, uh, SS-whatever—"

"Kennedy."

"—knows that you collared someone called Natalie Cutter. So what?"

"So I was told to check her out and report back."

"And you found me," Kate said. Her arms tightened defensively across her breasts. "I don't like where this is going. You said you could keep your confidential informant *confidential.*"

"I have."

"Then what's the problem?"

"Two problems."

She waited tensely.

"The first one is this," he said, reaching over to the Mandel file and tapping the envelope he'd brought with him. "It was faxed to the hotel for me."

"What is it?"

"Lab work from the trunk of a rental car."

Kate flinched and said hoarsely, "Lee's dead, isn't he?"

"We can't be sure until we find a blood type match from his medical files, or better yet, a DNA match from hair follicles on his brush or comb in his apartment. Or maybe he cut himself shaving and the trash hasn't been emptied. We won't know until we get a look inside."

She nodded tightly. "How soon?"

"I've applied for warrants. There shouldn't be any problem, as a crime strike force gets precedence over routine Bureau stuff. One day, two, maybe less. Depends on who the judge is. The lab is working with some faster tests for DNA, so once we get the warrant, it shouldn't be too long. I hope."

"Do you think it's Lee?"

Sam hesitated, shrugged, and said, "I think it's a real good bet."

"How good?" Her voice was raw.

"Ninety-nine percent."

She sagged. "Even though my common sense said he was dead, I kept hoping . . ."

He reached toward her, then let his hand fall away without touching her. "We won't be certain without lab confirmation."

Kate made a broken sound that could have been a laugh or a sob.

"The bad news," Sam said neutrally, "is that the instant the blood work gets into the system, Lee's file will be updated. If—and we're by no means certain—your ghost caller has access to FBI records, he'll know that the file is active again."

"But he won't know I'm the one who forced the case to be re-opened," Kate said quickly.

"You're assuming he's reasonable and won't blame you." Sam held up a hand to stop her protest. "That's an assumption I can't make. Even if I could, it's just a matter of time—short time—until your name is connected to the case again."

"Why?"

"Kennedy is getting restless about my CI," Sam said.

"So?"

"There are the Bureau rules, and then there's the way things really work. The reality is that Kennedy dislikes me, Bill Colton would love to shove you down my throat, and he's just competent enough to track you down the same way I did."

"I wondered about that. How did you find me?"

"I saw you with Gavin, got his name from his badge. Showed your picture—"

"What picture?" Kate cut in.

"I got one from the hotel security cameras. Gavin recognized you right off. My SSA—Kennedy—has a copy of the photo, which means good old Bill could take it and show it around until he gets your real identity just like I did."

Kate absorbed that in silence. Then she squared her shoulders. "It should be all right. No one will get information from Uncle Gavin. He leaves today." She looked at her watch. "In two hours I'm going to meet him in the Royale's lobby and take him to Sky Harbor."

"You're going to be seen with the one man who can identify you as Katherine Jessica Chandler, aka Natalie Cutter, aka the woman who is probably my CI, aka the woman who is number one on someone's hit list? Wow, that's really a bright move, sweetheart. Do you have a death wish you haven't told me about?"

"God." Kate raked fingers through her hair. When Sam put it that way, being seen with Gavin probably wasn't the brightest idea she'd ever had. "Okay. I'll call him and—"

"I'll call him," Sam interrupted. "And while I'm at it, I'll tell him not to talk about you to anyone and to call me if someone asks about you."

She started to argue, thought about Lee, and shut up. "There must be *something* I can do besides get ahead on my backlog of stone-cutting," she said finally.

"What you should do is go to a motel and tell nobody but me where you are. I'll pay for it in cash so there won't be a credit record. No way to trace you."

"That's ridiculous. There's no—"

"There's every reason," he cut in roughly. "All that stands between you and some asshole with a knife is the false identity of Natalie Cutter."

"So far, so good," Kate said through gritted teeth.

"What happens when I ask you to start making the rounds of the traders with me?"

She looked startled. "Are you asking me?"

"I'm thinking about it. Sure as shit I'm not getting much on my own. How many of the traders know you on sight?"

She shrugged. "Not many."

"How many is not many?"

"Here? At this show?" She frowned. "None of the traders who were working with Purcell know me."

"For these small blessings we are thankful," Sam muttered. "How about the ones who are setting up as we speak?"

"It depends on who's manning the booth for the various traders."

"I'll get a list."

"Does that mean you're asking me to help you?"

He said something savage under his breath. "I'm asking you to put your ass on the firing line, yes."

"How am I going to tell the difference?" she asked ironically.

"I hope to hell you don't find out."

Chapter 36

Outside Scottsdale
Friday
3:15 P.M.

Kirby sat behind the wheel of a baby-white SUV with heavily tinted glass windows. There was a rental agreement on the passenger seat next to the cut up panty hose that would make his features impossible to identify if he got unlucky with witnesses. On the floor lay the electronic recorder he'd used to catch the frequency of the courier's key and then to program one of the many blank keys Kirby always had. Now all he had to do was get within ten feet of the courier's car and open it with his homemade radio key.

The nice thing about machines was that they were reliable. Stupid, but reliable. Like the mud artfully splattered in the little SUV's wheel wells and across the back bumper and license plate. Not enough mud to attract a cop's attention, but like pulling nylon over your head, it made a useful ID damn near impossible.

As for the rest, according to the rental papers he was Dick Major, head of production for Western Trails Enterprises. He lived in Hollywood and had a California driver's license. At the moment he wore a black Stetson over his temporarily dyed black hair, had fake face fur that itched like fire ants, and a snub-nosed thirty-eight in his boot holster.

And sweat. He wore a lot of that too. He was parked in the laughable shade of a desert "tree" that was shorter than he was. But the parking slot gave him a great view of the New Tires—FAST garage bay. The courier had brought his car into the shop on three tires and a rim.

Kirby had been as relieved as the courier to finally get to a tire store. It had been a bitch to follow a car at twenty miles an hour on the freeway and not get caught. The only good news was that he'd nailed the key signal when the courier locked the trunk before putting the car on the lift.

This time Kirby wouldn't have to stroll through a parking lot with a tire iron tucked along his leg. He could open the trunk the easy high-tech way.

Waiting for the opportunity to get the job done, he shifted in the narrow seat. Cheap rental cars were anonymous, and damned uncomfortable after the first twenty miles.

Change the fucking tire, go to a gas station to piss, I'll key the trunk, and we'll all go home.

The courier's car finally came down off the lift and drove away. Kirby watched him pass up two gas stations with minimarts and a local café that advertised five kinds of beer. When the courier took the shortest route back to the freeway, Kirby knew he wasn't going to have a choice. If he wanted the package, he'd have to take it in the Royale employee parking lot.

He hesitated, then decided if it was shift change when he got there, he'd write off the shipment, turn in his car, and go back to being Jack Kirby. But if it wasn't. . . .

I'll take it.

Adrenaline spiked. He liked the familiar kick, harder and better than any caffeine, any coke.

He opened the glove compartment, took out a silencer, pulled his gun, and screwed the silencer in place. The gun didn't really fit back in the boot holster this way, but if he had to fire the piece it wouldn't make enough noise to bring every cop in creation on the run.

Even so, using a gun was risky.

It's worth it.

He was betting Branson and Sons had cleaned out the vaults to put together a second shipment. That meant he was a lot closer to a quiet life in Venezuela, fishing the Orinoco and making occasional trips to the bank in Aruba.

Smiling, Kirby waited and dreamed of fish rising out of a dark river to take his lure.

Chapter 37

Scottsdale
Friday
3:30 P.M.

"I always wondered how I'd look as a green-eyed redhead," Kate said.

"Dynamite," Sam said. He set the parking brake and looked at his made-over companion. "I thought your skin would give you away, but it's pink rather than olive, even without makeup."

"My ancestors were Welsh, Irish, and Scots, not Mediterranean." She watched the hotel parking lot activity without really seeing it. "Used to gripe me no end to have black hair, dark eyes, and a fish-belly complexion. I wanted gorgeous olive skin the way most girls want big breasts."

Sam smiled. "How do the contacts feel?"

"Not nearly as comfortable as advertised."

"Use the drops I bought at the drugstore."

"I did."

He reached for the door handle. It was that or reach for her. As he was trying real hard to keep everything at a professional level, he'd better stop touching her at every excuse.

"Ready?" he asked.

She blew out a breath. "Yeah. I don't think even Uncle Gavin would recognize me."

"Don't count on it. You have a way of looking sideways at a man and almost smiling that is unforgettable."

Kate looked startled, then pleased. "Really?"

"Don't sound so smug. It could get you killed."

"Hey, after a girl's been turned down, she takes her satisfaction where she can."

"I didn't turn you down."

"Then why am I unsatisfied?" she retorted.

"Kate—"

"Forget it. I'm trying to."

She shot out of the car and smoothed her lightweight black slacks and black silk tank top into place. Because she knew what hotel air conditioning was like, she had a loosely woven green silk shawl over her arm. It wasn't her usual meet-and-greet outfit, which was why she was wearing it. Ditto for the big leather tote and the platform sandals that brought her forehead up to Sam's cheekbones instead of his chin. Her earrings were green amber set in silver. A silver chain set with hunks of green and gold amber was clasped loosely around her waist.

If Sam's first reaction to her outfit was any indication, she looked pretty damn good.

With that and a dollar I can get a cup of bad coffee. I sure as hell can't get laid by Special Agent Sam Groves.

Sam slammed the car door. "Kate—"

"Branson and Sons is opening a booth today," she said over his attempt to talk. "Do you want to start there?"

Sam wanted to finish what he'd stupidly started back at Kate's house. But that wasn't on the table. Catching a murderer before he killed Katherine Jessica Chandler was.

"Sounds good," Sam said through his teeth.

He pulled the dark Stetson farther down on his head and shook his Levi's down over his cowboy boots. His weapon harness was concealed by a jacket that didn't have pearl buttons but managed to have a western look anyway. As far as he was concerned, simple disguises were always the best. Something always came unstuck on the elaborate ones.

"Wait a minute," he said. "I thought Branson and Sons lost their goods when their courier was hit."

"They did," Kate said. "They sent another one."

"How do you know?"

"They didn't have a choice if they wanted to stay in the show. Last I heard, they're staying in the show. So either a courier came or one will arrive real soon."

With that Kate set off at a brisk pace—or as brisk as she could manage in platform sandals—across the employee parking lot.

Sam didn't have any trouble in the cowboy boots, because they were his own, legacy of a misspent youth on his uncle's Arizona ranch.

"Is that big bus really your headquarters?" she asked when Sam caught up.

He didn't bother to look toward the motor coach, whose generators were working hard to keep everything cool inside. "When we're not in Sizemore's hotel suite, yeah."

"You guys sleep in the bus?"

"Not if we want to keep our jobs," he said. "We have plebe quarters at the back of the hotel overlooking the parking lot and restaurant grease vent. Since my roomie is Bill Colton, I don't spend much time hanging around there. Sleep, shave, shower, and split."

"Colton? Who fixed that?"

Sam shrugged. "Luck of the draw. We have two other Phoenix agents on temporary assignment with the crime strike force while we're here for the show."

"Are they like Colton?"

"They're solid, hardworking, politically savvy federal agents, the kind who make the bureaucratic world go around. Without them, we wild cards would be shit out of luck."

Sam ran a plastic key card through the employee entrance e-lock and held the door open for Kate. When she walked past him, he said in a low voice, "You're not the only unsatisfied camper, Kate. Don't push my buttons and I'll stay off yours."

She gave him a sideways look. "I couldn't push your buttons with a sledgehammer."

"Listen—"

"Hey, hold it for me, would you?" a woman called from behind Sam.

He turned, saw a twenty-something female wearing a bar hostess outfit—white ruffled shirt halfway unbuttoned, tight red pants, black half apron with a pad and a pen sticking out of the pocket. He held the door open for her as requested.

"Thanks." The woman brushed by Sam a lot closer than she had to and asked in a low voice, "You work here long, darlin'?"

"Just started."

"Check out the lounge a little later, okay? I have a break in two hours. Gotta run. I'm late."

Kate saw the exchange but couldn't hear it. Not that she needed to. Body language said it all. The woman had done everything but stick her hand in Sam's pants.

When he got closer, Kate fanned herself and said, "Whew. And I thought it was hot in the parking lot."

Sam made a sound a lot like a snarl. He looked irritated and embarrassed and altogether in a lousy mood. He took Kate's elbow and hustled her past the employee lockers to a service elevator. He swiped his card again. The doors opened. He shoved his key in a slot, punched the button for the top floor, and waited until the doors shut.

Then he grabbed her.

"What—" she began.

An impatient, hungry male mouth closed over hers. He tasted of coffee and something hotter, something primitive and demanding. She pushed her hands inside his lightweight jacket and grabbed the first thing she could to keep her balance.

He felt her fingers weave around the weapon harness and called himself twenty kinds of fool. And then he crowded her up against the side of the wall and leaned into her female heat.

The elevator bumped to a halt.

Sam dragged his mouth from Kate's and hit the control that would hold the doors closed. "I told you to stay off my buttons," he said roughly.

Kate blinked, gulped at air, and wanted to hit him almost as much as she wanted to jump him.

"Bullshit," she said. "That waitress was all over your buttons and you didn't—"

"She wasn't you," he cut in. "You're different." He lowered his forehead to hers. "God help me, Kate, you're different. I think about you when I should be thinking about the job."

She closed her eyes and was glad to have the elevator wall for support. "I know. You'd be fired."

"I'd survive getting fired. You wouldn't survive getting killed."

Chapter 38

Scottsdale
Friday
4:45 P.M.

Sam surveyed the men gathered in Boris Peterson's suite and wondered why it was women who wore the high-end pretties and men
who bought, sold, traded, and cut them. In this gathering of dealers,
as in her chosen profession, Kate was odd woman out.

"And I thought the Bureau was an old-boy club," Sam said quietly.

Kate started at the brush of his lips against her hair. Even two
hours after the meltdown in the elevator, she was unsettled. She
didn't like that, but she sure had liked kissing Sam.

"I'm used to it," she said. "I don't even notice it anymore."

"Some of the women in the FBI say that."

"Do you believe them?"

"No."

"Smart man," she said.

"Sometimes I'm downright stupid," he said under his breath.

Kate didn't want to get into that again. If it pissed her off that he
thought kissing her was *downright stupid,* then she could just stuff
it under her red wig and ignore it.

And him.

Although she did owe him some good karma for having the connections to get invitations to private showings, the ones she hadn't been invited to. It was an opportunity she wasn't going to waste by thinking about a man who kissed her stupid one moment and called himself stupid the next.

So stop thinking about him.

Kate blew out a breath and concentrated on the room. Not including the guard at the door of the suite, there were about sixteen people. The murmur of conversation as men discussed the merits of various gems didn't quite drown out the all-news network on the television in the corner. On tables everywhere finished gems were displayed in individual see-through boxes with electronic tags embedded in the clear plastic. The boxes made it easier to handle the gems. The electronic tags made them harder to steal.

Some fool might try to grab a prime stone anyway, but there was a guard at the only exit, right next to the portable electronic "gate" that would start screaming if an active tag set it off. As all tags were active until passed through a device only one employee of the Butterworth Gem Trading Company had access to, shoplifting wasn't a big problem.

If a potential buyer wanted to examine a stone more closely, someone from Butterworth would escort the customer to another room, where a variety of microscopes, light sources, polariscopes, and the like were set up. Once a Butterworth employee zipped a gem's protective box through a device—rather like a CD at a music store—the box opened and the gem was ready for serious study.

"Ms. Collins," a man's voice said from across the room. "You seem to be at all the best private showings today."

After an instant Kate remembered that she was Ms. Collins and smiled at the approaching man. She'd met Carter outside the door to Branson and Sons' locked suite—the notice on the door had said to try again in a few hours. Kate, Sam, and Carter had gone on together to the next private showing. Then as now, Carter was casually and expensively dressed in gray silk slacks and shirt. The watch on his wrist was a Rolex Oyster. The twenty-carat cabochon star sapphire in his ring was a high-quality Burmese blue. His haircut was straight out of a southern California trendsetting Hollywood magazine. On him it looked good.

"Mr. Carter," she said. "Nice to see you again. Did you have any luck buying that ruby?"

White teeth flashed. With barely a glance at Sam, Carter put his hand on Kate's arm and urged her toward a nearby table.

"That fifty-carat ruby?" Carter sighed and shook his head. "The dude was in love with it. Same for the matched peridot. Gorgeous goods, but he wanted the moon and the stars for it. Even my Hollywood clients won't pay that kind of money. There's no investment potential if you buy too high."

"Too bad. Have I missed any good untreated sapphire rough or great finished blue sapphires?"

"That's what I wanted to show you," Carter said, smiling down at her. "There's a lovely hunk of umbra yellow rough over here. Not the sort of thing I would recommend to my clients—I only do cut stones—but I thought of you immediately."

Sam hoped that what he was thinking of Carter didn't show. As far as Sam was concerned, Carter was slick as snot and twice as useless. Once the man had learned that Sam was the striking redhead's bodyguard rather than her husband, lover, or date, Carter had started putting moves on her. Sam didn't have to be a trained investigator to figure out what was on the oily bastard's mind.

It wasn't business.

Kate felt Sam's eyes drilling holes in her back. She was divided between a purely feline pleasure in his irritation and a desire to tell him to have a little faith in her taste in men. Or maybe Sam thought she was too stupid to notice the indentation on Carter's left hand ring finger where a wedding band had worn a groove into his flesh. Whether the ring had been freshly removed for play or freshly divorced, Kate didn't care. Either one spelled Big Trouble for any woman smart enough to read the signs.

Carter led Kate to the side of the room where samples of rough gems were laid out in groups according to kind rather than color. These specimens weren't boxed. They simply had an electronic tag glued to an inconspicuous part of the rough, where the common stone matrix showed through the valuable gem material.

She looked at the rough and then at the employee who was hovering nearby. "May I?"

"But of course." He hurried forward. "Would you like a loupe?"

"No thanks, I brought several."

Kate pulled a 10x loupe from her big purse and examined the piece of intense yellow sapphire that had come from one of East Africa's mines. No matter how many ways she turned and changed the lighting on the stone, some of the beautiful hazing that was the hallmark of untreated sapphire glowed in the gem. Unlike Asian sapphires, the yellows and oranges of East Africa didn't have to be heated to deepen the natural color.

There were flaws in the rough, but none that would interfere with cutting a stone that would end up between thirty and forty carats, depending on the skill of the cutter. At thirty carats finished, the price on the rough was about break-even for the cutter. At forty carats, there was a good profit.

"Microscope, please," Kate said.

Sam kept an eye on the room while she examined the rough more closely. Carter hovered like a vulture expecting a juicy meal. The rest of the people glanced at Kate, but nobody stared or seemed to watch her any more than any good-looking woman was watched in a roomful of men. The men were here for business; if they'd wanted a meat market, they'd be down in the bar or bribing the bellmen.

What a putz, Sam thought as he watched Carter hover over Kate. Almost touching her, but not quite. Nothing to call him on. No excuse to step all over his shiny Italian shoes.

". . . a flat tire, of all things," a man's voice said behind Sam. "Can you believe it? The price we pay for couriers and the cheap bastards don't even rent good cars for a delivery."

"Branson and Sons will pay for it," the man's companion said. His eyes were on a long table of finished gems. "They're losing the best action. We've had a day to look over everyone's goods, we've made

our choices, and if Branson doesn't get his act together, there won't
be any money left at this show for him."

"Yeah, especially as everyone knows that the best of Branson's
stuff was already clouted."

"Yeah? Do you know anybody who *hasn't* been hit?"

"Not me. Not for two years." The man's knuckles rapped against
a nearby wood table for good luck.

Sam listened as he kept watching Carter with part of his attention. If the putz got any closer to Kate, he'd be touching her.

". . . believe the price he asked?"

Sam glanced over. Two more men were making their way slowly
down the long table of cut gems.

"Oh, I believe it," the second man said. "A big piece of finished
kunzite, great color and clarity, and the brilliance. Wow. That took
one hell of a fine cutter to pull it off. Kunzite is even more temperamental than emeralds."

"But he wouldn't even consider looking through my inventory for
a possible swap."

"Try him after the show. If he's still got the stone, he might feel
more like trading."

Sam listened and watched as people drifted by in pursuit of a
deal that would leave them better off than they'd been before they
walked into the room. Nothing unusual about that. Just human nature, impure and not simple at all. That was the good news. The bad
news was that no one in the room made his instincts sit up and howl.
Most, if not all, of the conversations meant nothing in particular to
him. Maybe Kate would be able to drag some wheat out of the chaff
of whining and gossip.

Maybe not.

A lot of investigative work was a sheer waste of time. It was the
nature of the beast. You never knew where a trail would lead until
you followed it to a dead end.

Kate appeared in front of him.

Carter was about two inches behind her.

"Cash, please," Kate said, holding out her hand.

Sam pulled out the wallet he'd filled with cash. Getting the money had damn near wiped out her bank accounts and his own, because he hadn't dared to put in a request for FBI undercover funds to establish his confidential informant's stature on the buying and selling circuit.

And Kate had made it painfully clear that credit cards and checks weren't welcome. Cash and carry. Period.

He handed the wallet over to her without a flicker, as though he didn't have any money at stake. But while he was doing it, he made sure that Carter got a good look at the weapon harness Kate's "body-guard" wore. Maybe seeing the gun would take some of the zip out of the jerk's joystick.

With no expression, Sam watched Kate count out bills. When she handed the wallet back to him, he put it away. Two minutes later the rough was wrapped up and stashed in her bag.

Without saying a word, she went back to the table that held a rough rainbow of colors.

Sam followed, crowding out Carter just for the pleasure of it. The TV in the corner was running a banner across the bottom: Live from the Scottsdale Royale. Sam gave up on Carter for the moment and eased closer to the TV. There was a medium close-up of an earnest blonde holding her exaggerated lips close to a microphone. He couldn't hear all of what Tawny Dawn said, but he heard enough.

"Sources close to the investigation . . . the Purcells were involved with the South American gangs . . . plaguing the jewelry trade." Tawny turned aside. The camera shifted. "FBI Special Agent Mario Hernandez, could you tell us . . ."

Sam bit back a curse. Kennedy must have his balls in a twist if he was playing the old "try the victims if you can't try the crime" game for the news vultures.

At least now Sam didn't have to call Mario or Doug. Not much doubt about what they were going to tell him.

He still didn't want to hear it.

*Sorry you got the short straw, Mario. But look at it this way—
you're learning how to handle TV reporters.*

Carter made his move on Kate, closing the last two inches of
space between them. About three seconds later Sam stepped hard
all over Carter's loafers.

"Watch it!" Carter said angrily.

"Stop crowding her," Sam said in a voice only Carter could hear.

The man might have been pretty, but he wasn't stupid. He took
one look at Sam's eyes and backed off all the way to the other side of
the room.

Sam resumed watching and listening to the men milling around
while Kate looked at a piece of deep blue rough. She went through
four different loupes from her bag, examining the rough as thor-
oughly as she could without a microscope. Then she put the rough
down and shook her head.

"I asked to see only natural rough," she said distinctly.

The sound level in the room dropped.

"I'm sorry, Ms. . . . ?" the Butterworth employee said.

"Collins," Kate supplied.

"Ms. Collins, you're mistaken. This is a fine Burmese blue, untreated. I have the certificate to prove it."

The employee reached into a drawer beneath the case. A moment later he pulled out a piece of paper with a Swiss lab certifica-
tion of 43.7 carats of blue sapphire from Burma. He slapped it
down in front of Kate.

She read it with the kind of speed that said she'd seen a lot of
gem certifications.

"Very nice," she said evenly. "There's just one problem."

"Really. What would that be?" the employee asked. His voice
said he didn't believe her.

Though no one moved closer, everyone was quiet, listening. It
wasn't uncommon for a stone to be questioned, but it was always interesting when it happened.

"Untreated Burmese blue with origins as described in that certificate would have pyrrhotite inclusions," Kate said evenly. "I haven't found any hint of them with even my 40x loupe. Perhaps you could point them out to me?"

The employee's mouth opened, closed, and stayed that way. He picked up the disputed piece of rough. "Excuse me."

He headed in the direction of the room that held equipment for close examination of merchandise.

Conversation around the room picked up again, but there was a hushed expectancy that hadn't been there before.

Sam looked at Kate. She was looking at another piece of sapphire rough—orange this time. He hoped that she wasn't planning on buying it. Their joint bank accounts really couldn't afford this kind of high-stakes poker.

"Another purchase?" he asked in a low voice.

"No."

The room went quiet again.

"Looks pretty to me," Sam said in a normal voice, glancing at the radiant orange rough in her hand. "Isn't it natural?"

"It's natural. As a specimen, it's very nice."

"But?" Sam prodded. Money was one way of establishing credentials. Knowledge was another. He figured they had a hell of a lot more knowledge than money. Might as well underline it for the peanut gallery.

"With rough, I'm looking for a profit after cutting," Kate said in a voice that carried just enough to reach everyone in the room. "The zircon inclusions in this rough show the classic halo with a dark center, proving that the color is natural, not heat-treated. But the way the inclusions are placed . . ." She shrugged. "The inclusions were radioactive, which stressed the surrounding sapphire. Bottom line is I don't see a reasonably safe way to cut this rough that would yield a profit."

"Would another cutter?"

"Not so far," she said dryly. "This is the seventh show I've seen the rough in. Like I said, great color for a natural specimen, about the best I've ever seen. But it's priced like Butterworth expects whoever buys it to end up with a fifty-carat cut-and-polished gem or at worst three ten- to twelve-carat stones. In my opinion, whoever cuts this will be lucky to end up with two five-carat stones. They'll be very nice stones, mind you, but they won't cover the cost of the rough."

More than one head around the room nodded.

The employee came out of the other room. The look on his face said the verdict had gone to Kate.

"Ms. Collins," the employee said, "thank you for calling our attention to a potential difficulty with this rough. We will recertify before we offer it for sale again."

"Wise choice," she murmured. "Do you have any other excellent quality *natural* Burmese blue?"

"I was just bringing some out," he said, leading Kate toward a table at the edge of the room. "Our buyer was quite pleased with these."

Conversation around the room resumed. Most of it centered around the sharp-eyed redhead who had a gift for sapphires. Gradually, the chatter returned to normal.

". . . told me that his wife told him that Johnny boy got caught in the wrong sheets."

"That explains it."

"What?"

"He's in a real trading mood. Divorce lawyers are expensive. Same thing happened to . . ."

Quietly, Sam checked his cell phone. Three calls. Doug, Mario, and someone from the Miami office. He looked at his watch. Florida was getting ready to close up the office and head home.

Sam hit the callback feature. After a few rings the phone was picked up.

"Special Agent Mecklin."

Sam said, "You called me about an hour ago, regarding some interviews I asked you to make."

"What's your name?"

"Where's your head," Sam said in a low, deadly voice.

"Oh. Can't talk, huh? Sorry. I was getting ready to leave and was thinking about my kid's birthday party. Don't make me late, huh? The old lady would have my balls for breakfast."

"Tell me something I care about."

The man at the other end of the line put out his cigarette and flipped through a notebook. "Okay. Are you Special Agent Groves?"

"Yes."

"Right. We interviewed every pawnshop employee and owner in Little Miami. Only one gave a flicker. Name of Jimenez, street name Seguro. Said some killer blonde with rocket ship tits tried to sell him a stone that matched the sapphire you're looking for."

"And?"

"He declined. Said he was afraid it was hot and sent her on her way. Since we had to threaten to report Seguro and his sixteen cousins to the local Homeland Security guys to get that much out of him, we weren't in a position to push him any more. Want us to go back?"

Sam thought fast and remembered Kate's professional website. "There's a photo on the web. You have a printer?"

"I'll just put it on my handheld data log."

While Sam gave Mecklin the URL, he looked over at Kate. Nobody was crowding her. "Soon as you get the info, go back to Little Miami and get a sketch of the person who sold it to Seguro."

The other agent hooted. "I don't think this asshole's eyes ever got above her tits."

"Try anyway. Sweat him if you have to. I want a description. And I want his full background and anything you have on his cousins. Connections past, present, and assumed. Rap sheets. Everything. Got it?"

"When?"

"Yesterday. Day before would have been better. Or do you want to hear it from my SSA and SAC?"

"Shit. There goes the party."

"Is your house on the way to Little Miami?"

"Yeah. So what?"

"So you have to change clothes and pick your toes or whatever. Show up at the party long enough to keep your balls and make your kid smile. Then download that photo and get your ass back to work. I want to have breakfast with that sketch."

Sam punched out. He looked at the remaining two messages. He'd already figured out why Mario had called, and whatever Doug had to say, Sam still didn't want to hear it.

Expressionless, Sam let the gossip drift around him and wished he was in Miami, questioning Seguro Jimenez about the blonde with rocket-ship tits.

Chapter 39

Scottsdale
Friday
5:20 P.M.

"Are you sure you can stand another one?" Kate asked Sam. "We could wait and be the first on the floor tomorrow when the whole show opens."

He shrugged and drank some more bad hotel coffee. "I'll survive another one. At least the word got out real quick that you have a good eye for sapphires."

"Nobody gossips like folks in the gem business." Kate looked at her list and stuffed it back in her purse. "Branson will have to wait for tomorrow, assuming his courier finally arrives. I've saved the best sapphire dealer for last. Colored Gem Specialties International. They cater to the collector market rather than the investor. They're the ones whose A-list has every collector in the world who can drop a million on a nice piece of goods. The rough for the Seven Sins probably came from them. If the stones had been finished when they hit the market, CGSI would have been the most likely to buy and sell them."

"Saved it for last, huh?" Sam said. "Did you want to give the gossips enough time to make the grapevine hum?"

"Yes."

He leaned closer and said too softly for anyone to overhear, "Always thinking. You'd make a good agent."

"I make a better cutter. No committees, no meetings, no nasty-grams. I just put a piece of rough on a dop and set up the angle that meets the lap. Repeat until stone is finished."

"If it was that easy, everyone would do it."

"Everyone does. Especially the retired grandparents."

"Yeah? How can you make a living then?"

"I didn't say everyone did it *well*."

Grinning, Sam left his coffee and a tip on the hotel café table and followed Kate to the elevator. He was getting good at that—following her. Any man who wanted a female to walk one step behind him wouldn't last longer than a few minutes with Kate Chandler.

Just one more of the things he really liked about her.

Another was remembering her in the elevator, the way the top of his head came off with a simple kiss, the way she wrapped around him like he was the only thing in the world worth having.

Deep-six that memory. File it under Mistake—Big and Stupid. Forget it.

Yeah, right. Just like he'd forget the sideways, remembering kind of glance Kate gave him the second time today that they'd found themselves alone in an elevator. Their eyes had only met for an instant, but it had been enough. Too much. Working with a woody was distracting.

Work. Yeah. Work. That's what he should be thinking about. For instance, as her bodyguard for the day, he should be the first one through doors.

The doors to the elevator closed.

They were alone again.

"Much as I like following you—" he said.

"This damn wig—" she said.

They both stopped.

Kate wondered if Sam was as desperate to find a sexually neutral topic as she was.

"—as your 'bodyguard' for the previews," he said, "I should be checking out places before I let you through the door."

"Oh. Right." Hurriedly, she tried to think of something else to say. Something impersonal.

"What makes you think Colored Gem Specialists International handled the rough for the Seven Sins?" Sam asked quickly.

"Um." She scratched carefully beneath the back part of the wig, trying not to dislodge it.

He didn't look at her. He told himself he couldn't smell her elusive, maddening perfume. He told himself he couldn't still taste her. He told himself a lot of lies while he watched the floor numbers crawl by as though they held the secret to winning the next big lottery and weren't going to give it up anytime soon.

"There are a lot of gem traders," she said finally, prodding another part of the wig, "but only a handful that would be able to purchase and resell world-class rough and finished goods."

"Why didn't you mention that before?"

"I didn't think it mattered. The rough wasn't stolen from CGSI. They don't make regular deliveries in any sense of the word, so they haven't suffered the losses bigger, less specialized traders have."

"Did you approach CGSI at any other show since Lee went missing?"

"They weren't showing anywhere. The Scottsdale event is new to the high-end circuit. CGSI wants to show the flag in case there's a rich collector out here who's been living under a cactus and hasn't heard of them. Then there are the German collectors and cutters. They turn out for anything that's within driving distance of red-rock country, which means that Arizona is a big favorite with them."

"So no one here is likely to recognize you?"

"No. I've never bought anything from CGSI. Couldn't afford it."

"You still can't. Keep it in mind."

"Don't look so worried. Bodyguards are supposed to be calm yet alert."

He said something under his breath and rapped on the closed door of room 1516. The door opened just enough to show a two-inch slice of someone who had all the welcoming qualities of a junk-yard dog.

"Ms. Collins and bodyguard," Sam said, and hoped the man wasn't as familiar as he looked.

The guard closed the door to a slit, flipped through a list, and opened the door. He was wearing a weapon harness and the attitude of a man who was used to being armed.

It was Bill Colton.

Neither man showed any recognition of the other, but Colton looked at Kate like he was memorizing her.

Sam had no doubt that he was.

Kate gave the guard a glance and nothing more. She headed straight for the table that had every color in the rainbow except red. Unlike other dealers, CGSI didn't divide rough and finished goods. Rather they left them together to reinforce and enhance each other. If the buzz in the room was any example, it worked.

Wondering how to warn her about Colton, Sam stood near Kate when she bent over the sapphire display.

"Who was that?" she asked quietly.

Once again, Sam was grateful that Kate was smart rather than slow. "My roomie."

"Your . . ." She remembered his earlier sardonic summary of Colton. "Oh, shit."

"Something like that."

"Want to leave?"

"The damage is done. Let's see if something good can come out of it."

"Some gorgeous stones would come if we could afford the rough," Kate said wistfully.

Sam looked at the display. Even to his untrained eye, the gems seemed brighter, cleaner, more colorful than anything he'd seen before. He whistled softly.

"Yes," Kate said, running a fingertip lightly over a deep blue gem that exactly matched the color of Sam's eyes. "This is like going to the Smithsonian and lusting after their gems."

"Good thing I have control of the wallet."

Kate rolled her eyes.

The table just beyond Sam held rubies in every shade, tint, and tone of the color called red. Two men were standing close to it. One man was looking. The other was talking.

"It's the gem of the future, I tell you," the man said emphatically, pointing to the ruby display. "Emeralds are tainted by politics, sapphires are just too common, and diamonds aren't worth investing in because DeBeers isn't propping up the market anymore what with all the new synthetics. That leaves rubies. And these, my friend, are *rubies*."

"Salesman?" Sam murmured against Kate's hair.

Her breath caught at the stir of warmth. "Not unless it's used cars. I'm betting the silent one is an investor and the noisy one is a trader who has an 'understanding' with CGSI."

"He brings a live one to the cash register, he gets part of the kill?"

Kate laughed softly. "Bingo."

As they had in the last five private showings, Kate studied the stones and Sam studied the people. There was no one who was wrong for the time or place. No one who spent too much time studying the security arrangements. No one who—

"Seven Sins?" asked a man behind Sam. "Never heard of them."

"Not many people have," another male voice answered. "The only one who ever saw them was the cutter. And McCloud, of course."

By slow, painful degrees, Sam turned until he could see both men from the corner of his eyes. They looked like everyone else in the room—American or European, dressed well yet casually, intent on making a profit. The one who knew about the Seven Sins was dark haired and had the kind of tan that suggested he lived in the south of Florida or spent his life on Arizona golf courses. The other man was bald, plump, and had shrewd eyes.

"Arthur McCloud?" the bald man asked.

"You've heard of him?"

"Hell, yes. He outbid me for a piece of ruby rough I'd have given anything except too much money to own."

Teeth flashed in a rueful smile as the dark-haired man shook his head. "That's McCloud. He outbid me for some fabulous blue sapphire rough, the kind people once cut into gems and then worshiped along with the idol."

"He has the last bid and the best collection of finished goods outside of the biggest museums," the plump man said emphatically. "But last I heard he was buying emerald rough from sunken Spanish ships. Just a rumor, mind you. There aren't any legal shipwreck explorations that I know of right now."

"I heard the same thing." The dark-haired man shrugged. "I'm not into emeralds. But around Thanksgiving of last year, McCloud called me up and crowed about the Seven Sins he'd stolen out from under my nose. That rough I wanted had been turned into seven untreated ultra-fine blue sapphires of different weight and cut, with a perfect color match across the stones. Biggest one was just under one hundred carats."

The bald man's jaw sagged. "Untreated? Ultra-fine color? My God. You're sure?"

"Yeah, I'm sure. I should have bid higher. I didn't think a cutter could get that much from the rough. I figured six big stones, tops, and nothing over fifty carats."

"Who did the cutting?"

"A woman, if you can believe it."

The bald man grinned. "I believe it. You ever see my wife's work?"

"No, but I sure wanted to see the Seven Sins."

"Bet you left drool marks all over them."

"Never got that close."

"What happened? You piss off McCloud?"

The dark-haired man shook his head. "He called me a few weeks later and said that for insurance reasons, he's not letting anyone look at any part of his collection for a while."

"Odd."

"Collectors are odd. That's why we're collectors."

Sam drifted over toward the door, Colton, and the guest list.

"Dark-haired guy with the tan," Sam said quietly.

"The one standing next to the short bald man?"

"Yeah. Who is it?"

Colton looked like he wanted to refuse, but didn't. He scanned the guest list and said, "Jeremy Baxter, no company affiliation. Room eight-eighteen."

"Thanks." Sam turned away.

"Wait," Colton said. "What'd he do?"

"I'll get back to you as soon as I know."

Sam crossed the room to Kate. "How much longer you need here?"

She looked up. "You heard them too."

"You're so quick it's scaring me. Yeah, I heard them."

"Wonder how many other people McCloud called."

"That's just one of the things I'm going to ask him."

"While you're at it," Kate said, "ask CGSI who the other losing bidders on that batch of rough were. One of them might have been mad enough to kill."

Sam smiled slowly. "I like the way you think."

"Now *I'm* scared."

Chapter 40

Scottsdale
Friday
5:40 P.M.

Kirby drove his rental car into the Royale employee parking lot a few moments after the courier did. He stayed back several car lengths, saw where the courier parked, and drove on by without so much as looking in the courier's direction. The usual order of the day would be for the courier to go inside and check in with Sizemore Security Consulting while leaving the goods securely locked in the trunk of the car. Then, depending on the wishes of the consignee, the courier could sign over the package to Sizemore's company and get an escort for the walk from the parking lot to Branson and Sons' suite, or the courier would get an escort for the walk from the parking lot to the hotel safe.

Whatever the protocol, it wouldn't matter to Kirby. He would be in and out of the trunk in twenty seconds. Thirty-five seconds, max. By the time the courier and escort came back to the parking lot, Kirby would be on his way to Sky Harbor to dump the rental car and the itchy disguise.

He turned down one aisle between parked cars and stopped when he was a row over and directly opposite the courier's vehicle. He put the SUV in park and left the engine running with the key in the ignition. With the expertise of a surgeon or a dentist, he snapped on exam gloves. A few quick yanks on the stretchy hosiery pulled it into place, blurring his features. He put the cowboy hat back on, furthering hindering any useful identification. Then he hit the key he'd programmed with the courier's code.

The courier's rental car flashed its lights in reply.

Party time.

Chapter 41

Scottsdale
Friday
5:40 P.M.

A man came in through the employee door, brushed by Sam and Kate without a look, and hurried down the corridor leading to the lobby. The door closed hard behind him, emphasizing his rush.

At the same moment, both Sam and Kate reached out to open the door leading to the employee parking lot. Gently, he pried her fingers off the hand bar.

"Men first," he said.

"Since when?"

"Since I became your bodyguard, remember?"

She stared at him.

He leaned toward her and said quietly, "When you're under-cover, you're never out of your role, remember?"

She blew out a breath. "Right. You go first."

"Oh, shit! I can't believe I did that!" echoed down the corridor.

Sam and Kate turned around to find out what was going on. The man who had been in such a hurry to get into the hotel a moment ago was now in a fever to get out.

"Excuse me," the man said running down the hallway. "I have to—right now!"

"Last time I heard that," Sam said to Kate as they jumped back out of the way, "it was in a men's room with all the stalls occupied."

The door slammed.

Sam opened it again. Kate made an ironic "after you" gesture to him and followed him out the door to the employee parking lot. Sam's car was across the lot, near the miserable shade of light pole. They started for the car, cutting between the rows.

Thirty feet down the third aisle between rows of vehicles, a small SUV sat in the center of the lane like a cork in a bottle. The driver's door was partly open, as though someone had given up on finding a closer parking spot and simply parked illegally to go into the hotel for a quick errand.

"What a jerk," Kate said as she started across the blocked aisle. "What if someone comes back before he does and wants to leave?"

Sam didn't answer. He was suddenly, intently, studying the rows of cars to their right.

"Hey! What are you doing?" yelled someone off to the left.

It was the man from the hallway, the man in a hurry. He was running and yelling.

Sam turned and took it all in with one quick look, time slowing to a crawl, everything sharp and distinct in the reddish light of the setting sun.

Thirty feet away, a man in cowboy hat, boots, and surgical gloves had a crowbar under the trunk lid of a parked car.

The man from the hotel was dashing toward him, shouting.

Then it all speeded up as the cowboy bent down and yanked a gun from his boot. The courier went facedown. The cowboy leaped toward the illegally parked SUV. The engine revved and tires squalled.

The car was coming right at them.

Sam yanked Kate just as she literally threw herself away from the parking aisle to get clear of the speeding SUV. She slammed into the side of a parked car so hard her wig flew off.

Sam was a heartbeat behind her, covering her.

"What—" Kate asked breathlessly.

Metal caromed off metal with a sound like a thin scream.

A nearby windshield turned into a maze of cracks.

Sam didn't need the hole in the center of the web to tell him what was going down. With one hand he shoved Kate to her hands and knees between parked cars. His other hand held his weapon. He didn't expect to hit the cowboy, but he could at least keep the bastard too worried for any more wild shooting. Ignoring Bureau policy, Sam fired two fast shots at the fleeing SUV.

Unlike the cowboy's gun, Sam's made enough noise to bring men pouring out of the FBI motor coach.

Sam grabbed his badge with his left hand. He held both hands high and in plain sight.

"I'm FBI!" he yelled at the agents. "There's a man down by the black Mercedes!"

Two agents broke away toward the Mercedes.

Three more came at a run toward Sam, weapons drawn.

"Stay down," he said to Kate. "They're feeling edgy."

"*They're* feeling edgy. *We're* the ones who were shot at!"

"They don't know that yet. Did you get a look at the license plate?"

"Oh, sure. Would that be when you slammed me up against a car or while you held my face to the pavement?"

"You okay?" Sam asked, but he didn't take his eyes off the men who were closing in on them.

"How the hell would I know?"

"I'll ask you again when the adrenaline wears off. Stay down until I tell you otherwise."

Whatever Kate said was lost when one of the agents yelled, "Sam? Is that you under the cowboy hat?"

"It's me, Doug."

Immediately, Doug signaled for the agents with him to head for the black Mercedes.

"I've got a civilian here," Sam said, "so don't be surprised when she stands up."

"She armed?"

"No."

"You both okay?"

"We're working on it." Sam holstered his weapon, anchored his badge holder in his front jeans pocket so that the shield still showed, and hauled Kate to her feet.

She didn't thank him. She was too loaded with adrenaline and aftershocks to worry about being polite. She wanted to scream. Hit something. Shake. Hide. Scream some more.

So she forced herself to lean against the car and act like she spent part of every day almost getting killed.

"The other civilian looked like he was hit," Sam said to Doug.

"By you?" Doug asked.

"No."

"We only heard two shots, evenly spaced. They sounded like they came from a thirty-eight."

"Those were mine. The cowboy had a silencer. I wasn't close enough to see make or model of the gun, but even muffled, it had enough punch to knock down a man at ten feet, minimum."

Doug holstered his gun and looked toward the Mercedes. Someone over there was yelling for the paramedics. Somebody else had a cell phone to his ear, probably talking to the cops.

Kate started forward to see if she could help with the wounded man. Her knees wouldn't cooperate.

Without looking away from his supervisor, Sam casually propped her up against the car. She didn't know whether to thank him or hit him.

Breathe, she told herself. *Slow and deep. You can do it. Hell, even a baby can do it.*

Sam gave her a worried look.

She bared her teeth at him.

"What'd you see?" Doug asked Sam.

He turned away from Kate. "White Subaru Forrester, this year's model, heavily tinted windows, clean except for the wheel wells and license plate, which were muddy."

"Convenient," Doug said, not surprised.

"Yeah. No plate in front. Dirty plate in back was Arizona. I'm betting it's a rental. One man in a cowboy hat and boots, surgical gloves, jeans and a medium-blue work shirt, a stocking pulled over his face, dark, short beard underneath. Caucasian, Hispanic, possibly Eurasian. I couldn't see the eyes. An inch or two shorter than me, slim build. Shot right-handed. Had a boot holster."

"He say anything?"

"No."

"Impression?"

"A pro. He'll dump the car wherever his own is parked, throw his hat and boots in his own trunk, and vanish."

"Shit. Just what we needed." Doug looked at Kate for the first time. "Who are you?"

Sam stepped in front of her, blocking Doug's view.

"She isn't here," Sam said.

"Mother," Doug muttered. "Get her out of here. Then get your ass over to my office. One hour, max."

Chapter 42

Scottsdale
Friday
6:30 P.M.

"That's the best you can do?" Sizemore asked harshly as he opened another beer. High-test beer in a classy, ice-dripping bottle. A snap of his thumb and forefinger sent the cap sailing toward the trash can. The cap fell in and rattled over empty bottles and cans.

It had been a long day.

Ignoring her own tightly drawn nerves, Sharon took a deep breath and tried one more time. "If you dialed back on the beer and—"

"If you did as you're told rather than getting in my face," he cut in savagely, "none of this would happen."

She put her hands on her hips even as she gauged his alcohol level and temper. By the color of his face, both were high. He'd loosened his collar and tie, but otherwise was dressed exactly as he'd been every workday since he joined the Bureau.

Maybe she should just pack it in and head for that tropical beach and let dear old Dad sort out his own mess.

Soon, she promised herself. *Very, very soon. But until then . . .*

"The courier," she said with deadly precision, "is awake and doing very well. Three hurrahs for him."

"I'd be leading the cheer if the fool had seen anything."

"To be fair," she said, "he was rattled by the flat tire and being late. So he rushed into the hotel to tell us he was here and get an escort to—"

"Yeah, yeah," Sizemore interrupted. "Then the fool remembers he didn't lock the car and runs back into the parking lot." He made a disgusted sound and took down the level of beer in the bottle by a third. "Some fucking courier."

"The point is," Sharon began.

"The point is, we look like Keystone Kops," Sizemore said harshly. "Courier doesn't lock the car. Thief uses a remote key to open the trunk, only he locks it because it was already *unlocked*. Big laugh out of that one. Ha ha. So the thief thinks his key is bad and goes to work on the trunk with a tire iron."

"We—"

Sizemore swallowed beer and kept talking. "Courier runs out of hotel to lock the trunk, which is now locked, thanks to the thief. Second big laugh. Ha ha. Thief dumps courier with a silenced gun. Then Special Agent Sam Fucking Groves leaps to the rescue and shoots at fleeing SUV, which is against agency policy for Chrissake."

Sharon waited for her father to run out of venom. Or beer.

"Agents come flying out of the HQ like bats out of hell," Sizemore continued, took a long swallow, then another. "And where is Sizemore Security Consulting in all this? Picking our ass, that's where. The only time we'll get mentioned on the news is when they do the 'laugher' at the end of the show."

"So that's why you've been ducking reporters."

Ignoring her, he drank, belched, and fired the empty beer bottle at the wastebasket. It hit with a loud sound. He walked over and kicked the wastebasket halfway across the room, making a real racket. Bottles and caps bounced over the hotel's luxurious carpeting.

"Some office manager you are," he snarled at Sharon. "You should have known that—"

"How am I supposed to know what the whole FBI can't find out?" she cut in.

"It's your job to know! Hell, ask Jason. He knows fucking everything about what's going on in the gem business and he can't wait to bend your ear. I should have fired his ass last year when he asked for his second raise in ten months."

Sharon didn't know which was worse, her headache or the anger gnawing in her stomach. Sometimes getting in her father's face worked, because it was about the only thing he respected. But not when he was halfway drunk.

"The point is," she said, "the intact package was delivered by Sizemore Security Consulting to Branson and Sons. That matters more than a few seconds on local TV news feed."

"Yeah?"

"Losing another package in the parking lot of the hotel would have been a public relations disaster. Which brings up my next point."

Sizemore twisted the cap off another bottle of beer and turned his back to her.

She was used to it. She kept talking even as she braced for what her words would bring. In truth, part of her was looking forward to it.

She just might let it all go, yell back, and to hell with little things like long-range security and enough money not to spend her life dreading bills.

"I know you don't want to hear this," she said clearly, "but it has to be said. There's a leak somewhere that—"

"That's *bullshit.*"

"—we need to stop," she finished.

"You've checked the couriers and guards again and again. So have I." Sizemore sent the bottle cap spinning in the general direction of the prone trash can. "You've run their credit cards and debit cards and checking accounts. Nothing but Joe Citizens, every last one of them. If their accounts don't show unexplained cash, then no cash worth chasing is coming in. *It's not our leak.*"

"If the leak isn't with us, then it's with the FBI."

Sizemore started to explode, then looked thoughtful.

Abruptly, Sharon realized he wasn't nearly as drunk as he

seemed. Like her—like any good agent—he could be a game player when it was worth the effort.

"Yeah, you're right," he said. "It's gotta be Groves."

Her brown eyebrows rose. "Interesting. Any particular reason or was that just the first name you thought of?"

"Don't run that bitchy mouth on me," Sizemore said. "You're not too old to get slapped and I'm not too old to do it. I gave you a job when nobody else would touch you with anything but his dick and don't you forget it."

How can I? You remind me twice a day. But that was old history, so all she said aloud was, "Why do you think Groves is the leak?"

"Why do you care?"

"We can't afford to be embarrassed by more screwups," she said. "We were lucky not to lose the second Branson and Sons package. If I've missed something, I want to know it."

"Groves was in the parking lot."

"A coincidence."

"Yeah?" Sizemore took a long drink. "Groves has a CI and he's not sharing the information with anyone, including Kennedy. Then Groves shows up in the parking lot just in time to stop a robbery and be a hero. Coincidence my ass. He's got a line into the gangs that we don't. I want his CI before something happens that makes us look like more of a donkey's asshole than we already do."

Sharon was quiet for a moment. Then she nodded. "All right. How?"

"I'm betting the CI is Natalie Harrison Cutter."

"The woman he caught swapping stones?"

"Yeah."

"You think he flipped her, that she's his informant in return for not getting arrested?"

"The timing is right." Sizemore reached into the breast pocket of his suit and handed Sharon a picture. "This was taken off the security cameras."

She gave it a comprehensive glance. "Ms. Cutter?"

"So Groves says, only no one by that name is registered at the hotel or for the gem show."

"False name?"

"That's what I'm assuming. Nobody in the FBI data banks popped under that name either."

"What about Arizona law enforcement?" Sharon asked.

"Zilch."

"Did anyone get a look at the citizen who was with Groves in the parking lot?"

"The SAC said she was facedown between the cars. Female. Caucasian or Hispanic, under fifty."

Sharon tapped the photo with her fingernail. "From what I've heard, the female Groves was with in the hotel was a green-eyed redhead, late twenties, early thirties. Other than the age, the rest is wrong for Cutter."

"The hair was a wig. Don't know about the eyes."

"A wig? How can you be sure?"

"Kennedy told me they found a red wig in the parking lot near where the female had fallen."

"So I'm looking for a Caucasian or Hispanic female around thirty whose eyes may or may not be green—colored contacts are easy to get. What about height? Weight?"

"Five-foot-five or -six. One-thirty to one-forty. Not a stick."

"Good for her," Sharon said. "Anything else?"

"Shit, you want me to connect the dots for you?"

"Fine. I'll show her picture around as soon as I finish the paperwork on the—"

"Give me the damn thing," Sizemore cut in, grabbing the photo. "I'll take care of it myself."

Chapter 43

Phoenix
Friday
6:30 P.M.

Kirby parked the white SUV in the east economy lot at Sky Harbor. He'd already ripped off the fake beard and stuffed it in the cowboy hat along with the panty hose. Now he switched boots for running shoes and shoved all the leftovers in a small nylon duffel. When he got out of the car, nothing of his disguise remained except the dark hair and jeans—which hardly stood out in Arizona—and the surgical gloves he wouldn't remove until he shut the car door.

The bullet hole on the rear panel that had seemed to be as big as a baseball while he was driving on the freeway looked insignificant in the long golden light of a desert evening.

Snub-nose guns are no damn good past ten feet. But at least the bastard didn't get a window. That would have been hard to hide.

And getting shot would have been even worse.

Kirby peeled off his gloves and stuffed them in his pocket. Then he walked toward the shuttle stop and went inside the parking building, where cars could be sheltered from the sun on a first-come, first-serve, pay-more basis. He took the shuttle to the airport, got out at the first stop, and headed for the nearest bathroom. He flushed the face fur in one stall, walked to the next airline terminal and the next john, and flushed the gloves. Three times. While he was at it, he took care of most of the hair color with paper towels and water from the toilet. He dumped the panty hose in a closed trash container at the food court. In another restroom he sat in a stall, shredded the rental contract and fake ID, and flushed until there was nothing but water. Since no one was in the restroom, he rinsed the last of the hair color out in one of the sinks.

Duffel in hand, Kirby caught a shuttle to the west economy parking lot, where he'd left his own car. He would be back at the hotel in time for dinner.

Chapter 44

Scottsdale
Friday
7:00 P.M.

Doug pushed back from the clever yet cramped desk space in the motor coach, glared at Sam, and wished that Ted Sizemore lived in the deepest part of hell. A sealed part. No possibility of communication.

Especially with SSA Patrick Kennedy.

"You're late," Doug said.

"Traffic," Sam said.

"Yeah, yeah. Everybody talks about it and nobody does anything about it. Shit." Doug drummed his fingers on the desk. "We've got a problem."

Sam didn't figure it was the traffic. "Sizemore?"

"We look like horses' asses. That's the problem."

"And Sizemore looks better?" Sam asked. "Did anyone in the FBI know when the courier was due?"

"We're trying to find out. As close as Kennedy and Sizemore are . . ." Doug grimaced. "Who the hell can be sure? This has clusterfuck written all over it."

Sam didn't argue. He'd been thinking the same long before the crime strike force reached Scottsdale.

"Level with me about your CI," Doug said, pinning Sam with a bleak look. "Did she know?"

"No."

"That quick?"

"Yes."

"We found a red wig in the parking lot. Know anything about it?"

"Should I?"

Doug's hand slammed down on the desk. "Don't fuck with me on this one."

"If anything goes on official records *anywhere,* my CI will be targeted by the same man who did the Purcells."

Doug became very still. "You're certain of that?"

"As certain as I can be without attending a funeral."

"Are you saying that the murderer wears a badge? Is that why you don't want your CI's name known to the FBI?"

Sam chose his words very carefully. "I don't know."

Doug waited.

So did Sam.

"You're heading for some time off without pay," Doug said flatly. "Talk to me."

"I need your word that you won't tell anyone. And that includes Kennedy. Otherwise I'll take the time off without pay and the nastygram in my file and any other punishment the Bureau dreams up."

"Shit. I don't believe it. Colton is right. You're fucking your CI."

"No."

Sam figured the fact that he'd like to jump Kate was none of the FBI's business. If he wondered how long it would be before he took her up on the invitation in her eyes, well, that was his problem.

There was a long silence.

"Colton is saying that the redhead he saw you with is your CI," Doug said finally.

"It's a free country. Even jackasses get to bray."

Another long silence.

"Okay," Doug said. "Nothing we say leaves this room. And Christ help us both if Kennedy finds out. Now sit the hell down. I'm tired of looking up at you."

Sam took some files off a chair and sat on the edge of it. He was a long way from being relieved or relaxed. He trusted Doug with his life, but he hated having to trust Doug with Kate's.

"My CI saw this coming after the parking lot shootout," Sam said. "She gave me permission to tell you and no one else. I told her you would keep your word."

Doug heard the rest of what wasn't said: if Doug went back on his word, he and Sam would sort it out personally rather than sniping at each other through the FBI bureaucracy.

"You sure you aren't sleeping with her?" Doug asked.

"Damn sure."

"But you want to."

"If the Bureau starts cracking down on 'want to,' we won't be able to field a single agent."

Doug almost smiled. "Did your CI know about the shipment today?" he asked for the second time.

"No."

"Did you?"

"No."

"Then how do you explain the fact that you were in the parking lot with a woman wearing a disguise?"

"Bad luck. Or good luck, depending on your point of view. Bad luck in that she was nearly killed. Good luck in that the courier would have bled out before he was discovered."

"You'll take an oath that it was a coincidence that you were in the parking lot when the attempted robbery went down?" Doug asked.

"Yes."

"Hard to believe."

"Why? If coincidences didn't happen, we wouldn't have a name for them. Hell, we have agents coming and going through the parking lot all the time. It could have been anyone that stumbled across

the robbery. Besides, like I said, being spotted didn't do me any fa-
vors. Or her."

Doug put his elbows on the desk and rubbed his eyes. He was
getting too old to go four nights in a row on too little sleep to keep a
college student alive during finals.

"Okay." Doug pinched the bridge of his nose, opened the belly
drawer, and went looking for aspirin. When he found three, he
looked up. "What were you and your CI doing at the hotel?"

"Looking at the best of the private showings."

Doug popped the pills in his mouth and grimaced. "Why?"

Sam stood and drew a paper cup of water from the cooler standing next to the door.

"Drink this," he said to Doug. "Watching you dry-swallow aspirin
makes my throat hurt."

"Doing it is even worse. Thanks."

Though he'd rather have paced, Sam sat down again. "This is
where her life goes on the line."

Doug hesitated, then nodded.

"Remember that Florida courier case five months ago?" Sam
asked. "The one that kicked off the whole crime strike force?"

"The McCloud shipment. Courier took it and ran."

"That's what somebody wants us to think."

Doug settled back in his office chair and fiddled with the paper
cup. "What's your version?"

"It was staged. The courier—Lee Mandel—likely is somewhere
in the swamp feeding crabs."

"Then who took package?"

"Whoever killed him." Sam made an impatient motion, cutting
off Doug's next question. "My CI didn't believe the stage dressing.
She started asking questions, pushing, forcing the FBI file to stay
open. Then, just after the file got updated again a few months back,
she gets a call on her answering machine telling her to stop pushing
or die. The caller used a voice distorter. CI couldn't even say for
sure whether it was a man or woman."

Doug's fingers stilled. "Just after the file was updated?"

"Yes."

"You think it was someone inside the Bureau."

It wasn't a question.

Sam hesitated. "All I know for sure is that whoever made the call had access to Bureau files. He knew when something was updated."

"Could be a hacker."

"Could be Superman and his X-ray eyes," Sam retorted. "Look, I didn't want to believe it either. But potentially it explains a lot."

"Like?"

"Like why we keep coming off looking like schmucks on this job. If someone inside is feeding information outside, we're fucked."

"Okay, that's one possibility." Doug said it like there was a bad taste in his mouth. "Could be one of the gem traders or courier companies, couldn't it?"

"Not unless my CI is lying."

"What does that mean?"

"She knew what Lee Mandel was carrying, so—"

"She's the one who stole it," Doug said quickly. "Hell, even the FBI doesn't know what was in the frigging package."

"She knew because she cut the gems Mandel was supposed to deliver to McCloud."

Doug opened his mouth. Closed it. Thought hard. "She's a cutter?"

"A damn good one. But everything I've learned in my years of investigating tells me that she didn't do it."

"Then who did? Who else knew what was in the package?"

"Her stepfather. He owns the courier service Mandel was working for at the time he was hit."

"Mandel Inc.?"

"Yes."

"Run him."

"I did," Sam said, resisting the urge to point out that he wasn't some apple-cheeked rookie. "Mr. Mandel has my nomination for citizen of the year. He wears his seat belt and his parking tickets are paid promptly. So are his taxes. He was audited once on a random basis. Government ended up owing *him* money."

"He needs a better tax accountant. What do his company books look like? You want a warrant?"

"He's cooperating," Sam said. "So far our accountant hasn't discovered anything but data-entry errors, and the majority of them favored the clients."

"So that's why you had me sign a request for a forensic accountant and refused to tell me who or where or why."

"I was protecting my—"

"You forget that my dick is in the wringer along with yours," Doug snarled. "Keep talking and maybe I won't chop yours off. Who else knew what was in the shipment?"

"Mandel did, so his lover might have."

"Is that your cutter?"

"No. Mandel was gay."

Doug blinked. "Hand me Mandel's file. It's on the floor next to you."

Sam sorted through the stacks until he found the right file and passed it over the desk. "It won't do you any good. Mandel was so deep in the closet that no one but his lovers knew. And my informant. They were half brother and sister through the mother. Mandel's father is my informant's stepfather. Lee didn't tell anyone but her that he was gay."

"What does his lover say? Did he know about the package?"

"He denies it. He's still crying over Mandel. They were planning to be married June eighth, the anniversary of their first date."

"Check him out anyway."

"An agent in Los Angeles is doing just that." Sam gave up trying to sit and stood with his thumbs hooked into the back pockets of his jeans. "Nothing worth reporting so far. Norm Gallagher—Mandel's lover—has a junior partnership in an investment firm that specializes in managing money for 'alternative lifestyle' clients. Everybody knows Norm is gay and no one gives a crap. In other words, he's not being blackmailed, doesn't have a gambling habit, doesn't do drugs, and is helping to take care of his ailing parents, who knew he was gay before he did."

"Dead end," Doug summarized.

"I told them to keep digging, but I'm not holding my breath waiting for any big revelation."

Doug grunted. "Okay. Your snitch—"

"Confidential informant," Sam cut in. "Snitches are lowlifes. She doesn't fit that profile."

"Whatever. She knew what was in the package, but didn't do the courier, Mandel. Her stepfather knew the timing, but he didn't do it either, pending new evidence. Who else knew?"

"McCloud."

"You think the brother-in-law of a sitting president is a murderer and a thief?" Doug asked in rising tones.

"I have an agent working on a follow-up interview with McCloud."

"Holy Mary, mother of God." Doug put his face in his hands. "And my name is on the request for interview, right?"

"You're my SAC."

"I'm looking at early retirement in Fargo." Doug straightened and sighed. "Well, I'll finally be able to try cross-country skiing."

"Don't forget ice sculpture."

"You're thinking of Minnesota. North Dakota doesn't have that much water. Tell me somebody else besides McCloud knew about the shipment."

"According to him, he didn't tell anyone," Sam said.

"Do you believe him?"

"No. I think there might be an insurance issue if he ran off at the mouth about deliveries. Whatever. It probably doesn't matter. Couriers get clouted all the time and the thief doesn't know until he opens the package what the prize is."

Doug picked up a pen, looked like he wanted to break it, and set it aside. "You're not making me feel any better."

"Story of my life."

"Change it. Make me feel better."

"My CI found one of McCloud's missing stones in Mike Purcell's display case," Sam said.

"Which one?"

"An emerald-cut blue sapphire as big as your thumb. Bigger actually. You have small hands."

"Blue sapphire? Aren't they all blue?"

"Don't start. And no."

Doug's eyes narrowed. "Wait. Wasn't there something about a Natalie Cutter switching stones on Purcell?"

"Yeah. I caught her on the second switch."

"Back up. You lost me."

"She was—and is—trying to prove that her half brother, Lee Mandel, isn't a thief who took off for the tropics with a big-boobed blonde on his arm."

"You said he was gay."

"He was," Sam said. "Apparently, whoever was out setting up false leads for us to follow didn't know that. Like I said, Mandel was way deep in the closet."

"Okay." Doug pushed back and fiddled with a paper clip. "So you're assuming whoever clouted Mandel didn't know he was gay. Go back to Purcell's sapphire."

"Again, this doesn't leave the room. If it becomes general knowledge in the strike force, we take a big step back from catching the guy."

Doug nodded.

"McCloud's shipment was seven blue sapphires that had been cut and polished in seven different shapes by my CI. He called them the Seven Sins."

"Seven stones worth a million bucks."

"My CI says that's only what McCloud had in the rough and in her work. Market value would be at least twice that, maybe more. Depends on who fell in love with the stones and how hot the bidding got."

Doug straightened one curve of the paper clip.

"The important thing is that somehow Purcell ended up with one of the Seven Sins," Sam said. "My CI proved it when she palmed the real stone, left the synthetic, went home, and studied the stone and the photographs she'd taken of it before she put it in the courier's pouch."

"No doubt that the two stones were the same?"

"None."

Doug nodded and went to work on the next curve of the paper clip.

"When she was certain," Sam said, "she took the real stone back and swapped it for the one she'd left."

"Why?"

"She's not some lowlife thief," Sam said impatiently. "She just wanted to have evidence that the stones were the same so that the FBI could squeeze Purcell and make him talk."

Silence.

Doug took the last curve out of the paper clip and spun it between his fingers. He was looking at the faintly rumpled line of metal, but he was thinking about something else. Whatever he was thinking, he wasn't happy about it. He looked like a man sucking on a turd.

"But before I could get to Purcell, somebody else did," Sam continued. "I've had Mario going through Purcell's papers—what few he had—but he hasn't run across any mention of a big sapphire purchased in the past five months, or any big cash withdrawal or transfer of funds that might, could, and should have been involved in Purcell getting his hands on a stone like that."

Doug made a snarling sound. He could see where Sam was going. He really didn't want to be taken there.

"I figure Purcell had had the stone for at least two months, maybe more," Sam said. "You want to hear my reasoning?"

"Not yet." The words came through Doug's clenched teeth.

Sam chose his next words very carefully. He didn't like where he was going any better than his SAC did.

"Purcell flashed the stone around some other gem shows before this one in Scottsdale," Sam said. "No problems. He showed it here.

No problems. And then I caught a woman doing a stone swap and Colton shot off his big mouth about it at the strike force meeting in Sizemore's suite. By the time I ran down the real identity of Cutter and the reason for the swap, Purcell was dead, and so was any chance of the FBI finding out how a bottom-feeder like Purcell got his hands on a really choice bit of goods."

Doug began putting a curve in the straightened paper clip.

"Just to put the cherry on the cake of my investigation," Sam said, "Purcell's killer does the Colombian necktie dance, and suddenly Kennedy and Sizemore are seeing South Americans behind every door."

"You don't think it was the South Americans?"

"Purcell didn't handle Colombian emeralds or drugs. Why would they whack him?"

"To shut him up."

Sam made an impatient noise. "If the Mandel hit was South American, it was one of a kind. Trunk wasn't forced. Courier vanishes instead of being left with a mouthful of his own genitals as a warning to others. Mandel's car is turned in to the rental company—after a shampoo—late at the airport. You ever hear of South Americans returning a rental car for a dead man, much less washing it?"

Doug put a second curve in the mangled clip.

"Rumors of a blonde with big boobs begin circulating," Sam continued relentlessly. "Mandel's name is dragged through the mud. He's pretty close to his family, but he never calls home, never gives a hint that he's okay. He's totally silent, yet all the cops seem to 'know' that Mandel is in Aruba or Rio, bouncing on the mysterious blonde. Have I mentioned his gay lover? He doesn't hear from Mandel either."

Silence.

The paper clip broke. Doug fired the pieces into a trash basket.

More silence.

"All right," Doug said finally. "I'll keep backing up your requests and ducking Kennedy. Did your CI save the answering machine message?"

"The one with the threat? Yes."

"Send it to the lab."

"I did."

"Anything?"

"Not so far."

Doug looked Sam straight in the eyes. "Get this son of a bitch. Get him fast."

"Tired of the headlines?" Sam asked.

"Fuck the headlines. If the leak is in the Bureau, you're a dead man walking."

Sam had already figured that out. What he hadn't figured out was how to keep Kate from getting killed along with him.

Chapter 45

Scottsdale
Friday
7:15 P.M.

It had been a long time since Sizemore had retired from the FBI, but he hadn't forgotten the moves. He never would. He still lived and breathed the Bureau.

"I'm doing a follow-up on an interview your manager had with FBI Special Agent Sam Groves," Sizemore said at the lobby desk. "Is Madeline Dermott on duty?"

Forty seconds later Sizemore was being let in through a side door to the manager's office. When the desk clerk introduced Sizemore as an FBI agent, he didn't correct the clerk. Instead, he held out his hand to Madeline. A brisk shake, a professional smile on both sides, and they were down to business.

"How may I help you?" Madeline asked.

"Tuesday afternoon Special Agent Sam Groves interviewed you on the subject of this woman," Sizemore said, producing the photo. "Her name is Natalie Harrison Cutter."

"I remember. She wasn't registered here at the hotel or for any of the conventions that are currently on our books."

"Hate it when that happens," Sizemore said, smiling easily.

Madeline smiled back and confessed, "In this case, I was relieved.

I didn't want anyone who was suspected of something by the FBI to be registered at my hotel. And the other one is gone now too."

"Other one?"

"The other one Mr. Groves wanted to talk to. His name was Gavin . . . Gavin . . ." Madeline turned to the computer. Her beautifully manicured nails flew over the keyboard. "Gavin Greenfield. Florida."

"Greenfield. Of course." Sizemore gave Madeline an appreciative look. "Is that the Greenfield who lives in Miami or was it . . . ?"

Madeline glanced at the computer screen. "Coral Gables."

"Odd. He hasn't been answering his phone at that address. Could I check my number against the one he left with you?"

"Certainly." Madeline turned the screen so that Sizemore could read it.

He memorized the number and then said, "Well, that explains it."

"What?"

"Someone reversed the last two numbers when they gave it to me. Happens all the time. Thank you."

"You're welcome. I'm always happy to cooperate with the FBI."

Sizemore smiled again and let himself out of the office. He went to a quiet corner of the lobby, pulled out his cell phone, and keyed in the number he had memorized. It was answered on the third ring.

"If this is another damned telemarketer," the man began.

"It isn't," Sizemore interrupted. "I'm following up on the interview you had with FBI Special Agent Sam Groves."

Silence, followed by, "Who are you?"

"More to the point, who is Natalie Cutter to you?"

"Special Agent Groves told me if anyone wants to ask questions about her, they should call him. Since you're in the FBI, I'm sure you have his number. Good-bye."

Gavin Greenfield hung up with emphasis.

Sizemore sat for a few minutes, thinking about various ploys he could try on the uncooperative Mr. Greenfield. Lacking a badge, he really didn't have any leverage. All he knew for sure was that Greenfield had heard the name Natalie Cutter before.

That, and the fact that Sam Groves didn't want Greenfield to talk about her.

Sizemore went back to the lobby desk. Once more, the clerk took him to Madeline's office.

"Sorry to bother you again," Sizemore said, "but there's a problem. Not with your records, but with ours. I'm assuming you keep a list of calls each guest makes?"

"Of course. Phone calls used to be one of our big profit centers. Not so much now since so many people use mobiles."

Sizemore hoped that Greenfield didn't have a mobile phone. Sizemore himself hated the things. He only put up with them because they were useful.

"Did Mr. Greenfield make any calls?" Sizemore asked.

The manager's fingers raced over the computer keyboard. "Oh, yes. Quite a few. Here, I'll print it out."

"Thanks. That would be a big help."

List in hand, Sizemore went up to his suite and started up the computer he rarely used, because he had the same love-hate relationship with the machine that he had with cell phones. He plugged into the Internet and went to a site that listed the addresses of all telephone numbers. Sites like this were one of the reasons he'd learned to use computers. Saved an investigator all kinds of time.

Most of Greenfield's calls had been to his home in Coral Gables. Several others were to furniture outlets. Two were to a residence in Glendale, Arizona. That number was listed to K. J. Chandler.

Sizemore wrote down the name and address, switched over to a map site, and entered the Chandler address as a destination and that of the hotel as a starting point. Very quickly a map appeared on the screen. After a few fumbles he managed to attach a portable printer to the computer. He printed out the map, studied it, and checked his watch. Assuming anyone was home, he'd have to allow at least an hour for the round trip and interview.

He'd be late for dinner with Kennedy.

Sizemore left a message for Kennedy at the desk and headed out.

He only got lost twice on the way to K. J. Chandler's house. Phoenix was growing so fast that maps were out-of-date before they were even printed. L.A. had been like that once, but no more. The state taxed everything that moved, and if it didn't move the state taxed it twice as much.

The more Sizemore saw of Phoenix the more he liked it.

By seven o'clock he was driving down a suburban street lined on both sides by that rarity in Phoenix—thirty-year-old houses. Unlike older homes in L.A., the landscaping on these hadn't overwhelmed the yards. One hundred and sixteen degrees in the summer was a real effective way to shut down plant growth.

Reverting to old training, Sizemore didn't stop at the address. He simply drove by it, looking at other house numbers as though he hadn't yet found his destination.

Without seeming to, he got a good look at the Chandler house. The first thing he noticed was a sign right in the front yard telling the world that this place was protected. At least he didn't have to get out and examine the doors and windows to be certain that they were wired to an alarm system. Not that it really mattered. Nothing kept out real pros. The best you could do was slow them down.

None of the other houses he'd passed had anything more than faded NEIGHBORHOOD WATCH signs on every block.

"Interesting," Sizemore said to himself. "Wonder what she's hiding? Or maybe Chandler is the kind of female who hears about a rapist on the evening news and is sure he's coming to her window next even though the rapist is working a county fifty miles away." He shook his head. "Women. I'll never understand them."

Sizemore turned right, went over a few blocks, and came back at the address from a different direction. The exterior of the house had told him that Ms. Chandler wasn't going to be as quick to cooperate as the hotel manager. He wouldn't try knocking on the door except as the last resort before a black-bag job.

Halfway up the block from the house, with the residence behind him, he parked and watched the house in the rearview mirror. He

debated the risks of using the ceremonial badge he'd been pre-
sented with at his retirement. Representing himself as an FBI agent
could get him in a world of hurt—but only if he was caught.

Another car turned onto the street. American make. A few years
old. Basic model.

It fairly screamed government issue.

The car stopped in front of the Chandler place. Sizemore
watched Sam Groves get out and go to the door. No doubt about the
identity, even in failing light. Groves had a my-balls-clang way of
moving that irritated the hell out of Sizemore.

Two seconds later Sam was inside the house.

Bingo.

Sizemore drove off, planning the ways he would search various
official and unofficial records for K. J. Chandler.

But first he'd take the time to rub his smart-ass daughter's nose in
the fact that he'd found out about the CI while she was putting on
makeup to go out with that shitheel Peyton.

Chapter 46

Glendale
Friday
8:00 P.M.

As soon as Kate shut the door behind Sam, she automatically began locking up. He watched her with brooding eyes and an intensity that would have made her nervous if she'd been looking at him.

He was sure looking at her. He noticed everything about her. She was wearing an emerald-green bathrobe. Her feet were bare, her hair loose. She smelled of something that was almost lemon, almost spice. He saw every nick and scrape on her hands from the parking lot, saw the faint bruise along her cheekbone, and the scratch along the vulnerable line of her neck. In the space of a breath he felt again the rage that had shaken him when he realized she was seconds away from being killed.

"You sure you're okay?" he asked. "Maybe you should see a doctor."

She turned and leaned against the door, wishing she'd worn heavy sweats instead of the slippery robe that revealed too much skin. But she was damned if she would pull the neckline higher and the hemline lower, fidgeting over her clothes like a girl on her first date.

Besides, Sam looked tired, shuttered, anything but a man watching a woman he wanted.

No news there. The cop is in control. Over and out.

"Like I told you every few seconds while you drove me home," she said, "I'm fine."

"You were shaking." He'd been shaking too, but that wasn't something he wanted to talk about.

"Ya think?" she said, widening her eyes. "The next time someone tries to kill me, I'll be sure to keep a stiff upper lip. Lower one too."

Sam groaned and did what he'd needed to do earlier and hadn't dared because he knew what would happen; he reached for her. Earlier he'd wanted to be able to tell the truth when Doug asked the question about sex and Kate. If Sam had touched her earlier, he knew he wouldn't have let go. Then he would have had to lie to Doug in order to stay close enough to Kate to keep her alive.

But now wasn't then. Sam ran a fingertip over her lips, brushed it gently against her bruised cheek.

"Damn, Kate, you scared me to death."

Her breath stopped at the turmoil revealed in his eyes, in the fine trembling of his finger. The cop wasn't in control right now. Maybe in the next second, but not *now*. She wanted to lean into him, to hold him, to keep on holding him until there was nothing left in her mind but the taste and scent and feel of him.

She didn't move.

She didn't know what she would do if she reached out only to have him turn away from her again.

"You've got me confused with the guy trying to run us down," she said huskily. "And shoot us. I keep forgetting that part."

"Kate," Sam whispered.

"What?"

"Nothing." He leaned closer. "Just Kate."

She shivered when he whispered the last words over her lips, which were trembling again. Not with fear, but with the need he aroused in her just by being alive, by being Sam.

Close enough to taste.

His lips brushed over hers, brushed again. The tip of his tongue traced her mouth.

Hands clenched at her sides, she didn't move.

"Kate?" He lifted his head. "I thought you wanted me."

Her eyes opened almost black with emotion. "And I thought you didn't want me."

"You thought wrong. I want you so much it scares me."

"Same here. But you keep backing away."

His hands slid into the thick black hair that had fascinated him from the first time he'd seen it settle sleek and heavy and faintly wavy on her shoulders. Tonight it was warm and damp from the shower. He leaned in until his lips were almost touching hers.

"If I back away far enough," he asked, "will I reach the bed?"

She almost smiled, almost laughed, and completely gave up trying to keep her distance from him.

"Sam," she said.

"What?"

"Just," she kissed the corner of his mouth, "Sam."

One of his hands slid from her hair. His arm went around her hips, recklessly pulling her close for the kind of knees-to-forehead embrace that told her he'd given up trying to hold her at arm's length.

"You sure you want this?" he asked.

She bit his lower lip. "Are you?"

"What does it feel like?"

She smiled. "It feels like you're wearing your holster a little low."

He gave a crack of laughter and held her hips even closer, tilting her into his erection. "You sure?"

"Let me check."

He caught her hand and looked at her. "Last chance."

"For you or for me?"

"You. I was lost right after I met you."

She blinked. "You sure hid it well."

"Self-preservation." Slowly, caressingly, he let go of her hand. "How about you?"

Her hand drifted lower, settled, shaped, measured. She let out a long breath she hadn't been aware of holding. "Sam, I don't know if I'm checked out for this caliber. I'm used to, uh, twenty-twos."

"I'll show you all the fine points of handling and safety."

She gave a shaky laugh. "You sure?"

"I've never been more certain of anything. It will be good, Kate. For both of us."

She took a deep breath. "Okay."

He looked at her, saw she meant it, and felt a combination of tenderness and lust that nearly brought him to his knees.

"Bedroom, couch, or floor?" he asked.

"Okay," she said again.

He bent and joined their mouths in a deep, mutual exploration that left both of them breathing hard.

"Bedroom," he said finally. "I don't want you bruised anymore."

"Only if you start stripping on the way there."

He smiled down at her. "Stripping, huh?"

"As in peeling off layers of clothes until we're even."

"Even?"

"All I'm wearing is this robe."

His eyelids half lowered. His breath hesitated as he looked at her from pink toenails to sleek calves, inward curving waist, and the shadow between her breasts that had been making him want to howl. And as he looked, he shrugged out of his suit coat and kicked it aside. Her hands were already on his weapon harness, tugging at it as much in frustration as in any real attempt to unfasten it.

"Here," he said, guiding her fingers. "And here."

Her hands went lower. "What about here?"

A shudder went through him like lightning. "Wrong gun," he said thickly.

"You sure?"

"Only if you want to get as far as the bed."

"If it's the floor, you're on the bottom."

"Deal."

He kicked aside the last of his clothing and reached for her robe. The look on her face stopped him.

"Something wrong?" he asked.

"Just enjoying the, um, manscape."

"The what?"

She licked her lips. "Male landscape."

Her robe came off with a swift motion of his hand.

"Female scenery is outstanding," he said, following his glance with his hands, his mouth, until he was on his knees in front of her. He ran the back of his hands inside her legs from her ankles to her thighs, gently prying them apart. His thumbs caressed the black cloud of female hair, parting it. "If I'm going too fast for you, let me know."

She started to ask what he meant, then felt the slick, searching caress of his tongue. She made a sound that could have been a throaty cry of surprise or pleasure or both tangled into one. A few moments later her knees loosened, then buckled as waves of heat slammed through her, shaking her, tormenting her with what was just beyond her reach.

"Sam, I can't—stand—anymore."

"Come down here and tell me that."

She felt his hands on her hips, urging her down. She went eagerly, desperate for more of what he'd given her. When he reached for the slacks he'd thrown aside, she dragged them closer for him.

"Want to play dress-up?" he asked, pulling a condom out of his pocket. "Or you want me to do it?"

She reached for the packet, saw her hands were shaking, and laughed. "You better do it."

"What if mine are shaking too?"

"Impossible."

"They were earlier."

"When?" she scoffed.

"In the parking lot. I thought I'd lost you." He opened the package and sheathed himself quickly. Then he caressed her slowly and deeply, teasing her and at the same time testing her readiness to accept him. His thumb circled the sleek knot of flesh that silently begged to be touched. "But I didn't lose you, did I?"

She couldn't answer. Heat was spilling through her in quicksilver pulses that unraveled her breath and her body.

Smiling rather fiercely, he pulled her down over him and pushed into her, eased by the liquid pulses of her release. The fit was tight, slick, perfect, everything he'd dreamed of when he first thought of opening her legs and pushing in deep. He clenched his teeth against the demanding, overwhelming lure of his own need. He wanted to savor every bit of her, wring the last drop of her ecstasy, feel—

But it was too late. He couldn't stop the heat exploding up from the base of his spine, demanding that he drive into her again and again while the world went red and black and wild around him.

With a final shivering, clenching sigh, Kate slumped over Sam's chest and lay there trying to breathe around the sweet pressure of him filling her. Aftershocks of completion kept rippling through her, surprising her, breaking her breath into pieces.

"Sorry I was so quick," Sam said, running his fingertips down her spine. "I've been dating myself too long. I'll do better next time."

"Quick. Jesus. You destroyed me." She let out another breaking breath and kissed his neck, licked it, liked the taste, licked it again. "I've been dating myself too. You feel good inside me, Sam. So damn good. Perfect."

"Not the wrong caliber after all, huh?"

"Are you laughing at me?" she asked lazily.

"Would I do that?"

"Yeah." She bit him. "But I forgive you."

"Does that mean you'll let me do it again?"

"Laugh at me?"

"Eventually."

She felt him moving slightly beneath her, opened her eyes, and saw his hand patting around, trying to find his slacks without disturbing her. She leaned to the side to help him get closer to the slacks, liked the way it felt at that angle, and wiggled a little.

His breathing changed. "Um, darling?"

"What?"

"Condoms are only good for one round, remember?"

"The problem has never come up before."

"Well, it's come up now, but good."

She smiled. "I noticed."

With a slow reluctance that almost ruined Sam's good intentions, Kate lifted herself off him. "Okay."

"The last time you agreed with me, we ended up on the floor."

"With you on the bottom."

Sam got to his feet, winced, and said hopefully, "Bed?"

"With you on the bottom?"

"Any way you want me." He grabbed a fistful of condoms from his slacks.

"Mmm," she said, opening his hand and stirring the small packages. "Let me count the ways. One, two, three, four . . ."

"I offer rain checks."

"So do I."

He pulled her close, kissed her even closer. "It's a deal."

Chapter 47

Scottsdale
Friday
9:00 P.M.

A cell phone rang, interrupting Sam and Kate just as they were thinking about dragging themselves out of bed to make a late dinner.

"It's yours," Kate said.

"I'm trying to ignore it."

"Is it working?"

Sam cursed and stalked into the living room where his cell phone was still attached to his belt, which was still attached to his slacks, which weren't attached to him. When he recognized the number, his irritation vanished. He didn't know what Lee Mandel's godfather wanted to talk about, but he doubted it was good news. He punched the answer button.

"Special Agent Groves."

"This is Gavin Greenfield. Sorry to bother you on a Friday night, but you told me to call if anyone questioned me about Kate or Natalie Cutter."

Sam's gut clenched. *So quick. Jesus, this killer is scary.* "Yes. Who called?"

"He didn't leave a name."

"Tell me as much of the conversation as you remember. Word for word, if possible."

"I answered the phone," Gavin said. "He told me he was following up on an interview with you."

"Did he use my name?"

"Yes. He called you FBI Special Agent Sam Groves."

Sam frowned. Most civilians were happy with less than the full title. "Go on."

"I asked him who he was, just like you told me to."

"And?"

"He didn't tell me. He just asked me who Natalie Cutter was to me. I told him since he was in the FBI, he should ask you. Then I hung up. Did I do the right thing?"

"Yes. Do you remember him representing himself to you as a member of the FBI?"

Gavin hesitated. "No. When he said it was a follow up on your interview, I just assumed . . ." Then, anxiously, "He was FBI, wasn't he?"

I hope not, but I'm not betting Kate's life on it. "Thank you, Mr. Greenfield. You did just right. If anyone else calls, please let me know immediately."

Sam hung up, held the cell phone in his fist, and grappled with the sickening feeling that the killer was two steps ahead of everyone.

Especially Sam Groves.

"What is it?" Kate asked.

He looked at her standing in the doorway, naked and beautiful. Vulnerable. His gut clenched.

"You mentioned rain checks," he said.

"You want one?"

"No, but I'm asking for it anyway."

"It's yours." *And so am I.* But that was something Kate wasn't ready to say aloud.

Sam reached her in three long strides and pulled her into his arms. Instead of the passion and driving strength she'd come to expect from him, she found herself held gently, rocked against his chest.

"I have to go back to the hotel and take care of some things," he said, his voice as rough as his hands were tender. "I don't want to. But if I spend the night here, they'll yank me off the strike force." He tipped her head back and looked into her eyes. "You understand?"

She nodded.

"I want you to put my cell phone number in your speed dial so that all you have to do is punch connect to get me," he said. "Okay?"

She nodded again.

"Don't let anyone in here except me, and only if I'm alone," he said. "If I'm not alone, call 911 and take your gun off safety and don't open the door. Okay?"

"Sam . . ."

"Promise me, love."

She gave up. "Okay."

"If anyone knocks or calls or does anything that makes you uneasy, dial me no matter what time it is."

"Sam, who just called?"

He hesitated, not wanting to make her as uneasy as he was. Then he told himself he was a fool. She couldn't protect herself if she didn't know what was going on.

"Gavin," Sam said. "Someone called him, asking about you."

He watched understanding take the light from her eyes.

"I see," she said huskily. "That was quick."

"Kate, I'll stay if you—" he began.

"No," she cut in. "It's all right. I don't want you taken off the strike force." *Leaving me with men I have to trust and can't, because I'll be wondering which one of them is hand in hand with a killer.* "I'll do whatever I have to." She stood on tiptoe and kissed his lips. "Be safe."

He pulled her close and held her, just held her, trying not to think about how fragile life was.

Chapter 48

Scottsdale
Saturday
4:00 A.M.

Sam awoke to the hotel phone ringing. And ringing. He looked at the bedside clock, then at the other bed. Empty. Colton must have the graveyard shift tonight.

Sam grabbed the phone. "What!"

"I'm very sorry, sir," the night clerk said quickly. "A fax just came in for you. The cover letter said it was most urgent. I—"

"I'll be right down."

He disconnected, rubbed his sandpaper face, and told himself to hang tough, it was only a few more years before he could dump his shaver in the trash and never look back. He went to the bathroom, splashed cold water on his eyes, and grabbed the jeans he'd dumped on the floor after he finished drawing up diagrams of who knew what and when regarding various couriers and deliveries. Then he'd looked at them and wanted to bang his head against the wall.

He had enough suspects for a dental convention—and a headache to match.

He still had one. Four hours' sleep wasn't enough.

I'm getting too old for this shit.

But not all of it. He smiled when he remembered how he'd spent the best part of last night with Kate. She liked it all the ways he did, hard and fast, slow and mind-blowing, slipping and twisting and turning until there wasn't any breath in his lungs but hers. . . .

He splashed more water on his face and then reset the hotel's complimentary automatic coffeepot for cook right now instead of at seven A.M.

Barefoot, still buttoning the shirt he hadn't bothered to tuck in, his hair looking like it had been stirred rather than combed, and his weapon harness hanging loosely on his shoulders, Sam rode the elevator to the lobby.

The clerk took one look at the man walking out of the elevator toward the desk and glanced nervously toward the lobby guard.

Sam fished his badge holder from his rear pocket and said, "Special Agent Groves. You have a fax for me."

The guard and the clerk relaxed.

"Yes, sir. If you'll sign here . . ." The clerk pushed a form and a pen toward Sam.

He signed for the fax, wondered if the ten bucks per page charge included the fancy sealed folder with the hotel's logo, and took the papers up to his room. The welcome smell of coffee greeted him. He tossed the folder on the bed, poured a cup of coffee, drank it, and poured another. That took care of the free coffee provided by the hotel. If he wanted more, he'd have to wait until the maid came to refill the coffee basket in maybe nine hours, or he could order from room service and watch Doug's blood pressure spike at the expense report.

Sam reached for the phone. "This is two-twelve. Send up a pot of coffee. Black."

He hung his weapon harness on a chair and went to the bed. Sipping on the lethal black brew, he opened the folder. The cover sheet informed him that the contents were privileged information not to be read by anyone without clearance from the FBI.

"This better be good, Mecklin," Sam said, "or I'm going to call you at four A.M. tomorrow and sing every frigging verse of the 'Battle Hymn of the Republic.'"

Sam scrubbed away a yawn and turned over the cover page. It lifted, slid, and came to a rest halfway to the hall door.

He ignored it.

The first sketch showed a flashy female figure with light eyes, Dolly Parton hair, and tits to match. Caucasian, if you could trust the artist's rendition of a description given by an unhappy citizen remembering what had happened five months ago.

The second sketch showed the same busty female with dark hair and dark eyes, as Sam had requested. He studied it for several minutes, but couldn't pin down why she looked kind of familiar. Caucasian, Hispanic, either was possible. Which meant that better than half of the female population of the United States between the ages of twenty and fifty could fit the description.

No wonder she looked familiar.

He tossed the sketch on the unmade bed. The third and fourth sketches surprised him. Each showed the same person, absent makeup and wig, with a man's haircut and shirt. The result was a subtly effeminate man with a lean build and ordinary looks. The third sketch was of a blond male with light eyes. The fourth version was dark and dark.

Sam whistled silently. *Wonder if Lee Mandel looked like either of these.*

Only Kate could help him on that, and it was too soon to wake her up. Unless he was in bed with her.

Don't think about that. It will fuzz what's left of your brain.

He set the sketches in a row across the foot of the bed and reached for the folder again. The remaining two pages were a summary of both interviews with Seguro Jimenez.

When Sam finished reading, he threw the papers on the bed and grabbed his cell phone. It took three separate people and a lot of attitude, but he finally tracked down Mecklin.

"The stuff arrived," Sam said.

"You woke me up to tell me that?"

"Sorry," Sam said. "Thought you'd be awake, having just sent me the fax and all."

An indistinct grumble was Mecklin's only answer.

"I just wanted to verify some facts with you," Sam said. "Did Seguro think the person trying to pawn the sapphire was a transvestite?"

"If you read the interview summary you know he couldn't be pinned down."

"You were there," Sam said. "What did you think?"

"Seguro Jimenez is a switch-hitter. He doesn't care what gender as long as he's not the catcher. He liked what he saw, male or female. So now we have the whole population to look at, male, female, and undecided."

"Did Seguro say anything that would make you think the he/she act wasn't comfortable in the costume, like maybe it was a temporary disguise?" Sam asked.

"No. In fact, he thought the tits were made-to-order, expensive drag queen stuff for a guy that didn't want to take estrogen shots and have breast implants in order to attract straight men. That's why the dress had a high neck—jiggle can be put in bras, but real cleavage is tough to fake close up and bare."

"So is the rest of the equipment," Sam said.

Mecklin gave a snort of laughter. "Yeah, can you imagine a dude who's expecting to find pussy between his date's legs and finds jingle bells instead?"

"I don't want to imagine it, thanks. Did Seguro come any closer to admitting that he bought the stone?"

"That solid citizen? Hell, no. He's a real prince. He sent the tits and the stone right back out the door. Funny thing, when we showed Seguro a photo I printed of the stone, his eyelids flinched. He recognized it. I'll show it around to the others tomorrow, but my money is on Seguro being the fence."

"Okay. Tell me more about his family."

"They're pimps, cons, thieves, and a few stone killers."

"Sounds like part of every immigrant group I've ever heard of, including my ancestors. What else?"

"We're still looking at it, but right now I'd feel good about saying he's kissing cousins with cousins who are kissing cousins of the Santos gang."

"Ecuadorian?"

"Yeah, but they're like the Chinese. They have arms of the family in all major cities in the U.S. Nothing formal. Just friends of friends of relatives. If you don't know a homeboy, you don't get in the front door."

Sourly, Sam wondered if Mecklin had been talking to Sizemore. "You think it was a gang hit from the word go?"

Mecklin paused long enough to light up a cigarette and blow out a plume across the receiver. "No. I used to work L.A. I read the Mandel file after I got your request. Different MO entirely."

"Hallelujah. Someone who understands little things like MO," Sam said under his breath.

"What?"

"Nothing. If Seguro did fence the gem, where would he do it? Miami?"

"Too close." Mecklin exhaled heavily. "None of his family here had the right connections. But he married a woman whose maiden name was de Santos."

"De Santos and de los Santos? Same crew?"

"Yeah. The longer you're here, the less likely you are to keep the full name. First to go is 'los.' Next is 'de.' We have a lot of Santos."

"Are the ones we're talking about from Ecuador?"

"Same country. Same rural town. The de Santos have been bringing in everybody but the village idiot. I can't prove it, but my gut says Seguro Jimenez sent the stone to L.A. and his wife's family."

"Who?"

Mecklin sighed another stream of smoke. "Most likely is José de Santos, who works in the jewelry district laundering drug money through gold purchases. It could be Eduardo de Santos, who works as head cutter for Hall Jewelry International and, if street gossip is true, has a nice little sideline reworking stolen gems passed to him by his extended family."

"How big is this sideline?"

"Nothing much. A little skimming here, a little trimming there. More like a hobby and a retirement account than a profession. It's his way to become a respected *patrón* in his little village in Ecuador."

"Must be my lucky day," Sam said. "Finally."

"Why?"

"You actually know L.A. and gangs."

"I worked drugs in southern California with a DEA task force and some immigration guys back when it was called the INS. Same players, different merchandise."

Sam hesitated. "Your name wasn't in the Mandel file, but the Miami office handled it."

"I was transferred two months ago."

"L.A. to Miami." Sam tried not to be jealous. He'd gone from L.A. to Seattle to Phoenix. A clear downward spiral. "Antiterrorism, right?"

"Yeah."

"Fast track to the top."

"Tell my wife," Mecklin said. "She hates the Bureau."

"You ever met a wife that didn't? Same goes for the husbands of the female agents."

Mecklin muttered something.

Sam hesitated. "I need someone like you, but I have to tell you up front that the only fast track I'm on has Fargo written in big letters at every station. Still interested?"

"I'm listening."

But not committing.

Sam didn't blame him. Nobody joined the Bureau to end up in North Dakota.

"If I call L.A. and ask for follow-up on the de Santos clan," Sam said, "I might get it sometime this century and I might not, no matter how many priority stamps are on the request."

"Who'd you piss off in L.A.?"

"Hurley."

"Christ Jesus." Mecklin coughed. "I'll back-channel it and see what I can do."

"Thanks."

"No promises," Mecklin said. "They're all real busy covering mosques and their asses for the time when something blows up. And it will."

"Die or fly, let me know."

"I will. And Groves?"

"Yeah?"

"Thanks for sending me to my kid's party. She had a grin when she saw me that I'll never forget. Makes all the rest of the shit I work with not quite so ugly, if you know what I mean."

For the second time Sam was jealous. He didn't even have a wife to yell at him when he came home late, much less a kid to grin and be happy to see daddy.

"You're welcome," Sam said. "If something pops I'll keep your name out of it."

"Do that." Mecklin blew out a long breath. "Hurley. Of all the people to piss off. You know he's going to be director in a few years, don't you?"

"Yeah."

"I'll write to you in Fargo."

Chapter 49

Scottsdale
Saturday
9:10 A.M.

The biggest difference between Kennedy's "office" in the motor coach and Doug's was that Kennedy had a working television, four phones, and not a computer or file in sight. None of the phones had a number known to any media, which right now meant that Kennedy's office was the most peaceful space occupied by anyone in the crime strike force.

The escape wasn't total. The muted TV showed Tawny Dawn's eager features in a replay of yesterday's news. That was the problem with cable news 24/7. There just wasn't that much *new*, much less newsworthy. Repetition, speculation, sensation, and self-promotion filled the gaps. Tawny was good at all of them.

A line of print crawled across the bottom of the screen as she breathlessly asked Sam Groves about the horrible shootout in the parking lot. And by the way, how did you miss the man if you fired twice?

"Civilians," Doug said. "They watch too much TV. They think a pistol is a rifle and every cop is a helluva shot, especially when someone's shooting back and you have enough adrenaline in you to light up a city."

"Yeah, but at least she's kicking the right mutt," Kennedy said. "The prick has it coming. CI my ass. Colton is right. Groves is fucking her."

Doug made a noncommittal sound, relieved that Kennedy was focused on the CI rather than on the fact that Bureau policy decreed that agents not shoot at fleeing vehicles.

"The media is short-stroking this for all it's worth," Kennedy said. "Two couriers down, two grandparents dead—"

"Last I heard," Doug interrupted gently, "the grandparents worked with South American gangs."

Kennedy shrugged. "Yesterday's news. Today we have four—count 'em, four—victims of a violent crime wave that's sweeping the entire yada yada yada."

"Nothing new there."

"How about you?" Kennedy said, killing the TV with a snap of the remote control. "You have anything new?"

"All gem deliveries are present and accounted for."

"Screw the stones. I want the guy that did the Purcells. I want some real evidence to tie the Purcells to the South American gangs. I want the guy that whacked the courier in Quartzite."

"She died last night."

"You think I don't know? It led the news this morning. They have a continuous loop of Tawny interviewing the grieving husband and sister at the hospital. Thank God the bitch didn't have kids. That's all we'd need."

Doug grimaced and waited for Kennedy to get to the point, whatever it was. Doug didn't think the boss had called him there just to complain about the media. Doug knew he was coming real close to getting a second nastygram in his file over Sam Groves. Doug hoped, fervently, that it wasn't going to happen right now. He didn't want to be the one who shoved a CI into the line of fire.

Neither did he want his own ass swinging in the breeze.

Damn Sam Groves anyway. How did I let him talk me into this? Again!

Kennedy rearranged the ashtray on his desk, fiddled with a

lighter, and finally gave in to the nicotine urge. He unlocked his desk drawer and scrounged around way in back until he came up with a dog-eared pack that had two cigarettes left in it. He was going to quit some day. He was sure of it.

But not today.

He lit up, drew down hard, and expelled a long, satisfying plume before he asked, "How long are you going to put up with this CI crap from Groves?"

"I'm not sure what you mean, sir," Doug said.

"Bullshit. Just because that's what Groves is feeding you, don't expect me to eat it and like it."

Doug resisted the urge to shift his feet or put his hands in his pockets. He'd really hoped for a few more days before he balanced on the edge of this particular abyss.

"Special Agent Groves is following Bureau policy in regard to his CI," Doug said. "Considering the amount of violence associated with our present investigation, it's natural that he would be concerned for the safety of his CI and therefore have a particularly strong interest in keeping the CI's identity under wraps."

"How do you know he isn't just jacking off on his own?"

"Groves has a history of closing cases. I trust his record."

"He has a history of being a pain in the butt," Kennedy said.

"Yes, sir. A useful pain."

Kennedy grunted. "Do you know the informant's identity?"

"Not quite."

"What the hell does that mean?"

"I know enough," Doug said carefully, "to be comfortable with the position that the CI will be able to do our strike force some good."

"So make me comfortable too." Kennedy flicked the cigarette against the ashtray and pinned Doug with the kind of glance that made grown men sweat.

"The CI won't do us any good dead," Doug said.

"That's supposed to make me comfortable?"

"We have good reason to believe that if the CI's identity becomes known," Doug said, "the same people that murdered the Purcells will murder the informant."

"I'm not suggesting we call Tawny and put it on the nightly news," Kennedy said curtly. "We'll keep it in the family."

"Sir, you know that leaks are inevitable."

"Are you saying you don't trust me?"

"No, sir. Not at all." Doug thought quickly about the safest path through this minefield without blowing up his career. "I'm saying that, even with the best will in the world, the more people who know a secret, the more likely it is to end up on the news."

"Are you refusing to tell me what you know?"

"No, sir."

Kennedy waited.

Silently Doug cursed the impossible position he was in. "All I know is that Natalie Cutter had some information that might have led to some other information that would be useful to the strike force. Groves is following up."

"Colton ran the Cutter name on his own," Kennedy said. "He found a whole lot of nothing."

"That's what Groves told me after he ran the name."

"What else did he tell you?"

"He said that his informant might be able to help with the Mandel case in Florida," Doug said.

"Mandel, Mandel, Man— You mean the courier that ran off-shore with McCloud's package?"

"It's possible, perhaps even probable, that the courier in that case was murdered."

"Fuck me!" Kennedy's fist slammed down on the desk. "That's all I need, another murder under my nose. You find Groves. Get his ass in here. He can talk to me or he can turn in his credentials and piece. I don't much care which happens. You get that?"

"Yes, sir."

Doug turned away and was nearly hit by someone opening the door from the narrow hallway. Sizemore rushed in, barely pausing long enough to nod at Doug as he slammed the door in his face.

"Remember Natalie Cutter, the woman who switched the stones?" Sizemore asked Kennedy.

"Yeah."

"Her real name is Katherine Jessica Chandler."

"And I care because . . . ?" Kennedy asked.

Sizemore grinned. "She's the CI that Groves has been hiding. She goes all the way back to the courier in Florida. Lee Mandel. His half sister."

Kennedy shot Doug a deadly look. "Get that son of a bitch and bring him here. *Now*."

Chapter 50

Glendale
Saturday
9:10 A.M.

Sam spread the sketches on a worktable that Kate had cleared for him. She hovered at his elbow, looking at the papers and smelling like sex. It was making him nuts.

And he savored every breath he took.

What am I going to do about her?

The only idea that came to mind was expressly forbidden by the Bureau's rules for dealing with informants.

The other ideas he had weren't mentioned by the Bureau but were still illegal in some states.

"Okay," he said, telling himself he couldn't really feel the heat of her body, couldn't taste her breath. "You recognize anyone?"

"No."

"That was quick."

Kate glanced at him, at the smoky dark blue eyes and a mouth that could light fires, beard shadow on his cheeks just waiting for a woman's appreciative palm. Abruptly, she turned back to the sketches.

Much safer.

The cop was in full control again. The man wanted to come out and play, but it wasn't going to happen.

Damn it.

"I was looking at these while you laid them out," she said, gesturing to the sketches.

He pushed the drawing of the slender male closer to her. "You sure? None of these look even faintly like anyone you know?"

"Yes."

"Not even this one?" he insisted, pushing the drawing at her.

"Not even that one," she said patiently.

"Well, hell."

"Who are they?" she asked.

"They're different takes on the same person. He/she tried to pawn one of McCloud's Sins in Miami soon after Lee vanished."

"Which one? The one Purcell ended up with?"

"Yes, but I can't prove it yet. Not courtroom proof."

Kate's mouth flattened. "So this is Lee's murderer."

"Maybe," Sam said. "And maybe he/she is just one link in the corrupt chain."

Kate studied the sketches silently. Intently.

"I'm not asking for a cross-my-heart-and-swear-to-God match," Sam said. "Do any of these sketches even *remind* you of anyone?"

She shifted one of the work lamps and stared some more. "I'm sorry," she said finally. "I can't help with this."

"None of these sketches even faintly resembles Lee?"

Her head lifted and she turned sharply toward Sam. "Is that what the pawnshop said? That this is Lee?"

"Not in so many words. The person came in dressed as a woman, but a lot of what was up front wasn't real. He/she had light blue eyes and blonde hair, just like the woman Lee was supposed to have run off with to Aruba."

"Wait a minute," Kate said. "Let me be sure I've got it straight. The he/she had light eyes and blonde hair?"

"Yes."

"Millions of people have light eyes. The ones who don't can buy colored contacts. Ditto for hair. So what?"

"So how close is this sketch to Lee Mandel?" Sam asked. "Forget the hairstyle and color. Concentrate on bone structure, thickness of the lips, the line of the jaw, and nose and eyebrows."

"That's just it," Kate said. "Lee was broad shouldered, raw boned, with a crooked nose and a wide mouth and . . ." Her voice cracked. She cleared her throat. "This sketch is nothing like Lee," she said neutrally.

Sam's thumb brushed away the tear Kate hadn't been able to hold back. "Sorry, darling," he said. "But I had to be certain." He licked her tear from his thumb. "My SSA isn't going to like the idea that Lee is a victim rather than a thief."

She took in a ragged breath that owed as much to Sam's gentleness as to her grief for Lee. "W-why?"

"Why am I touching you?" Sam asked wryly. "Because I can't help it." He stepped back, beyond reach. "As for Kennedy, if Lee is a victim, the FBI looks stupid. Again."

Kate leaned back against the worktable. It wasn't enough. She braced her hands on the lip of the table. The man took her breath and the world away one instant, and regretted it the next.

Last night hadn't changed anything.

"Damn it, Sam," she whispered.

"Yes," he said. "Damn it. Wrong time. Wrong place. Right woman." He blew out a long breath. "My fault. I'm supposed to be trained, disciplined, and walk on water." He shoved his hands in his jeans. "Anyway, my SSA is going to shit a brick when he finds out about you and Lee."

"When will that be?"

"The instant we get a DNA match from Florida," Sam said reluctantly. "I can't hide you past that."

"I know. You told me."

"I'm sorry."

"You told me that too." She smiled sadly. "It's all right, Special

Agent Sam Groves. I wanted to make the FBI pay attention to Lee's death. I succeeded. If anything happens to me because of that, it's my doing, not yours."

Sam opened his mouth to tell her how wrong she was.

His cell phone rang.

He yanked it out of his back pocket and glared at the number. *My SAC. That's just fucking beautiful.*

Sam wanted to pretend that he wasn't home. Hell, he wanted to pretend he wasn't even on the same planet.

But he was.

Sam hit the green button. "What's up, Doug?"

Kate watched Sam's expression change from irritated to furious.

"I'm on my way," Sam said. "I'll take Kennedy's heat and then I'm heading right back to Kate's. Once I get there, I'm staying with her until we bust the mutts that are killing people right and left. If that's a problem for the Bureau, you know what you can do about it."

Sam punched out on the connection before his boss could answer.

"What happened?" Kate asked. "Did someone else get murdered?"

Not yet, he thought savagely. "Ted Sizemore couldn't leave well enough alone."

"Meaning?"

"The son of a bitch tracked you down the same way I did. He knows your name, your face, your address, and everything else about you that's in any public record anywhere. And he's not under any compulsion to keep it to himself. As a civilian, he can broadcast it on the news."

Kate leaned a little harder on the worktable. She kept hearing that eerie voice telling her she would die. She closed her eyes, took a deep breath, and pushed away from the table.

"Well, you told me it might happen," she said. "Now it has."

Sam's only answer was a fist hitting the table hard enough to make the sketches jump. With a vicious word he picked them up, stuffed them in the Mandel folder, and put it under his arm.

"I have to report to the motor coach," he said. "When I leave, lock up behind me and lock up tight. Load your gun and keep it handy. Don't open that door for anyone but me. And I mean *anyone*. I'll be back as fast as I can."

"What if your boss won't let you?"

"Then he won't be my boss anymore."

Chapter 51

Scottsdale
Saturday
9:48 A.M.

The door to Kennedy's office was yanked open before Sam could even knock.

"Good morning," Doug said neutrally to Sam.

But the SAC's eyes both apologized and warned.

"It's morning," Sam agreed. He ignored Sizemore and nodded to Kennedy. "I understand you want to talk to me."

"I sure as hell do. It's one thing to have a CI. It's another thing to deliberately sabotage a crime strike force investigation."

"I haven't."

"Like hell you haven't," Kennedy shot back. "For three days you've concealed information from me."

"That's not correct," Sam said evenly. "The Bureau gives me the right to keep a CI's identity secret."

"Not when keeping a snitch under wraps makes a crime strike force look like a horse's ass!"

No matter who was right, Sam couldn't win a bureaucratic pissing contest with his SSA. All he could do was try to stay in a position to protect Kate. Which meant that he had to find a way to tell

Kennedy the bad news about leaks in such a way that he didn't go ballistic.

Yeah. Sure. That would happen right after Sam ate coal and shit diamonds.

"Her life has been threatened," Sam said, keeping his voice calm and professional. "Given the murders that have taken place already, keeping her identity a secret was SOP."

"Standard operating procedure, my ass." Kennedy scrounged in the desk drawer for his last cigarette.

Doug picked up the lighter and waited. When his boss found the cigarette, the lighter would be ready. A small thing, but maybe it would take some of the fire out of Kennedy's temper.

The lighter clicked. Kennedy took a hard drag.

"Just when were you going to tell me?" Kennedy asked sarcastically. "When the case was closed?"

"I would have told Doug if and when I got a positive DNA match on the blood in the rental car trunk and Lee Mandel."

"What rental car?" Sizemore and Kennedy asked as one.

"The one Lee Mandel drove from the airport and somebody else likely returned to the airport a day late."

"Why wasn't I told about this?" Kennedy asked.

"Because I won't know it's true unless and until I get a DNA match."

"If there was blood in the trunk of the rental car, it could have come from a badly wrapped pot roast," Sizemore said with a shrug. "Big fucking deal."

"It wouldn't be the first time," Sam agreed. "That's why I wanted to wait for the labs."

Doug took a cautious breath and began to think his career might survive. The help from Sizemore was unexpected, but in this business you took aid and comfort where you found it.

Kennedy treated himself to another steadying drag on the cigarette. "Tell me what else you have."

"The trunk wasn't forced," Sam said. "If Mandel didn't do the job himself, it was done by someone sophisticated enough to record the electronic key code and make a duplicate."

"So what?" Sizemore said. "How does that help us in Phoenix, where we have mutts popping trunks and shooting in the parking lot?"

"The cowboy in the parking lot had a duplicate key that he'd already made," Sam said. "He didn't reach for the tire iron until he thought he'd made a bad key. If the courier hadn't run back out, the cowboy might have pulled it off. He's a real pro. Who's to say that the same thing didn't happen in Florida, except that Mandel was killed, stuffed in the trunk, and hauled off for swamp burial?"

Sizemore grunted.

Kennedy said, "What does this have to do with a gem-swapping con artist? Is she good for it?"

"No," Sam said quickly. "She's the woman who cut the Seven Sins—seven very expensive sapphires—that Mandel was carrying when he disappeared. She didn't believe he'd stolen them, so she's been following the gem circuit, waiting for the goods to turn up. Purcell had one of them. She swapped it for a synthetic, took the real one home, and matched it with her working photographs. No doubt about it. Purcell had a stone that had last been seen with a missing courier. She swapped the stones again, because she'd never been trying to steal, just to identify what had already been stolen. I caught her after she'd replaced the original."

"How did Purcell get the stone?" Kennedy asked.

Sam had to admit that the SSA had good investigative instincts. He understood linkage in a way Colton never would. "We're checking that out right now."

"What do you have, *right now*?"

"A pawnshop in Little Miami, a blonde with big fake tits, and a pawnshop owner who swears he never touched the stone. Said owner has family in L.A. who would be able to put the stone in circulation."

Kennedy nodded. "Nail it down. And be sure to put everything— names, dates, witnesses—in a report with a copy to Ted. He's real well connected in L.A. Might as well save the taxpayers some money."

"I'll get on it as soon as I have the report," Sizemore said.

"Fake tits," Kennedy said. "Is it some kind of drag queen? A courier laying a false trail?" He flipped quickly through the file. "Here the tits are again. And here."

"Mandel was supposed to have left for parts unknown with a blonde with big tits on one arm and the package under the other, right?" Sam asked Kennedy.

Kennedy looked at Sizemore, who shrugged.

Sam flipped through the Mandel file and pulled out the sheet he had highlighted. "According to this witness—whose name, by the way, seems to be lost—Mandel was keeping company with said blonde. Someone, again unnamed, saw a couple that might match the Mandel-blonde description leave a car at the airport rental agency."

"So?" Kennedy said.

"Lee Mandel is gay."

Kennedy looked at the end of his cigarette and then at Doug, who shook his head, silently telling his SSA that it was news to him too.

"Give me that file," Kennedy said.

Sam handed it over.

There wasn't any small talk while Kennedy read through the file with the speed and intensity of man who has seen a lot of files like it. When he was finished, he wasn't smiling.

"I see a lot of stuff that wasn't in my file," Kennedy said.

"The moment your file is updated, Kate Chandler is nominated for the lead role in a turkey shoot," Sam said.

"Says who?"

"The last time the FBI's Mandel file was updated," Sam said, "she got a threat on her answering machine—stop pushing on the Mandel case or die. Mechanical voice distorter. The lab is working on it, but nothing has come back to me yet."

Kennedy didn't take one second to get to the bottom line. He gave Sam a narrow-eyed glare. "Where's the leak?"

"I don't know."

"Guess," Kennedy said flatly.

"Someone on the crime strike force," Sam said.

Doug braced himself for the explosion that would end Sam's career, and probably his own.

Twin blazes of color appeared on Kennedy's cheekbones. He opened his mouth to tell Sam what a miserable piece of shit he was.

But Kennedy hadn't gotten where he was by ignoring all inconvenient facts—just most of them. Some of those unhappy facts had a way of biting you on the ass if you ignored them. The line of Sam's investigation was shaping up to be a career breaker.

Or, handled the right way, a career maker.

The silence was punctuated by the subtle sounds of a man smoking, knocking ash off, smoking some more. Thinking fast and hard and mean.

Sam's cell phone rang. He looked at the caller ID, answered, and listened. It didn't take long. He punched out and faced Kennedy.

"It wasn't a pot roast," Sam said.

"Mandel?" Doug asked.

"No doubt of it. Local law enforcement will begin searching the favorite dumping grounds for bodies. After five months . . ." Sam shrugged. "Flesh gone, bones scattered by tide, storms, and predators. We might get lucky, find something, and have closure for Mandel's family, but I wouldn't put money on it."

Sizemore shook his head. "I hate those swamp jobs. Worse than cremation for evidence."

Everybody looked at Kennedy.

"All right," Kennedy said, standing up. "Here's the way it's going to be. That file gets updated and it gets updated right now, along with a full summary by Special Agent Groves of where he has taken the investigation and with what results, tentative, imaginary, or solid. I want it all."

Sam nodded.

"Include a summary of your conversations with your CI," Kennedy said. "You can leave her name out of it."

"That won't be enough to keep her safe," Sam said. "Whoever is behind these murders isn't stupid. They'll connect the dots very quickly. And then they'll try to kill Kate."

"Does your snitch have any more information that's not in the file?" Kennedy asked.

Sam heard what wasn't said: *If you've wrung the snitch dry, who cares what happens to her?*

"My CI isn't your average mutt," Sam said, stepping into Kennedy's face. "She's the kind of victim that would make Tawny Dawn light up like a Christmas tree. You want to look bad on the six o'clock news—as in seriously fucking stupid? Cut my CI loose. I guarantee the result will destroy your career."

"Are you threatening me?"

"No."

Sam met Kennedy's furious glance, held it, and waited. After a long, tight time, Kennedy nodded.

"All right, Groves. We'll do it your way. Hide her name or put it in bold face in the file. Put it on the nightly news for all I care." Viciously Kennedy stubbed out his cigarette. "As of now, you're responsible for keeping your CI alive."

"Twenty-four/seven?"

"Yes."

"One man isn't enough to—" Sam began.

"I'll be sure to explain that to Tawny Dawn," Kennedy said, "while I wring my hands on camera about federal budget cuts and rising crime." He smiled thinly and faced an imaginary camera. "Just think, this lovely young woman and her valiant FBI escort would still be alive if not for a stingy Congress and a penny-pinching—"

Sam was already out the door, running for his car and the woman who had trusted him with her life.

"I want your report in two hours," Kennedy yelled after him.

Sam's only answer was the kind of hand signal that would have gotten him fired if Kennedy hadn't already figured out a better way to get even.

Doug turned to Kennedy and said, "At least put in for witness protection for the CI."

"She's a snitch, not a witness," Kennedy said.

Sizemore shrugged. "Hey, Doug. Save the taxpayers a dime and stop worrying. She's living in a fortress."

"What do you mean?" Doug asked. "And how do you know?"

"I went there. She's wired to a local alarm company. She'll be fine."

"Against a murderer who works for the Bureau?" Doug retorted.

"We don't know that," Kennedy shot back. "Right now, it's a possibility, that's all. Just a lousy possibility."

"Christ, man, we're talking about a woman's life," Doug said.

"Maybe. And maybe Sam Groves is leaking info through his CI to make us look bad," Sizemore said.

"Do you really believe that?" Doug asked, astonished.

Sizemore shrugged. "Like your boss said, lots of possibilities, and right now that one is as good as any other. Groves isn't a team player. He's got an ax to grind with the Bureau."

Kennedy laughed shortly. "This time the son of a bitch can grind it on his own thick skull."

"What if Sam is right?" Doug said.

"Then we'll nab the perp," Kennedy said. "If Groves isn't right, his ass is fired and he gets the blame for every foul-up so far. Either way, it's win-win for me."

"SOP," Doug said through his teeth.

"You have a problem with that?" Kennedy asked.

"Would it make any difference?"

"To me, no. To you?" Kennedy shrugged. "You want to get fired along with him, be my guest."

"You're not the only one with friends in high places," Doug said. "Don't threaten me."

"You want a pissing contest?"

"I don't want a dead CI on my conscience."

Kennedy smiled coldly. "Then you better pray your pet agent is as good as he thinks he is."

Chapter 52

Glendale
Saturday
1:15 P.M.

Under cover of her eyelashes, Kate looked up from her polishing wheel and glanced toward Sam, who was sitting at a table along the wall, working at her computer. He'd started to work right after he showed up on her doorstep hours ago with a bunch of files and a grim look around his eyes. He hadn't said much in the way of hello then.

He hadn't said anything since.

Whatever he was working on had turned him into a man who radiated the kind of barely leashed fury that made people wary on a primal level.

Without warning he hit the send key, shoved back from the computer, and glared at the screen like he was thinking of putting his fist through it.

"Finished?" she asked.

He grunted.

"Mind if I check my e-mail?" she asked. *It's my computer you're using, after all.*

"Oh, yeah, I'm finished," Sam said. *Now I can go from bad to worse. Jesus, I really don't want to be the one to tell her about Lee.*

"My SSA can print out as many damn copies of my report as he wants. All he has to do is remember to open his e-mail."

"You muttered something about a fax when you first got here," she said.

"Fuck the fax. It's time the Bureau entered the twenty-first century."

Kate let out a breath. "You ready to tell me what happened?"

"I thought you wanted to check your e-mail."

"It will keep."

Abruptly, Sam stood up. "I work for a prick."

"Um, okay. That makes some days worse than others. Anything else I should know?"

Sam didn't want to tell her what had happened in Kennedy's office any more than he wanted to tell her about her half brother. But there wasn't any choice. It was her life.

And he was about to punch a big hole in it.

"I just updated your half brother's file," Sam said levelly.

Kate braced herself against the worktable and waited.

"The DNA match was right on," Sam said. "It was Lee's blood in the trunk of his rental car."

She closed her eyes and said, "No mistake?" Then she looked at Sam. "None?"

He touched her hair, then let his hand drop, not trusting himself. He wanted her so bad he was having trouble standing up straight. That wasn't what she needed now. She needed a cop, not a lover with a woody.

"I'm sorry," Sam said. "There's no way to be absolutely positive unless we get lucky in the swamp or screw a confession out of his killer. That said, I have to tell you if Lee's alive, it will be the first time in my career that blood found in a trunk led to a happy reunion."

She bit her lip, blinked fiercely, and said, "I have to call Mom."

"I'll do it."

"No, I—"

"It's easier coming from a cop," Sam cut in roughly. "The family can get angry, yell, swear, cry, let it all out. They can't with you."

"But—"

"After I'm finished, I'll hand the phone to you." He touched her cheek lightly. "Please, Kate. It will be easier on everyone."

Reluctantly, she nodded her head.

Sam hesitated, but there wasn't any help for it. He needed her, and he needed her thinking, not crying. "Before I call, get me McCloud's number, the one you used to report your progress with the stones."

"How did you know?" she asked dully.

"The man had a million bucks invested. It stands to reason he'd want regular reports."

She went to her computer and opened an address file.

He looked at her bent head and the tight line of her shoulders and wished there was something he could do that wouldn't make her feel worse.

"I'm sorry," he said.

She nodded and scrolled through names on the screen.

"I mean it," he said.

"I know." Her voice was hoarse. "It's just . . ." Her shoulders moved almost impatiently.

"Yeah," he said. "It's just that being sorry doesn't change anything."

She looked over her shoulder at him. "It changes my opinion of the FBI. Or at least some of them. One of them. The best one. You."

Sam gave up and opened his arms. Kate stepped into them and held on, held on hard. Then she let grief wash through her.

"My head knew that Lee wasn't coming back," she said when she could talk again. "Yet I couldn't help hoping, can't help asking . . . God, Sam, are you sure?"

"As sure as I can be without a body." He brushed his lips over her cheek, the corner of her eye, tasted tears, and felt his own throat close. "Kate, I don't think Lee's remains will be found," he said roughly. "I'm sorry. I know in some ways it would make it easier, give closure, but the swamp and five months make finding anything a very long shot. Do you understand?"

She nodded, took a ragged breath, looked up at Sam. The concern she saw nearly made her cry all over again. Somehow, some way, she had slipped under the cop's guard and touched the vulnerable man.

She stood on tiptoe, kissed him gently on the lips, and said, "Thank you."

His mouth turned down at one corner. "For what? Fucking things up from start to finish?"

Her smile trembled, but it was real. "For being honest, for caring, for being here when other men would have grabbed their career and run for the hills. For being Sam Groves." She cleared her throat. "A good man. Very good." Her fingertips touched his lips. "I'll get McCloud's number for you."

Sam watched the stiff line of her back and neck as she bent over the computer. He wanted nothing so much as to hold her again, to protect her from a world that ate innocence as a snack before moving on to a more satisfying meal of violence and death.

You can protect her better as a cop than a man.

Too bad he wanted to be both with her.

"This is the number," Kate said. "Want me to write it down?"

Sam gave the highlighted number a glance, which was all it took for him to put it in his own personal memory bank. "I have it. Check your e-mail while I call your parents."

She flinched, nodded.

"I can do it here or in the living room," Sam said.

"Living room." She looked straight at him. "I trust you to be as good with them as you were with me."

His fingertips traced the line of her jaw, touched her lips, and then he turned away to make the kind of call every cop hates.

There was no good way to tell parents their son was dead.

Chapter 53

Scottsdale
Saturday
1:50 P.M.

"Jason, you know we'd fall apart without you," Sharon said into the phone even as she skimmed her computer screen. She was—as ordered—working from her father's suite so that she'd be available if he needed anything. Peyton was sitting six feet away, drinking beer and eating pretzels, killing time before his three o'clock appointment. "Especially now, with all the trouble. The next time Dad yells at you, think seagull, okay?"

The man at the other end of the line looked toward the ceiling of his office at Sizemore Security Consulting. He didn't rate a window, but he didn't resent it. Only the big boss had one.

"I'd rather think of a raise," Jason said.

"Works for me. I'll bring it up the next time he isn't chewing the scenery over something."

"I can't wait that long."

Sharon sighed and wondered if all men were prima donnas, or just the ones she was unlucky enough to meet. "Look, you know I'm doing everything I can for you."

"And I'm doing the same for you. Winnowing truth from gossip in the jewelry trade is more art than science. I've sent a lot of business to Sizemore, and kept a lot of bad prospects from ever getting through the front door. You know that as well as I do."

Peyton got up and wandered over to Sharon. While he looked at the computer screen, his beer-cool fingers played with the hair curling against her cheek. She clicked to the next page of the document, reading, thinking, and listening all at once.

After a moment, Peyton realized that she was vetting her father's e-mail. The document she was reading had been routed to SSA Patrick Kennedy and forwarded to Ted Sizemore. Something about Lee Mandel.

Peyton caressed Sharon's cheek while he read at top speed.

"Okay," Sharon said after Jason wound down. "I'll talk to Dad in a few days. Right now he's biting the head off everyone within reach, including his Bureau buddies. Asking for a raise now would be stupid."

Jason drummed his fingers on the desk. "A week. No more. I had a really good offer from Mandel Inc."

"I know." Jason hadn't waited two minutes to call her after the offer came in. Not that she blamed him. It was business, not personal. She clicked to the next page of the document she was reading on the screen and asked, "Is everything else okay?"

"My brother." Jason sighed. "Still looking out the window, waiting for his lover to call, and wondering what the hell went wrong."

Sharon hesitated again. Clicked to the next page. Read hard and fast, then reread to make sure.

"Sharon?"

"Still here. I'm just—"

"Multitasking as usual," Jason cut in. "I promised Norm I wouldn't say anything, but I've got to. His lover is Lee Mandel, the courier who vanished in Florida late last year."

Sharon froze. "Mandel? *Gay?*"

"Yes. Have you heard anything that I could tell Norm? He's really slammed by this. Waiting and not knowing is hell."

Sharon shook her head like a dog coming out of water. "Lee is gay. Oh, my God. I interviewed Mandel and never even caught a hint."

"Does it matter?" he asked curtly.

She shook herself again and thought hard, but all she said is, "Dad will flip."

"Lee isn't out of the closet, so don't tell anyone. Especially your father."

"Give me a few seconds." Sharon stared at the screen, frantically piecing things together. She quickly decided that nothing had been hurt and something might even be helped. "Dad would have my head if he knew what I'm about to do."

"He'll have your head anyway. That's just the way he is."

"Don't I know it. The Mandel file was just updated. Tell Norm to stop waiting and wondering. It wasn't anything he did or didn't do."

"What does that mean?" Jason asked.

"The Bureau is looking for Lee's body somewhere in the swamp on Sanibel Island."

Peyton's playful fingers stilled.

At the other end of the line, Jason closed his eyes. "Robbery or hate crime?"

"They're assuming robbery," Sharon said.

"This will kill Norm. He and Lee were going to be married in L.A. in two months."

"Shit, Jason. That really sucks. I'm sorry."

"You're sure that Lee's death wasn't a hate crime?" Jason asked. "Florida isn't what I'd call a hotbed of enlightened sexuality. When he was away from home and wouldn't be recognized, Lee occasionally went to gay bars just to unwind. Someone could have seen him in one, followed him."

"I'll make sure Dad brings up that angle with the Bureau."

"Good. Thank you," Jason said.

"Don't expect anything." Sharon rubbed the back of her neck and wondered if she'd make it to fifty before the hours killed her or she killed her father or she took everything she'd socked away and got the hell out of Dodge. "Frankly, from what I've seen of this case, Lee wasn't a martyr to anything but bad luck."

The door to the suite opened. Peyton stepped away from Sharon and went to greet Ted Sizemore. The two men loathed each other, but business was business.

"Thanks for the suggestion," Sharon said quickly. "I'll get back to you as fast as I can."

She hung up and smiled brightly at the two temperamental men in her life. She wondered how long she could balance them before her already raw nerves snapped. *I need a vacation. A long one.* But she couldn't afford to take one now. She'd just have to suck it up and keep playing the dutiful, obedient dumb woman to a world of needy men.

"Lee Mandel's file just came in," Sharon said.

Sizemore looked at Peyton. "I'm sure you'll excuse us. Business."

"Of course." Peyton smiled at her. "See you at seven."

"Maybe," Sizemore said quickly. "Maybe not. I might need her."

"And I *know* I'll need a break," Sharon said. "Seven."

Peyton shut the door behind him, leaving father and daughter to sort out who would be eating what, where, when, and with which male.

"Why don't you ditch that mutt and find a good man?" Sizemore said. "Have kids. Be a woman."

"Every man I know looks out for number one. Why shouldn't I?"

"Because you're a woman."

"So selfishness is lodged in the balls? Or is it the dick?"

"You're feeling bitchy. That time of the month?"

She smiled thinly. "At least my moods are predictable." She stood up and waved her hand at the computer. "SA Groves's summary of his CI, Lee Mandel, and the fact that Groves is still holding out for his Teflon gang as the perp for a lot of the courier hits, including Mandel."

Sizemore scanned the report with a speed that belied the alcohol puffiness of his eyes and jawline.

"Can they track the stone from Florida to Purcell?" Sharon asked while her father was reading.

"They're working on it. The pawnshop owner that supposedly turned down the stone has connections to L.A., where Purcell had his home base."

"So they're thinking this mutt sent the stone through the South American version of the old-boy network?" she asked impatiently.

Sizemore nodded.

"What about the transvestite?" she asked. "Was he local?"

"They're showing sketches around to find out."

"Sketches? I haven't seen any."

Sizemore clicked on the last page of the document. Four sketches had been scanned in. He zoomed in on them one at a time.

Sharon stared intently at each sketch in turn. The I-need-a-vacation headache behind her eyes settled in for a long stay. A drink would have helped her overstretched nerves, but Sizemore didn't allow her to drink on the job.

"Anything?" he asked.

"No. You?"

"I've met a few drag queens in my life, but not this one." Yet Sizemore kept staring at the sketches, frowning.

"Could it be Lee Mandel laying a false trail?" Sharon asked after a moment.

"Not if he was already dead," Sizemore said. "Besides, the CI says the sketches aren't Mandel."

"Natalie Cutter?"

"Whose real name is Kate Chandler, who happens to be Mandel's half sister. If anyone would recognize him, she would."

"Well, that just adds a real gloss to this cluster," Sharon said, shaking her head. "The half sister has been a regular fountain of false leads. How did she get back into the game?"

"She's the CI."

"She's a nutcase!"

"The Bureau doesn't think so. And neither do the DNA results. The only good news is that somebody is trying to kill her."

"Excuse me?"

"Death threat. Mechanical distorter. Lab is working on it now."

"Waste of taxpayer money," Sharon said quickly. "Even if they stroke a voice out, no court will accept it. Too many choices. If you use x frequency for your template, you get x voice. If you use y, you get y. If you use a cat, you get a cat."

Sizemore shrugged. "You never know. The lab has pulled more than one white rabbit out of a hat."

"Nutcases, mutts, and white rabbits," Sharon said, throwing up her hands. "I don't believe this shit. What is Kennedy *thinking*?"

"He's covering his ass for all he's worth. He's damn good at it too. He's isolated Groves and Chandler in such a way that no matter what happens, Kennedy wins. That's one smart son of a bitch."

Sharon thought her father had the son of a bitch part right. "Now what?"

"The Bureau is shaking the tree to see if some Ecuadorians drop out."

"Here?"

"L.A."

Sharon frowned and thought fast despite the throbbing in her head. "Why L.A.? Purcell and the stone?"

"Yeah. It all comes back to the stone." He grabbed a beer, twisted off the cap, and raised the bottle in sardonic salute. "Here's to the color of death."

"What?"

"Blue. Sapphire blue."

Chapter 54

Scottsdale
Saturday
5:15 P.M.

Kirby sat in his locked hotel room, staring at his palm.

A rectangular blue eye stared back at him.

"Wish you could talk," he said. "I'd sure like to know why the Voice wanted Purcell killed and you cut up into smaller stones."

Light shifted and shimmered over the stone as though it was alive, breathing. Blue on blue on blue, deeper than time, a well with no bottom, hypnotic.

Kirby had sold the rest of Purcell's stones to Peyton, but not this one. He kept thinking he could use the gem as a twist on the Voice. If not, well, it was worth a lot of money in a few markets he could think of. Saudi Arabia, for one.

"I'd sell you and head for Rio or Aruba," he said to the gem, "but I think that would be a fast ticket to hell if the Voice starts squeezing me. You've got to be good for more than money, right? I sure as hell don't need the Voice following me into retirement."

Or hiring some soldier to kill me.

But that was something Kirby didn't want to say aloud, even in the privacy of his locked room. He moved his hand, making the stone flash like blue lightning.

"You know what I mean?"

Whatever the stone knew it kept to itself.

From the bedside table came the bleat of Kirby's cell phone. He fisted his left hand around the stone and grabbed the phone with his right.

No caller ID.

The hair at the base of Kirby's neck stirred. *Does the Voice know I'm double-crossing him?*

"Yeah?" Kirby said into the phone.

Eerie mechanical tones said, "I need someone in L.A."

"Why?"

"Some mutts from the de Santos gang are walking down the wrong streets."

"So?"

"José de Santos. Eduardo de Santos. José launders Colombian money in the jewelry district. Eduardo takes hot gems for Peyton Hall and cuts them into cold stones."

"How do you know?" Kirby asked.

"Why do you care?"

"I don't," Kirby said quickly.

"Take out the de Santos. José gets a necktie. Do whatever you want with the other one. They're stealing from the wrong people."

"How much is it worth for me?" Kirby asked.

"As much as you can take on the job."

"No cut for you?"

"I'll get mine on the other end," the Voice said.

Kirby wondered what that meant but knew better than to ask that question.

"You have a pencil?" the Voice asked.

"Sure," Kirby said. He stuffed the stone in his pocket, grabbed a pad and pencil from the bedside table, and started writing addresses as fast as the Voice recited them. "Are these recent?"

"Eduardo hasn't moved in ten years. José might be more of a problem. Maybe Eduardo can help. Just do them fast."

"Anything else?"

"Kate Chandler, Phoenix."

Kirby wrote the address quickly.

"Make it look like rape-murder," the Voice said.

Kirby didn't like that. "Rape? Too many ways to leave evidence behind."

"Wear a rubber."

"But—"

"It's worth a hundred big ones in your Aruba account."

"A hundred thousand?" Kirby asked.

"You heard me. If you can't get it up for rape, use a broomstick. Just don't make it look like a hit."

Kirby felt the shape of the stone in his pocket and wondered if it was time to get out. "I want that hundred thou in my account tonight."

"You'll get it when I see her body on the news."

Kirby hesitated. Three murders. Boom boom boom. Then the Purcells before that, and the courier. A lot of death dirtying up what had been a fairly clean game.

It sounded like something was coming apart.

"Cash up front or find another man," Kirby said.

The silence stretched so long that Kirby was afraid he'd misjudged. Sweat gathered under his arms.

"Agreed. Do them within twenty-four hours and you get fifty extra."

The Voice disconnected.

Kirby pulled the sapphire out of his pocket. For a long time he sat with the gem in one hand and the cell phone in the other.

"Time to retire," Kirby said.

But first he had some work to do.

He punched a number into the cell phone. It was picked up quickly. *Rancheria* music blared in the background. A woman's smoke-roughened voice sang along in Spanish.

Kirby would like to have handled both ends of the job, but he couldn't do that and collect the bonus, no matter how often there were flights between L.A. and Phoenix. So he'd give L.A. to Tex

White. That way if there was any splashback from the Colombians over their pet money launderer, White would take the heat.

"What's up?" White asked before he bothered to say hello.

Kirby could tell from the sound of the other man's voice that he was halfway soaring on cocaine. Or maybe just plain old meth. Whatever. It didn't matter. White would never have any money to get out of the business. It all went up his nose. He'd gone from righteous soldier to plain old mutt.

But that wasn't Kirby's problem. After this one, he wasn't going to use White again. After this one, he wasn't going to use anyone again. He was heading south.

"Another job," Kirby said. "You interested?"

"What's it worth?"

"Twenty."

"Twenty? What kind of courier carries that kind of small change, even wholesale? We talking wristwatches here?"

"Not a courier. Two mutts in L.A. Eduardo de Santos and his cousin, José de Santos. Old José gets a necktie. Do the other one any way you want."

"Gimme the addresses."

"Remember. José gets a necktie."

"Yeah, yeah. I hear you. Gimme the fucking addresses."

Kirby read off the numbers, then disconnected and began thinking about the job ahead. As he did, he pulled out the sapphire and rolled it in his palm caressingly. Blue flashed and gleamed, flashed and gleamed, an unblinking death's eye watching everything with equal clarity.

After a long time he put the stone back in the smuggler's pocket he'd rigged in his underwear. He'd cracked too many safes to ever trust anything valuable to one, and the sapphire was the most valuable thing Kirby had ever owned.

He suspected it was also the most deadly.

Chapter 55

Sam wasn't a Bureau hacker, but he'd been taught by one how to get the easy stuff off the 'net. Financial and tax records were nearly always available through one website or another. It was just a matter of knowing someone's Social Security number, the mother's maiden name, and the date of birth, which were usually available on other websites.

He could have asked the Bureau to do it. He still would if he had to. And he could just imagine Kennedy going nuclear when the director asked what in the hell the Bureau was doing prying into the private life and finances of the president's brother-in-law—without a warrant.

Sam went back to burrowing into private files. Finally, he stretched and sighed.

"Well, I can tell you for certain that Arthur McCloud isn't worried about where his next Rolls-Royce Silver Cloud is coming from," Sam said. "He's richer than God and is closing in on Bill Gates."

Kate looked up from the piece of intense yellow sapphire rough she'd been studying while Sam used her computer. "Did you think he wasn't?"

"Always a possibility. Insurance scams are more common than ticks on a Georgia hound."

"Somehow I can't see Art killing anyone, even for a million dollars."

"Most people just hire it done," Sam said absently while he accessed another website.

"You make hiring a killer sound as easy as getting a housecleaner or a gardener."

Sam glanced at her with world-weary eyes. "Easier, actually. It's all a matter of connections. If you have them, getting someone whacked is cheaper and a lot simpler than getting a good nanny. Of course, if you want a pro to do the job rather than some mutt with a drug habit and a gun, you pay more. A lot more. But I haven't heard any complaints from the people depositing money in overseas accounts."

Kate was silent for a few moments before she finally asked, "Do you like the world you live in?"

"A lot less than I used to, why?"

"It's . . . ugly."

"Some good guys have to live there or everyone would be forced to. You drink all the coffee?"

"Yeah."

"Now that's ugly."

She smiled without meaning to. "I'll make some more."

"I think it's my turn."

"I'll trade a fresh pot of coffee for a smile."

He smiled the same way she had, without meaning to. They kept taking each other by surprise.

"And a rain check on a hug," she added. *Since right now you're about as huggable as a porcupine.*

"Three hugs."

"You drive a mean bargain." Kate set down the intense yellow rough and picked up the empty coffee carafe. "I'll be back with more coffee. You want something to eat?"

Sam thought about it and realized that lunch hadn't had much appeal for him. Talking to the Mandels had been tougher than he expected. Probably because Mrs. Mandel had sounded so much like Kate.

And then Sam tried not to wonder if Lee had sounded like his father. If the half brother had had Kate's quickness and courage. If—

"Sam? You hungry?"

He wasn't, but he knew he should eat something besides coffee grounds or he wouldn't be much good to anybody. "Is the rest of my lunch sandwich still in the kitchen?"

"Does the garbage disposal count as 'in the kitchen'?"

"How about some chips?"

"How about some fruit, cheese, crackers, and a nap before dinner?"

Sam didn't answer, because Kate had thrown the last question over her shoulder before she disappeared in the direction of the kitchen. He picked his cell phone up from beside the computer and punched in the number for Jeremy Baxter's hotel room. Sooner or later he'd get lucky and catch the man changing clothes or using the john.

"Hello?"

"Jeremy Baxter?" Sam asked.

"Yes."

Sam pulled a big yellow pad closer and picked up a pen. "This is Special Agent Sam Groves of the FBI," he said. "I have some questions about seven blue sapphires called the Seven Sins."

"What's this about?"

"I'm not free to say at this time."

Silence, a sigh, and a soft curse. "They were stolen, weren't they."

"I'm not free to say."

Baxter hesitated.

"If you have any doubt about my identity," Sam said, "go to the big black motor coach in the employee parking lot, knock on the door, and ask for Doug Smith. He'll show you credentials and vouch for me."

The sound of ice rattling against a glass came over the line. Sam could visualize Baxter thinking and swirling the contents of a near-empty drink.

"Okay," Baxter said. "But I don't know how I can help you. I don't know anything about the stones besides the name and the fact that Art McCloud owns them. I never got to see them once they were cut."

"Do you know anyone who did?"

"Art and whoever appraised them for insurance purposes. And the woman who cut the stones, of course."

The FBI had already vetted the insurance appraiser back to the sixth grade and come up with nothing, but Baxter didn't need to know that.

Kate's vetting had been even more thorough.

"What about fellow collectors," Sam said, "friends, girlfriends, anyone?"

Ice rattled against glass again. "Art has friendly competitors, not friends. As for family, I never met any outside of the newspapers. Girlfriends? I've never heard any gossip about any,"

The FBI had, but none lately and certainly none who'd had hard feelings about their severance pay.

"How about unfriendly competitors?" Sam asked.

"Oh, he pissed people off by having more money than a Saudi prince. But no one was laying for him that I know of. It just irritated us that he could outbid us without really thinking about the bank account. Thank God all he liked were sapphires and occasional rubies."

"Did you bid against him for the rough that was cut into the Seven Sins?" Sam asked.

"Yes, for all the good it did me."

"Who else was in the bidding?"

Kate walked in as Sam started writing quickly on the legal pad she used to make notes about whatever piece of rough she was working on. She set food and coffee near the pad.

He reached for the coffee. Phone tucked between shoulder and ear, he sipped coffee and wrote and asked questions. "Who handled the rough?"

"CGSI. Colored Gem Specialties International. Anything else? I have an appointment in a few minutes."

"I'm trying to pin down a show that was held the second week in November."

"There were several. Cut gems or rough?"

"Which ones did you attend?" Sam asked without missing a beat.

"Only the one in Fort Worth that featured Russian estate jewelry. Amazing goods. Really amazing. Of course, they knew what they had. I only bought a few old emeralds. Basilov cleaned up."

"He was there?"

"Hell, he put the thing together and got some guys in from Singapore and Hong Kong who still had money. Like I say, he cleaned up. The Asians are finally getting into colored stones for investment, as well as their traditional pearls and jade."

"Any of the other regulars there too?" Sam asked. A moment later he began writing quickly. Then he stopped writing and started putting checks next to names Baxter had already given him. "And that was from the eighth through the ninth of November?"

"Yes, but everyone who knew ruby from spinel left after the first day. There were no previews, so it was nonstop from eight in the morning until nine that night. After that, the good stuff was gone. Excuse me, but I really have to go now. I'll be late."

"Thank you for your help," Sam said. Then added quickly, "Someone might be calling you on a follow-up."

"Whatever, just not now."

Baxter hung up.

Sam finished his cup of coffee and reached for the pot.

Kate put a plate of cheese, fruit, and crackers underneath his hand and looked at him.

He took the hint and started eating. Once he got past the first few crackers and some really prime red grapes, he began to realize just how hungry he was. He ate faster, with real interest. When he discovered salami hidden under the cheese he grinned.

"Did you get anything from Baxter?" Kate asked.

"A lot more than I got from the tight-ass citizens at CGSI." Sam swallowed salami and chased it with cheese and a swallow of coffee. "I'm going to enjoy dropping a warrant on them. Any of these names familiar to you?"

She scooted her work chair closer to him and looked at the names. "The names, yes. The people, no. They're collectors and traders. I've cut stones for two of them."

"Are they clean, dirty, crazy, what?"

"You mean would they kill for the Seven Sins?"

"Yeah."

"I don't know them well enough to say."

"Guess." Sam crunched into a grape and reached for some cheese. "If you had to start, which name would you draw out of the hat?"

Kate frowned over the list. "Basilov, I guess. He came on the scene five years ago out of nowhere."

"In his case, nowhere was Georgia, former Soviet Union."

"He has a lot of cash to spend. He's not like Art—he doesn't buy what he falls in love with and to hell with 'value'—but Basilov's a real force when it comes to buying choice material."

Sam swallowed some coffee and said, "I'll tell the boys to start with him."

"Did you talk to Art?" Kate asked curiously.

"Yeah, while you were on the phone with your mom."

"Was Basilov one of the names you got?"

"I got zip from McCloud. He said if he felt like talking to anyone in the Bureau, he'd get in touch with the director."

"Ouch," Kate said.

"Yeah. Nothing personal, from all I know about the man. He's just a prick with money and connections."

"I suppose it would be tactful for me to disagree with your description of Art, seeing as how I've worked for him in the past."

Sam smiled as he snagged some more cheese and grapes. "Only if you want to cut more stones for him in the future."

"Arthur McCloud is a fine, upstanding—"

"Yada yada yada," Sam cut in. "If I'm ever privileged enough to talk to him, I'll be sure to tell him you defended him to the last gasp of hypocrisy."

Kate looked at the dates Sam had circled. "Eighth?"

"November."

"When Lee . . ."

"When Lee was murdered," Sam said evenly. "Yes."

Kate flinched.

Sam knew he sounded cold. He also knew from experience that dancing around the reality of death didn't do anything except draw out the painful process of acceptance.

"I didn't mean that the way it sounded," he said, standing up and drawing her close.

"I know."

Her breath was warm against his neck. Her body was warm against his. And if he didn't let go of her right now, he wasn't going to let go of her until it was way too late.

"Anyway," he said, stepping back and grabbing a handful of grapes, "according to Baxter, the same people who were likely to know about the Seven Sins, the same people who bid for the rough, were all in Fort Worth on the day Lee was killed."

"Convenient," Kate said bitterly.

"Maybe, maybe not. I get the feeling a lot of these people go to a lot of the same sales."

She sighed. "Yes, they do. Sorry, I didn't mean to imply. . . . It's just that I'm . . ."

"Yeah." He looked away because it was that or reach for her. If he did that, he'd be making love to her instead of trying to save her life. As much as he wanted her, it was no contest. The cop won by a mile. "I'll check out every name, but I'm not counting on it going any-where. Whoever killed Lee wasn't buying stones in Fort Worth on the eighth."

"The car wasn't turned in until the ninth."

"The car didn't kill him. Someone who was on Sanibel Island be-fore noon on the eighth did, someone who knew Lee's habits, someone who either called Lee away from his lunch or screwed up popping the trunk so that Lee saw or heard, came running, and got killed."

"Why?" Kate asked starkly. "Why not just rob him or beat him up like the other couriers?"

"That's the million-dollar question," Sam agreed. "Of all the couriers, his is the only one whose body was hidden. Why? The answer is our killer."

"What do you mean?"

He fiddled with his coffee cup, thought about not telling her, and decided she'd do better with the truth than with well-meaning evasions.

"I think whoever killed your half brother is part of a group I call the Teflon gang. I think they're American. I think they have someone on the inside of the gem trade. Way inside. I think Lee must have recognized whoever robbed him in Florida. I think that's why Lee died." Sam looked up. His eyes were as grim as the line of his mouth. "And I'm afraid the gang has someone on the inside of the crime strike force too."

"You don't mean just someone with ambition and media contacts and loose lips?"

"I mean someone who knows just what he's saying and just what the results will be."

Kate closed her eyes for a moment, then opened them. They looked the way she felt—angry and afraid and determined. "What can we do?"

"First I'm going to put you in a safe place."

"Already taken care of. Look around you, Special Agent. Deadbolts and locks and alarms everywhere. What's second?"

"I want to move you to another place."

"I don't want to go. I'm safer here than I would be in a motel room going nuts staring at bad art and wondering if the next guy coming through the door will be you or a killer with a badge. I mean it, Sam. I'm staying. I'm safer here."

"I'm just one man. I can't protect you twenty-four-seven."

"I'm just one woman who can put bullets into man-shaped targets at twenty-three feet with either hand."

Sam lifted his eyebrows. "Did the targets have guns?"

"Our instructor said that came under the heading of postgraduate work, and she hoped to hell we never had to do that dance."

"So do I." Sam looked at his watch without really seeing it. Whatever the readout said, it didn't matter.

There wasn't enough time.

But whatever it was, it was all they had. "Okay, we'll do it your way until that doesn't work anymore. Then we'll do it mine."

Kate ignored the chill that was gathering under her skin. "Sounds good."

He almost laughed. Nothing sounded good to him but grabbing her and running like hell. Too bad that being on the run wouldn't get the job done.

"We're going to make a list of everyone Lee knew in the jewelry trade," Sam said. "Then we're going to make a list of everyone on the strike force. Then we'll see how much the lists overlap."

"What if they don't?"

"Then we make a list of friends of friends. Somewhere, somehow, there's a link between Lee and the FBI."

"There's always a pattern, is that it? Like cutting rough?"

He smiled slightly. "That's one way of putting it."

"So all we have to do is throw away the facts that don't matter."

"All." Sam laughed wearily. "Yeah, that's all. Hope you weren't planning on much sleep. It's going to be a long night."

"Sleep? What's that?"

Kate took the yellow pad, flipped to a new page, and drew a stark black line down the center of the page. In neat block letters, she started writing down the name of everyone Lee knew in the jewelry business. Sam was right. It was going to be a long night.

But at least she wouldn't be spending it alone.

Chapter 56

Glendale
Saturday
11:08 P.M.

Kirby was driving a dark blue rental car when he closed in on Kate Chandler's house. The Lexus wasn't flashy, but it was a long way from an urban beater. A man in a suit driving an expensive car was assumed to be a solid citizen returning from a late flight. He was a lot less likely to be stopped and questioned by a cruising squad car than some mutt in dirty jeans driving a clapped-out Ford.

If anyone noticed that Kirby was wearing a black turtleneck under the suit coat, that his pants were black jeans instead of true slacks, and that he was sporting black running shoes instead of loafers, it still wouldn't matter. Lots of middle-level workers dressed like that in the west.

The briefcase on the seat next to Kirby was glossy leather and entirely fitting for the car and the dark suit. The fact that the case was packed with burglar's tools didn't show on the outside.

Everything was looking routine until he saw the plain four-door sedan parked in front of Kate's house. The Voice hadn't said anything about a guard on the female, but the car might as well have great big letters on its side announcing "This turd on wheels is official property."

Only cops drove cheap American sedans.

Shit.

For a few seconds he thought about turning around, driving away, and to hell with the money, but he was revising his plans before the idea of walking out had a chance to take hold. It wasn't just the money, although money was always useful. It was just that he'd been . . . anticipating.

Warm flesh. Cold steel. Screams that never made it past duct tape. Panicked eyes. The scent of blood, the hot spill of it, the rush that told him he was still young.

Nothing wrong with a man enjoying his work.

He drove by the parked car. He couldn't see anyone through the windows. Maybe the cop was stretched out in the back of the sedan, sleeping on the job. Maybe he was an off-duty cop and her boyfriend and was inside the house. Either way, no alarm would go out on the sedan's radio. But if the guy was inside the house, that was different.

Kirby thought about it as he scanned the surrounding houses. None of them had lights on. In neighborhoods like this, most of the people who lived there were old and went to bed early or young and had the kind of jobs that got them up at dawn. In the end, young or old, everyone went to bed before ten.

The target house had lights on. Unlike the neighbors, somebody was up and around.

Son of a whore. Decent people are asleep by now.

He memorized the houses in the immediate area, their approaches, their fences. The target house had empty lots across the street. They wouldn't be empty long because a developer's big sign announced that apartments were on the way. Kirby didn't care beyond the fact that the sign might provide cover for him.

He drove on, turned right, and turned right again on the next street. The house directly behind the target was weather-beaten, unlit, and had a FOR RENT sign stuck into the dead lawn. The houses on either side were dark, with older cars parked in the driveways.

After another drive around the block from the other direction,

Kirby went to a bar he'd spotted in a small shopping center a mile away. He sat in the parking lot and dialed up White's cell phone. A little help might be smart.

No one answered.

He dialed again, hung up, then called a third time. It was their prearranged signal to pick up even if you were jumping the old lady.

No answer.

No voice mail either. Not that Kirby would have left a message even if he'd been able to. The business he and White did together wasn't the type that you felt good about leaving voice mails.

So it can't look like a whack job, and she either has a guard or a boyfriend that drives a government special.

Cursing silently, Kirby considered the possibilities. If she'd been alone, he wouldn't have cared about the lights being on, but she wasn't alone and he did care. He'd have to wait until the guard or boyfriend or whatever left or they got tired of screwing and fell asleep.

And here he'd been all psyched up and ready to go.

He got out of the car, locked his briefcase and suit coat in the trunk, and walked toward the bar. In his dark clothes, he was just one more shadow in the parking lot.

Chapter 57

Glendale
Saturday
11:35 P.M.

The wreckage of mostly eaten pizza and too many cups of coffee lay across one of Kate's worktables. Another table was covered with Sam's files. A third sprouted sticky notes with information that hadn't yet been assigned to a category. Kate sat at the fourth table with tablets labeled Prime Suspects, Persons Unknown, Last Resort, When Pigs Fly, Active, or Pipeline scattered in front of her. Sam was right next to her. Because neither of them had the skill to display complex linkages on the computer, they were working the old-fashioned way—legal tablets, pencils, and erasers.

And sticky notes. Lots and lots of sticky notes.

The computer was within arm's reach for the times when Sam needed to get public—or not so public—information on the people they were discussing.

"Okay," Sam said, "it's your turn to read. Take it from the beginning."

Again? Kate wanted to bang her head on the table, but silently reached for a yellow tablet instead. When Sam had told her that a lot of investigative work was a waste of time, Kate hadn't really believed him. She did now.

"June of last year," she said in a flat voice, reading the time line they had been working on for too many hours already, with nothing to show for it but a headache and dirty coffee cups. "Arthur McCloud buys blue sapphire rough at a CGSI auction. Six bidders. Presumption is that McCloud bragged about Seven Sins to one or more of the unsuccessful bidders. Same six bidders attended a different auction in Texas on the day Lee is presumed to have been killed and the sapphires stolen."

"Put those bidders on the Last Resort list," Sam said, lifting a cup of cold coffee. "Even if they bailed on the morning of the Texas auction instead of the afternoon, they'd have had a hell of a time getting in place in time to pick up Lee at the airport and follow him to the SoupOr Shrimp. So far, their alibis look good. Someone in headquarters is running their financials for me. If something pops, we'll take a look at it. Until then, forget it."

Kate pulled pink sticky notes with six names listed and put them on a legal tablet whose heading read Last Resort. None of the notes had opportunity or means written across the bottom. The motive—greed—was represented by a big G on each note.

"In addition to McCloud, three other people were known to have information about what was in the missing courier's packet," Kate continued. "The cutter, the owner of Mandel Inc., and the owner's wife. None of these four—"

"They don't even make the Last Resort list," Sam finished when Kate paused to turn to a new page. "McCloud has no motive except money, and he's got plenty of that. Money isn't a motive that flies with you or your parents. And even if it did, there's not one clue in anyone's financial records that hints at money from a questionable source. Yes, we have a forensic accountant working on your family in case I missed something, but my gut isn't buying it. Without motive, opportunity and means don't add up to spit. Put those four names on the When Pigs Fly list."

Kate duly transferred the white sticky notes to another legal tablet with the appropriate heading.

"It's probable, but unproved," she continued reading, "that Norm

Gallagher knew what Lee was carrying, and when. As for motivation, so far there isn't any. I haven't been able to reach Norm to ask him if he knew." *I haven't even been able to tell him that the FBI is assuming Lee is dead.*

Not that Sam would have let her. That was privileged information. Even her parents had promised to tell no one about their son's near-certain death.

Sam peeled the note with Norm's name off the table and pressed it onto the tablet labeled Active.

"Approximately two days after the courier's death," she read, "Seguro Jimenez is approached by a man or a woman who may or may not have been blonde and blue-eyed. Said unknown person had one of the Seven Sins. Seguro claims not to have purchased it."

Sam reached out, pulled the red sticky note with Persons Unknown on it, and stuck the note to a third legal tablet, which was labeled Prime Suspects. Seguro's name, on a pink note, went to another tablet labeled Pipeline.

With a stifled yawn, Kate went back to reading aloud. "The first investigation into the missing courier was conducted by . . ."

While she recited the dreary facts that had led nowhere in an investigation that had interested the various local, state, and federal cops not at all, Sam watched Kate with a gentleness and hunger he kept hidden from her. If nothing else came of the past tedious hours, at least she could now recite the facts surrounding her half brother's death without flinching. It wasn't much, but he'd learned through the years that a little something was a whole lot better than nothing at all.

She flipped the page without transferring any sticky notes anywhere. None of the investigations had turned up anything worth pursuing, period.

"You think the coffee is done yet?" Sam asked.

"I think you drink too much coffee."

"You too. You want a cup?"

"What do you think?"

"I think the coffee is ready."

Sam went to the kitchen, inspected the state of the coffeemaker, and decided it was close enough for government work. He poured two mugs and headed back to the workroom. As he did, he automatically checked the status lights on the alarm system.

All green.

"Want some pizza with it?" he asked, setting the mug in front of her.

She shook her head, frowning at something on the page in front of her.

"You sure?" he asked. "There might not be any left if you change your mind in a few minutes."

She half smiled and waved toward the remains of their hasty dinner. "I'm sure. Knock yourself out."

He pulled the mostly empty pizza box closer and settled in to clean up everything but the grease spots on the cardboard. While he chewed, he listened, waiting for the instant when the same facts assembled in a different way would lead to new insights, new suspects, *something.*

When Kate got to the part where she received the death threat, he tried not to think about how satisfying it would be to strangle the cowardly son of a bitch.

I have to catch him first. One fact at a time, one step at a time, go over it again and again, repeat as necessary. Something will pop.

It has to.

Kate transferred another red note to the Prime Suspects tablet. This note said Person Unknown/Death Threat. When she started to recite the list of dealers who had attended the same conventions in the months since Purcell surfaced with one of the Seven Sins, Sam interrupted.

"I've got Mario on those," Sam said. "Unless a name appears on another tablet heading, put them all under Long Shot."

Both of them already knew that none of the dealer/civilian expert names appeared under any other heading, except for Peyton Hall, CGSI, Purcell, and Sizemore Security Consulting. But even after their names were stuck to the Active tablet, the tablet labeled

Long Shot still sprouted so many notes that it looked like a drunken checkerboard.

"What about Mandel Inc.?" Kate asked. "They're civilians."

"Your parents said no one in the organization had access to the courier routes, times, or goods."

"Someone could have hacked into the files."

Sam almost smiled at her determination to treat everyone as an equal suspect. When he'd told her that each time they went through the facts again, they had to treat it like the first time, he hadn't expected the level of intensity and unrelenting concentration she'd given to the job.

"The Mandel Inc. computer that deals with routes, couriers, and so on, isn't connected to the Internet, so it can't be hacked into," he reminded her. "Only your parents have the computer entry code. Same for Sizemore's company and CGSI. Unless you tell me something new, your parents stay in the When Pigs Fly category. The jury is still out on the rest of the folks."

"Okay." Absently, Kate rubbed her neck. "Now we're at the part where it gets complicated. Your turn."

Without meaning to, both of them looked at the table that was nearly covered with sticky notes waiting to be assigned. Many of the names were duplicates, which was one way of keeping track of how many "hits" each name had in the course of the investigation, and whether the hits came under motive, opportunity, and/or means.

Sam picked up his own tablet and began reading. "Crime strike force personnel. Pending further investigation, assumed motive is money."

Another flurry of notes were lifted from the table and put into tablets. All but one name went into the Active category. Sam's name went on the Last Resort list.

"When Pigs Fly," Kate said, yanking off the note and putting it on another tablet.

"What if all this is an elaborate ruse on my part to—"

"Oh, bull," Kate interrupted. "Don't waste my time."

"What makes you so certain?"

She rolled her eyes, then saw that he was serious. "There are some things a man can't fake."

"Emotions? Darling, I hate to tell you but—"

"Erections," she said succinctly. "You might screw me once just because I was handy and you were horny, but it takes real passion to do it four times in a row."

"Stamina too."

"Exactly."

"For you too."

"You noticed?"

He smiled and touched the corner of her mouth. "I noticed."

She kissed his fingertip. "And you're gentle with me. At least you are now that you don't think I'm a crook. You weren't very nice before that."

"I'm not paid to be nice."

"See? There you go. But you're nice to me and you're innocent." She looked at the tablet he was holding. "How many of the people on the strike force had a previous connection to Lee or Mandel Inc.?"

"As far as we can discover from your parents' records, no one."

"What about Sizemore Security Consulting?" Kate said. "Lee worked for them a couple of times."

"Sizemore's company isn't part of the strike force."

"Puh-lease. Are you telling me that the Legend doesn't know everything that jerk Kennedy knows?"

"No. I'm telling you it's an informal rather than a formal connection."

"Yeah, yeah, yeah," Kate muttered. "Any more formal and they'd be married."

Firmly she pulled up a slip with Sizemore's name and stuck it to the Active file. Then she wrote "/Lee" on the note and looked at Sam defiantly.

He was smiling.

Then he took Kennedy's name and wrote across the bottom of the note "/Lee?" The note went next to Sizemore's in the Active category.

"Why?" Kate asked.

"They've been sharing information for thirty years. We're better off assuming shared knowledge than burying our heads in the sand."

"I've always thought that sounded way uncomfortable."

"What?"

"All that sand in your eyes."

Sam shook his head, picked up his tablet, and began reading again. "As much as I'd like to pin a rose on Bill Colton, so far all I have against him is his sweet personality. He'd cut my throat, and yours, to become SAC, but otherwise he's clean."

Kate took the note with Colton's name and put it on the Active tablet.

"Why?" Sam asked, reaching for the note. "At best he's a long shot."

She pushed his hand away. "I don't like him."

"You've never met him."

"I saw him. That was enough."

"A woman of rare perception and taste."

Smiling, Sam went back to reading. "On to the civilian component. Sizemore Security Consulting had the means and opportunity to take out most of the couriers. Exceptions are noted next to the courier's name."

Kate looked down the list of couriers. Nineteen in all. It shocked her each time she confronted it. Then she reminded herself that it was less than one percent of the jewelry courier runs in the U.S. in the same time period.

"No connection to Lee, though," Sam said. "But the motive is there. Money. Sizemore's company has been in a steady decline for six years. Extra cash here and there would be welcome."

"But thanks to all these couriers getting hit when they were under Sizemore's supposed security net, Sizemore is getting a bad reputation among its client base," Kate said. "Whatever he got in the short run wouldn't be worth ruining his own business, would it?"

Sam grimaced. "You're sure about the reputation thing?"

"Very. People in the jewelry trade gossip. Sizemore Security Consulting isn't getting any compliments."

"Well, damn. Unless he's gone around the bend, he doesn't have an obvious motive. Or maybe he's socking away the proceeds of crime for his retirement."

"Does that fit with his personality?" Kate asked.

"I'm no shrink, but it's not sounding real good to me. On the other hand, who knows what makes people go postal? He could see old age closing in on him and all he has to fend it off with is an FBI pension and a failing company. And beer."

"True. And from what you said, he's certainly arrogant enough to be a crook."

"Yeah." Sam looked off into a distance only he could see. "In some ways the line between cop and crook is a lot thinner than we like to think about, much less talk about."

After a moment Sam shrugged and moved Sizemore's name from Active to Suspect. At least it was a name rather than an unknown person or persons.

"What about the other people at Sizemore's company?" Kate asked. "Even if he's innocent as a baby's smile, there could be someone inside the company using or selling information, couldn't there?"

"We're checking into that. So far no good. The son is a hard worker who wants to please Daddy. The daughter is a hard worker who keeps the operation together. The third in command, Jason Gallagher, is—"

"Who?" Kate cut in, surprised.

"Jason Gallagher."

"I think—I can't be certain—but I think Norm's brother is a Jason. At least, his nickname is Jase."

"You never said anything about a brother."

"That's because I don't really know much about Norm, except that Lee is—" She stopped abruptly, then continued after only a brief pause, "Lee was over the moon about him. That's all Lee talked about when he called me. That and the fact that Norm was urging him to tell Mom and Dad. Norm's family was very supportive of him." Frowning, Kate pulled the clip out of her hair and rubbed her scalp as though that would stimulate her memory. "Lee said that was something he and Norm had in common. Jase supported Norm and I supported Lee. Given the context, I just assumed that Jase was Norm's brother."

"Fair enough. And that would certainly connect Sizemore's company with Lee in a big way," Sam said. "If Lee told Norm what was in the courier packet, and Norm told his brother Jase, who also happens to be Jason Gallagher, and Jason mentioned it to his boss . . ."

"That's a lot of ifs," Kate said dubiously.

"Yeah. But it's a link we didn't have before. Let's see if it goes somewhere."

"Are you going to call Jase?"

"First I'm going to be sure that we have brothers. If we do, we'll assume linkage."

"Why not just ask Jase?"

"Because if Sizemore is dirty, Jase could be dirty too."

Kate shifted unhappily. "Are you saying that Jase set up his brother's lover?"

"I'm saying I don't know who's dirty and who isn't. Until I do—or can at least make a reasonable guess—I'm not going to go broadcasting my suspicions."

"But they were going to be married."

It took Sam a moment, but he made the connection. "Look, Jase could have tipped someone, or Sizemore could have, or someone else who had the information, without intending to harm anyone but the insurance company. Up until Lee died, the couriers weren't killed."

"What changed that?"

"Good question." Sam fiddled with a piece of pizza crust and stared into the middle distance. "The Purcells were killed to keep them quiet about where they got the sapphire. I think the female courier was roughed up to change the MO so that the cops would assume South American gangs were at play, rather than the guys I call the Teflon gang. The female courier happened to have a thin skull, so she died. The courier who was shot in the parking lot is just one of those things that go down when crooks carry guns. A screwup. Otherwise it was a classic Teflon job—homemade remote key, inside information on the courier and the route, the courier isn't around for the grab, no one is hurt, in and out and gone in thirty seconds."

"How many of these nineteen couriers fit that profile?"

"Twelve, if I'm right about the female courier and the parking lot screwup, and one or two others where the MO is mixed."

"What does your boss say about your theory?"

"My SAC says that his boss told him that when we round up all the South American mutts, and the courier hits continue, then and only then will Kennedy start looking under his maiden aunt's bed for Teflon ghosts."

"Got it. Kennedy's not impressed."

"Neither is Sizemore. Kennedy controls the Bureau information pipeline, so nothing gets in the files that would make him unhappy. Sizemore has the media in his pocket, which only feeds the frenzy for South American gangs."

"That's what you meant when you said facts that don't agree with the brass don't make it into the final report."

"Yeah."

"It's a wonder anything ever gets done."

He smiled wearily. "It's not just the Bureau. It's human nature. We don't like the bearer of bad news. We reward the folks bringing good news. Guess which messenger gets ahead in the world?"

Kate just shook her head.

"Okay," Sam said, "next civilian under investigation is CGSI. Raul Mendoza did a preliminary on them and came up with nothing interesting. Ditto the accountant. Only thing of interest is that they handle their own courier and security information, always."

"Dad has tried to interest them in using his company. No sale."

"Tell him not to take it personally. Sizemore got the same treatment when he tried to include them in his security umbrella for this show. They told him to go crap in his mess kit. A few other security companies tried, but they weren't gem and jewelry specialists."

"Is CGSI any better off for doing its own security?" she asked.

Sam turned and went to work on the computer keyboard. "They've been hit once in four years. South American gang MO. That was two years ago." He tapped out a rapid series of commands, calling up an FBI evaluation of various companies involved in the gem and jewelry trade. The screen changed to a graphic representation. "Considering the amount and value of the stuff they move, CGSI is doing much better at not getting hit than the average company with the same volume of goods."

"That doesn't make Mandel Inc. or Sizemore Security Consulting look very good, does it?"

For a moment, Sam didn't answer. "No, it doesn't. But it could just be a factoid. It's too soon to tell."

"What's a factoid?"

"A fact that doesn't mean anything in the larger scheme. If you get enough of them and they all point in the same direction, then you take a closer look."

"I see." Kate picked up a pencil and made a little circle on the Mandel Inc. and the Sizemore Security Consulting sticky notes. Then she put circles on each employee's note.

"What are you doing?" Sam asked.

"Entering factoids."

"You're going to drive yourself crazy."

"You say that like it's a bad thing."

Gently, he tangled his fingers in her hair. "You doing okay, darling?"

"No. How about you?"

"Want to take a time-out?"

"Right after we finish with the civilians."

"They have a lot of cross-references and factoids," he warned her.

"That's okay. I have a lot of pencils."

He looked at his watch. "Go sharpen them while I call in some names to fingerprinting."

"What names? Why?"

"My personal six most-likely suspects. I want the lab to compare any prints on file with whatever they got off the rental car."

"Isn't it a little late—and on Saturday night?" she asked.

"Not a problem with Kennedy's pull."

"I didn't know he was behind you."

"Neither does he."

"He'll be pissed."

Sam smiled grimly. "How will I tell the difference?"

Chapter 58

If the neighborhood had been quiet a few hours ago, now it was dead. A few night-lights glowed in a house here and there, and the dusty old streetlights pushed small gold halos into the darkness. After that, it was completely dark. Even the fingernail moon had already set.

Headlights off, Kirby parked in the driveway of a rental house in back of the target's address and waited, wishing he had brought his beer with him. But that would have been stupid. He shouldn't even have had the beers he'd drunk while waiting for the bar to close, but there hadn't been any choice. Bartenders and barmaids notice the patrons that don't drink. He didn't want to be remembered.

After five minutes of watching the street, Kirby felt confident that if anybody had noticed him, they didn't care. No house lights came on. No doors opened to the street.

Quietly, he opened the car door. Nothing flashed on because he'd already pulled the fuse controlling the interior lights. No dog barked at hearing his footsteps, because his soles were soft and he was walking lightly. He soon reached the garage, went over the low fence down a narrow side yard, and along the backyard. Every step of the way, chest-high shrubs with thin leaves and long thorns plucked at his dark clothes. Beneath the black ski mask, he was sweating with a combination of beer and adrenaline.

The lot next door to the target house had more of the thorny shrubs scattered across the bare land. Instead of avoiding them, he used their thin cover to blur the outline of his silhouette against the sandy dirt. It wasn't a conscious decision but past training that kept him moving at a slow and steady pace, gliding from shrub to shrub until he reached the target.

The first thing he noticed was the wires on all windows and doors.

The second thing was the alarms.

He smiled.

People slept deeply when they were guarded by wires and alarms. It made his job easier, once he was inside. And he would get inside. Security depended on electricity, which could be outsmarted by crossing the right wires. Same for alarms.

The really sweet thing about residential alarm systems was that they had a thirty-second grace period built in. In thirty seconds he could short-circuit the two wires on a window, taking it out of the alarm loop. Then he could cut a big hole out of the glass and take a look around. If she had motion sensors, he could deal with them too.

Thirty-second alarm delays made his life easy.

He took one last look around. Smiling at the glittering rush of his blood that heightened all his senses, he opened the briefcase and went to work. His heartbeat picked up in his eagerness to feel the woman's softness and terror when his knife bit into her.

Chapter 59

Glendale
Sunday
2:25 A.M.

Sam woke up with a rush of adrenaline that told him something was wrong. He didn't know what it was, but he knew it was real.

Next to him, Kate stirred briefly, then went completely still. The change in her breathing told him that she was awake. Wide awake. Whatever had pulled him out of sleep had done the same to her.

The alarm panel above the bed showed green at every station.

Sam didn't believe it.

Slowly, he brought his lips to Kate's hair. When he spoke it wasn't a whisper, which would carry in the stillness like a hiss of steam. His voice was a bare thread of sound that went no farther than her ear.

"Don't move," he breathed, reaching for the weapon harness he'd left right by the bed. "I'll check out the house."

"My gun," she murmured, shifting carefully as she spoke. "Where?"

She reached down and under the bed and came up with a handful of metal. "Here."

The gun was smaller than his, but by no means a girly weapon. It would do just fine putting a hole in someone's bad intentions.

"Don't shoot me by mistake," Sam murmured.

"Same goes."

"Stay here." His hand tightened in her hair. "Promise."

"Unless I hear shots."

He wanted to protest. He shut up because he knew he wasn't going to win and arguing could give them away to whoever was prowling around outside in the yard.

Or in the house.

Jesus, I hope not.

But Sam wasn't going to count on it. Whoever had managed to get close enough to wake both of them up and yet not trip any of the alarms was a pro, not some careless hype breaking into homes for drug money.

Naked as the gun in his hand, Sam walked silently to the closed bedroom door and listened.

And listened.

All he heard was his own light, slow breathing and a softer whisper in the room behind him that was Kate's careful breath as she sat up in bed.

From somewhere in the house came a muffled thump. If Kate had had a cat, Sam would have thought the sound came from a feline jumping from the kitchen counter to the floor. But Kate didn't have a cat . . .

Silently, Sam waited, judging the danger of staying put versus trying to get past the squeaky bedroom door handle and into the rest of the house. He opted to stay and let the attacker come to him. Assuming there was anyone out there.

He really hoped there wasn't.

A slight rustle from the bed told him that Kate was on the move. He glanced briefly over his shoulder. Her naked body was a paler shade of darkness sliding off to his right. He wanted to tell her to stop, to get in the closet, to go out the window and run like hell— do anything except quietly position herself so that if the door opened quickly, slamming into him, she would have a clean shot at the intruder.

And even as Sam wanted her to flee, he silently saluted her pragmatism. She knew that the bedroom door handle squeaked, that neither one of them could get out without giving away the game.

So they waited.

A few minutes later there was another muted noise, not enough to worry about except that both of them knew there was no reason for anything in the house to get up and move on its own.

The door handle turned slightly, squeaked softly.

Stopped.

Sam had already taken the safety off his gun. Distantly, he was aware of adrenaline firing up his blood, sharpening his senses, picking up his heart rate, his body silently demanding that he *do something*.

All he could do now was wait and pray that there was only one man testing the door, and that the attacker never had a chance to get close to Kate.

The handle turned more. Squeaked.

Stopped.

Kate felt cold sweat slide down her back and turn slick along her ribs. She ignored it along with the wild beating of her heart. Her instructor's words ran in her mind like a jingle from an obnoxious commercial.

When you can't run, use the gun. When you can't—

Squeeeak.

Silence.

The door handle was halfway turned. A little more patience, a few more squeaks, and it would open.

When you can't run, use the gun.

Without realizing it, Kate silently took off the safety and assumed the shooting stance that had been drilled into her during the hours of practice that had left her hands numb and her arms aching.

Did the targets have guns?

As she'd been taught, she shoved thought aside and let her body take over.

Squeak—squeeeak.

Her gun came up as though someone else was holding it, someone else training it on the door to the right of Sam, someone else waiting. She had a hard time believing it was happening to her.

It isn't real. Just another practice. Just—

Waiting.

Waiting for the *squeeeak* and the sliding shadow of darkness that would be a man intent on killing her.

Waiting.

The door moved with dreamlike slowness, opening into the room.

"Don't shoot!" Sam yelled to Kate even as he slammed into the door with the full force of his body.

A man cried out in fear and anger and pain. He left arm was caught in the vise of the door. The knife in his hand gleamed dully.

"FBI," Sam shouted. "Drop the knife!"

Kirby twisted and threw himself at the door, trying to get his arm free and throw his attacker off balance.

It almost worked. Sam had been expecting the man to retreat rather than attack. If Sam had had any doubt about what they were up against, he no longer did.

Not only a pro, a well-trained one.

Sam grunted with effort and put his weight into the door. "If he gets past me, start shooting and don't stop until he does. Got it?"

"Yes." Thin, flat, the voice didn't sound like Kate's, but her understanding was clear.

"Last chance, asshole," Sam said. "Drop the knife!"

Kirby went slack.

Sam shifted to reach for the knife.

On the other side of the door, Kirby lunged forward. His entire body slammed into the door, knocking Sam back an inch. Just one.

Way too much.

Kirby yanked back his trapped arm. Instead of running away, he drew back and hit the door like a pile driver. It splintered away from its hinges. Off balance, Kirby staggered into the bedroom.

Sam bent under the impact of door and attacker, rolled, and scissored his legs. He didn't connect the way he'd wanted to, but he managed to knock the attacker off balance again.

Kate looked for a target. All she saw was a windmilling kind of darkness rushing around the open doorway.

A knife blade sliced through the air and thunked into the wall so close to her cheek that the metal felt hot and cold at the same time. She gave a startled cry.

Sam shot twice quickly, then twice more. In the small room it sounded like four cherry bombs going off on top of each other.

The man on the floor jerked and went still.

"Sam, are you all—"

"Not yet," Sam said harshly to her. He went to where the man lay and bent down far enough to wedge the muzzle of his government-issue Glock up under the intruder's chin. Even if the man was playing possum, now he couldn't move without getting his head blown off. "See if the lights work," Sam said to Kate. "If they do, don't look real close."

The lights worked.

She tried not to look. It was impossible. There was blood and . . . *something* . . . everywhere. The intruder was dripping scarlet everywhere he wasn't black. Bone gleamed in an open wound.

Her stomach turned over.

"Damn, I told you not to look," Sam said. "Breathe through your nose and hiss it out through your teeth. It will help the nausea."

He ought to know. It was how he was keeping his stomach in place. Then he glanced up briefly and saw the blood on her cheek.

He stopped breathing.

"Kate. You're bleeding."

She blinked. "I am?"

"Your cheek."

She touched her cheek with her free hand. Her fingers came away red. Vaguely, she became aware of a burning sensation. She probed more deeply.

"Just a little cut," she said. "I'm fine."

"You sure?"

"Yes."

"Okay." Sam started breathing again. It felt good. "Find my cell phone. Punch one and then two. When Doug answers, tell him what happened. Can you do that?"

She wiped her bloody fingers on her bare thigh and looked everywhere but at the man on the floor. "Yes."

Kneeling, Sam put the fingers of his left hand lightly on the attacker's neck where the arterial pulse of life should be. If it was there, his own heart was beating too hard for him to pick it up. But all in all, he didn't think there was a pulse to be found.

Fuck.

He'd been looking forward to questioning the mutt.

Grimly, Sam began the job of going through the would-be assassin's clothing, looking for anything that might identify him. No wallet, which didn't surprise Sam. Pros don't make it easy for cops. There was a remote car key with a rental tag on it in a front pocket of the man's bloody slacks. Nothing else. No credit card, no money, not even change in his pockets, which could have jingled and given him away.

Automatically, Sam patted the body down for other weapons.

It took him about forty seconds to find the sapphire.

Chapter 60

Scottsdale
Sunday
8:00 A.M.

"What do you mean Eduardo's dead?" Peyton demanded.

Sharon looked up from the breakfast she'd been sharing with Peyton until the phone rang. Without glancing over, he gave her a gesture that told her to stay put and be quiet. She shrugged and went back to her waffle.

"Geraldo?" Peyton pressed. "Was it a heart attack?"

In Los Angeles, his uncle sighed and looked at his sister. Peyton's mother shook her head, silently saying that she didn't want to talk to her son right now. This was business, and Geraldo de Selva's job was to take care of things, because the Blessed Mother knew that Peyton was too busy lifting skirts to keep his attention on business. Like father, like son.

"Regrettably," Geraldo said, "it appears that Eduardo was involved in a little gem-cutting on the side. Family business, if street gossip can be believed."

Peyton believed it. He just hoped that Geraldo wasn't listening on the same street corners as his nephew.

"The de Santos . . ." Geraldo hesitated. "Well, people say they have many interests, few of them legal. A cousin of Eduardo's in the jewelry district also died last night. Rumor says that he took too much of the money he'd been laundering for the drug lords. They left their mark on his body."

"How?"

"Colombian necktie." Geraldo sighed. "Mother of God, they're brutal men."

"What about Eduardo?"

"Dead, as I told you."

"But was he in with the Colombians too?"

"We don't know. His throat wasn't cut, if that's what you mean. He was tortured, then strangled."

Peyton grunted. "Damn it. I've been training him for years. How did it happen?"

"We don't know that either. All we know is that his body was in the cutting room when the janitor came by earlier. I'm on my way now to meet with the insurance agent and assess how much was stolen."

"Stolen." Peyton's voice was flat.

Sharon's eyes narrowed but she didn't move or say a word. If Peyton wanted her to know, he'd tell her. If she wanted to know and he wasn't talking, she'd find out in bed. It was a simple arrangement for both of them. That was why it worked.

"I'll take the next plane out to L.A.," Peyton said. He was thinking hard and not liking any of the conclusions he came up with. The only good news was that none of the off-the-books gems were on the Hall headquarters cutting floor right now.

"No, no, stay there," Geraldo said quickly. "Your mother wishes you to take care of business in Scottsdale. There's nothing for you to do here and much to do there. You know how important it is to get more rubies at the right price for our Christmas promotions."

Peyton thought about arguing, but didn't. He'd never won an argument with his mother; no reason to think today would be his lucky day. "Tell me if you learn anything more. I still can't believe Eduardo is dead."

"Yes, it's difficult," Geraldo said. "But greed brings all men to death."

"All men get there anyway," Peyton said. "Might as well get there rich."

Geraldo laughed in spite of his sister's frown. There were some things only men understood.

"Call after you and the insurance agent go through the building," Peyton said. "Give my love to Mother."

He hung up and stared for a moment at the phone.

"Bad news?" Sharon asked, taking the last bite of waffle.

"My head cutter was murdered last night."

Sharon's fork hit the plate with a clatter. "Like Purcell?"

"I don't know. I hope not. There was some valuable stuff in the cutting safe."

"Did he have the combination?"

"Yeah." Peyton shrugged. "I got tired of being there at six-thirty every morning to open the damn thing."

Sharon hid a smile. Peyton hated to get up early. She didn't love it much herself, but she didn't fight it the way he did.

"What was that about Colombians?" she asked. "Was it a courier kind of hit?"

Peyton added more coffee to his cup, dumped in some cream and sugar, and started to pace. "Eduardo's cousin was found with a Colombian necktie. Before that he was rumored to be laundering drug money through the Hill Street gold market."

"Must have pissed someone off."

"Yeah. I'm just wondering who."

She shrugged. "Why do you care? You don't deal with the Colombians, do you?"

"Just want to make sure that no one is trying to muscle in on the business," Peyton said, sidestepping her question. "The way L.A. is today, you have enough ethnic gangs around to make nineteenth-century New York's problems look like squabbles on a playground."

Sharon shrugged. "I think of it as job security."

"I think of it as a pain in the ass."

She pushed away the rolling room service table and patted the bed next to her. "Come tell me all about it."

"I thought you said you had some work to do for your father."

"It will wait."

He glanced at her computer on the bedside table. Before breakfast had come, she'd been following some interesting threads on various couriers. He hadn't planned on hitting anything so soon, but after Eduardo's death in the cutting room, he'd have some ground to make up.

He kissed Sharon with lips that tasted of coffee. "I'll take you up on it tonight. Go ahead and work now. I've got some things of my own to do."

Sharon pulled her computer into her lap, settled against the headboard, and called up a file. The mattress gave in heavily as Peyton settled next to her, his own computer in his lap. Soon she was immersed in her work, trying to connect courier thefts with the information the FBI had. She knew how much her father wanted to break the case before the Bureau did. And she wanted to be the one who gave him facts every step of the way.

From time to time Peyton glanced at her computer screen. If she noticed and looked at him, he just smiled at her, kissed her, and went back to his own computer without a word.

The companionable silence was broken only by the click of keys.

Chapter 61

Scottsdale
Sunday
1:10 P.M.

Kate looked at the black motor coach with its blanked-out windows and grimaced. "Why do I feel like I'm about to be thrown in irons and grilled like a cheese sandwich?"

Sam smiled faintly. "Not you. Me."

"What for?"

"Oh, they'll think of something."

The door opened before Sam could reach for it. Doug stuck his head out. "Took you long enough."

"I wanted a doctor to look at Kate's cheek."

Doug glanced at the thin line across Kate's cheekbone. "Not deep enough for stitches. Already scabbed over. Clean. Looks good to me."

"You sound just like the doctor," Kate said, "but if you try to give me any more shots, I'll go for your throat."

Doug's smile flickered, then settled. "Sam said you were a tiger."

Her smile turned upside down. "Was that before or after I threw up?"

Sam wanted to gather her in a comforting hug, but he couldn't. Not in front of the boss. "You didn't throw up."

"I wanted to."

"So did I."

She gave him a look of disbelief.

"What?" Sam said. "Do you think I shoot men on a weekly basis?"

"I—I didn't think." She looked at him and saw the new lines around his eyes, the new shadows, the pallor beneath the strength. *Why did I assume it wouldn't reach him the way it reached me? Because he's an FBI agent?* She wanted to touch him, comfort him, tell him she understood and it made him all the more a man to her. She kept her hands and thoughts to herself. Doug might be a friendly boss, but he was still Sam's boss. "I'm sorry," she said to Sam.

"Don't be," Doug said, gesturing Kate inside. "Jack Kirby was a miserable piece of shit."

"Then you have an ID?" Sam asked, following Kate up the steps.

"Oh, yeah. Kennedy will fill you in."

"Don't try to tell me the mutt was Ecuadorian," Sam said under his breath.

"Nope," Doug said with faint malice. "Pure d American, born and raised in southern California and educated by the U.S. Army, and from there to the DEA. Spent a lot of time undercover."

"Army? Was he a Ranger?" Sam asked.

Doug paused in the act of reaching for Kennedy's door, which was partway open.

The door opened fully. Sizemore stood there looking impatient and curious at the same time. Obviously, he'd been listening.

"Why do you think Kirby was a Ranger?" Sizemore asked Sam, closing the door after everyone was in the room.

Sam gestured Kate in and looked at Kennedy, who nodded curtly.

"Answer him," Kennedy said.

Same old shit, Sam thought. *Sizemore and Kennedy and to hell with the rest of us.*

Sam looked at Sizemore and wondered, really wondered, if he was dirty. Or if Kennedy was. Much as the idea appealed to him on a purely personal level, on a professional one it had no appeal at all.

"Kirby fought like he'd been trained," Sam said evenly, "and I don't mean the usual smash and slash method they teach army grunts. He was unexpected. Quick. I was damn lucky to take him down."

Kennedy grunted. "You always had high marks in shooting and unarmed combat, as well as in case clearances. It added up to just enough to keep your head above water with the Bureau."

Why do you think I did it? Sam asked silently. *You think I got off on punishing myself at the firing range and gym?*

"Anyway, the mutt's ex-Ranger," Kennedy said. "Fingerprints just came back. Army, then DEA. Retired with pension and two ex-wives to support. He ran with another ex–Special Forces type, one John White. A SEAL. White is a sweet piece of business. Barely got an honorable discharge."

"So he was a U.S. citizen?" Sam asked.

"Yeah. At first we thought he was South American with an alias, but it didn't come down that way. Maybe some of his pals. We're checking it."

"What did he do to get bounced out of the military?" Sam asked.

"Some really expensive special-ops equipment went missing one night," Doug said. "White was the only one who could have taken it. But considering his past good service to the country, yada yada yada."

"They cut him loose," Kennedy said. "He left the country and worked around the world. South America, mainly."

"Mercenary," Sam said.

Kennedy shrugged. "Fancy name for a thug with an automatic rifle."

"Okay, so Kirby was American, ex–DEA, with two ex-wives to support and he hung with former special-ops men," Sam said. "Anything else?"

"We're checking into that right now," Sizemore said.

"Does he have a record?" Sam asked Kennedy, ignoring Sizemore.

"Kirby is clean. White has been smacked for speeding, drunk and disorderly, beating on his girlfriends, that sort of thing," Doug said when Kennedy just glared at Sam. "Clean for last six years, which is interesting, because his only job is about one step above burger flipper, yet our preliminary investigations indicate he spent money on cocaine and women."

Kate looked from face to face. Even without Sam's terse explanations in the past, she would have known that Kennedy didn't like Sam, and Sizemore positively despised Sam, and Doug was trying to oil the troubled waters.

"Kirby and White lived in L.A.?" Sam asked Doug.

"Santa Ana."

"Close enough," Sam said. "Was either of them ever hired by or connected in any way to Sizemore Security Consulting, Mandel Inc. or—"

"What the hell are you suggesting?" Sizemore snarled, shoving his face into Sam's.

"I'm *saying* that Kirby was hired for a hit on Kate by someone who has a stake in keeping this investigation swimming around in the toilet until the department flushes it—and us." Sam's voice was calm, but his whole body radiated a desire to pick Sizemore up and throw him through the closed door. "Someone, by the way, who's in a position to know every fucking thing the Bureau knows as soon as the Bureau knows it."

Sizemore's face turned red and his hands fisted. "Are you accusing me?"

"Should I?" Sam asked.

Doug stepped between them. "Nobody is accusing anyone. Right?"

Sam met Doug's eyes for a long minute, then nodded. "There are several people and/or organizations that might be dirty," Sam said. "Sizemore's company is just one of the pack."

"Why, you son of a bitch!" Sizemore yelled, reaching for Sam around Doug's sturdy body.

Sam shook off Sizemore's grip with a swift motion of his hands that could just as easily have broken the other man's wrists.

"Back off," Kennedy said in the kind of voice that reminded everyone the SSA had once been in the Marines. *"Both of you."*

The words penetrated Sizemore's anger. He visibly reined in his temper.

Sam hadn't lost his temper, but he'd really been looking forward to doing it all over Sizemore.

"Ted," Kennedy said. "I need a few minutes, okay? I'll call you."

Sizemore shot a deadly look at Sam and Kate, then turned around and left the small room. The motor coach's floor vibrated from the weight of his angry steps.

Without a word Kennedy opened his belly drawer, reached in back, and pulled out a pack of cigarettes. Doug had a lighter ready. Still saying nothing, Kennedy took a deep drag, and another. Then he pinned Sam with a steel-gray glance.

"I assume you have proof backing up your accusations," Kennedy said with deceptive mildness.

"Courtroom proof?" Sam asked. "No."

Kennedy's lips flattened. "It's too late to be coy. You better have something besides a big mouth."

Kate reached into the oversized purse she'd brought with her. She took out a sheaf of papers and put it on his desk.

The SSA glanced down, saw the lines and handwriting, and frowned. "What's this?"

"Special Agent Groves and I spent a lot of time trying to figure out who knew what and when," Kate said carefully. "This is the result. It suggests some new avenues of investigation."

"Give me the bottom line," Kennedy said impatiently. "And it better be good, Groves, or you're finished."

Sam reached into his pocket, pulled out a sealed, transparent evidence holder, and put it on Kennedy's desk.

Emerald-cut blue sapphire, as big as a man's toenail, the gem inside the plastic drew light into its depths and returned it as blue fire.

Kennedy looked from the gem to Sam. "Is this what I think it is?"

"Yes."

"Judas Priest."

Kennedy picked up the papers and began to read.

Chapter 62

Scottsdale
Sunday
1:30 P.M.

Sizemore stalked into his hotel suite, only to find that Peyton was there with Sharon.

"I need some time with my office manager," Sizemore said through his teeth.

Peyton knew an invitation to leave when it was shoved in his face. "Dinner at eight?" he said to Sharon.

"She'll be busy," Sizemore said.

Sharon started to argue, then saw the pallor beneath her father's fading flush of anger.

"She," Sharon said coolly, "doesn't know what she'll be doing at eight." She stood, kissed Peyton, and said softly, "I'll call you as soon as I know what's going on."

He shrugged and left without a word.

"All right," Sharon said as soon as the door closed. "This better be more than the usual 'Why are you hanging with that shitheel?' harangue."

Sizemore grabbed a beer, opened it, and drank most of it in three long swallows. He wiped his mouth and said, "Groves is trying to frame me for the courier deaths."

Sharon's eyes widened. Her skin went as pale as her father's. Cold sweat gathered on her spine. "What? *What?* He's crazy! What's his so-called evidence?"

"I don't know. Kennedy kicked me out of the office before they got down to it."

Slowly, she sank back down onto the couch. "There must be something then. Groves is a wild card, but he's not stupid."

A beer bottle slammed into a wastebasket. Sizemore grabbed another brew out of the ice and opened the top with a savage jerk of his hand. "There's something."

"What?"

"I know Jack Kirby."

"Kirby, Kirby . . ." She frowned and drummed her fingers against her leg. "Do I know him?"

"He was on the task force with me in Florida when I took down the South Americans. I don't think Groves knows it. Yet. So was John 'Tex' White. He'd been with the army working on taking down the Colombian gangs."

"So what? That was a long time ago."

Sizemore looked bitter at the dismissal of his greatest moment, but didn't argue the point with her. "Yeah, well Kirby is a PI and he's working a case here and I had a drink with him a few days ago. Someone must have seen us together. Kirby and White still hang together, I guess."

"Who cares?" she said impatiently. "You have drinks with a lot of people."

"None of those people got shot to pieces by Sam Groves while trying to kill Kate Chandler."

Sharon took a breath, shook her head, and took another. She felt like the top of her head was coming off. "Wait. Back up. I'm missing something." At least, she really hoped she was. "When did all this happen?"

"Kennedy just kicked me out of his office."

"No. The killing. Or the attempted killing. Or whatever." She stood up and started to pace. "What a cluster."

Sizemore didn't argue. He just drank long and deep, telling himself that he was just thirsty, that's all. It wasn't that his mouth was dry with fear. It couldn't be that. He had nothing to be afraid of.

How could this happen?

"Talk to me," she demanded, turning to face him. "And put a cork in the beer. If word of this gets out, Sizemore Security Consulting is ruined."

He ignored her until he finished the second beer. Then he reached for a third.

With startling quickness, Sharon stepped between her father and the vat of icy beer. "No."

He started to shove her aside, only to find that she was stronger than she looked.

"It's my life too," she said angrily. "Tell me what's going on and then you can drink beer until you're too drunk to care about anything but the next beer."

Sizemore started to explode, then decided she was right. The beer could wait.

"This is much too important to screw up with a father-daughter shouting match," she said.

He shrugged. He hated when she was right, which was a hell of a lot more often than he gave her credit for.

"What do you want to know?" he muttered.

"This Kirby dude. Where is he now?"

"The morgue."

She let out a long breath. "Well, that's going to make it hard to question him."

Sizemore gave a laugh that was more like a grunt. "Maybe that's the whole idea. Dead man, no witnesses but Groves and the CI he's shagging. Easy enough to point the finger at someone else."

"Kennedy has known you too long to buy their bull."

"I hope so." Sizemore looked at his watch. "I expected him to call by now to apologize."

She frowned and narrowed her eyes at something only she could see. "So you have a vague connection to Kirby and Kirby is dead. What else could Groves use against you?"

"There's a leak somewhere on the crime strike force. Groves wants to pin it on me."

"How?"

"How?" he repeated sarcastically. "Shit, use your head for something besides blowing Peyton. I run a security operation. I have access to a lot of courier information."

"So do other people. The CI's father, for instance. Is Groves barking up that tree?"

"I don't know."

"What about the couriers themselves?"

"You think they set themselves up to be killed?" Sizemore asked in rising tones.

"Maybe they just expected to get part of the take and they got killed instead. Besides, most of the couriers never even know anything has happened until they check the trunk. They report the theft and walk away perfectly healthy. Only the insurance companies cry."

Sizemore frowned. "And we look like dickheads."

"Maybe Mandel Inc. was working with dirty couriers," Sharon continued. "Maybe the son found out and something went wrong."

"You think the man killed his own son?"

"Read the Bible. Hell, read the newspapers. It happens all the time. Maybe no one meant for anyone to get hurt," she said, waving her hand impatiently. "Maybe that's just the way it turned out. Shit happens."

Sizemore pulled at his lower lip with his thumb and forefinger. "I like it. Can we prove it?"

"I don't know." She went and sat by her computer again. "But if we put our minds to it, we might be able to inflate the theory enough to keep us afloat."

Chapter 63

Glendale
Sunday
5:30 P.M.

"When do you think he'll call?" Kate asked.

Sam shifted, lifting her to a more comfortable position on top of him. They'd flipped a coin for top or bottom and he'd lost. Not that he was complaining. The floor wasn't uncomfortable, exactly. It was just that the bed was a lot more accommodating.

Or had been. Right now the bedroom smelled like industrial strength cleaners. Kate wouldn't even look at it.

He didn't blame her.

Besides, the living room floor had a lot to recommend it. Convenience, for starters. Oh, yeah. It was convenient. He smiled at the memory. He liked having her come apart in his hands, his arms, both of them too hungry to make it more than three steps inside the front door to shut off the alarm. He could get used to that kind of heat and loving.

Who are you trying to fool? You're already used to it. What are you going to do when this is all over? Ask her to make ice cubes in Fargo with you? Because that's where you'll be until hell freezes solid or your twenty years are up, whichever comes first.

But until they broke the case, he had Kate, all warm and soft, covering him like a dream.

"Sam?"

"Mmm?" he asked, running his thumb down her spine to the alluring shadow between her buttocks.

She moved her hips and both of them took a swift breath.

"Kennedy," she said breathlessly. "When will he call?"

"I don't know."

"Do you think he'll believe the connections we made?"

"He doesn't have much choice. But just in case . . ." Reluctantly, Sam lifted Kate and slid out from under.

"What?"

He dropped her slacks on top of her and zipped up his own. "Back to work."

"Slave driver."

"You weren't complaining earlier."

She smiled and slanted him the kind of glance that told him she was remembering the second time, when she'd begged him to finish and he'd just kept on moving slow and easy and deep until she came so hard she almost blacked out.

He grinned.

"You look real smug," she said, pulling on her thong.

"All your fault."

"Yeah?"

He slid a fingertip down from her belly button to the crease where her right leg joined her body, then lower, lower, skimming lightly, like a tongue tasting. "Yeah."

She blew her hair out of her face. "Keep that up and it will be round three."

"You have an optimistic view of my ability."

She grinned and nipped lightly on his chin. "All your fault," she said, repeating his words as she stepped into her jeans. "In fact—"

Sam's cell phone rang. Since he'd never made it all the way out of his pants, everything was still within reach. He pulled the cell phone off his belt and looked at the code. "Mecklin."

"Is that some kind of exotic curse?" she asked.

"No. It's an agent in Florida."

Kate measured Sam's expression. Playtime over. Back to work for both of them. "Okay, I'll make some sandwiches while you talk. I wouldn't want your, uh, ability to flag for lack of food."

He was smiling as he answered the call. The smile didn't last past Mecklin's first words.

"Somebody is closing down the pipeline."

"Which one?" Sam asked.

"The sapphire one—Florida to L.A."

The last of Sam's sexy good humor vanished. "Who? Where?"

"Remember the de Santos cousins I told you about in L.A.?"

"Eduardo and José, the cutter and the launderer?"

"Bingo. They were murdered last night."

"Any suspects?" Sam asked.

"In José's case, given the necktie, they're looking for a Colombian connection."

"Any mutt with a knife can do a necktie."

"Yeah," Mecklin agreed. "Gotta love copycats."

"What about Eduardo?"

"Torture and strangulation."

Sam grunted. "Anything at the crime scenes?"

"Blood and dead bodies."

"How are the cops treating it?"

Mecklin laughed without humor. "Like two cold cases in the making. Everyone is talking to the usual suspects, knocking on nearby doors, filing reports, and all the rest of the brain-dead routine. Like I said—the cops know a case that's headed for the cold files. They'll save their energy for something they have a chance of solving."

Sam couldn't blame the locals. There were lots of murders in L.A. When someone with known gang connections died, not a whole lot of sweat or tears got used up finding out who and when and why.

"Okay, they got the L.A. end of the pipeline," Sam said. "Was Hall Jewelry robbed?"

"The cutting room was busted up some, the safe was opened. Nothing left but a couple of stones that got spilled on the way out."

"What kind of stones?"

"How the hell would I—wait."

Sam heard the other agent tapping at a computer keyboard.

"Red," Mecklin said after a minute.

"Red?"

"Stones. The stuff that was dropped on the floor was red. That's all that the cops said. If you need more information, wait for the insurance report."

"No thanks. I was hoping for blue stones. Wonder if the murderer was too."

"What?" Mecklin asked.

"Nothing. Just thinking aloud. What about Seguro Jimenez, the Florida end of the pipeline? Is he okay?"

"According to his wife, he's visiting family in Ecuador."

"You believe her?"

"I believe that the grapevine got to Seguro before I did," Mecklin said. "I believe he already knew about the de Santos murders. Either he had a part in them, was afraid he was next, or he *was* next and we haven't found the body. Any way it comes down, he's gone somewhere that we can't get to him."

"End of pipeline."

"Looks that way. Sorry I don't have better news."

"I'll take what I can get. Keep on Seguro. If you hear he's back in town—"

"I'll be on him like a streetwalker wanting out of the rain," Mecklin cut in.

"Thanks."

Sam punched the end button, saw the battery was low, and went to the suitcase he'd brought to Kate's house. By the time he'd set up the charger and plugged it in, then unloaded his files and computer onto various worktables, Kate appeared in the door of the workroom. She was carrying a tray of sandwiches and fruit. A big pitcher of iced tea unbalanced the tray.

"I'll take that," Sam said, lifting the pitcher.

"Thanks. That should keep us going until the coffee is ready."

He looked at the half gallon of tea. It had been hot outside, but not that hot. "Thirsty?"

"Sure am. Gee, I wonder why."

He smiled slowly. "Same here."

"You wonder why?"

"I know why I'm thirsty. Want me to tell you?"

Her lips turned up in a very female smile. "Sure, but only if you're not going to slip into cop mode at the wrong moment."

"Is there a right moment?"

"Last night was a good one. It saved our butts." She handed him a thick sandwich made from the leftovers of last night's chicken. For the first time in hours, looking at food didn't make her stomach flip. "Did, uh, Meckler—"

"Mecklin," Sam said around a big bite.

"Mecklin have anything interesting to say?"

"Two men died in L.A. last night."

"And this was unusual how?"

"They were the two men most likely to have handled the big sapphire on its way to Purcell."

Her hand hesitated before it reached a sandwich. "How so?"

"One laundered Colombian money through the gold market in L.A. The other was a cutter in L.A. Both were de Santos, cousins of a cousin of a friend of a cousin to Seguro in Florida, the man who insists he didn't buy the big blue gem from the her/him act."

Kate blinked, almost smiled, and said, "I want a big kiss."

"Why?"

"I understood that."

A corner of Sam's mouth turned up. "I'll owe it to you. Every time I get my hands on you, we end up on the floor."

"Or against a wall."

He grinned and kept taking big, efficient bites of food.

"Were any more sapphires found?" Kate asked as she took a cautious nibble of sandwich.

"No."

"Anything to connect the deaths with Purcell?"

"Does a necktie and torture count?" He saw the look on her face and kicked himself. "Sorry, darling. I keep forgetting you aren't a cop. You sure handled yourself like one last night."

"Pure, undiluted practice. I was terrified."

"Why do you think repetition and drills are such a big part of any cop's or soldier's training?"

"I was still screaming in my mind," she said.

"You think I wasn't?"

"I don't know why that makes me feel better, but it does. Even if it isn't quite true." Kate blew out a long breath and returned to her sandwich.

Sam had already finished his and was looking hopefully at the tray.

"Go ahead," she said. "I'll be lucky to eat this."

He scooped up the last sandwich and went to the worktable where he'd spread out his files.

"Why hasn't Kennedy called?" Kate asked.

"You mean to grovel?"

"Yes."

"Don't hold your breath on that. He's probably checking facts and then checking them again while he looks for other explanations. He sure as hell isn't going to be eager to pull the trigger on his old buddy Sizemore."

"Neither are you."

Sam didn't argue. "Sizemore is a prick, but that's not a good enough reason to ruin his reputation. The evidence we have is largely circumstantial. And . . ." After a moment, he shrugged.

"And what?"

"And I'd like a backup position if Kennedy doesn't go for our interpretation of the facts."

"What backup position?"

"Good question." He looked at the files and tablets and sticky notes. "Let's hope we find an answer."

Chapter 64

Scottsdale
Sunday
8:10 P.M.

Kennedy's expression was grim. His office was wearing a shroud of cigarette smoke. The ashtray looked like a funeral pyre.

"It'll never stand up in court," he said the instant Sam and Kate walked in.

Sam looked at Doug.

Doug looked like he had a toothache.

"What's the problem?" Sam asked, turning back to Kennedy.

"Circumstantial," the SSA said succinctly. "All of it. No hard evidence. Any defense lawyer could shove it up our ass."

"If it was only one circumstance or two or three, sure," Sam said. "But no one else had the information that Sizemore did. Not us, not—"

"What about Mandel Inc.?" Doug asked. "They had it."

Sam's fingers pressed against Kate's wrist, warning her to be quiet.

"Doesn't fly," Sam said.

"Why not?" Kennedy demanded. "They sure as hell knew their son was carrying the goods their daughter cut."

"You're out of your bureaucratic mind!" Kate said, ignoring Sam's silent warning. "Dad wouldn't kill his own son!"

"Nobody's saying he meant to," Kennedy said calmly. "Ninety-nine percent of courier heists don't even result in a hangnail to the courier, much less death. Something just went wrong."

"Like what?" she asked sarcastically. "Lee tripped and broke his neck and a flock of vultures carried him off to the mangrove swamp for a snack?"

"Look, Ms. Chandler," Kennedy said. "I know how hard this is on you."

"You don't have the faintest idea. Last night someone tried to kill us and I ended up with blood and bone and—*stuff*—all over the—" She took a sawing breath. "Never mind. That's not important. The point is that my father wouldn't kill my brother."

"Admirable sentiment, and quite expected," Kennedy said. "But I could think of several scenarios in which your brother's death would be required. Regrettable, I'm sure, but still necessary."

"Name them," she said through pale, tight lips.

Kennedy looked at Doug.

Doug looked right back at him.

"If the heist was supposed to be clean and quiet," Sam said evenly, not wanting Doug to get in any more trouble than he already was, "and Lee happened onto the scene and recognized his father or some other Mandel employee, then Lee had to die, right? But since it's basically a family business, the father is the most likely suspect."

Kate wanted to object. The pressure of Sam's fingers around her wrist made her think better of it. That and the clear sense that he was a breath away from losing his temper and going right over the desk after Kennedy.

"Very good," Kennedy said sardonically. "I guess you haven't lost your perspective after all."

Sam ignored him. "Or Lee could have been in on it from the start, and his father found out, they argued, and Lee ended up dead."

Kennedy nodded.

"Or Lee could have been innocent and his father wasn't," Sam continued. "Argument, same result."

Again, Kennedy nodded. He reached for another cigarette, lit it, and began to look relaxed for the first time.

Doug didn't. He just kept looking at Sam as though he expected the other man to pull his weapon and start shooting.

"The only problem with those scenarios," Sam continued in his dangerously neutral tone, "is that they assume a single death unrelated to any other courier heist, which we know isn't the case."

Kennedy threw the lighter on his desk. "What are you talking about? Of course the heists are connected. Even if the MOs are mixed—hell, I'll give you your goddamn Teflon gang—there's not one single reason to assume the Florida hit was a one-off."

"I agree," Sam said. "Which leads us to the second problem."

Doug braced himself.

Kennedy picked up a letter opener and tested its edge. Not sharp enough. Not nearly as sharp as Sam Fucking Groves. "I'm listening," Kennedy said, putting down the tool.

"The outstanding features of the courier heists I've concentrated on were technical skill, inside information, and the kind of training usually associated with special law-enforcement and/or military teams. That's what makes them Teflon. They're smarter and a lot better trained than your average mutt. Or their boss is. Kirby was smart, but I don't think he was the boss. He didn't have a way to get the inside information unless someone gave it to him. Someone who was already inside."

Kennedy grunted.

"Mandel Inc. certainly has the technical skill to make remote keys," Sam continued, "and in some but not all cases, the inside information, but not one Mandel employee has ever had law-enforcement or military special-ops training. I can guarantee that the intruder last night did. Which brings up the question, How did Mandel get into the ex–special ops community? Those boys are as clannish as they come."

Kennedy took a long pull on his cigarette and didn't argue. There was no point.

Yet.

"Kirby had the kind of training that would get him into that community," Sam said. "Right?"

"Sizemore didn't," Kennedy said flatly. "He went into the Bureau right out of university. You're wasting my time."

Sam kept talking. "Kirby, and the pal he hung with, White, were part of Sizemore's crime task force, the one that took down the South Americans."

Kennedy's eyes narrowed. "So what?" He stubbed out his cigarette. "So were a lot of men."

"The Bureau is tracing them now," Sam said. "We came up with one other guy—Stan Fortune—who's living in L.A. near Kirby. He was army, special ops, ten years after Kirby. Discharged because of injury. Bitter about it. Joined the DEA, went undercover in Florida, and made people nervous. They gave him a desk job. He quit."

"It happens," Kennedy said. He fiddled with another cigarette but didn't light it.

"He was one of Sizemore's informants on the famous task force. Kirby found him for that job."

Kennedy grimaced. He wanted to get up and leave, but he couldn't. *Damn it, Ted. What the hell happened?*

There was no answer but the sound of Sam's voice telling everyone what Kennedy didn't want to know.

"So far, every unhappy loner we've traced from the good old crime task force leads back to Kirby," Sam said relentlessly, "who worked with Sizemore, who has information of the kind that would be valuable to mutts wanting to knock over couriers."

"Ted didn't know about the McCloud sapphires," Kennedy said flatly. "He had no way of knowing. It was a Mandel Inc. job all the way—father, daughter, brother."

"Lee's lover was Norm Gallagher, whose brother works for Sizemore's company in the home office," Kate said. "Sizemore easily could have known."

Kennedy's fingers gripped the lighter so hard his knuckles went white. With an impatient snap, he lit up the cigarette and sucked hard. "Circumstantial."

"It's one more straw—the one that broke the camel's back," Sam said. "I'm asking for a warrant to go through Sizemore's computers and a forensic accountant for the company books. Do I have to go over you?"

Kennedy closed his eyes. When he opened them, he hit the intercom switch on the phone and said without inflection, "Send him in."

A moment later the door opened and Ted Sizemore stepped into the office. One look at his face told Sam that the other man had overheard every word that was said in Kennedy's office. But it wasn't anger Sam saw on Sizemore's face, it was confusion.

And fear.

Sizemore went straight to Kennedy. "I swear I didn't do it. You have to believe me." Tears leaked from his eyes. *"I swear it!* Hook me up to a machine, you'll see. I'm innocent! Groves is framing me!"

"If it isn't you, who is it?" Sam said. "Someone at your firm?"

"I—I—no," Sizemore said. "It can't be."

"Why?" Kate asked. "You were ready to accuse my whole family." Sizemore just shook his head.

"Ted," Kennedy said quietly, "at this point it looks like your firm is the only source of information that accounts for the high-tech and nonviolent—until Mandel—courier heists. Help me out on this."

"I can't," Sizemore whispered. "I don't understand—" His voice broke. "Any of this. I just don't. Give me a lie test. I swear—" Sizemore's voice broke. He didn't try to say anything again. He just shook his head.

"Doug will take care of the paperwork you need for warrants and such," Kennedy said to Sam. "It will go through highest priority. Satisfied?"

Sam looked at Sizemore. All swagger was gone. There was nothing left but an old man with tears on his face.

Not very satisfying at all.

"Put some more men on White," Sam said. "Maybe he can tell us something useful. And if Sizemore doesn't object, I'd like to see the background checks and personnel files of everyone in his company with access to sensitive information."

Sizemore said, "Go ahead. I'd help you, but you don't trust me."

"In my shoes, would you?"

Sizemore flinched. "No. God help me, no." He grabbed a piece of paper from Kennedy's desk and scrawled a string of numbers and letters. "This is my entry code to the company computer. You can access it from your own laptop." Sizemore handed the sheet over and said bitterly, "Have fun."

Chapter 65

Glendale
Sunday
11:40 P.M.

"Hey," Kate said, coming up behind Sam as he hunched over his computer, clicking through Sizemore Security Consulting personnel files. She sank her thumbs into the knotted muscles of his shoulders and leaned in, trying to loosen him up. "You can't do it all at once."

"I'm missing something. I have to be."

"Why?"

He let out a long sigh and spun the office chair around so quickly that they bumped knees.

"You haven't said a word about Sizemore since we left Kennedy's office," Sam pointed out. "What's wrong?"

She looked at Sam's haunted blue eyes and heavy beard shadow, the weapon harness worn over a wilted T-shirt, jeans tight over his strong thighs. She wondered what would happen after the case was closed, how much she would miss the man who had become such an important part of her personal landscape.

"Why do you think I haven't said anything?" she countered.

"Same reason I think I'm missing something. Neither of us feels as good as we thought we would about Sizemore taking the fall."

Slowly, she nodded. "You know him better than I do. If he was guilty, wouldn't he be more likely to bluster and shout?"

"Instead of crying?"

"Yes."

Sam stood and prowled the workroom barefoot. Light gleamed and slid over the weapon harness with each stride. He was like an animal pacing the walls of a cage.

Her dark eyes followed him, wanting to help, to hold.

"That surprised me," he admitted finally. "I was expecting fists and boots and curses. But he looked . . ." Sam shook his head, not knowing how to say it.

"Bewildered," Kate said.

"Yeah." Sam swiped a hand through his short hair, leaving a wake of dark spikes. "Jesus. What if I'm wrong? I don't want to ruin the man's life just because he's a prick."

"If we're wrong, the jury will let him go."

Sam made a sound that was too harsh to be laughter. He spun around and looked at the woman who filled out her blue blouse and jeans the way a woman should. Her dark eyes were serious, her hair an unruly cloud around her intent face. The intelligence and emotion in her made him want to pull her close and hold on until everything else went away.

But everything wouldn't go away. It never did.

"Do you really believe that good-guys-always-win shit?" he asked.

"No. But I'd like to."

He smiled thinly. "So would I, but I can't, so I settle for not being one of the bad guys. And that's how I'm feeling now, like a bad guy."

"What have you come up with so far?" she asked, gesturing toward the computer.

"Sizemore Security isn't doing real well. The whole family had to take a salary hit this year."

"All the more reason for him to do something crooked."

"Yeah." Sam frowned.

"Drop the other shoe."

"I'm no forensic accountant."

"I've noticed. Yum."

He gave her a surprised look, saw the humor and female approval in her smile, and couldn't help grinning at her. Then he looked back down at the computer screen.

"Nothing I see here is out of line for Sizemore's income from salary and retirement," he said. "If anything, he's pretty modest about what he spends."

"What about Jason?"

"You think he'd kill his brother's lover?" Sam asked.

Kate closed her eyes briefly. "I don't think anyone set out to kill Lee. I think it just, well, happened."

"Murder two instead of murder one?"

"Whatever. If I'm right, then personal motives are irrelevant. Other than greed, of course, or whatever it is that drives a crook."

"All kinds of things do," Sam said, "but I get your point. Motive in this case isn't as important as means and opportunity."

"Right. Jase could have given the information to someone accidentally or intentionally. If it was an accident, well, that's not much help. If it was intentional, then the money has to come to him somehow. Same for anybody else in the company."

"That's just it," Sam said. "If it came in through the company books, I can't find it."

"What about their private accounts?"

"Same old same old. Sonny, Sharon, and Sizemore all live well within their means. Sonny never went into the military. Sharon didn't have any special-ops contacts."

"What if someone else had access to the company computer code so they could see 'secure' information?"

"The two most likely—Jason and Ms. Tibble of accounting— aren't in hock and don't have expensive tastes. They don't have any obvious connection to the ex-military old-boy club either."

"Unlike Kirby," Kate said, flipping through a file, "who had four bookies and two ex-wives. Or like White who bought more cocaine than he earned changing tires for a repair shop. Kirby and White had plenty of ex-military contacts but didn't have the connections to get courier information on their own. They could have just followed guys coming out of jewelry stores, I suppose."

"That's what the South American gangs do," Sam said, "which leads to a grab bag of items. Everything from watches to wedding bands. But the Teflon gang only does the high-end, anonymous stuff, or stuff that can be made anonymous by reworking. They have an inside track to the trade. So if it's not Sizemore, who is it?" Sam smacked his hand down next to the computer in frustration. "I'm missing something."

"Then so am I, unless the professional accountants can get more out of this than we have."

"We're still waiting for warrants on Sonny, Sharon, Jason, and Ms. Tibble's private accounts. Those forensic accountants are good. If it's there, they'll find it."

"What about Sizemore?" Kate asked.

"He waived his rights. He's working with the Bureau accountant."

"Which means he isn't guilty or he's real sure he's buried the evidence where no one can get to it."

"That takes the kind of arrogance I didn't see in him earlier."

"Yeah." Kate rubbed her eyes, trying to remove the picture of a shattered, weeping Sizemore. It didn't work, any more than rubbing her eyes wiped out the memories of last night's blood and fear. "Even though you fixed the alarms around here, and everything's been cleaned up, I'm not real eager to go back into my bedroom and try to sleep. Knowing how fast Kirby got in . . ." She shrugged. "It just doesn't make me feel sleepy."

"Kirby was a pro. Most mutts aren't nearly that good."

"I suppose that's meant to be comforting. All I have to do is not think about the fact that your Teflon gang is made up of pros who are better than most mutts."

Sam acknowledged that with a wry twist of his mouth. "There

are two agents parked out front, two in the garage, and four more patrolling nearby streets. Even if someone wanted to pull the same trick twice, it won't happen."

"My mind knows that. The rest of me isn't buying it." She put her hands in her pockets and moved restlessly around the workroom. Her jeans made a rubbing noise with each step. "I think I'll make some coffee."

"Now who's the one drinking too much caffeine?"

"You're a good influence," she said, heading for the kitchen.

Sam's cell phone rang. He looked at the number and answered fast.

"Hello, Doug. What do you have?"

"Tex White."

Thank you, God. "Did he lawyer up?"

"Sure did. Then he traded information for taking the death penalty off the table."

"Death penalty? For what?" Sam asked.

"The murder-for-hire of Eduardo Pedro Selva de los Santos."

Sam whistled. "You sure?"

"Peyton Hall is. He made the ID on some of the stuff we found in White's apartment. There were blood traces on some shoes in the closet. Cocaine makes you think you're invincible, which makes you careless."

"Stupid."

"That too. The bloody shoes are when the bust went from possession of cocaine to murder one. White doesn't want the death penalty and we'd already connected him with Kirby, so we clubbed him with the murder-for-hire angle."

"So Kirby was the boss?"

"Looks like it," Doug said. "Funny thing, though. The agents searching Kirby's hotel room in Scottsdale found a digital phone."

"Digital? No chance of eavesdropping then."

"We all should be able to afford digital," Doug said.

"Try convincing the budget office."

"I have. Anyway, the intriguing thing is that Kirby had a record feature on his phone. Like voice mail, only he could activate it by punching the pound key at any time during a conversation."

"Anything of interest recorded?"

"Oh, yeah. Seems like Kirby wasn't always the boss. At least once that we know of, he took orders from someone who used a mechanical distorter."

"Kate's death threat," Sam said instantly.

"Looks like it. Only this time, the weird voice wanted two other people dead in addition to Kate."

"Two? José and Eduardo?"

"Yeah."

"So you're figuring that either White or Kirby was good for Lee Mandel's murder too?" Sam asked.

"Not White. He'd never heard the name. Didn't know McCloud or the missing sapphires, didn't know Kate Chandler, and hadn't been to Florida since they put out a warrant on him for jumping bail on a DUI hearing three years ago."

"Maybe White was lying about that."

"Why bother? He'd already cut his deal with us. Kill two, kill three, kill thirteen, no matter," Doug said. "You only get one life sentence without possibility of parole."

"What about Kirby then? He had the sapphire."

"That's how we're seeing it."

Sam hesitated. "So we're thinking Sizemore was the guy on the distorter?"

"Sizemore or anyone who had access to knowledge stored on his computer."

"And the ability to be accepted by the old-boy ex-military types," Sam pointed out.

"Yeah. Sizemore fits all the requirements. Why aren't you sounding happy about it?"

"Because I'm not."

"Your gut?"

"I guess."

"You've got an interesting gut," Doug said, "or have you already heard from Kennedy?"

"Heard what?"

"Sizemore never lifted the needle on the lie detector. Not once. We go to trial with what we have now and his lawyer will kill us."

Chapter 66

Scottsdale
Sunday
11:45 P.M.

"You sure you can't spend the night?" Peyton asked Sharon as they stood outside his hotel room door. "You know I don't mind if you work."

"That's why we've lasted so long," she said, smiling and shifting the computer case to her other hand. "You let me be me." Her smile faded and the nerves she'd been trying to hide showed in the line of her mouth. "Not tonight. Dad needs me."

"What's going on, honey? You can tell me."

"No, he'd never forgive me."

Peyton smiled without humor. "Then the rumors are true."

"What rumors?" she asked sharply.

"That Ted Sizemore got caught with his hand in the jewelry jar."

Sharon looked away and told herself that there was still time, it would be all right, everything would be all right. "Where did you hear that?"

"You should get out more. It's the talk of the trading floor."

She drew a swift breath and shook her head as though he'd slapped her. "There's not one bit of proof!"

"He may be a son of a bitch, but he's still your daddy, is that it?"

She just looked frayed and jumpy as a feral cat.

"Listen," Peyton said urgently. "You don't have to go down with his boat. We can find a way to put your expertise to work. I'll finance you through this mess. Change the name of the company. In a year or two people will forget and you'll be running your own security operation. Hell, you run it now. Your daddy's just the front. We can get through this. Together."

For a long moment she looked at Peyton's earnest face and intent eyes. If she didn't know better, she'd swear he really cared about her, perhaps even loved her. But she knew that at his core, he didn't care about anyone but himself, which meant he was after something. Maybe sex. Maybe something else.

Maybe she'd give it to him.

Maybe she wouldn't.

"I'll think about it," she said tightly. "Thanks."

Peyton kissed her with something very close to relief. "We're a great team. I don't want to lose that."

She slid out of his arms. "I'll call you tomorrow."

He watched her stride down the hallway between rows of framed flower prints and heavy wallpaper. Her shoes didn't make a sound on the thick rug with the hotel's logo woven in gold against a red background.

"Sharon?"

She looked over her shoulder.

"Don't wait too long, honey. I don't want things to change."

She understood what Peyton didn't say—if her father went down, she'd go down with him unless she started damage control very quickly.

And if she went down, her affair with Peyton was over. He'd regret it, but he'd drop her just the same, because hanging on would shadow his reputation, which would cost money. Business first, last, and always.

Men were predictable. Heartbreakingly, humorously, hatefully predictable.

"I won't," she said.

She supposed most women were predictable too.

If there was a god, he or she must be laughing its ass off over all the predictable monkeys running in circles, whining and clutching their gonads.

Sharon wasn't going to be one of them. It was time to cut the losses and change to a new game.

"Peyton?" she said, turning around.

He stopped in the act of closing his hotel room door.

"Breakfast tomorrow?" she asked. "Eight o'clock."

"Sure thing, honey," he said, smiling widely. "Your room or mine?"

"Yours. You get better service than I do."

Chapter 67

Glendale
Monday
7:30 A.M.

Kate woke up stiff and yet content at the same time. She didn't know whose bed she was in, but it was as warm as it was cramped. Then she heard Sam breathing, felt him all around her except for her back, which was pressed hard up against the old couch she kept in the workroom for those times when she was too tired to care about where she slept.

She opened her eyes. The world was a blur with brilliant blue sapphires at the center.

"You awake?" Sam asked.

She blinked. His face was so close to hers she couldn't focus. "Looks like it. How about you?"

"Working on it."

"You're working, period. I can feel the vibes."

"Just thinking," Sam said.

"That's what most of your work is. Thinking. So . . . whatcha thinking?"

"That Peyton Hall and Sharon Sizemore eat dinner together a lot."

Kate tried not to yawn. "Old news. Years old."

"So the affair's over?"

"No. It's just old news. Peyton has a well-earned reputation as a hound. He's married, has a long-term mistress—that's Sharon—has had two- or three-week flings all along the way, and he regularly does the one-night dance with bar girls and dumb secretaries."

"Nice guy," Sam said.

"Your irony light better be on."

He smiled. "It is. So, do you think he and Sharon talk much about business?"

"Probably. After five or six years together, what else—" Abruptly, Kate went silent. "Peyton Hall? You think he's the one?"

"I think we take another look at him. Real close. If we find a solid connection to Kirby or White or anything military, then we have something to go with."

"What about Sizemore?"

"What do you mean?"

"You really don't think he's guilty, do you?"

Sam sighed. "I'd love to nail his arrogant ass to the wall, but not for something he didn't do. Before we arrest him, I have to look at every other possibility. I don't want to ruin someone just because I can't stand being in the same room with him."

"Someone in Sizemore's company has to be passing along information. You think it's Sharon?"

"I don't know. She's been stupid about men before, but leaking information goes way beyond stupid. It's called being an accomplice. Hell, maybe Ms. Tibble did the nasty with Peyton and wants to do it again, so she passes out tidbits."

Kate snickered. "How do we start?"

"I want to take another look at Peyton's bank accounts. Wouldn't hurt to look at Hall Jewelry either."

"Back to hacking, huh?"

"Yeah." He put himself nose-to-nose with her. "Coffee?"

"You asking me to make it?"

"I sure am."

"You'll owe me," she warned.

"I love it when you go all dominatrix with me." He pulled back enough that she could see his grin.

She tried not to laugh, then gave up when he kissed her nose and walked naked to the bathroom. She really was going to miss this early morning intimacy, having something to think about besides work, having someone to laugh with, to touch, to talk with, to. . . .

Does he feel the same way?

With an impatient sound she stood up and went to make coffee. The kitchen floor felt cold under her bare feet. When she bumped into the refrigerator, its smooth chill made her jump back. Being butt naked had some disadvantages.

While the coffee cooked, she went to her bedroom, which was still mostly torn up. Bed moved. Carpet gone—Sam had done that after the cops left. She couldn't bear looking at it. Even with the carpet out, she still wasn't happy. Quickly, she pulled on underwear, grit-stained jeans, and a blue work shirt that had been bleached so often that the only real color left was pale cream. She left the bedroom in a rush, wondering if she would ever be comfortable in that place again.

Sam was sitting at the keyboard with the cell phone tucked between his ear and left shoulder. He'd put on jeans, period. The rest of him was naked and wonderfully tempting. Whatever he did to keep himself in shape showed in the fluid shift and bunch of muscles each time he moved. His fingers raced over the keyboard with more force than necessary to depress the keys.

"Okay, good . . . no, wait," he said into the phone. "Go over that bit again." He listened, typed, nodded, and typed some more. "Got it. Any other shortcuts I should know?" He listened, grunted, and scribbled madly on a pad next to the keyboard, which already had a lot of previous scribbles on it from his other forays into hacking. "Thanks, Jill. If that doesn't do it, I'll call again."

He punched off and smelled the coffee before Kate put it under his nose. "You just saved my life," he said, grabbing the cup.

"Sounds like I was second in line. She helping you again?"

"What? Oh, Jill." Sam grinned. "The Bureau only has the best, thank God. There's a way to get into Hall's computers. At least, it should work. Nearly all business software is based on the same program, and that program has some frigging big holes in the security."

"That's good?"

"Hope so." Sam drank the rest of the steamy coffee in three big swallows. "We'll find out."

He went back to work at the keyboard. Kate watched while screens and minutes raced by, codes asked and answered, until finally he settled back and sighed. "Be damned. It worked. The personnel files are mine."

"Legally?"

"Don't ask, don't tell."

Kate took the hint and shut up. She drank her coffee, refilled both cups, and walked up and down between the worktables. The beautiful piece of yellow sapphire was mounted and ready to be studied with various devices, including an old-fashioned magnifying glass. The sooner she got to work on the sapphire, the sooner she could pay Sam back for his unintended loan to buy the pricey rough.

Not that he was pushing for the money. He hadn't even mentioned it. Maybe he'd like to go partners in the finished work as well. She turned to ask him, but before she could, he was talking to her.

"Jack Kirby. Son of a bitch. He worked for Peyton Hall."

"Kirby was a licensed private investigator, wasn't he?" Kate asked, frowning.

"Yeah? So?"

"So there could be a legitimate reason. Kirby could have worked for a lot of people."

Sam grunted. "Let's see what Sizemore says."

"What? You're going to tell him?"

"Actually, I think I'll let him tell *me*."

Chapter 68

Scottsdale
Monday
8:30 A.M.

Sizemore opened the door with a beer in one hand and attitude sticking out all over him.

"You sure I don't need my lawyer?" Sizemore said with something close to a sneer.

"You want him, call him," Sam said, brushing past Sizemore. "We'll wait inside."

Kate followed Sam into the suite.

Sizemore kicked the door shut behind her hard enough to make the frame vibrate before he turned to face Sam.

"I don't need my lawyer to deal with a mutt like you," Sizemore said. "You're not worth two hundred bucks an hour."

"Neither is your lawyer."

Kate rolled her eyes and stepped between the men, looking Sizemore right in the eye.

"Before you two start clawing and pulling hair," she said, "let's get a few things out of the way. You don't like Sam. Sam doesn't like you. Big flapping deal. People do business all the time with folks they despise. That aside, do you have any problem talking to us?"

Sizemore looked surprised. He glanced over Kate's head at Sam. "Do girls these days go to a special school to learn attitude?"

"The good ones are born with it," Sam said.

"Huh. Well, I hope the fucking you get is worth the fucking you get. Never was for me."

Sam couldn't help it. He looked at Kate and grinned.

She grinned right back at him.

Sizemore shook his head. "I'll never understand women, or men who understand them, for that matter. Beer, anyone?"

"I'll pass," Kate said.

"Me too," Sam said.

Sizemore lowered himself into his favorite chair and said, "Your party. Your tune."

Sam pulled up a chair for Kate but didn't sit down himself.

"Assuming that the leaks came from your company," Sam said, "and assuming that you weren't the source, who was it?"

"Hell, I've got twenty employees and a bunch of couriers who only work on a job-by-job basis." Sizemore took a drink. "Could be any of them."

Sam looked at the dark skin ringing the other man's bloodshot eyes. "Is that the best you can come up with after a sleepless night or did you spend the whole time drinking?"

Sizemore flushed and visibly bit back what he wanted to say.

"How many people at your company have access to every file on your main computer?" Sam asked.

"Four," Sizemore said sullenly. "Me, Sharon, Jason, and Ms. Tibble."

"Of those four, who has access to the ex-military old-boy club?"

"You know the answer as well as I do."

Sam waited.

"I'm the only one!" Sizemore said. He slammed his empty bottle in a nearby wastebasket—a bottle because this morning he'd started in on the high-test brew early. He put his head in his hands. "I'm the only one and I didn't do it."

Sam made a subtle gesture to Kate. Time for the sort-of-nice cop to step in.

"Did you know that Peyton Hall employed Jack Kirby?" she asked.

Slowly, Sizemore's gray, shaggy head came up. "What?"

"According to information we have," Kate said, "Peyton used Kirby for occasional background checks for Hall Jewelry International."

"Kirby never mentioned it," Sizemore said. "But why would he? I only saw him a few times in the years since the strike force."

"What about Peyton Hall?" Sam asked.

"Putz."

"No argument here," Kate said, thinking about the man's reputation with women. "Do you think some of his pillow talk with Sharon might have been about business? Sizemore Security Consulting business?"

"Sharon knows better than to talk out of school," Sizemore said roughly. "Oh, she might have let something slip here and there, but she's not stupid."

"Except with men?" Kate asked gently.

Silence stretched.

And stretched.

Abruptly, Sizemore came to his feet. "Most of the time when I see Peyton, he's leaning over her, looking at her computer screen while she works. He could get a lot of information that way. Hell, he could even have her security code. And Kirby would be all Peyton would need to hire a bunch of badasses for the dirty work."

Sizemore grabbed the phone and punched in Sharon's room number.

No answer. He waited long enough for the hotel operator to break in and then hung up without leaving a message.

"Sharon's not in her room," he said.

"Where else would she be?" Sam asked.

"She should be here. She knows we're leaving. Or we were,"

Sizemore said bitterly. "I don't know if I'm going to be allowed near an airport until this is over."

"If Kennedy hasn't had you arrested by now," Sam said, "then he isn't going to."

Sizemore shoved up his shirtsleeve and held his wrist under Sam's nose. "I'm under house arrest. Or hotel arrest, to be precise."

Sam looked at the "bracelet" Sizemore was wearing. It was the latest word in keeping track of people without putting them behind bars. Sizemore couldn't get away if he wanted to. The band on his wrist let the Bureau track him anywhere on the planet.

The red flush on Sizemore's face said that he was humiliated by the bracelet, but it was better than being fingerprinted and put in prison.

"Kennedy's good at covering his ass," Sam said.

Sizemore's mouth flattened.

"Is Peyton Hall still here?" Kate asked quickly.

"Sharon had breakfast with the putz," Sizemore said. "Didn't say anything about him leaving before tonight. The last of our clients will be out of here by then." He looked at his watch. "She's late. Should be here by now."

There was a light knock on the door and the sound of the lock and the door opening.

"Dad? I've been thinking. It isn't easy to say, but—" Sharon stopped cold when she saw Sam. "What are you doing here—gloating?"

"They came to talk about who else could have access to Sizemore Security Consulting information," Sizemore said.

Sharon took a deep breath, like she'd been hit. Fear or tears glittered in her eyes. Her fists clenched at her side.

"I've been wondering about it too," she said jerkily. "I was awake most of the night. Thinking. About connections. About who could and who couldn't." Visibly, she struggled to control herself. It took a few moments, but she managed. Swallowing hard, she said in a hoarse whisper, "I—Peyton. I'm so sorry, Dad. It's Peyton. The bastard has been using me all these years."

Sam narrowed his eyes. "What makes you say that?"

"We had breakfast together. He wanted me to walk away from my father." She took a hitching breath and looked at Sizemore, not at Sam. "I was—upset. I went to get some antacids out of his computer case—he always keeps them there because—oh, shit, that doesn't matter. I grabbed the bottle and dumped some on my palm and—and—*this*." She held out her right hand, opened it.

A brilliant blue oval flashed against her shaking hand.

Kate's breath came in with a sharp sound.

"Is it?" Sam asked tightly.

"Yes." She looked at Sharon. "Were there others?"

"Yes, damn it! I didn't know what to do. I was—all those years with him." She swallowed and wiped impatiently at her eyes. "I left the other stones where I found them and came to tell my father." She squared her shoulders and glanced at Sam. "It will be all right now, won't it?"

Sam didn't answer. He was too busy talking into his cell phone.

Chapter 69

Scottsdale
Monday
9:15 A.M.

"I think you should have stayed with Sizemore," Sam said to Kate as they waited in the hotel hallway for an elevator.

"Not a chance. Once the warrant for Peyton came through, I was out of there."

"Sharon didn't last that long. Said she had to pack. I thought they weren't leaving until tomorrow."

"Do you blame her for sliding out? When Sizemore wasn't ripping into her for being stupid, he was telling everyone in the room how he broke this case single-handed. Talk about a putz. Sizemore in full swagger is more than any woman should have to take."

Sam and Kate stepped onto the elevator at the same time.

His cell phone vibrated against his belt. He'd switched it to silent mode so that he wouldn't be bothered during the arrest of Peyton Hall. But the damn thing tickled.

He looked at the call window, frowned, and decided it would have to wait—which was the message he sent by punching the answer button and then disconnecting instantly.

"Stay in the hall until Peyton is cuffed," Sam said to Kate when the elevator slowed.

"Oh, please." She rolled her eyes. "He won't try to fight. He's way out of shape."

"Guns don't need gym memberships."

Kate shut up.

As soon as the elevator stopped at Peyton's floor, Sam looked outside. No one was in the hallway except Doug, who was waiting at the bank of elevators for Sam to arrive.

Peyton's suite was only three doors down. Sam pulled his Glock and held it down the side of his right leg. Unless someone was looking for it, the gun was both hidden and ready to use.

His cell phone vibrated back to life.

Shit.

He punched it on and off again.

"Stay here," Doug said to Kate.

Without waiting for an answer, the SAC set off down the hallway.

"Please," Sam said.

She gave him a smile that was all teeth, folded her arms, and leaned against the wall. "I'll be a good girl."

"Just stay put," Sam said. "That's all I ask."

He caught up with Doug. When they reached the door, Sam stepped to one side while Doug knocked on the door.

No one answered.

Doug knocked again, harder.

"Who is it?" Peyton called from the other side of the door.

"Federal Bureau of Investigation," Doug said. He pulled out his badge holder and dangled the gold shield in front of the spy hole where Peyton could see it.

"Just a minute."

The sound of the door bolt being flipped to open position was followed by the handle turning. Peyton Hall's handsome, rather soft face appeared in the opening. His designer linen shirt was unbuttoned, as were his slacks. Apparently, the belly pushing over his belt wasn't happy under pressure.

"What can I do for you?" Peyton asked. He opened the door

enough to show that he was being cooperative, even though he hadn't invited anybody inside.

If he had a weapon, it wasn't in either of his hands.

Sam saw the tension around Peyton's eyes and mouth. It was at odds with the professional salesman's smile. Anticipation purred along Sam's nerves. He was really looking forward to taking down the asshole who had killed Kate's brother and tried to kill her too.

Doug smiled at Peyton and said, "It won't take long. Could we come inside?"

Peyton glanced quickly at Sam, who was careful to keep the Glock out of sight and the predatory light out of his eyes.

"This is Special Agent Sam Groves," Doug said casually, waving a hand in Sam's direction.

Peyton frowned. "Yes?"

Two doors down, a couple emerged from a room and walked toward the elevators. They gave a long, curious glance at the three men who didn't look particularly chummy. From farther down the hall came the calls of maids as they exchanged gossip over fresh towels. The elevator doors opened and someone stepped off with too much luggage and a tired child.

Praying silently that the civilians got the hell out of the way *fast*, Sam turned slightly, keeping his weapon hidden.

"There's not much privacy out here, is there?" Doug said to Peyton, glancing from the man's bare chest to his bare feet and back. "Your choice, of course, but wouldn't you be more comfortable talking to us inside?"

"Uh. Yeah." Peyton stepped back.

Sam moved between Peyton and any potential weapon in the room. Though Sam didn't reveal his gun, it was there, ready.

"I don't have much time," Peyton said to Doug. "Got a plane at one o'clock and I'm not finished packing yet."

"This won't take long at all, Mr. Hall," Doug said, grabbing Peyton's right wrist and pulling it behind his back in a swift movement. "You're under arrest for the murder of Lee Mandel."

Peyton was too shocked to struggle when his left hand joined his right behind his back. Doug pulled out plastic restraints, wrapped them around Peyton's wrists, and cinched down hard enough to bite into flesh.

"What the hell?" Peyton said, staring over his shoulder at Doug. "There's been some kind of mistake! I don't even know this Medlon or Meddle or whatever the—"

"Mandel," Sam said curtly, holstering his Glock. "Lee Mandel."

With brisk efficiency, Sam went over Peyton for weapons while Doug did the Miranda chant—with variations required by recent court decisions—for the benefit of all the lawyers that were sure to come.

"Mandel. Fine, whatever," Peyton said. "But this is crap. I'm no saint, but I pay my taxes on time. You can't just come in here and arrest me."

"Actually, we can," Sam said, stepping back from Peyton. Then, to Doug, "He's clean."

Peyton tried not to think about his hidden accounts in Aruba and the gems that were reworked after Kirby and Eduardo's cousins got them from wherever they did. Thinking about it made his nerves skitter.

"This is ridiculous," Peyton said. "I want a lawyer right *now*."

Doug took Peyton to the phone, punched in the number he recited, and held the phone to his ear so that he could talk.

While Peyton was whining to his lawyer, Sam dropped a search warrant on the coffee table and went to work.

"Wait!" Peyton said when Sam opened the computer case. "You can't do that!"

"Tell him," Sam said to Doug.

"We also have a warrant to search this room and everything in it," Doug said politely. "Would you like me to explain it to your lawyer?"

"Fu—" Peyton stopped abruptly as it occurred to him that telling a federal agent to fuck off wasn't the best way to present the case for his innocence. "At least tell me who the hell it is who died and why you're framing me for his murder." Then, into the phone, "Bob, you gotta help me. These clowns just aren't listening!"

The look on Peyton's face said that he didn't like the advice his lawyer gave him: *Shut up*.

Belatedly, Peyton realized it might be a good idea. Nobody had talked about any overseas accounts, so this was all just a mistake. A scary one. Really, really scary.

A mistake, that's all. He'd never killed anyone. Robbed them, sure. Tipped off some bad dudes about where and when the pickings were good, yeah.

But he hadn't ever pulled the trigger, so he wasn't guilty.

Plastic ties cut into his wrists. His stomach heaved. It wasn't supposed to be like this. He was supposed to go to Aruba, not some federal lockup where the only women he saw were in his dreams.

"My lawyer wants to talk to you," Peyton said through pale lips. Then, almost desperately, he leaned closer to Doug. "I've never killed anyone. You have to believe me!"

Doug didn't bother to answer. He put the phone against his own ear and started going through everything from the numbers on the warrants being simultaneously exercised in L.A. and Scottsdale, to the specific federal laws that had been violated in the death of Lee Mandel.

Sam didn't listen. He'd heard it all before, so he just kept on exercising the rights granted by the search warrant. He unzipped Peyton's fat black computer case and pulled out the laptop. Though tempted, he set the machine aside for later investigation and began going through the multitude of zippered pockets that covered the inside and outside of the case. It took a lot of fiddling to be sure he looked at everything. He'd seen less elaborate Chinese puzzles.

"Look, at least tell me about this Lee Mandel," Peyton said to Doug. "The name sounds kind of familiar, but hell, I know a lot of people. Where did he die? How? C'mon, help me out."

Doug put his hand over the receiver, closing out the lawyer. "Mr. Hall, I've noted your objections. Your lawyer has noted them. Do us all a favor and shut the fuck up."

Sam's cell phone quivered into life again, tickling his belly. He ignored it because he'd just come across a shape that made his heart kick. He dug deeper in one of the side pockets and came up with an antacid container. Grinning like a wolf, he popped off the cap of the wide-mouth bottle and tipped the contents onto the coffee table.

Bright, brilliant, sapphire blue winked among the powdery white discs.

"Bingo," Sam said savagely, watching the prisoner rather than the gems.

Peyton was staring at the display with wide eyes and a dead-pale face. He swallowed hard. Twice. "Where did that come from?" he managed.

"You saw where it came from," Doug said. He tugged on Peyton's arm. "Let's go."

"No, they're not mine! Somebody else—"

"That's what they all say," Doug cut in, disgusted by the lack of originality in criminals. "I suppose you're going to tell us the maid put them in there?"

"I don't know." Peyton looked at the gorgeous blue sapphires and began to sweat visibly. "I've never seen them before in my life."

"Yeah, they grew there, like mold," Sam said. "Funny, I never get fine gems growing in my Tums."

"I don't even take antacids! Check with my doctor. He gave me something much better—"

Sam's cell phone kept vibrating. He tore it off his belt and snarled, "What!"

"This is the—"

"I know who it is," he broke in. "What do you want?"

"That list you gave us?"

"Yeah?"

"We got a match on three partials from the trunk of the courier's rental car."

Sam smiled coldly. "Kirby? Or White?"

"Neither."

"Peyton Hall? Ted Sizemore?"

"Close. His daughter."

Sam looked like the phone had just pissed in his ear. *"What?"*

"Sharon Sizemore. Right thumb, right index."

Sam remembered Kate standing alone in the hallway, waiting for them to arrest the wrong murderer.

He headed for the door at a run.

Chapter 70

Scottsdale
Monday
9:25 A.M.

Kate shifted against the wall and wondered how long it took to arrest someone. Then she remembered that the room had to be searched. She felt like banging her head on the wall. If she'd thought of that sooner, she would have argued harder against being left out in the hall. Not that it would have done any good. Sam had a stubborn streak in him that was as wide as hers.

It was one of the things she really liked about him.

A sound caught Kate's attention. Hopefully, she looked down the hall toward Peyton's room. All she could see was a maid's cart piled high with towels staggering down the hall toward the elevators. The young woman pushing it was too tiny to see over the towels. She barely missed a guest backing into the hallway close to the elevators, towing a suitcase.

"Watch it," Sharon said sharply.

"Sorry, *señora.*"

Sharon tugged her bronze jacket into place over her bronze trousers and black blouse, and headed for the elevator. She saw a casually dressed woman there, leaning against the wall as though waiting for someone. She looked familiar.

With a mental shrug, Sharon punched the down button. Whoever the woman was, it no longer mattered. Nothing did. She was out of here.

Kate smiled automatically at Sharon Sizemore even as she wondered if the other woman knew how badly she'd been used by her boyfriend.

The two women waited for the elevator with the forced politeness of strangers sharing a public space. Kate was relieved when she saw Sam striding down the hall toward her.

"That was fast," Kate said. "Did you—"

Then she saw the Glock held down along his right leg.

Kate had a really bad feeling. It might have been the grim line of Sam's mouth. It might have been the flicker of raw fear in Sharon's eyes when she saw the weapon.

Sharon reached inside her purse.

Sam started to lift the Glock.

The elevator door opened. Two kids holding pool towels and plastic swim goggles looked out.

Sharon yanked a snub-nosed gun from her purse and leaped toward the open elevator.

Without stopping to think, Kate threw herself at Sharon, knocking her to the side. The elevator doors jammed on her suitcase, tripping Kate.

Sam got to the elevator just as the two women hit the hall floor, each slugging and kicking for an advantage. Kate had been hamstrung by the suitcase just long enough for Sharon to get on top. He saw the flash of a gun in her hand and lashed out with his foot. Sharon screamed as her wrist broke.

She was still screaming when he kicked the gun away from her, yanked her head back by the hair, and rammed the muzzle of the Glock under her chin.

"Don't move," he told her. "Don't give me an excuse."

Sharon looked at his eyes and went completely still.

"You all right, Kate?" he asked without looking away from his prisoner.

"Yes. What about the kids?"

"They're fine, thanks to you." He glanced for an instant at the children. "Right, girls? Don't worry, I'm FBI. One of the good guys."

Kate looked at Sam's blazing eyes and the gun jammed under Sharon's chin. The older girl looked at him too. Then the girl shoved the suitcase out of the way, the elevator doors slammed shut, and the car went down.

"Guess you didn't look like a good guy," Kate said.

Chapter 71

Phoenix
Evening
Five days later

Kate sat on a hunter-green leather couch and watched Sam walk in
from the condo kitchen carrying two steaming mugs of coffee. Like
the condo's decor, he was relaxed and masculine. He handed her
one mug, picked up the TV remote from the coffee table, and settled onto the couch next to her. Right next to her, thigh to hip to
shoulder. She leaned into his solid warmth and sighed.

"You make better coffee than I do," she said, saluting him with
the mug.

"I grind my own beans."

"Yikes. Way too much trouble."

He kissed her nose and nibbled at the corner of her mouth.
"Good is never too much trouble. Great is worth all kinds of effort."

She smiled and took a bracing swallow of caffeine. The last two
weeks had been long on adrenaline and short on sleep.

The television flickered to life. It was one of the plasma types,
two inches thick and four feet wide.

"Your TV makes mine look like it belongs in a museum," she said,
yawning.

"It does."

"It still works. If something works, I don't throw it away."

"I've noticed." He looked at her intently. "You're loyal."

"So is a cocker spaniel."

He laughed and wondered how he'd gotten through the years before he met Kate.

Life hadn't been as good, for damn sure.

"Look, that's Kennedy," Kate said, pointing at the TV.

Sam looked. "Yeah, that's Kennedy." Front and center and being adored by Tawny Dawn's wide, wide blue eyes.

The camera angle shifted, drawing back.

"And there's Doug Smith, and . . ." Kate hesitated, trying to remember.

"Raul Mendoza," Sam said. "He's the strike force's federal entry from Homeland Security."

"Who's that other one?"

"A Phoenix PD captain. Ralston, I think."

"Where's Mario?" Kate asked, frowning. "He's Phoenix PD."

"At home with his wife and kids, if he's lucky."

"But didn't he really help with—" Kate objected.

"The whole crime strike force wouldn't fit on a TV screen," Sam said before she could finish her question.

Kate reached for the remote and switched on the sound.

"—being here tonight with us," Tawny said in an unusually husky voice. "I know how tight your schedule is."

Kennedy nodded, managing to appear both busy and gracious.

"He looks more important on camera than in person," Kate said.

"Are you saying you like him at a distance?" Sam asked dryly.

"Yeah. The more the better."

"We're all sleeping soundly again in Phoenix, thanks to the FBI. Mr. Kennedy, could you tell us in your own words how you cracked this murderous gang?"

"The usual way," Sam muttered. "Underlings and gofers."

"Ssshhhh. I want to hear."

He rolled his eyes and took a drink of coffee.

"First of all, I want to make it clear that although it is an FBI supervised crime strike force, we had the help of the Bureau of Homeland Security and many police departments across the United States, from New York to Florida, Chicago to Phoenix to Los Angeles."

"Cut to the chase," Kate said under her breath.

"That is the chase," Sam said. "Just one big happy family of crime busters taking a bow in front of the taxpayers."

"Working together, we brought to justice one of the most vicious gangs it has ever been my misfortune to discover on American soil."

"The Teflon gang," Tawny said eagerly. She knew a good sound bite when she had it in her mouth.

"Exactly." Kennedy gave her the kind of smile a man gives a dog that does tricks on cue. "This evil gang wasn't content with robbing couriers and hardworking businessmen. When the crime strike force started closing in on them, the Teflon gang began murdering people who had information the gang wanted kept secret."

"Is that what happened to the Purcells?" Tawny asked.

"I'm not at liberty to say for fear of prejudicing any future jurors."

Annoyance flashed over Tawny's face. "I understand that there is a connection between the Teflon gang and two recent murders in Los Angeles, those of José de Santos and Eduardo Pedro Selva de los Santos."

"Yes. We believe that the Teflon gang overlapped with the South American gangs that have been preying on couriers."

"Is that true?" Kate asked, turning to Sam.

"It is now."

". . . investigating multiple leads that show cross-connections among the gangs," Kennedy continued.

"But really?" Kate insisted.

Sam hit the mute button. He'd heard enough self-serving bull- shit for one evening.

"The whole point of a press performance like this," Sam said, "is to define what is real for public consumption now and in the future. Kennedy was forever publicly baying after South American gangs. He can't just suddenly admit this crime spree was completely home- grown, now can he? Wouldn't look good."

"And that's what it's really all about," she said, waving her hand at the TV. "Looking good."

"Everyone up there will get an 'attaboy' letter from the president within a month. Promotions soon to follow."

"But you were the one who did most of the work!"

"So what?"

Kate opened her mouth. Nothing came out.

"I bet you were going to say something about 'fair,'" Sam said, giving her a hooded look.

"Um . . ."

"I cut a deal with Kennedy that I'm happy with," Sam said. "That's all the 'fair' I care about."

She sat up straighter. "What deal?"

"I wouldn't give interviews about Ted Sizemore's murderous daughter who only brought along one pair of exam gloves, slit the fingertip on a sharp piece of trunk, and ended up leaving some partial prints on a car rented by Lee Mandel." Sam took a sip of coffee. "I wouldn't talk about how she milked Sizemore Security Consulting of information, used it to fatten up several overseas accounts, and stole the Seven Sins to frame her lover Peyton Hall for everything, including Lee's murder."

Kate's mouth opened.

Sam kept talking. "I wouldn't tell any reporter how John 'Tex' White admitted that Kirby received orders from a mechanical voice, including the orders to kill the de Santos men. I wouldn't tell reporters about the voice distorter, blonde wig, and gel bra the cops found in Sharon's L.A. condo. I wouldn't tell anyone how Peyton Hall was humping Sharon and at the same time taking information off her computer screen, information he used to beef up his own overseas account by cutting deals with the damned South American gangs, including money laundering. And that was as close as the whole mess got to Kennedy's wet dream."

"Sharon and Peyton. What a pair."

"They deserved each other."

Kate frowned and watched the politic words crawl across the

bottom of the TV screen. "Why did she do it? Did she hate her father that much?"

Sam appeared to consider the idea. "I think she hated the old-boy club as much as she hated her daddy. She wanted to prove she could make fools of them."

"She did, for a while. And then they made a fool of her."

"Did they?" Sam asked. "Left on his own, Kennedy would have booted this case to the far side of the moon. It took a stubborn, gutsy, and very bright woman to bring down Lee's murderer. That's you, darling."

"And a stubborn, gutsy, very bright FBI man with her."

Sam laughed humorlessly. "Not very bright or I'd be lined up on the TV with Kennedy's pets."

"That was the rest of the deal, wasn't it?" she said after a moment of silence.

"What was?"

"You don't get any credit, public or private, for breaking the case." Her voice rose angrily and she swiped her hair away from her face. "That stiff son of a bitch Kennedy gets it all."

"He can have it. I got what I wanted."

"Yeah?"

"Yeah."

"What was that?"

"You."

Kate blinked.

"Kennedy had already cut my transfer orders to Fargo," Sam said. "I didn't figure you'd want to work gems in North Dakota, so I made a little deal with a big horse's ass and the transfer papers were shredded. Of course, I can't guarantee I'll keep out of FBI trouble for the next three years, ten months, and seventeen days . . ."

"But who's counting, right?" she asked, smiling.

"Wrong. I am. That's a long time to stay on Kennedy's good side."

"Does he have one?"

Sam shrugged. "I haven't found it yet."

"Don't kill yourself looking for it. As long as you bring me coffee, I'll happily cut gems anywhere."

He gave Kate a long look, the kind that made heat uncurl through every part of her.

"You sure about that?" he asked intently.

She met his eyes. "Very sure."

"I'll hold you to that."

"I'd rather be held by you."

"It's a deal."

Date Due

JUL 01	SEP 28 05	
	OCT 28 '05	
JUL 28	AUG 01 06	
AUG 30	OCT 19 06	
SEP 06		
OCT 22		
DEC 13 2004		
JAN 03		
JAN 10		
JAN 26		
FEB 02		
FEB 16		
MAR 16		
JUL 05		

BRODART, CO.   Cat. No. 23-233-003   Printed in U.S.A.